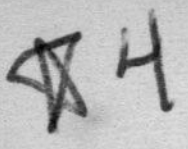

SPELLBOUND

"Talcott. That's all you think of, isn't it?" Adam said, his voice growing cool. "You can always use the Talcott name to hide behind, can't you?"

Bryony stiffened. "I have no need to hide. I have pride in my family. Talcotts founded the Hollow. Talcotts have always cared for the people here."

"And a Talcott is all that you are?"

"What do you mean?"

He moved closer. "You're more than a name. You're a human being in your own right. You're a woman. Doesn't that count for aught in your world?"

Bryony stood her ground, her pride assaulted. "I possess a mind of my own if that's what you mean. But I am the last of the Talcotts. I have a duty and a desire to carry on our work here to the best of my ability."

"Your work?" Adam smiled, but not with any good humor. "Ah, yes. The Talcott magic."

Coral Smith Saxe

LOVE SPELL NEW YORK CITY

LOVE SPELL®

August 1994

Published by

Dorchester Publishing Co., Inc.
276 Fifth Avenue
New York, NY 10001

Printed in the United States of America.

Enchantment

Chapter One

"Beware a South Winde if your Purpose bee Love. Its prodigious Heete may stir the Soule to such a Passion that no Thing may quench it. Choose instead a West Winde for Love Undying. Or stay Indoors till the Feeling subsides."

—*Cassia Talcott, from her* Compleat Booke of Spelles, Herbes, and True Wisdom.

Rural Pennsylvania, 1787

The place looked sane enough.

That was Adam Hawthorne's first thought as his coach rattled into the tiny frontier hamlet of Cold Springs Hollow. There was the usual conglomeration of small stores and houses, an inn, a blacksmith's shop, and a white-steepled church clustered around a central square of grass cut by narrow footpaths. Nothing out of the ordinary. The farms he'd passed on the way to town had looked neat and prosperous, the livestock sleek and contented. It was early spring and small freshets and creeks gurgled down the length of the valley, ending in a deep, sapphire pond at the southern end. New leaves were hazy suggestions of green in the trees. It was an idyllic, winsome sight.

But Adam was not a painter, a farmer, or a romantic poet. He'd come to this little valley for one purpose only: to find and discredit the Hag of Cold Springs Hollow. And he wasn't fooled by the calm, picture-perfect image of the area. Anyone, anywhere could be taken in by so-called witches, warlocks, sorcerers, soothsayers, and conjurers. Any place could be a harbor for these frauds. He knew that very well from extensive personal experience.

The coach shuddered to a halt outside an inn that sported a weathered sign with a crude picture of a black spaniel wearing an absurd, comical smile. The Laughing Dog Inn and Tavern, Adam read on the plaque by the door. Established 1688; nearly a hundred years ago. That made this place much older than he'd reckoned by the look of it, but he knew that the Hags of the Hollow went back for generations.

"Carry yer bags in, sir?"

Adam nodded to the coachman, who hefted Adam's trunk and satchel and led the way inside.

The common room spoke of the age of the place, with its rough stone fireplace and crude wooden benches polished smooth by the posteriors of numerous patrons over the decades. A short, bespectacled proprietor hurried out from the kitchen to greet them. He stopped when he saw Adam and his eyes widened to saucer size.

Adam stood, somewhat discomfited by the man's sudden, awestruck pose. "Is there something wrong?" he asked, glancing around him to see if he had blundered into something unawares.

"N-no. No, sir." The innkeeper shook himself to life and hurried to take the satchel from the coachman. "Welcome to Cold Springs, sir. I'm Jonathan Leary. My wife Demelza and I, we keep this place. May I show you to a room? You are staying, aren't you?"

"Yes. Not long, but for a few nights, I expect. My name is Hawthorne."

"Hawthorne," the man echoed. "Very good, Mr. Hawthorne. Just this way. We actually have a private room that's free just now, if you'd like to see it."

Adam gave his assent and he and the coachman followed Mr. Leary up the steep stairs to the second floor and down the hall to a west-facing room. The place was quite small, but clean, neat, and well-furnished with simple country furniture. After the bone-rattling coach ride over the rutted highways and muddy tracks of southern Pennsylvania, the quilt-covered bed and plump pillows beckoned to Adam.

"I'm going to rest for a while and I don't wish to be disturbed," Adam told Mr. Leary. "What hour is supper served?"

"In your room, sir, you may have it most any time. We have few staying guests just now. In the common room, we serve between the hours of five and half-past nine. Venison tonight, sir."

"I'll be down."

Adam signaled to the coachman to set his trunk down near the bed and took his satchel from the innkeeper. As he paid off the coachman and dismissed him, he glanced casually at Mr. Leary. "I've heard there's a famous witch in these parts. What can you tell me about the Hag of Cold Springs?"

Leary beamed. "That'd be Mistress Bryony Talcott. She's our Hag."

"Does she live in town?"

"Oh, no, sir. Talcotts have always lived at the south end, by Crystal Pond. Talcott Farm is one of our finest old places."

"Does she come into town much?"

The man shook his head. "None too often. Folks either come to her or she visits around. Comin' on spring like it is, she's powerful busy saying words over the plantings and helping out with the gardens and animals. Don't know what we'd do without her." He gave Adam a wary look. "Would you be friend or kin to the Talcotts?"

"Neither. Just a visitor. Thank you for your aid, Mr. Leary. I'll see you at supper." Adam produced a coin out of thin air, it seemed, and pressed it into the innkeeper's hand.

"Just as you say, sir." The man hesitated for a moment, gaping at the coin, seemed about to say something, then pocketed the coin and scuttled out the door, as if bent on some urgent purpose below.

Adam shrugged out of his dusty jacket and sat to pull off his boots. He glanced about him and gave a nod of satisfaction. He'd arrived at last. He felt the thrill of anticipation he always felt when he embarked on a new project like this one. Something told him that this time he'd have a challenge on his hands, and Adam Hawthorne was a man who liked a challenge.

So the Hag of Cold Springs was out "saying words" over the crops, was she? And no doubt charging a lion's share of the profits from each field, if he knew anything about her sort. A so-called witch didn't garner the finest place in the county without demanding a handsome charge for her "magical" services, money from the pockets of poor people who desperately wanted to believe that magic could protect or release them from the cruel realities of life.

This was Adam's mission in Cold Springs, as it was his mission in life: to seek out the frauds who preyed upon the hopes and fears of helpless, needy people, offering them shams and potions and all manner of tomfoolery in place of real aid or comfort. It seldom took him long to unmask the humbug. What was much harder, he knew, was convincing those who'd pinned so many of their fondest hopes on the charlatan. From what he knew, this Bryony Talcott and her whole family had been duping the citizens of Cold Springs Hollow for generations. It could take some doing to show the local citizens how badly they'd been misled.

He lay back on the comfortable bed and felt himself sink deep into puffy eiderdown. He stretched his long legs with a yawn. He'd bring down the Hag of Cold Springs, he vowed, and perhaps collect a tidy sum in friendly wagers for his troubles. His true satisfaction would come, though, in knowing that he'd won a small victory in the fight against ignorance and blind superstition. And he'd fulfill a vow he'd made to himself years ago.

He'd meet the Hag. And she'd rue the day that Adam Hawthorne crossed her crooked path.

Bryony Talcott settled herself cross-legged on the parlor floor and looked around at the objects she'd arranged before her. There was a ceramic cup of her father's good brandywine, a small silver bowl of dried corn, two candles—one red and one white—and a small piece of parchment tied with a green satin bow. She smoothed her simple white gown around her, shook her hair about her shoulders, and took a deep, quieting breath. Closing her eyes, she assumed an attitude of studious concentration.

"I seek knowledge, will, and courage," she intoned, her face highlighted in the candlelight. "I call upon the east wind to blow fresh breezes of change into my life. I call on fire to warm this—

Oh, drat!" she exclaimed, jumping up. "I just knew I'd forget something."

She hurried to a sideboard and rummaged in the drawer. She drew out a carved wooden box and flicked open its bright brass clasp. From it she took a small polished stone of a warm, honey color. She closed the box carefully and carried the stone back to her circle of objects, then resumed her cross-legged position on the floor.

"I seek knowledge, will, and courage," she repeated. "I call upon fire to guide me, to give me strength and clarity." Gingerly, she lifted the brown quartz between her thumb and forefinger and waved it over the candle flame. "I light a red candle for life and strength," she said, regaining her concentration. "I light a white candle to burn the past and all its problems to white ash. Let the flame heat and—Ouch!"

She dropped the hot stone and sucked at her burned fingers. "How did Mama manage this?" she muttered, pulling her hand out to examine the afflicted digits. "I'm sure I'm following the ritual properly, but it's just not working."

She tried again. Picking up the parchment, she untied the ribbon and began to read aloud. "In the face of the east wind, under a waxing moon, I pray that the Creator should give me the strength and the power to learn my true—"

A frantic pounding sounded at the front door, halting her ceremony once more. With a sigh, Bryony dropped the parchment on a low shelf above the candles, scrambled up, and hurried to the entry hall. A woman stood on the step, hair and clothing in disarray.

"Sorry to be callin' so late, Miss Bryony," the woman said breathlessly. "But Desdemona's time's come and she's havin' some trouble. Can you come right away?"

"Yes, of course, Mistress Addison. Just let me put on my shoes and get my cloak."

Bryony passed through the parlor, fluttering the candlelight in her wake. In the kitchen, a plump gray cat eeled around her ankles while she bound her hair back from her face with a bit of twine. "Not very elegant, I know, Soot," she told the cat, "but Desdemona won't mind, I guess."

Soot *firrupped* in response and cleared away as Bryony slipped her feet into a pair of worn shoes and grabbed her cloak from the peg on the wall. "Mind the house while I'm gone, old fellow. And try to find the mouse that's been at the malt, will you? I declare, you're the laziest old puss in the whole of Cold Springs Hollow."

Soot flicked his tail, uttered an indignant *errowwrr,* then settled down to seek solace in his dish of milk. Bryony grabbed her bag of medicines and charms and hurried to the front hall, where Sarah Addison waited, bobbing up and down with impatient anxiety.

"I've got my wagon outside; no need to hitch up yours," she told Bryony as they went down the wide front steps of the Talcott house. "Edward's with her now, tryin' to hold her off till we get there. I won't feel right about our Desdemona givin' birth without the Hag bein' there, I told him."

They drove off in a puff of dust, guided on their way by a huge, late April moon. Inside the house, Soot the cat came to sniff the cup of wine Bryony had left on the floor. He took an experimental taste, sneezed, and backed away with a wrinkled nose. As he turned to leave the displeasing stuff behind, his tail swiped at the parchment on the low shelf. The paper floated down, caught flame in the red candle, and fizzled to ashes on the clean floor. Soot watched in fascination until the last tiny ember faded out; then he stretched, yawned, and returned to the warmth of the kitchen hearth and the comforting proximity of his food dish.

Jonathan Leary plunked himself down in the chair and slapped his palms on the table. He glanced around at the three older men who sat at the table in the lamplight of early evening. "I tell you all, it's him. He's the one. First thing he asked me was did I know the Hag!"

"Slow down, Jonathan," said Matthew Cowley, resting his elbows on the tabletop. "Tell us from the beginning."

"He came in the coach, from up over the hill—the northern pass. He walks into this place just like he appeared out of a book or something."

"How'd he look?" asked Lucas Rutledge, dryly. "And don't tell us none of that storybook stuff and nonsense."

"Tall, more than average by a long foot. Reddy hair, but dark, like old rosewood or cherry. Clean-shaven, dressed all in brown. And his eyes—" Jonathan paused for dramatic effect, his own eyes blinking wide behind his spectacles. "His eyes were green as new grass in June. Just like Matt said they'd be."

Marcus Tupper spat. "A green-eyed stranger. Could be anybody. Doesn't mean he's the one. You know the old saw, 'Cold weather and knaves come out of the north.' "

"I tell you, it must be. He fits the description of the man that Matthew saw in his vision the day our Bryony was birthed." Jonathan gave an emphatic little jump in his chair. "And he gave me a coin he pulled out of nowhere!"

Matthew raised a weathered hand. The men turned their attention to the man who was their senior by ten years. "Now, Marcus, you may have a point. Even though it does seem like all the signs are falling into place, we can't be sure until we've talked with the man."

"He's out there now, having his dinner by the fire." Jonathan jerked his head toward the front of the inn.

Matthew pushed to his feet. "I believe I'll go introduce myself," he said mildly. "It's only fitting to greet strangers in our little town."

"Do you think this Hawthorne fellow knows about the signs?" Lucas asked.

Matthew shrugged. "Dunno. I'd guess not. But Beryl Talcott confirmed what I saw that day, and she was never wrong at foretelling. If he's all

Jonathan says, he's the one. Things'll be settled once and for all."

"Praise be," said Lucas.

"Don't speak too soon," Matthew warned. "There's more to the vision, remember? If this is the man, we're in for bad times, as well as good."

Bryony sat back on her heels in the straw and wiped her hands on a damp piece of toweling. "There you are, Mistress Addison," she said with a weary smile. "Mother and babies all well and doing fine."

Sarah Addison leaned over and counted the little bodies wriggling up to find their first meal. "One, two . . . three . . . four . . ." She paused. "Four piglets? Just four?" She looked at Bryony in wonder.

"Well, four's not unusual. And every one of them is strong and hale, not a runt among them." Bryony tried to be cheerful.

"Yes, I suppose that's some consolation," Sarah agreed grudgingly. "And Desdemona's chipper, to be sure, 'specially after you came and talked to her. Still, it ain't like the old days, back when your—"

"I'd best be getting back now," Bryony said, rising in haste. "I have to be up before sunrise tomorrow to say words over Remy Tompkins's fields. Spring's coming on so fast, I can hardly keep up with all the blessings and the incantations."

"Oh, to be sure, child. I know it's busy work bein' the Hag. You'd best be gettin' along to your bed."

Bryony winced at the goodwife's use of the term Hag. True, she was by right of birth the Hag of Cold Springs Hollow, but she was far from being a true Talcott in the sense of all that name implied. Almost twenty years old, the last living Talcott, and it seemed she could hardly work a spell for the curdling of milk. Twenty years old, unwed, unspoken for, and so far lacking in any hint of a true calling to the magic that was supposed to be her heritage. Her recently singed fingers and this parsimonious litter of piglets were painful testaments to that fact. The prodigious Lady Desdemona Addison had never produced fewer than six at any birthing attended by previous Talcotts.

"Here, take the lantern, child," Sarah was saying. "And thank'ye for coming to help. It probably wouldn't have gone so well without you."

And then again, maybe it would, Bryony thought.

"You go home and get some rest, now, dearie. You look like you been rained on, inside and out."

"Thank you, I will. Now, be sure to give Desdemona the potion I gave you. Pet her and be sure to say words over her every night and morning for three days."

"Which words?"

"Oh, it's not too important. Say grace, if you like. Just be sure to give thanks for the bounty you've been given. That way you're sure of getting another litter just as good."

"Or better."

"Or better," Bryony said with an inward sigh. "Good night, Mistress Addison."

"'Night, dear."

Sarah watched as Bryony's lantern bobbed away into the night, following the path across country to Talcott Farm. Then she turned and went back into the barn.

"Thanks for the bounty we've been given, eh! Hmph! This's more like a snack than a feast. Four piglets, indeed!"

Sarah looked around then, as if worried that someone might have overheard her ungracious words. "Oh, well, I suppose she's right—the little 'uns are all healthy and Desdemona come through it better'n she began. Maybe our Bryony just isn't a dab hand at piggin', is all. Heaven knows where we'd be without the Talcotts in this hollow."

She knelt down in the straw and clasped her hands. "Dear Lord, thank you for the four fine piglets you've blessed us with today, and for our Desdemona's good health. May she continue to produce fine, healthy litters in thy name. And if you could see your way clear to makin' the chickens produce like they used to, we'd be obliged." She paused, then added: "Bless our Bryony Talcott, Lord, and look after her. She can use your help, and I think you know what I mean. Uh . . . world without end, amen, amen."

With that, Sarah rose from the straw, took the other lantern, and went into the house, leaving the stately Lady Desdemona Addison to blissfully snore beside her newborn babes.

Bryony walked home in the light of the setting moon, the breeze fluttering her hair but failing to soothe the unsettling feeling within her that there was something important she had left undone. Or perhaps it was something she'd done wrong. Whatever it was, she could sense there was a change coming, and she wasn't entirely sure that this change would be to the good. Whatever it was, it pricked at all her senses and danced, just out of reach, at the corners of her mind. She shivered a bit, pulled her cloak closer about her, and hurried for home. If a change was coming, she'd best get ready.

"Evening, sir. Welcome to Cold Springs."

Adam looked up to see a tall man in his later years standing by his table. He hadn't seen or heard the man approach, but that didn't surprise him, for the inn was crowded and noisy with diners and drinkers and chattering folk. The man's face was tanned and seamed with many years in the sun and air, and his hair was moonlight white, but the eyes under the heavy white brows were a snapping, brilliant blue.

"Good evening to you. And thank you." Adam motioned to the bench opposite him. "Join me in a mug of ale, if you please?"

He was fully prepared to make himself friendly with all the people of the hollow, however feeble or benighted they might prove. It would help him to learn more about how to go about repudiating this witch who was said to hold the whole community in thrall.

"Thanks. Don't mind if I do. Matthew Cowley's the name."

Adam signaled to Leary to bring another mug of ale. "Adam Hawthorne. I just arrived in town this afternoon."

Matthew chuckled. "I'd hardly call Cold Springs a town. More like a smudge on some old wanderer's map."

Adam smiled and produced a heavy silver coin from his sleeve. He flipped it, caught it, then began to make it "walk" over and under the fingers of first one hand, then the other. "Maybe so," he said to Matthew. "But Cold Springs is known outside of the hollows around here. I've heard a whole family of witches is said to live around here."

Matthew cocked his head. "Where'd you hear such a tale?"

"Up north. Man by the name of Nicodemus Harper told me he visited here almost ten years ago."

"Harper. Harper. No, can't say that I recall aught by that name, but I could've been fishing that day." Matthew accepted his mug of ale with a nod of thanks to Leary. "What brings you out from the big city, if I may ask?"

Adam returned the man's bland smile. "I'm a magician. I'm looking to ply my trade a bit and work my way down to Virginia."

"A magician?" Matthew's eyes crinkled at the edges. "Well, now, that's a mighty unusual line. Mighty unusual. But there's plenty of folks here who'd pay to see your work."

"Are there?" *I'll just bet there are,* Adam thought to himself. "That's good to hear. I've been in some places where people are a trifle edgy about magicians. Smacks of blasphemy and sorcery, they say."

Matthew nodded. "Yep. There's good Scripture-reading folks in these hills and valleys. But we're used to wizardry here, and we welcome a bit of entertainment of an evening, besides. Though we hold by the Scriptures, too, of course."

"How long have you lived in the hollow?" Adam continued to maneuver the coin over and under his fingers.

"Only my whole life. Born and raised."

"Then you must know the Talcotts."

"Oh, yes. Everybody around here knows them. Friend of the family, are you?"

"No, just curious. Like I said, Nicodemus Harper mentioned them to me. And the innkeeper said something about a Hag?"

"Yep. That'd be our Bryony Talcott. She's our Hag now."

"Is she here tonight?" Adam scanned the room, his eyes lighting on two old women hunched over a game of dice in one corner.

"Bryony? No, no. She'd not have time these days. Too busy gettin' ready for the spring." Matthew's gaze followed Adam's and he frowned in puzzlement.

Adam tucked his coin away and turned back to the remains of his dinner. "I'd like to meet her," he said as casually as he could. "I'd like to meet someone who can do real magic."

"Yours isn't real?"

"Well, no. I'm just a performer. I do sleight of hand. I only make people think that it's magic."

Matthew's frown deepened. "What's the difference?"

"What's the dif—" Adam sat back, astonished. This was a response he hadn't expected. "It's pretty evident, isn't it? I just do some fancy juggling and if I do it properly I fool people's eyes. They think they've seen something mysterious and wonderful. Magic."

"And what our Hag does is real, not fooling anybody?"

Adam felt pinned by Matthew's brilliant eyes. He wanted to say yes; he wanted to say no. How was he to answer such a question without showing his hand? And just who was this fellow?

Adam answered slowly and carefully. "As I've never seen the Hag nor what it is that she does, I'll reserve judgment. But I'd still like to meet her. It seems she's highly regarded around here."

"Oh, that she is. She's one for the books, is our Bryony."

"Would she come here to see a performance tomorrow night? I've arranged it with the innkeeper here."

"She might. I can stop in on her on my way home tonight. Might do her some good to get out and have a bit of fun. Gets kinda lonely livin' all alone, as I can attest." He eyed Adam cautiously. "You a married man, Mr. Hawthorne?"

"No." Adam almost bit his tongue. What had made him say that? It was true, certainly, but it wasn't exactly smart to go telling that truth to any stranger who came along. Especially a stranger who might have an unmarried daughter or a spinster niece.

"That's as I expected," Matthew said. "A young buck like you doesn't want to be tied down, I reckon."

Adam smiled. "Something like that."

Matthew quaffed the last of his ale and stood up. "Thank you kindly for the drink and the chat, sir. I'll be sure to tell Bryony and any others I might come across that there's a new magus in town and he's doing a show here tomorrow night. Pleased to make your acquaintance."

Adam rose, shook hands with the older man, and Matthew departed. He watched as Matthew made his way through the cheerful, crowded inn, greeting almost everyone in the place and being hailed by all as he passed.

A nice enough gent, Adam thought. He hoped he'd look as bright and fit when he reached that age. Matthew Cowley looked as if he could plow all day and dance all night and sleep like a babe after it all. He also seemed to know the Hag fairly well. No doubt they were playmates together as children.

Bryony Talcott, of course, would not be so hale or handsome. Oh, she might be hale, as a horse or a cow, but the Hag would be a crone, he knew, left alone because of her curious ways, shunned by ordinary folk, perhaps taking on her identity as a witch to make up for what she lacked in comeliness and charm. The "witch" of Westover up in New York had been just that sort. Adam had unmasked her within a week, much to the surprise and gratitude of the farmers she'd been bilking for many a year.

He finished his drink in silence, pondering his options. Once he'd met the Hag, he'd know more, of course, but it sounded like she purported to have powers over the crops and the cattle in this valley, if everyone was calling on her to "say words" over their plantings. Such cases were always harder to discredit than mere tea-leaf readers and table-levitators. More often than not, frauds like Bryony Talcott had built up a history of superstition in their communities and by carefully fostering it over the years—the Hag had to be at least fifty years old—they were able to claim that it was their influence that rendered up good harvests. Of course, they never accepted similar responsibility for a poor harvest. That, they would say, was God's will, or they would blame the deluded farmer for not following their instructions properly. Everything was always fixed so that they couldn't fail.

But there were ways of exposing such charlatans. Adam knew that reason and the strong evidence of what people could see, hear, taste, touch, or smell for themselves would prove that this Hag had been gulling them all along. Adam didn't have to prove that they *couldn't* work magic, usually. As often as not, he'd challenge the practitioner to prove, absolutely, that he or she *could* work magic. It never failed.

The Hag of Cold Springs Hollow—what a title. Bring on the wretched old bat, her thought, handling a coin once more with his long, dexterous fingers. He'd show everyone what a miserable cheat she really was.

He frowned for a moment, recalling the time when he'd first spoken similar words aloud. His mother had slapped him. His father had stalked from the room. But he'd done what he said he would do. He'd shown them that the false healer they'd hired was nothing more than a conniving old thief who'd preyed on their grief and desperation and then just taken their money.

He shook himself out of his reverie. No use going over that now. He'd come a long way since then. And many people had shown their gratitude to him for his work. He was good at what he did, and he intended to prove it once again in this pretty little hollow, perhaps in this very inn.

He rose, paid for his meal, and went upstairs to unpack his trunk. He had a magic show to prepare. Tomorrow night, the Astonishing Balthazaar, magician to the imperial courts of England, Europe, and the mysterious East, would dazzle the locals with a display of tricks the like of which he'd bet they'd never seen before. And, he hoped, he'd snare himself a witch.

Outside the inn, the other three men waited anxiously as Matthew approached.

"Well?" demanded Lucas.

Matthew paused, looked at each face in turn. Then, slowly, he nodded. "Yep," he said. "That's him. That's the fellow who's going to marry our Bryony."

Chapter Two

"Nothing's surer: Followe Love and it will flee. Flee Love and it will followe Thee. You may somewhat resist its Spelle, with grimy Adornment and a noisome Smelle. I recommend garlick and Chicken Leavings; both are Simple and easily Obtained."

—*Cassia Talcott*

Bryony rose with the first hint of sunrise and went about the house in the dim light, gathering the things she needed for the day's ritual. She wasn't happy about this particular experiment; it went counter to much of what she'd been taught about magic as a girl. Where Talcott magic was always subtle, quiet, and at one with nature, this rite seemed to be noisy, extravagant, and, well, *smelly*.

Still, she was desperate, and the Obeah woman

she had visited in Cullers Creek had said that this was what the island people did to gain their magic powers. There didn't seem to be any reason why it wouldn't work in a valley, too.

Reverently, she donned a burlap gown that had been sewn together with grasses. The Obeah woman said she should use catgut, but Bryony had shuddered at the image of Soot or one of his companions being lost just to serve her personal needs. The Obeah woman had rolled her eyes and said never mind, marsh grass would do.

Bryony wore nothing else with the shapeless brown dress except an amulet that the Obeah woman had given to her. It consisted of a leather thong, from which dangled the dried feet of a rooster that the Obeah woman had said was the most potent and loudest she had ever known. The bird had perished of noble old age, she assured Bryony. She'd bound three of his rusty and ragged tail feathers into the leather at the top of the amulet and they waggled in the breeze as Bryony stepped out into the morning air. A small linen bag was nestled among the feathers and feet. It bumped gently on her breast when she walked, disturbing the contents. A smell as foul as dead skunk under a chicken coop wafted up with every step. For the sake of her magic, Bryony braved the stench, and it wasn't too long before her eyes stopped watering.

Soot came trotting up to greet her, fresh from his early morning hunt and roll in the dew. He took one sniff and backed off quickly.

"I know," Bryony said apologetically. "I don't like the smell, myself."

Soot sat down and watched her go, his tail twitching with indignation. Bryony gave him a wave from over her shoulder. She knew what he was thinking. Like all cats, he took it as a personal affront if his human altered her routine—or her scent.

Bryony did all she was told, venturing first to the marshlands and smearing her face and arms with the richest of the black mud found there—to be at one with the earth, Obeah Lulu had said. Then she perched in meditation on the rock by her private cove at the edge of Crystal Pond, trying to hear the voice of the rooster inside her, calling her powers to waken. Or at least, that was what the Obeah woman had told her to listen for.

All she heard was the rumble-chug of the bullfrogs residing in the tules and the indignant cries of a blackbird who coveted the rock for a sunning spot. Soon, the mud was dried and itching on her skin. She endured it for another hour, then rose to go on to the next stage of the ritual.

This part was not so ridiculous. She went to the woods near her farm, to a clearing that had long been used as a quiet place for prayer and sky-watching by her family. It was a spot full of peace and good memories. She cleared away some pine needles, took a hazel stick, and drew a circle in the center of the cleared space. Into the center of the circle she placed a big chunk of quartz, shining and clear, a raven feather, and a handful of rice from a little pouch she had placed under a rock the night before. She paced clockwise around the circle three times, then knelt to the north, east, south, and west. That done, she sat herself down, sang a hymn three times, and then sipped some of the water she'd brought from the pond.

She sighed. A whole day of this! The Obeah woman said that she must stay with the magic from sunup to sundown, or the spell would lose its power and perhaps even work against her. She knew about the importance of timing in working good magic, of course, but spending a day wearing mud and a pair of chicken feet dipped in asafetida—or something worse; she hadn't dared to ask—was more than she'd bargained for.

She brightened. But maybe, just maybe, this was what she needed. A whole day devoted to finding her magic. A whole day of sacrificing her comfort and her precious time might just be the way to prove that she was ready and worthy to learn what her true magical gifts might be. She would go on with the ritual. She would prove herself.

With renewed spirit, she moved on to the next task.

Matthew Cowley was waiting for him when Adam came downstairs to his midday meal. He rose and beckoned Adam to his table and offered to buy him dinner. Adam accepted, with thanks.

"How 'bout I show you 'round the hollow today?" Matthew asked, signaling to the server. "Unless you have other plans?"

"No," Adam said. "I'd enjoy that. From what I saw driving in, it looks like a fine place."

"Oh, that it is. You like to fish?"

Adam chuckled. "I haven't the patience. Sitting on a bank dangling a line and just waiting for something to happen isn't my sort of thing."

"Too bad. Crystal Pond is full of fish, ready to be cotched. But never mind, there'll be plenty to do. I trust you slept well?"

"Like a babe," Adam said.

Matthew ordered dinner for both of them, with generous mugs of cold cider. "I thought you would," he continued to Adam. "The womenfolk around here set great store by their pillows and featherbeds. They use the finest down, you know, and say the good words for sleeping over each and every stitch."

Adam groaned inwardly. But he knew better than to speak up too soon and reveal his plans before he had marshaled enough evidence about the Hag.

"From up Philadelphia way, are you?" Matthew asked.

"Yes." Adam wondered how he could tell.

"Hearing you talk and looking at your clothes put me in mind of it. Your speech has that kind of sound to it; I've heard it before. And your clothes, well, pardon, but they ain't fancy enough for New York or Charleston, nor sober and costly enough to be Boston-made. Yet they're fine and all, so that left Philadelphia."

Adam grinned. "Excellent reasoning." So the old man wasn't a complete half-wit, like so many he met on these trips. "Did you ask the Hag to come tonight?"

"That I did. Stopped by on my way home last night and caught her before she was retiring. She said she'd try but she had a long job of spellin' today."

I'll bet, Adam thought sarcastically. Hard work, that spelling. No doubt she'd be exhausted from counting up all her fraudulently obtained wealth. Perhaps he shouldn't wait. "Is there any way that I could meet her before tonight?"

"Oh, well, I hadn't thought of that, but maybe that'd be advantageous. Anxious to get acquainted, are you?"

"Yes, I guess you could say that."

"Well, that's fine. I'll tell you what. We'll drive about and see the hollow and as we're swinging back around toward town, we'll stop in at Talcott Farm and see Miss Bryony."

"Lead on."

The trip around the hollow was enlightening to Adam. Though the land was obviously rich and the farms seemed to be thriving, he observed the telltale signs of decay here and there. Some of the houses were in need of a whitewashing. Some fields that should have been plowed like the others were lying fallow. Two houses were clearly unoccupied, as if the owners had packed up and gone on to greener country.

The Hag must be losing her grip over the place, Adam thought. She must be desperate not to lose any more of her sheep, lest she be the next one to pack up and leave town. After generations in the same spot, it would no doubt be a grave hardship to train a whole new flock of sheep to her ways.

"There's been two hard winters," Matthew said suddenly. "Folks were hit bad by the freeze and by the fevers. The Kingstons from yonder farm went back north, after their sons all was killed by the fever. And the older Tompkinses—they just got disheartened when the frost did in their orchards. They went to relatives up in New York. Sorry to see 'em go. Good neighbors are hard to come by, though we all get along pretty well in this place."

Adam felt a small shiver in his bones. That was the second—or was it the third?—time that Matthew had spoken as if in answer to his thoughts.

He gave himself a mental shake. What nonsense. Matthew had seen him looking at the empty farmhouses and barnyards and easily concluded what anyone would be thinking about at such a sight. There was nothing mysterious about it.

"Yonder's my place." Matthew pointed to a fine old house, its unpainted clapboard sides silvered to a lustrous sheen. "Kind of a lonely place since my Julia died and my girls moved away, but it's still the best place for the likes of me."

"Looks like a good farm," Adam said. "Did you build it?"

"Me? No. 'Twas was my granddaddy's place. He married a Talcott, did you know? Not the Hag, o' course, but a Talcott woman, all the same. Rosamunda Talcott. Sweet as her name, she was."

Not like the current Talcott-in-residence, Adam thought. He doubted that anyone had ever paid court to Bryony Talcott. If they had, she'd be safely married by now and too busy to go about meddling with silly witchcraft.

"We'll take a drive up to the pond," Matthew said, guiding the horses back onto the road. "You're not a fisherman, but I think you'll find it a fine sight."

The horses made their plodding way up the gentle slope to where the road entered the woods. Tall blue spruces and lacy dogwoods with their first leaves of spring wove an archway overhead. The air was cool and still and fragrant with new growth. Adam couldn't help but savor the soothing effects of the air and sights around him. He drew in a deep, slow breath and let it out, feeling tension lift from his shoulders.

"Peaceful, ain't it?" Matthew asked. "This is an old, old place—you can feel it. Folks come here often just to get back to themselves when their cares get to be too much. Me, I come here daily. Keeps me right as rain."

"I don't doubt it," Adam said truthfully.

They emerged from the trees and climbed another rise. As they crested the slope, Adam smiled with sheer pleasure at the sight below. The pond was well named, for the waters looked as clean and blue as cut glass held up to the sunlit sky. Trees skirted the edges on two sides and hid small coves beneath their hanging branches. Birds darted about, trilling and calling, and cattails were just appearing in the shallows.

"Come here near every day, too," Matthew said. "There's a big old fella in those waters who's been toying with my line for years, now. Must be nigh onto my age, at least in fish years. I'll get him on my line for good, one of these days. Don't know what I'll do then, but I aim to do it."

Adam chuckled. "Sounds like a reasonable goal. And I can see why you'd want to spend so much time here. It's beautiful."

"Yep. A good place. Talcotts knew that when they came down into this hollow years and years ago. They knew this was sweet water and a place for magic-making. Founded a fine family and a fine little town."

"Who were the first Talcotts?"

"Oh, that'd be Darwell and Cassia. He come from over England way when they was shipping folks out 'cause they had too many mouths to feed. Found himself a wife up in Massachusetts colony—lovely Cassia—and brought her out here in the wilderness without so much as a map to guide them. Just took it on faith that Providence would guide them home. Which is just what she did."

Adam looked about him. They must have thought they'd found paradise, coming to this place after their long travels, he mused.

"Yep. Like the garden of Eden it was to them, though they didn't get kicked out of it. They got to stay and build their farm and raise up a crop of fine sons and daughters. And they all had the gift, every one of 'em."

"The gift?" Adam successfully ignored the prickling of hairs on the back of his neck as Matthew again seemed to echo and answer his own thoughts.

"A gift. Darwell and Cassia, they had several, and some of the others that come after—like Cavendish and Dandelion—they had more'n one gift. But mostly Talcotts get one true gift of magic and they make the best use of it they can."

"What kinds of gifts?"

"Well, the usual, of course. Water scrying, and dowsing, and seeing the future in smokes. Some had the gift of seeing through others' eyes, and some could read the cards—although cards and such aren't their line, generally. Some had the touch for birthing healthy animals and others could call forth plants from underground in half the time it would take 'em to grow. Things of that sort."

What a scheme, thought Adam. Each generation took on a new "skill" so that there was always a fresh claim to magic, never the same old trick that could wear thin and be shown up for the falsehood it truly was. These Talcotts were clever, if nothing else. They'd protected their own, decade after decade.

Matthew put a hand to his forehead, shading his eyes as he gazed across the pond. Adam looked and saw a figure just disappearing behind a greening willow.

"If I'm not mistaken, that's Miss Bryony over there. It's getting on sunset, so like as not she'll be heading home soon. Would you like to go across and meet her?"

A vision of Bryony Talcott flashed across Adam's mind, an image gained of many contacts with her kind. She'd be hunched and skinny, and hung with garlic to ward off the evil eye. Between her sagging breasts would be a talisman of rabbit's feet and horsehair, and she'd be forever stirring some noisome pot of greens and entrails, muttering incantations all the while. She'd have a voice like a man's and chin whiskers, besides. And she might, God help him, believe that she really could work magic.

But he'd come here to see her and to oust her from her throne as the monarch of this little valley. He had to face her sometime and the sooner the better.

"Lead on," he said to Matthew.

They wound around the pond, the horses seeming to know their way without any urging or direction from Matthew. They drew near the spot by the willow and Matthew drew the wagon to a halt. He dismounted and Adam followed.

They passed the willow and faced a clearing between the pond and the woods. There, a bent figure in ragged brown was swaying and waving her arms about like a windmill.

"She'll be through with her spellin' in a minute," Matthew said, looking at her with an expression of mingled pride and admiration.

The creature dropped her arms and fell silent. Her shoulders drooped and she seemed utterly forlorn. A moment later, she straightened and turned.

Adam raised his eyes and came face-to-face with the Hag of Cold Springs Hollow.

His heart sank. It was as bad as he had feared.

Hair the color of decomposing leaves was plastered to her head in some places and sprang out like corkscrews in others. Her torn, shapeless gown hung on her like a bag, and her hands, face, and bare feet were begrimed with mud. Around her neck was some hideous talisman of—ye gods, Adam thought—were they chicken feet? Pigs' tails? Or something worse? He hardly dared guess. She was crooning to herself again, eyes closed, and she flapped her hands in the air before her, as if shooing some unseen flock of contentious barnyard geese. Worse yet, they were upwind of the creature, and she smelled as ripe as a compost heap in late July.

He turned to Matthew, his mouth open, ready to beg off from this horrible sight. But the old man was simply grinning and nodding in the direction of the Hag.

"Yonder she stands," he said, pride unconcealed in his voice. "One for the books, is our Bryony."

Which books? Adam wondered, his shocked mind wandering helplessly into meaningless fields. Certainly not any literature of his acquaintance, unless one counted some of the more dire forebodings in the Book of Revelations.

Adam attempted a reply, but it came out as a halfhearted gargle. He was unable to resist the impulse to turn and look again at the wild woman who stood swaying on the green. It was like passing the site of a burning house or an overturned cart—he was compelled to gawk. And the scene before him was every bit as alarming as any roadside accident.

"Evenin', Bryony," Matthew sang out cheerfully. "Any luck?"

Bryony started and came to an abrupt halt. She'd been so absorbed in her final bout of chanting that she hadn't heard anyone approaching. Before her stood not only Matthew Cowley, a respected friend and a leader of the community, but with him was the handsomest man she'd ever beheld. His striking features and red-brown hair, lit by the sun's last rays, made her feel somewhat peculiar inside, as if she were tilting a bit on her feet. He stood as tall as Matthew and his shoulders overspanned Matthew's respectable spread by a good measure. And those green eyes! Like the willow leaves, they were, and yet piercingly bright and keen. He was like no man she'd ever imagined, let alone met. A shiver of pleasure and apprehension rippled through her at the sight of him.

And he'd seen her, of course. He'd seen her performing this ludicrous ritual and he was looking at her now as if she were a fish that had just crawled up onshore and offered him a hot biscuit. She wanted to sink into the spongy earth beneath her feet and tunnel her way home to bed.

"Where's my manners?" Matthew said, clapping his hands. "Miss Bryony Talcott, this is Master Adam Hawthorne of Philadelphia. He's new to these parts, but I guess you could figure that one out on your own." Matthew burbled on, oblivious to the discomfiture of both of his companions. "Master Hawthorne'll be stayin' at the Laughing Dog, o' course, and gettin' to know folks as they come. And he's a magus, think of that! He'll be doing some of his magic at the inn tonight, like I told you."

Bryony's voice, hoarse from singing all day in the wet air, came out as a husky croak. "Welcome to the hollow, Mr. Hawthorne."

Matthew gave Adam a firm nudge and he sprang to life. "It's a pleasure, Miss Talcott," he said, reaching for her hand. He braced himself and kissed the air over the grimy appendage with as much of his customary grace as he could muster. It was a sacrifice, but it would help his work to win her confidence as early as possible.

Bryony withdrew her hand and thrust it behind her back. "I—I must be going. Mistress Turner needs me in the morning. Good luck with your work, Mr. Hawthorne."

"Will you be there tonight?" Adam managed to get the words past his unwilling lips.

"I don't know," she said, her voice cracking violently. Humiliated, she hurried on. "It's so late and I must be up—ahem!—you know how it is, nice to meet you, good day, sir."

She put her head down and hurried past the two men, feeling the tips of her ears burning with embarrassment. Her bare foot struck a rock in the path and she staggered slightly, hopping on one foot for a short way. She hobbled off, dismayed and disturbed by the presence of the handsome Mr. Hawthorne and the awareness of his brilliant green eyes staring at her back. Whatever his reasons for being in Cold Springs Hollow, she devoutly hoped that she'd never have to face him again.

Adam watched her graceless exit and felt a moment of thin triumph. He'd been right. There was no escaping it. The woman was a grubby, demented, crow-voiced stumble-shins. It would not be putting too fine a point on it to say that she was indeed a bona fide Hag. And he would have to get close to her to unmask her—a most revolting notion.

He turned to Matthew in mute horror and resignation, but the older man was gazing after Bryony Talcott with rapturous pride and pleasure.

"She's a prize, lad," he said, nodding his head. "A prize."

Adam dressed with care that evening, taking time to install all his various devices within the pockets, sleeves, and linings of his flamboyant silk costume. He stood before the pier glass and tested the cuffs of his flowing, deep violet shirt. They looked tightly buttoned and secure, but his nimble fingers could hide or produce any number of items under their protective cover. The same could be said for his waistcoat, with its multitude of tiny colored stripes. It fit snugly from chest to waist and yet it concealed a multitude of props and provided a busy backdrop to fool the eye. He palmed a coin from one of its pockets and began to limber up his fingers by passing it over and under one hand.

He gazed at his face in the mirror for a moment. His green eyes held the spark of anticipation and challenge they used to hold before a performance, though these days his act was but a cover-up and a tool to help him with his more serious work. There was little left of the old delight of performing or the pleasure of sharing his skills with others.

Six years ago, he'd been fired with the pleasure of his work. He'd been the best magician, bar none, in all of these new United States—colonies back then. He was feted at the homes of the rich and powerful; he performed in the best theaters in New York, Boston, and his hometown of Philadelphia. He'd even performed in Europe. He was written about in the newspapers, a light note to add to the grim news of the war for independence.

He'd also put in his time in service of that war, taking an officer's commission when the time came. He returned home to Philadelphia, not a hero, but as one who'd acquitted his duty well. But while other men his age returned to their former lives and occupations, Adam Hawthorne put aside all his magic.

He was invited, then begged to perform, but he stayed in retirement in his parents' home, seeing no one and performing no magic. The rumor took on the air of truth—the career of the Astonishing Balthazaar was over.

But the magician in him did live on in his new profession, though he called upon it only as a cover. His magical training also gave him the insider's knowledge of how magicians and tricksters of all sorts made their money. He could expose and discredit most thimbleriggers, as he called them, in a matter of moments.

And he was called on to do just that with surprising frequency. Distraught families who'd been robbed of their life savings by a false healer, angry heirs who feared that Grandfather would squander his money on a fortune-teller who'd convinced him he was destined to marry a sixteen-year-old nymph, poor folks who'd given their mite to a traveling lightning salesman; all these and more sought the help of Adam Hawthorne.

Then there were the gamblers. The wagers were what paid the most, though Adam had earned enough as a magician to keep him in style for many a long year. A bet had been the instigation of this trip to Cold Springs. That night in the comfortable Blue Dolphin Club, back in Philadelphia, seemed an age ago now.

"A whole family of witches," Beau Weston had told him, setting his palms down on one of the Dolphin's heavy tables. "They've been running this entire town for generations. Nobody makes a move without them. Just the thing to challenge your witch-hunting skills, Hawthorne."

Adam had scowled. "I'm no witch-hunter. You won't find me persecuting innocent old people for muttering to themselves or keeping a pussycat. And I don't believe that I represent God on earth or that it's a sacred duty to do what I do."

"I know, I know," Beau said, straddling a chair and filling his brandy glass once more. "You do it for the challenge. And the money."

"And to help people who are being robbed," said Taylor MacLaren. "Don't forget that Adam doesn't take any pay beyond expenses if the people are poor. And most times not even that."

"Yes, well, there can't be too many rich folk in a godforsaken outpost called Cold Springs Hollow. It's off to the west of here—almost on the Susquehanna." Wade Sewall jabbed a finger at Adam. "Admit that the idea intrigues you. A whole family of witches. A whole town in their thrall. Why, the town even voted to levy an extra tax just so that they could keep on supporting these Talberts or Talbots. How's that for rascalry?"

"Sounds like politics as usual," Adam drawled.

Laughter had rung out around the table. The fire from the hearth lit the faces of the four men seated at the table, glinted off the good cut glass of their brandy snifters.

"Well?" Wade demanded. "What do you say to one hundred in gold, Hawthorne? Give us a chance to make back what you took from us on that Saunders fellow." He shook his head ruefully. "I could've sworn that he was the genuine article. As God is my witness, I thought the man really could rise up into the air of his own power. And he seemed so sincere when he prayed and all—claimed his power came from on high. His rigs and cables had me fooled."

"He had you fooled, old friend," Adam said with a smile, "because you are a fool. Despite everything I've told you about so-called magic and the supernatural, you cling to a childish hope that someday, somewhere, you'll get to see real magic."

"Oh, come now—" Wade began as laughter sounded again around the table.

"No, no, don't try to deny it. It's written in your eyes every time you see one of these fakers go into his act. You're saying to yourself: 'This time, yes, this will be the one.' Deny it if you must, but I know that's what you're wishing. I've seen that look on too many faces to mistake it." Adam settled his long frame into the chair, stretched his legs out to the side, and crossed his booted ankles. His face darkened momentarily.

"And you aren't wishing it?" Taylor's eyes were friendly, but probing.

"No," Adam replied. "I know there's nothing in this world that can't be proven to be the machinations of either nature or man. All you have to do is use your five senses along with good common sense and all will be made plain to you."

"And you never let your emotions get in the way?" asked Beau.

"I hope I do not."

"Yes, yes, all this philosophical talk is fine," said Wade. "But I'm a practical man. I have a hundred in gold that says that magic or not, you can't prove that these Talbots—"

"Talcotts," Beau interjected.

"—Talcotts aren't true witches. What do you say, Hawthorne?"

Adam shrugged noncommittally. "Who told you about these Talcotts?"

Beau and Wade looked at each other, exchanging triumphant smiles. "Nicodemus Harper," Wade announced.

"Nicodemus Harper!" Taylor exclaimed. "You're lying, you dogs."

"I swear it!" Wade cried. "Nicodemus Harper, deacon of the church, graduate of Harvard College, head of the First Bank, scion of the community—"

"—pillar of virtue and honesty," added Beau.

"That's right. We had dinner with him at Compton House and he told us all about it over sherry. He visited this Cold Springs Hollow five years ago and saw these Talcotts for himself. He believes in them utterly."

"Harper," Beau said, leaning forward. "The word of the most upright man in town. And the challenge, Hawthorne, think of it: uncovering a whole nest—hell, a dynasty!—of these rascals you hate so much. What a coup it would be for you."

Taylor chuckled. "He's got you there, Adam."

"See? Even MacLaren thinks you should do it."

Adam glanced at Taylor. They'd been friends for years, and Adam trusted and respected Taylor's thoughtful opinions. And Taylor alone knew the whole truth behind Adam's mission to repudiate all claims of magic.

Taylor considered for a moment, watching Adam's face. "I won't say I'm wholeheartedly in favor of your chasing off into the wilds. Those little towns out there can come and go like summer storms, and it's been five years since Nicodemus Harper visited Cold Springs. You need to learn more about it. But it may be the thing you need right now, the thing that will resolve this hunger for proof you've developed."

"There!" Wade exclaimed. "It's just what you need, Hawthorne!"

Adam frowned, his eyes still on Taylor's across the table. Slowly, he nodded. "All right. I'll do this much. I'll go talk to Nicodemus. If he can convince me that he soberly believes there's a whole town of these humbugs, then I'll consider going there myself." He paused. "And the price will be two hundred from each of you."

Wade and Beau glanced at each other, then back to Adam. "Done," Wade said. They shook hands all around.

Adam had straightened in his chair. "The first thing I need to know is where in the hell is Cold Springs Hollow?"

He'd found out, and here he was. Nicodemus had been utterly convincing and frank about his visit to this place and the wonders he'd seen there. Adam had known then that he had to come. If a fine man like Harper could be duped by these people, then what must be happening to the simpler, less knowledgeable folk in that hollow? It was too great a challenge to resist, as his friends had said. And too important to leave uninvestigated—his own wounds still stung.

Returning from his reverie, he slipped the coin he'd been manipulating back into its pocket, sorted through his magic equipment, and readied himself for his performance. He bowed low before the glass, a look of hauteur and mystery taking over his sharp-cut features. The transformation was complete. The Astonishing Balthazaar was ready to take the stage. The Hag of Cold Springs—he shuddered at the memory of her, smelly and bent—had best hang on to her broomstick.

Chapter Three

"Warding off Desire is like War—the Prudent Personne takes cover at the first Shotte. But, as Love and Desire have little to do with Prudence, I can only advise the Wary Soldier to find a cold-running Stream—and sit in It."

—*Cassia Talcott*

The inn was crowded by the time Adam signaled to the innkeeper to make his introduction. Matthew had effectively spread the word throughout the hollow, it seemed, and it looked as if half the township was squeezed onto the benches and lined up against the walls of the Laughing Dog.

"Ladies and gentlemen, it is my pleasure to welcome you to my humble establishment," called out Jonathan Leary, tapping on a wooden plate with a spoon. "We've got a special treat for you tonight.

For your pleasure and mystification, I introduce the Astonishing Balthazaar, imperial magician to the crowned heads of England, Europe, and the mysterious East."

There was a flash of blue light, a puff of smoke, and Adam stood before the crowd on a raised dais at the far end of the room. There were gasps and cries and a round of generous applause. Adam bowed low with a sweeping gesture, the silver and gold threads in his embroidered waistcoat glittering in the lamplight. Several of the women nudged each other, grinned, and dissolved into giggles. Several of the men crossed their arms, frowned, and waited for the stranger to prove himself.

They hadn't long to wait. Adam was in rare form. He began with clever tricks with fire and silks, bringing cheers from the children in attendance and murmurs of surprise from the adults. From there, he went on to ropes and balls, his long, nimble fingers moving with grace and ease, his body obeying his every command with energy and style.

In the middle of his performance, when he was doing some simple card tricks, he had the chance to glance out into the audience. He saw Matthew at the back of the room, tall and smiling, near the front door. A woman with dirty brown hair and a sallow complexion stood next to him, scowling. That would be the Hag, of course, he thought. She must be royally peeved that she had competition for the awe and admiration of her subjects, he thought.

He turned on his most charming manners as he moved through the crowd, involving the audience in various gambits with cards and coins. He joked and smiled, flirting with the goodwives and joshing with their husbands, winning friends as he went. He'd just about reached the back of the room, where Matthew and the Hag stood looking on, when he was brought up short by the hand of a giggling, slightly drunken maid. He looked about for an escape as he jovially tried to extricate himself from her grasp on his shirtsleeve. In another moment, she'd feel the many objects hidden in their copious depths, and she was just the sort to exclaim aloud about her findings.

". . . and that's all for that little game," he said, twisting around to his right. "Unless, of course, you, madam, would like to try your hand—"

He fell silent for the briefest moment, but the time seemed to slow to an eternity. The woman on his right lifted her head, and from beneath her broad, golden cartwheel hat a pair of the most eloquent and lustrous amber eyes gazed up at him. They seemed to speak to him of wonder and of pain, and of a kind of yearning that something deep within him answered to at once. He had an impression that the rest of her face was pleasant and sweet, and that the breasts that rose and fell beneath her gauzy shawl were softly and abundantly rounded, but all he could concentrate on were those honey-brown eyes, even as the black fringe of her lashes swept down to hide them from his view. He was jolted to his very depths with sudden desire and some other, newer emotion that he could not name. What on earth was happening to him? came the thought from the far edges of his mind.

"Or perhaps you, sir," he said hastily, forcing himself to pass the woman in the cartwheel hat and move on, making his way toward the back of the room once more. "Or you, madam," he said at last, steeling himself to look the Hag of the Hollow full in the face. After the luminous beauty of the other woman's amber gaze, the bloodshot, pea-green orbs of the Hag were a hideous insult to his senses.

"Never mind your silly games," the witch snapped. "I'm not getting paid to do your act for you. Get back up there and show us what you're made of."

Adam bowed, smiling. "A critic," he said to the crowd. "How charming of you to have her here to make me feel welcome."

The audience laughed and Adam threaded his way toward the makeshift stage once again, chatting and joking and juggling small objects along the way. He paused by the side of the golden hat, but couldn't make himself approach her with his foolish patter. Yet, as he finished his act, his eyes strayed often in her direction and he savored the few glimpses he had of her fresh, yet solemn countenance.

His finale took place outside, in the open space before the inn. He was to escape the bonds at his wrists and ankles and get free from a large grain sack that was stitched closed at the top—

before fire could consume the sack and Adam inside it. It was a trick he'd performed only a few times, and he knew it was risky, but he had the insane, adolescent wish to show off for the golden-eyed beauty. He also knew that such a stunt would attract the attention of the Hag and perhaps goad her into a competitive display of her own "powers."

He didn't dare look at *her* face, however, that face beneath the straw brim. He'd immediately spotted the hat in the crowd that was gathered around. He longed to look, but he knew that seeing her face would distract him from his task and that could be dangerous. Instead, he concentrated on a spot over the inn door as Leary and two other men tied his wrists and ankles and bound the sack tight with leather stitching. They hoisted him up on top of a pile of kindling and waited for Adam's word inside the bag.

"Now!" he called out.

With trembling hands, Leary put a light to the base of the kindling, and flames began to lick around the twigs and bark chips piled together at Adam's wriggling feet. Leary and another man lifted the curtain in front of Adam as he had instructed them, but the audience could still see both the top of the bag and the flames below.

An excited buzz started in the crowd as the little fire was fanned by the spring breezes. It spread to murmurs of alarm as the bottom of the bag began to blacken and scorch. Time seemed to stop, and some panicked voices called out for water to be thrown before it was too late.

"Help him!" a man's voice called from the back of the crowd.

"Water!" came another cry. A few of the men made for the well nearby.

Before they could return, another man rushed forward with a bucket of water and threw it at the fire, effectively dousing it. He grabbed the curtain and yanked it down, showing only a singed and empty sack lying on the smoking remains of the fire. The man turned and bowed low, barely concealing a smile that was none too humble.

It was a triumph. The crowd held silence for a full moment after Adam had made his bow, bucket in hand. Then they burst into a storm of applause and shouts. There was no need to prove himself further, at least not tonight. He bowed low, savoring, for the barest instant, the pleasure of having entertained and delighted with his skills.

The townspeople swarmed over him and carried him back into the bar, buying him drinks and shouting their praises. He was engulfed at once and was lost in the sea of cheering citizens. When he bobbed up and could see over a few heads, the golden cartwheel hat was gone. So were Matthew and the Hag.

Damn, he thought. Lost on both counts. He'd have to wait until tomorrow to discover the name of the lovely amber-eyed woman. And he'd have to wait to discover how the Hag had reacted to his performance and whether she saw him as a serious magus or not.

He permitted himself a few drinks and accepted the praises of the audience, then excused himself and took his trunk and equipment up to his room. Once there, he stripped off his showy clothes and packed them away hastily. He always felt awkward in them once he was offstage.

The sounds in the tavern below softened and then silenced as Adam stood at the window in the darkened room and gazed out at the dim landscape, just outlined by the fading moon. His thoughts flew far, to Philadelphia, where his family was no doubt preparing for bed in the big house where he'd been born and raised. His mother and father wouldn't be pleased to know where he was tonight; nor would they approve of what he was doing. He grimaced, then shrugged. This was his way. He'd do what he must, with or without their approval.

His thoughts flew near, to the image of a pair of lustrous eyes beneath the brim of a golden straw hat. It was as if she'd spoken to him out loud, saying so many things that he only felt, deep inside. And, silly and trite as it sounded, it was as if he'd met her before, as if they knew one another. But that was impossible. Not that it mattered. He'd know her soon—as soon as possible. She'd sunk a shaft of amber light all the way inside him and he could almost physically feel the spot where it had touched him. He couldn't leave here until he had seen her, spoken with her, touched her. . . .

"Bosh," he muttered, jerking away from the window. What was he thinking of? Romantic twaddle.

He hadn't come here to get entangled with some female, especially one of the softheaded lot who doubtless inhabited Cold Springs in record numbers. He had a job to do and when he was finished, he had to return to Philadelphia. He had business to settle with his family.

Still, it didn't hurt to daydream, he thought to himself as he drifted off toward slumber, enveloped in the soft quilts and eiderdowns on the bed. Honey eyes and a wide, sweet mouth. Honey eyes and a honey mouth . . . Honey and cream and peaches . . .

"Bosh," he whispered.

Bryony sat on the bed in her nightdress. Soot bounded lightly onto the coverlet and burrowed against her hip, molding himself to her shape in order to maximize the available body heat. Bryony stroked his head and kneaded his shoulders until the sleek gray cat began to rumble with pleasure. She sighed and sank back into the pillows she'd piled up behind her.

He'd been magnificent, she thought to herself. Though many of his tricks were simple parlor magic, he'd performed them with the utter conviction and stylish grace of a true magus. He had a gift, all right, whether he used it or not. She might not yet have her own gift, but one thing she could do was spot the gifts of others.

He'd looked so strong and certain, she thought. Like one of the tall maple trees outside her windows. Adam Hawthorne was certain of himself and what he was doing, never wavering the way she did, trying to decide upon the right thing to do.

He'd seen much of her, too, she knew. She'd never been very good at disguising her thoughts and feelings—it was one of the things she despaired of when trying to achieve the detachment necessary to work magic. Her emotions always seemed to get in her way.

He didn't seem to be at all affected by her awful appearance earlier in the day. He'd been quite welcoming tonight, in fact. She felt relieved.

"How will I see him again, though, Soot?" she murmured to the cat.

Soot snorted sleepily.

"Well, that's easy for you to say. Cats can go trotting about in the dark and yowl outside of someone's window. I'm not a cat and I can't change into one, either." She giggled at the thought of Adam's face if he looked down to see her perched on a fence outside his inn window, mewling and caterwauling for his attention. He'd be justified in shying a boot at her from the window.

But she longed to see him. Just see him. To watch that lithe, long body stride about and see the firelight glint off his rich, rosewood hair. To see his hands, elegant and tapering, yet full of subtle strength. Magic hands.

She wriggled into the bed. What was the matter with her? Why was she so keyed-up tonight? She seemed incapable of any thought that didn't revolve around willow-green eyes and broad, rippling shoulders. She'd hoped that hurrying away from the inn and going home to her ordinary bed in her simple room would banish the excited, somewhat breathless feeling she'd carried within her ever since her eyes had met his. But sleep wasn't coming and the direction of her thoughts disturbed her.

"Wait for your gift," her mother had told her not long before the fever had carried her away. "It will come. It's your gift that will make you whole, and you'll know it when it comes."

"Be patient, but be prepared," her Aunt Beryl had said when Bryony had asked her about the way to acquire her special talent. "If you let yourself be distracted, you may have to wait a long time before you can regain your path."

"What sort of distractions?" Bryony had asked.

"Other people. Other tasks. Oh, I don't mean that you should shut yourself off from others—part of the magic is in the giving. But your gift isn't found through others alone. You must find it through yourself. So beware of giving yourself utterly to anyone else until you are secure in your gift."

Bryony couldn't imagine giving herself totally to another person. She'd been on her own for three long years and she'd always been somewhat isolated by her status as a Talcott. She was accustomed to going her own way in her own time, even as she devoted herself to helping the other people in the hollow.

But tonight . . .

No. It was nonsensical. She was nothing to this Adam Hawthorne and she wasn't going to give herself to him, however intriguing he might be.

What would a magus such as he be doing in the hollow, anyway? He was just passing through on his way to someplace bigger and grander and more exciting. And she—she was going to keep on helping others and working in her gardens and practicing all the rituals and incantations and magical skills she had at her command in order to achieve her destiny: the special magical gift that would define her as a true Talcott and show her the path to her future.

She shifted Soot around and snuggled down under the covers. Soot stood for a moment, lifting his paws one at a time to get the feel of the territory, then padded up to nuzzle close into Bryony's side.

Bryony sighed as she scrunched the pillow into exactly the shape she preferred for sleeping. She was glad to have that matter put to rest. Adam Hawthorne was only a momentary ripple in the quiet stream of her life. She'd move on tomorrow, just the way she'd always planned: solitary, determined, and secure. After all, she was a Talcott. That was how it was meant to be.

Soot gave a sleepy snort, as if to say "Humans."

Adam rose and went out early that morning. He thought he'd go out to Matthew's farm and see if he could ascertain what impression he'd made on the Hag. Was she concerned at all about a new magus in town? Or would he have to put her to a greater test before she showed her true colors? The sooner he got on with his task, the sooner he'd be back in civilized Philadelphia, where there were at least some folk who understood and respected the practice of sound reason and common sense.

There was another reason why he was headed for the Cowley farm at such an early hour, though he wouldn't consciously admit it. He had to know the name of the beauty in the wide-brimmed hat. Despite his best efforts to banish her from his thoughts and concentrate on his mission to discredit the Hag, those wide eyes with their tender, yearning expression still haunted the back of his mind. Matthew knew everyone in Cold Springs. He'd at least be able to give her a name.

Adam quickened his pace over the southbound track that led to the Cowley farm and Crystal Pond. He was striding along with some force when a weathered stone marker caught his eye. It marked the entrance to a side road that led off in the opposite direction from Matthew's.

"Talcott," Adam murmured, reading the name carved in the marker. This had to be the road to the Hag's farm.

Here was an opportunity too good to miss. He'd visit the Hag unexpectedly and perhaps catch her in the act of concocting a false cure or cooking up a mess of smelly herbs that would do no more than sicken its intended recipients—causing them to be deeply grateful to her when they survived the damned thing! Or, if he could meet with her one-to-one, perhaps he could win her confidence as a so-called fellow practitioner of magic. Perhaps then she would even confide in him, sharing some of her low tricks of the trade. He was collecting quite a store of information that could serve him well in the future.

The road led through a graceful arch of overhanging branches, then opened out to a broad, green yard and some lovely, well-tended gardens. The main house at Talcott Farm was a handsome old structure of gray fieldstone. Neat, dark green shutters flanked the many windows that overlooked the lawns, and morning glories twined around the corners and wound up the chimneys. The outbuildings were of the same gray stone. The whole place was well kept and indicative of wealth, country prosperity, and simple good taste.

It wasn't exactly what Adam had expected after seeing the Hag. He'd expected a place that was as slovenly and ill-kempt as her person, and hung about with hexes and signs. But then, he thought cynically, she could afford to have the finest place in the whole valley, living as she did off the sweat and tears of others.

There was no one about the yards, so Adam strolled around to the back of the house. An enormous garden stretched almost from the back door to the far edge of the woods. Though it was early in the season, the garden was already lush with growth, and every sort of flower, herb, fruit, and vegetable had been planted there, from what he could see. There were orchards and pastures off to the south and east, though no animals grazed there. He wondered how such a vast place could thrive so well and yet seem so devoid of human presence.

A voice behind him caused him to turn. It was coming from the house. The corn-husk croak of the witless Hag, he thought. Adam cringed to hear it, even as his curiosity was aroused. Here was his chance to observe her unawares, revolting though she was.

He approached the side of the house, keeping out of sight of the open window. He glanced about, then crept nearer and waited beneath the sill to hear what she'd say next.

"You sit there like a good lad. It's time you kept your eye out for the mouse that's been stealing the malt, puss. Everyone here has to work for his living, remember?"

There came the sound of splashing water and the scrape of a pot against the hearth. The scent of something sweet and pungent wafted through the open window.

Adam couldn't resist it. He had to see what the crone was brewing up in her cauldron. He dropped to a squat beneath the ledge, then carefully, an inch at a time, raised himself to where he could peer into the room.

At first, he could see nothing but a large, high-sided wooden tub standing before a bright fire and a sleek gray cat seated nearby on a stool. He saw the ugly burlap dress and the grotesque amulet lying on the hearth. She was probably just having a wash. Lord knew she needed it, Adam thought, recalling the potent scent of her yesterday afternoon. He felt a twinge of disappointment that he hadn't caught the Hag in some silly ritual. It would have provided him with more information about how she gulled her victims.

What he saw in the next instant, however, was enough to provide him with food for thought for many a long day—and night—to come. He had to grip the window ledge with both hands to keep from toppling over backward into the geraniums.

The Hag of Cold Springs Hollow was rising from her bath like mist off a midnight lake. Dark hair, luxuriant and thick, streamed down her back and formed a satiny, wet cape over her shoulders. She faced the fire, but what Adam could see of her form was breath-stealingly lovely—perfect skin that put him in mind of a fresh peach, shapely, long legs, and the most exquisitely curved little derriere he'd ever had the pleasure to gaze upon. God help him, but he had a sudden, wild desire to take a bite out of her, just to see if she'd taste of sweet cream and summer peaches.

He was struck dumb with awe, rendered motionless with surprise and anticipation, set on fire with pure, elemental lust. She was turning his way, lifting her long tresses as she reached for a towel. . . .

"So, lad, I thought this might be where I'd find you."

Adam thought he would levitate straight up into the air as Matthew Cowley laid a heavy hand on his shoulder.

"Couldn't wait to get another glimpse of her, eh?" Matthew managed to turn him about and raise him to his feet with one swift movement. Adam almost shouted out loud with frustration at losing sight of Bryony Talcott's emerging form.

"Can't say as I blame you, son," Matthew said, keeping his voice soft. "But she is a maid, sir, and entitled to her modesty. There'll be time enough for the earthly things later."

"I didn't—I wasn't—" Adam couldn't help himself; he was stammering like a schoolboy. What was happening to him?

"'Tis all right, no harm done," Matthew said with bluff good cheer. "Come along with me whilst I collect some chokecherries from the Hag's garden. You'll see her later, I vow it."

Adam allowed himself to be led away from the window and its delectable sights. His head was reeling. The Hag—it was her, wasn't it?—was a beauty. Or, at least, she had the most beauteous body he'd ever seen. Her face still might be the sort that frightened beasts and small children. But that body . . . How had she managed to conceal it so effectively before? He'd been in Cold Springs Hollow only a matter of hours, and already he'd glimpsed two of the most beautiful, desirable women imaginable. Was there something special in the water here? In the air?

"Come along and have a visit, then, lad," said Matthew. "I need to get these cherries into some good brandy straightaway, while they're still fresh."

Adam felt himself straining in several directions at once as he followed Matthew through the berry patches that grew in lush profusion on either side of the path. He wasn't leaving the hollow until he'd revealed the Hag as a fraud—that was absolute. He'd come too far already to turn back in his errand. And he wasn't leaving until he'd at least learned the name of the honey-eyed beauty from the inn last night. That was small enough compensation for all his pains out here in this outpost of nowhere. Last of all, though she might be a cruel pretender with the face of Medusa, he wasn't leaving this hollow until he'd looked his fill at Bryony Talcott's beautiful body. Every slender, silken, peach-tinted, cream-sweet inch of it.

Chapter Four

> "An Acorne at the Windowe will help keep Lightning out. Those who insist upon standing out in a Storm, however, must take their Chances."
>
> —*Cassia Talcott*

Bryony settled herself on the grass knoll overlooking the pond. She'd done her morning chores at the neighboring farms, mostly blessings and incantations over the new-planted seeds, and now she was ready to continue her personal quest. One of the skills she had most admired had belonged to her old Aunt Coreopsis. Aunt Cory had been able to send her spirit out to inhabit the bodies of other people, thereby giving her an insight into how they thought and felt and viewed the world. Kything, she had called it, an old word that meant both knowing and revealing. The result of this practice was that Cory Talcott had been one of the most gentle, unjudging persons Bryony had ever known, for she had, indeed, seen the world from the other person's point of view. Bryony had tried it once, to no avail, but now she thought she ought to try once again, just to make sure.

She'd decided to send her spirit into Millie Beebe, the baker's daughter. Millie had always seemed like a calm, untroubled person, whose greatest concern was remembering when to take the loaves from the oven. Bryony thought it might be peaceful to be Millie. She'd borrowed a red sock of Millie's from off her clothesline, fully intending to return it with the existing hole neatly mended. She also carried a large blue feather, dropped from a swift-flying jay, and a poplar twig. The sock represented Millie, the feather represented the flight of Bryony's spirit, and the poplar branch would work its age-old magic in promoting spirit projection. All Bryony had to do was lie quietly and envision her goal.

But a friendly bumblebee had no knowledge of Bryony's intent. Attracted to the blue and red and green in her hands, it was plain that he'd assumed he'd bumbled into a nice little patch of spring blossoms. He zoomed in to investigate.

Bryony heard the buzzing by her left ear and brushed at it with the feather. This only served to redirect the bee over to her opposite ear. She swished at him with the sock. "Shoo," she whispered. "Go away."

The bee took an awkward lunge toward her nose. She blew up a puff of air to send him on his way, but he soon returned to her right ear. This was not going well at all, she thought. Why did her attempts at these rites always seem to spiral down toward the absurd? She gave a swat with the sock and a puff from her lips, hoping to overwhelm the winged intruder. No luck.

"Ah . . . good morning. Miss Talcott?"

Bryony went stock-still, the red sock falling to drape itself over her face. Oh, Lord, she thought. She knew that voice already. It was Adam Hawthorne. She also knew that she must look a complete fool.

She brushed at the bee one last time and scrambled up, her cheeks warming as she saw the tall man standing there, a quizzical look on his face. She smoothed her skirts and offered up a tentative smile. "Good morning, Mr. Hawthorne. We meet again."

Adam felt his heart lurch as he took in the full impact of the vision before him. This was Bryony Talcott—the Hag? His mouth felt suddenly dry. "I believe we do," he stammered. "Good morning."

He had no idea what he was saying, but he had to say something or else just stand there stricken by her, like a man turned into a block of wood. It was she—the beauty with the cartwheel hat. He took a step nearer and drank in the wondering expression in her magnificent eyes. God help him, the Hag of Cold Springs Hollow was quite possibly the loveliest creature he'd ever seen. As his gaze dropped to take in the rest of her once more, he felt a jolt of excitement within him. If not the loveliest creature, then certainly one of the most desirable. From what he could see now, and what he could recall of her figure rising from her bath, not only was she fair of face, but she possessed a body that would make a statue melt in her embrace.

What was he to do now? The word "bewitched" came, unbidden, to his mind.

"Master Hawthorne?"

Adam startled at the soft, husky sound of her voice. "Yes. I was—was not expecting to find you here today. I just left Master Cowley at his fishing spot."

"Ah." She smiled.

Adam smiled back. He continued to stare at her.

Ye gods, Adam thought, as another jolt of excited desire permeated his senses. Were there donkey ears sprouting from his head? If there weren't, there should be, because it was clear that he'd turned into a complete jackass. Taylor, Beau, and Wade would laugh themselves sick over this sight, were they here.

The thought of his friends, their wager, and his errand brought him up short. She was just a woman. A lovely one, yes, but still a woman, and a foolish, devious one at that. Hadn't he just witnessed an example of her nonsensical habits—lying on the grass, puffing and fidgeting? And wasn't she wearing some silly pouch about her neck? Doubtless it was full of chicken feathers and ground cat bones, meant to ward off the evil eye.

"Miss Talcott, I was just going to your house," he managed to say. "I hope I'm not finding you at an inconvenient time?"

"Oh. No, no, not really." She gave him another shy smile. "I very much enjoyed your work last evening at the inn. It was most impressive."

"Thank you. I believe we have something in common, then," Adam said. "I understand that you are a practitioner of the mystic arts, as well."

Bryony felt a pang at his reminder of her search. She started down the path toward the road. "Well, I don't know how mystical they are. But I am the Hag here, and I learned several skills from my parents."

"You're too modest," Adam said, falling into step beside her. "I understand that you work spells on the crops and animals here, tend the sick, prophesy the weather, and sell special remedies."

She nodded. "Yes, just the usual sort of thing."

Adam wanted to smile. The usual sort of thing. If such things were boasted of in the educated circles of his own Philadelphia, there would be no end to the laughter that would follow. Still, she seemed modest about her claims.

"What were you doing just now?"

"Up there? Oh, trying out a skill my aunt used to use. I wanted to see if I could send out my spirit and see the world through the eyes of another person. Kything, we call it. But you know how difficult that is, even for the gifted."

I do, indeed, Adam thought. About as difficult as getting a camel to lay duck eggs. "Did you have any success?" he asked, trying to keep the derision out of his voice.

"No, not really. I found myself too distracted. It may not be a skill that I'll ever master."

"I see. Where are you going now?" he asked.

"I was going to the pond. I often go there in the morning to scry the waters while they're still fresh and undisturbed."

"Scry the waters?"

"Yes. You know—looking into the water to see what is before you."

Water is before you. That should be obvious. Aloud, he said, "Oh, yes, of course. I've heard of it but I've never seen it done. May I watch?"

She frowned. "It will surely bore you," she said hesitantly.

"I assure you it won't."

She bit her lip, then nodded. "If you truly wish. But we must keep silence, you know."

"I won't say a word."

She led the way to the path that skirted the pond on the left bank and pushed through a low overhang of willow branches. They emerged by a small inlet fed by one of the streams running down out of the hills. Willows surrounded the tiny cove and new grass carpeted the bank. Royal purple marsh lilies bloomed nearby in the wetland above the pond, and a heron stood meditating in the shallows. The pleasure of the idyllic sight caught Adam unawares, and he stood still beneath the willow eaves and simply stared at the landscape before him.

"It is lovely, isn't it?" Bryony said. She spoke

over her shoulder, not even seeing him as he stood in awe. "I've been coming here since I was a child. It's my favorite spot to come to when things vex me or I'm worried about something."

"I can understand why. It's very peaceful."

Adam stirred himself and moved ahead to join her at the bank. A large, smooth rock formed a natural seat by the waterside. Bryony climbed up and sat down, cross-legged, her skirts modestly tucked beneath her legs. Adam sat beside her and reached down to dabble his fingers in the water that lapped on three sides of the rock.

Bryony caught his wrist just before his fingertips touched the water. He looked up in surprise.

"You mustn't disturb the water," she said. "It must flow in its own way. Otherwise the scrying won't be true."

"Ah. Yes, of course," he murmured.

She held his wrist for a moment, her slender fingers touching his pulse. She seemed about to speak. Adam felt himself pulling toward her, his eyes held by the serious, wondering gaze in her golden eyes. What was it about her that so disturbed him? How was it that the mere sight of her, the merest touch, could so disarm him? He was about to lean in further when she abruptly broke their contact, dropping his hand and turning to face the water.

"I'm going to begin," she said softly. "From now on, we must not say a word."

Adam nodded, relieved that the spell between them was broken and he was himself again. He settled in to watch her antics. If this was anything like her attempts to inhabit another person's body by batting herself in the face with a sock, then he was in for a most amusing morning.

Bryony did not move for quite a long while. She merely closed her eyes and sat utterly still on the rock, an expression of peaceful concentration on her face. The sun rose above the trees behind them, warming them and casting its light closer and closer to the water.

Adam watched, fascinated, as she lowered her feathery lashes until her eyes were half-shadowed. She began to hum a song, her voice low and sweet, her body swaying a bit in time to the music.

It's as if she's becoming part of the water and the sunlight, he found himself thinking. Even the birds seemed to be singing in counterpoint to her song.

Balderdash. The sun was starting to bake his brains, he told himself sternly. She was just sitting on a rock, looking at an overgrown mud puddle.

Her song halted and she sat silent for a while. Adam wondered if she'd fallen asleep with her eyes open. He reached out to touch her shoulder, and jumped as she suddenly turned to him with a soft but somehow sad smile.

"There," she said. "I've finished. I hope I didn't bore you. I can't think why you'd want to watch. I'm sure you must know all about this."

"Well, yes," he said, recovering quickly. "Yet I'd like to see more. It's always useful to observe how others work."

"Yes, it is. I always loved watching my father when he was dowsing. He was so careful that all the signs should be right."

Adam stretched out on the sun-warmed rock and propped his head on his hand. He couldn't resist challenging her. "Did you ever stop to think how your father knew where water was?"

"Oh, yes. He told me. There's water all over this area. You can tell that from all the little streams and creeks that bubble up throughout the hollow."

"So, there wasn't any real magic involved in finding water. It was just your father using his powers of observation and reason."

"Yes. In part. My father was a wise man and well educated. But it took his magical powers to find exactly where to dig to find the sweet water, for there are some streams that run out of the hollow that are skunk water. You can't always tell from the first taste."

"Skunk water?"

"That's what we call it. Sour. Smelly. Impure." Her nose wrinkled in disgust. "I remember when Rolly Bleeckerman tried to dig a well without my father's help. Everyone who passed his farm could smell how bad it was. He finally came to Papa when everyone refused to sit by him, even in church, because he insisted on washing in the awful stuff."

"And your father found sweet water for him?"

"Not more than fifty ells away. The hazel wands almost jumped out of his hands. No one was better at dowsing than Papa."

"I see." Adam sighed. The girl obviously adored her father and thought he could do no wrong. It would be impossible to reason with her on the subject of his magical abilities, or lack of them. The man was dead these past three years, according to Matthew, and it was clear that she still keenly felt the loss. He felt again the sense that he would have to choose different tactics with this so-called Hag.

"Well, I must get back to the house and tend to my chores. You'll be going back to town, I expect?" Bryony rose and brushed off her skirts.

"Yes, but I have a request, Miss Talcott. I'd like to come back and watch some more of your . . . magic." He had difficulty pronouncing the word, but he managed to get it out.

Bryony stopped abruptly. Adam drew up before her, almost caught off balance. "You want to watch me work?" she asked.

"Yes, I do."

"Why?"

He groped around for an answer. Fortunately, one came quickly to mind.

"Because I'm in a quandary. I'm a magician, yes, but what I do is more for the sake of entertainment. It's fine for an evening's pleasure, but I'd like to be able to do more. I'd like to learn about other forms of magic. The kind that you practice."

She turned and walked on, frowning. She stopped again, and this time Adam had to put his hand on her shoulder to keep himself from running over her. The sudden, pleasant shock of touching her caused him to jerk his hand away at once.

"There's something you should know about me." She was still frowning as she met his eyes.

"Oh?" Here it comes, he thought. The grand declaration of ultimate power.

"I don't do magic."

This caught Adam off guard. He hadn't expected a confession so early in the game. Had she guessed who he was and why he was here? "You don't?" he asked.

She chewed at her lower lip for a moment. "Well, yes, I do. I mean, I try to. I can do the little things that some call magic. Herb cures and reading the signs for a good harvest and such. But I can't do any of the important things. I don't have my gift yet."

"Your gift?"

"All of the Talcotts have a special gift. Only Darwell and Cassia, the first Cold Springs Talcotts, had several gifts. The rest of us get only one or two. My father's chief gifts were dowsing and spells of protection. My mother's were telling the future—in all ways—and healing. She truly had the sight. As I told you, Aunt Coreopsis could inhabit the bodies of others and see things through their eyes. Others could see the future in smoke, or speak spells to animals and plants. But I—I don't seem to have any real gift at all."

She looked so utterly sad as she made this declaration that Adam found himself moved to comfort her. But he caught himself just in time. She didn't believe she had any special magical gift, he thought. That meant there was room for doubt in her mind. She wasn't as sure of herself as he had first believed. He might have to reconsider his tactics.

He looked down into her liquid, light brown eyes and read the earnestness of her words. He saw the slight trembling in her slim shoulders and knew that it had cost her to make this confession to him. Obviously, she had a large part of herself invested in her work as the Hag. He again fought the impulse to reach out and comfort her.

Why should he care? he thought, steeling himself against his irrational impulses. She was a trickster, the same as all the others. Of course she had a great deal invested in her scheme. She preyed on hope and fear and weakness. She made her living by it. And what was worse, she even acknowledged that she lacked any real magical gifts, which somehow made it more reprehensible that she led others to believe in her. She didn't deserve his sympathy. She needed to be stopped.

"I'd still like to see what you do," he said coolly. "The people here certainly set store by you."

She turned away, not catching the icy contempt behind his words. "I know they do. It's quite a burden sometimes. I know they depend on me as the Hag but I don't know how much good I really do for them." She began to walk again. "Perhaps *you* could help *me,*" she said shyly. "If you watched what I do, perhaps you, as a magus, could tell me what I'm doing that's wrong and what I could do to find my true gift." She raised her hand to stop his quick protest. "I know that the magic you claim is only for show, but a gift is a gift and my parents always told me that we can learn from everyone."

Adam felt as if he were losing his own grip on reality. This was a twist in his path he hadn't expected. She was asking *him* to be her advisor in magic? He opened his mouth again to protest, then closed it. This was an advantage he hadn't thought of before. If he were to go with her and talk to the people she worked with, he could soon learn who was disgruntled with her work and would be willing to see her unmasked. He could see what sort of things she did and accumulate a list of ways in which she duped people. It would hasten his efforts.

Another thought came to him, unbidden. Would he also show her the ways in which she duped herself?

Brushing this uncomfortable notion aside, he smiled at her. "I'm sure you're only suffering a moment's lack of confidence," he said. "But, yes, I would like to accompany you as you go about your . . . work. And if I can be of service, then so much the better."

"All right," she said slowly. "Can you join me tomorrow morning? At six o'clock? I have incantations to make over some of the new plantings, and as you know it's best to do it while the dew is still on the ground." She told him where they would meet.

"Six o'clock, at the first farm south of town."

Adam bowed to her as they paused by the stone marker that pointed the way to her farm. "Your servant, Miss Talcott."

"Good day, Master Hawthorne."

Bryony watched Adam Hawthorne's retreating back until he disappeared from view. Her senses were still somewhat confused by the impact of his sudden appearance before her that morning, his dark hair slightly ruffled by the breezes and his long, elegant body clearly revealed in his simple shirt, waistcoat, and breeches. It was a sensation she'd never experienced before and it had taken some time to retrieve her wits after they'd wandered off on a rapturous inventory of Adam Hawthorne's numerous physical charms.

Now that he was not before her, his willow-leaf eyes probing hers, she was more able to consider what she had just done. She had invited him to accompany her on her errands about the hollow, to watch her work. The very thought made her shake, for more reasons than one.

For one thing, he'd soon discover that she was indeed a fraud. He'd learn in short order that she could only do the everyday, humdrum sort of magic that worked in barnyards and gardens and kitchens, that she couldn't even scry water in the age-old mirror of the Talcott vision, Crystal Pond. She couldn't perform any acts of real magic, and she felt sure that was what he wanted to see.

She felt a rush of shame. It had been difficult to admit to Adam Hawthorne that she had not yet found her true gift, or that she might never possess a gift at all. She had sensed no such self-doubt in him. When he was performing, when he walked at her side, when he spoke, she saw only a bright, supremely confident person.

But he had agreed to come. The idea of him traveling about the hollow with her, always at her side, always her companion, made her insides tilt again. She would have welcomed help from anyone with a claim to magic, but Adam Hawthorne's handsome face and powerful, lean build made it seem ever so much more exciting a prospect. More than once this morning she had fought the urge to reach out and stroke that rich, red-brown hair, to draw close and breathe in the warm, clean, male scent of him.

She followed the path to her house and went inside to prepare the midday meal for Lucius Dreyer, who would be coming to do some of the heavy work in the yards this afternoon. A good, home-cooked dinner was payment for the shy young fellow's hard work.

Why had she never felt such feelings for Lucius? she wondered, rinsing fresh greens in a basin. He was about Adam's age, he was single, he was nice enough. And as a hollow-dweller, they certainly had more in common than she and the city-bred Mr. Hawthorne.

But there it was. She simply didn't feel it. She'd never once wanted to reach out and touch the young farmer's sandy hair. Or his face. Or his shoulders, broad with work though they were. And Lucius hadn't pressed any sort of a suit because she was, above all, a Talcott and the Hag. His attentions were saved for simple-hearted Millie Beebe.

She looked down and saw that she'd washed the same piece of lettuce five times. She had been distracted. By Adam Hawthorne.

Guard against such distractions, she'd been told. If not, she could lose her chance to discover her gift. Was Adam Hawthorne worth such a price? She'd already noted a certain aura of danger about him, a feeling of ice and fire that made her senses tingle and spoke of a warring spirit within him. Was it prudent to welcome such a danger into her life?

She shook her head. She'd be on her guard. Besides, it was most unlikely that this strange newcomer harbored any equivalent thoughts about her—Adam Hawthorne seemed not only fearless, but utterly unfazed by her own physical presence. Besides, to risk her gift would be a great folly, for herself and for the people in the hollow, who counted on the Talcotts to make the magic that protected and fostered this place. It was a risk she wouldn't take, even for the sake of—what? Love? Pride? She felt pulled in several directions at once.

She fixed her mind on the serene white clouds that drifted across the sky outside the kitchen window. Silently, she vowed to maintain that kind of serenity and distance with the man whenever they met. She had a higher task to accomplish.

Still, she couldn't help thinking that the deep green tops of the garden-fresh carrots she was cutting were nothing compared to the green of Adam Hawthorne's eyes.

Chapter Five

"To discover Thy future Husbande: At Midnight of Midsummer's Eve, set the Table for Supper and leave the Doore to the House wide ajar. The Man sought will come inne and sitte. Do not, however, mistake a Varmint for a Husbande. Thy Neighbor's Cat will not serve well, as a Rule."

—*Cassia Talcott*

Adam spent the week walking at Bryony's side, watching her ply her trade with the hollow-dwellers. He'd asked her how it was that she went everywhere in the hollow by herself, day or night, with what seemed to be little or no fear for her safety.

She had smiled. "The people in this place all know me. No one would have reason to harm me. Also, I'm the Hag. Even if someone took a dislike to me, they'd be too fearful of touching me because of the Talcott magic."

"But if you met a stranger?"

She glanced up at him and he saw a quick, measuring light in her eyes. She was considering if he might be such a stranger, he knew. But in reply, all she said was, "I have many sources of protection."

They visited a number of farms around the area. Bryony walked the acres with the farmers and heard their plans. She carried with her a cloth satchel, in which she carried a small supply of her herbal remedies, a toy or two with which she regaled ailing children, and most importantly, the Book. Adam took to calling it the Book in his own mind, for she was seldom without it and she consulted it on virtually every occasion. Her "patients" watched with reverent attention as she thumbed through the thick volume and scanned the pages, which were covered with a fine, tiny script and lavishly embellished with illustrations. When they visited the farms, she would ask the owner of the field what had last been planted in that particular ground, what he or she had in mind for that season's crop, and whether or not they had observed certain signs about the premises.

"How are the birds faring?" she asked one.

The farmer squinted toward the trees that edged the field to the north. "Oh, fat and sassy, them. There's a crowd of 'em settlin' in on the field near ever' morning. Don't bother anything but the dirt."

"And the rabbits?"

"Now, they been troublin'. The wife's winter garden was chewed down to nubbins twice and they're havin' a go at the new stuff she's got in already. Seems like nothin's gonna keep 'em out."

"I see."

Bryony pored over her book for a moment or two as the rustic watched with anxious anticipation. At last, she looked up and made her pronouncement. "You must plant only corn in this field, and in the far field plant some of those new Irish potatoes that were so tasty last year. The third field you must leave to lie fallow, except for some small crop of vegetation that the rabbits may enjoy. Be sure to plant the corn within the next fortnight or the moon will work against you. The potatoes must wait until after the seventh day of next month for the moon to be favorable."

She took a small square of linen out of her satchel. From this, she extracted a pinch of what looked to Adam like salt, a blue vial of some liquid, and a paper packet. He wanted to groan as she placed herself facing east and mixed the salt and water from the vial in her hand. She poured the mixture on the earth before her, then drew two seeds from the paper packet. She breathed on the seeds, held them up to the sun, then buried them in the earth where the salted water had gathered in a small puddle. She straightened, raised her arms, and softly chanted something about freedom, life, purity, growth, and, Adam guessed cynically, fertilizer.

"There," she said at last, lowering her arms.

"And what will I say?" the man asked.

Bryony placed her book into the satchel and carefully set the satchel on a stump nearby. She closed her eyes and clasped her hands in prayer, and the farmer followed suit. Adam felt his training demanded that he bow his head as well, but he was too curious to miss this last bit of flummery.

"Bless this ground, O Lord," she said softly. "Let it yield substance and sustenance for this family and for all who share it." She looked up at the farmer. "Can you repeat that?"

The man did so, haltingly. Bryony nodded her approval. "Good. Say it over each field at morning, noon, and night."

"Even the fallow one?"

"Even that one. Unless you wish the coneys to take all your crops."

"Oh, no, Mistress Bryony." He looked genuinely alarmed, as if Bryony could call down a plague of cottontails upon his house with a wave of her hand.

"Very well. Give my best to your wife and daughters."

"I'll bring payment by first of the week," he told her. "The same as always?"

"That would be fine."

Adam and Bryony took their leave and made the rounds of other farms and households. At each one, her routine was much the same. All of the folk of the region seemed to regard her words and claims as gospel, and Adam surmised that they would no more consider ignoring her advice than they would come stark naked to church on Sunday.

Bryony and the Book seemed to have an answer for everything that concerned or ailed the community. Most of it was quite singular in nature. Like the woman who complained of hearing too much scandal from her neighbors, for example. Bryony prescribed two days with soft cotton wadding tucked into the ears, alternating with two days of holding a smooth, clean stone close inside the mouth. The troubles, she claimed, would abate within a fortnight, if the remedy were repeated with diligence. She concocted an herbal mix of marjoram, mugwort, garlic, and thyme for a traveler to wear about his neck on a trip to the far-off city of Baltimore. A young man who'd been unfaithful to his sweetheart received a ritual for cleansing his guilt with lavender and rue—and the stern admonition to remember his lady at morning, noon, and night. She birthed piglets and encouraged chickens and blessed every sort of event, large and small.

For these unique treatments she was paid in stewing hens, in honeycombs, in pennies, in willow bark, in fresh-baked muffins, and even in a song from a sweet-voiced young girl whose mother was struggling with the sickness of early pregnancy. Adam wondered how Bryony kept herself in shoe leather with such odd barterings. Was she hiding some other source of income from him?

More disconcerting for Adam, however, were the feelings he was hiding from Bryony and everyone else. Every day, on first sight of her slender figure, his body simply went wild on him. Every day, he would plan to speak deferentially, noncommittally to her, to keep his distance and his cool demeanor. But it was like he was a green youth again, hardening at the mere anticipation of seeing her! And if perchance his hand should accidentally brush against her or she turned suddenly and bumped into him—ye gods, it would start all over again. He took to wearing his longest waistcoat, which blessedly covered the evidence of his arousal, but which could not diminish its willful eagerness. That would take all his strength of mind and will, and their encounters each day took on a new element of strain and awkwardness.

At night, in sleep, his will was utterly negated. Visions of Bryony rising from her bath floated in and out of even his most mundane dreams. The more explicit dreams shocked him with their intensity. He would waken in the morning exhausted and frustrated both at the realization that it was only a dream and with his sudden lack of any control over a part of his life that he had long believed mastered.

He wanted Bryony Talcott. He ached with the desire. And the conflict of that longing with his mission to bring her low left him as tense and disturbed as a lake before a thunderstorm.

A week after his first visit with Bryony, they were at the farm of the widow Dinsmoore. The woman was a regular visitor to Talcott Farm, Bryony confided to Adam, and she never failed to bring a new ailment or trouble with her, along with the demand that Bryony "cure" it. She wanted to stop by today to see if the latest remedy had taken.

"I've been robbed, Miss Bryony," Biddy Dinsmoore said without preamble as Bryony and Adam approached her in her yard. "Somebody's taken my second-best washtub and I want my property back."

"I see," said Bryony. In spite of her current "crisis," the older woman was gawking at the tall figure standing beside her. "Mistress Dinsmoore, do you know Mr. Hawthorne? He's visiting here from Philadelphia."

The woman nodded as Adam made a short bow her way, but she was not to be swayed from her purpose. "Yep. I've seen him. Saw his show. But what are you going to do about my stolen washtub?"

Bryony motioned to the woman to sit down on the bench beside her. "Of course you've taken the matter up with the aldermen?" she asked gently.

"I have. And once again, they refuse to do anything about it. They say that unless I can show the thief, there's nothing that they can do. I just want my property back, so I'm asking you. What'll you do?"

Bryony considered for another moment. "Let me consult Mama's book about this," she said. "This is a grave matter and calls for serious measures."

"I should say so," Biddy said, giving an indignant bob of her head.

Bryony consulted the Book once more. "Let me see. Tapping . . . tasting . . . temper, ah, yes, here it is, theft. Hmmm." She read down the page, her finger following dutifully along the lines. The widow leaned over her shoulder, squinting furiously at the page. "Aha. Yes, just as I thought. Here is what we must do, Mistress Biddy." Bryony turned with a look of grave concentration on her face.

"I'm ready," said the woman, squaring her shoulders for duty.

Several hours later, Adam wished he'd stayed back at the Laughing Dog, his feet up before the great hearth, a mug of ale cradled in his hands. Instead, here he was, back at the widow Dinsmoore's, witnessing another of Bryony's "cures."

It was just before midnight. A fire burned high in the old lady's kitchen, and the two women stood before it, solemn and intent. Bryony was speaking.

"First of all, when the clock strikes twelve, you must take your left shoe, put a goodly amount of manure in its toe, and burn it in the fireplace."

Biddy Dinsmoore's face went a bit pale at this. "My shoe? But I've only just purchased these from Cobbler Timmons."

"Perhaps an old pair of your castoffs will do," said Bryony soothingly. "And they are fine boots, I must say. However, you must burn a shoe, with the manure, in the fireplace and say the words. Are you ready?"

The older woman scuttled away and came back with a woebegone slipper, mended over but long past service. Adam winced and wrinkled his nose as Biddy scooped fresh cow leavings into the toe of the slipper with a tin spoon and packed it in firmly. She wiped her hands on her apron and turned to face Bryony. "I'm ready, Mistress Hag."

"Good. Now, repeat after me. Oh, thou who robs the innocent lamb, feel the burn of thy conscience. Smell the foul odor of thy deeds. Never will you know peace and cleanliness again until you have returned all that you have stolen from me."

Biddy repeated the lines, with Bryony prompting. Then Bryony clasped her hands. "Now, cast the shoe into the fire!"

Adam bit down on his lip to keep from bursting out in loud guffaws. The sight of the two of them, so utterly serious, flinging muck-filled slippers into the fireplace in hopes of recovering a stolen washtub was almost more than he could stand. What a performer this Bryony was! And how reverently these townspeople viewed her antics! It was hysterical.

Tears soon began to roll down his cheeks. Not from suppressed laughter, but from the combined stench of leather and cow dung. *Ye gods!* He was going to suffocate.

"Now, while this burns to ash," Bryony said, taking Biddy's arm, "there is another thing that you must do in order for this ordeal to be at an end."

"Tell!"

"You must take one silver piece and put it into a metal box with a sturdy lid. Add to this a large handful or two of grain—perhaps enough to fill a goodly mixing bowl—and seal the grain tight in a leather pouch. Go and get these things now and Mr. Hawthorne and I will wait outside for you."

Gratefully, Adam followed her outdoors while the widow hunted up the necessary items. Bryony fanned her face as they stood out in the cool, fresh air of nighttime.

"A noisome spell," she said apologetically. "But a sound one. If this last cure is all Mama says it is in her book, then Biddy's fears may be allayed at last." She put her hands to her flushed cheeks and dropped her voice to a whisper. "I must confess, she can be a trial. This cure is as much for my peace as her peace of mind."

Adam nodded. "I can understand this."

Biddy came out of the house, a cloud of odoriferous smoke trailing her skirts. She had the metal box under her arm. "Now what?" she asked.

"Secure the box well," Bryony said, "and when we are gone, take and bury it well under the earth a little ways from your house. Say words of blessing and thanks over it. Cover it so that it looks as if the spot was never disturbed. Then leave it there."

"Will that help me get my things back?"

"Well, it might. And what is more, as long as you are the only living soul who knows where that box is buried, this spell guarantees that you can never be robbed of all you have. It ensures that you will never be without money or food."

"Are you quite sure?"

Bryony drew herself up proudly. "It is a tested spell and written in the Talcott book."

That seemed to suffice. They made their goodbyes and went out the gate to the road. Adam glanced back and saw the widow watching them, no doubt waiting until they were well out of sight and hearing to hide her treasure. He turned to Bryony and gave her a round of soft applause. She looked at him quizzically.

"Most entertaining," he drawled. "And most enlightening. I had no idea that shoe leather and dung held magical properties."

Bryony felt heat rise to her cheeks at his slightly mocking tone. How would a real magus have handled the problem?

"Tell me," Adam continued. "What made you choose that spell? Wouldn't it have been more efficacious to hunt for the thief?"

Bryony shook her head as they turned onto the road toward her farm. "Most likely there is no thief. Every few weeks, Biddy loses a chicken, or misplaces her apron, or some such. She's lonely, and she doesn't see well, and she's forgetful. Also, she's consumed by the fear of poverty. I can't say as I blame her—her husband was no great hand at farming or anything else, and when he died, he left her alone with no stores and little money saved."

"How will getting her to burn her shoe change that?"

"It won't. But it may give her a feeling of power. That she isn't just a leaf tossed about in the storms of circumstance and old age. And when she finds the thing she thought was stolen, she'll have the peace of knowing that she retrieved it herself and that she didn't have to call one of her neighbors to account. For all her suspicions, Biddy is a good soul, at heart."

He stopped and drew closer to her, his eyes narrowed a bit. "And is this all you are called upon to do? Hand out comfort to the aged, treat infertile chickens, advise housewives on what plants to grow this season?"

"Well, yes, mostly. What is it that I should be doing?"

He came closer still. "I thought that you were the Hag, a witch," he said softly. "Aren't the Talcotts supposed to be workers of magic?"

"I told you," she murmured. "I don't yet possess my gift." She swallowed hard against the feelings that were rising in her, a feeling that she should run from this man. A feeling that she wanted him even closer.

"Ah, yes, so you said," he replied. "But don't the folk around here come to you expecting magic? Don't you take their money and their offerings?"

She looked at him, puzzled. "I do, when I know that they can pay. Sometimes the payment comes from a fund the town has set aside for those who can't afford to make any payment."

"Yes, I heard that. The town's council voted to levy an extra tax to support the Talcotts."

Now she was indignant. What was he driving at? "That money is not for our—my—support. I can well take care of myself. But I do need to send for special plants or ingredients that are not readily available in the hollow. I am at everyone's beck and call, night and day, as you have seen.

And people have their pride, as well. They expect to pay for services rendered, just as I pay for their services to me."

He gazed at her, his eyes dark and thoughtful. Absently, he took a coin from his pocket and began working it over and under the fingers of his left hand. Bryony watched his long, dexterous fingers moving with effortless grace and controlled strength. What would it feel like to have those hands touch her? Was that what he meant to do? Suddenly she felt a keen awareness that they were out alone together in the silence of night.

He took yet another step closer. He seemed but a breath away from her now, and he was gazing down at her with such a piercing stare that she hardly knew where to look. He was challenging her in some way—but what way? And why?

"Everyone pays willingly?" Adam asked.

"No, of course not. But that is the way of any business."

"Then this is a business, not a calling from above?"

Her innate sense of pride and courage rose to the fore. She summoned her composure and met his eyes with a steady assurance that she only half felt under the intensity of his gaze.

"I don't claim to be an angel or a miracle-working saint of old, if that's what you mean," she said quietly. "I use the skills that I learned at my mother's knee, at my father's side, just as Lucius Dreyer farms as his father taught him, and

Millie Beebe bakes with her family. I do hope that heaven smiles on my work."

He seemed to want to stare straight through her. She held her ground, struggling with the need to run from his dangerous eyes and the opposing desire to reach up and touch his stern, handsome face.

He seemed about to speak, then suddenly smiled and stepped back, though there was no humor in his eyes. She felt relief that he wasn't so close now, that she wasn't so swamped by the awareness of his powerful presence.

"I must be getting back to the inn," he said, his voice now coolly polite. "It is late and I have some . . . business I must attend to before this week's coach arrives."

"Will I—will you come tomorrow?" She wanted to bite her tongue for saying it, but she couldn't help it. She felt suddenly bereft at the idea of having him absent for any great length of time.

"I will."

"Oh. Perhaps then you can advise me in some of your methods. I imagine it will be somewhat different than the way in which my family works."

"Yes, I imagine that it will." He gave a short bow and left, his long legs carrying him easily down the lane toward the main road.

Bryony watched him as he went, his body moving with easy grace. She felt as if she had been holding in a flood of feelings while he was with her, and now, as she turned toward home, she found she was trembling. She wanted to sit down, but she compelled herself to keep going. The way her thoughts were going, she needed some focus to keep herself from being swept away in the strong tide of emotions that Adam seemed to rouse in her.

Was there ever such a puzzling man? These past few days, he had followed her about from garden to garden, farm to farm, his dark eyes observing her with the keen gaze of a hunting bird. Sometimes, when she looked up and met that gaze, she felt as if he were asking her a question, an important one, but that she could not find the words to translate it.

He asked keen questions aloud, too, but never volunteered either advice or information about himself. It piqued her curiosity that he never offered to take a hand in her work beyond carrying a basket or lifting something heavy for her—menial things, not magical. Was he merely modest or was he unwilling to share his knowledge with such an amateur as she? Indeed, if she so much as touched his sleeve, he withdrew from her as if he'd been stung.

She took the steps to her kitchen door slowly. She had no answers, only more and more questions.

She decided it was time to learn more. Then, perhaps, she wouldn't be haunted day and night by the image of willow-green eyes and long, elegant hands.

Things weren't going as Adam had planned at all. He was supposed to be finding ways to uncover all Bryony's underhanded tricks, the ways in which she duped people.

Instead, he was caught up in pondering her life, her family, her work. And, God help him, he was forever pondering all the possible combinations of lips and arms, slender hands and long, shapely legs. She was in his senses even now, filling his nostrils with her spicy scent of herbs and flowers, his ears with her soft, slightly husky voice, his eyes with the wonder of black-fringed golden eyes and peachy coloring.

Distraction! That was it, he told himself. That was what magic was all about—distracting the eye so that one couldn't see the truth of the trick. Smoke and mirrors. He was being distracted by her seeming innocence, by her womanly charms.

But it wasn't going to work. He had only to look carefully behind the facade to learn what he needed to know. And he had only to think of his family and the past to know why he must persist. He had to force the Hag to show her hand.

He found it helped a bit to think of her as a Hag. That way, he kept her in her place with the other frauds he'd dealt with in the past.

He needed to talk to the people of the hollow and find out just who had been "helped" by the Talcotts and who had not reaped such glorious benefits. Perhaps old Biddy Dinsmoore could tell him what he needed to hear. With their aid and information, he'd have a better idea of how to go about unmasking the Hag. He headed for the inn with renewed vigor.

He spent the next three days in a frustrating round of interviews with the local folk. Nearly everyone in the hollow, he reckoned, had availed themselves of the Talcotts' services. And while there were some, like Mistress Dinsmoore, who admitted that they were not always overwhelmed with good fortune as a result, none claimed harm or had a negative word to say about the family in general or Bryony in particular. For that matter, the widow Dinsmoore had even recovered her missing washtub.

Adam was beginning to wonder if his efforts were being wasted here. He couldn't find anyone who felt tricked by the Talcotts and their claims of magic—even though none of them could offer what he considered to be solid proof of their helping them, either. Indeed, he found many who held implicit faith in them. He hadn't found a single thing about Bryony Talcott that showed him she was anything more than an innocent dabbler in herbs and quaint practices. Where was the harm in what she did? he found himself asking.

But when he went to call on Matthew again, he heard what he had come to hear—an announcement that confirmed his suspicions that the seemingly normal outward appearance of the village of Cold Springs was only a veil. The very worst sort of mystical practices were going on within the ring of these fair green hills, practices that echoed back to the darkest days of the Middle Ages and the most grisly, decadent habits of ancient Rome—perhaps even earlier.

Adam had his evidence at last.

"It's the night of the corn sowing," said Matthew. "Darwell and Cassia Talcott celebrated it the first spring that they came here, in this very field. Ever since, we've honored their tradition and made the ritual every spring at planting time."

"A corn ritual?"

"Aye. No doubt you've seen such in your travels, or performed one yourself. We have to insure the bounty of the crop, so we choose a young lad and a lass to be joined this night and given to the corn."

Good Lord, Adam thought. A fertility rite! This was not only outlandish, it was downright heathen! He could just imagine the proceedings—a young couple forced to have relations for the "good of the crops," and then sacrificed to appease the gods of the corn. It was too much! Cold Springs Hollow was showing its true colors. They actually believed in the ancient, bloody acts of propitiation that were meant to keep the gods smiling and benevolent.

Well, he was having none of it. He would do everything in his power to stop these lunatics from humiliating—perhaps physically harming!—an innocent young girl and boy. He'd be at the corn ritual, all right. Cold Springs Hollow would never forget this night. And he'd unmask Bryony Talcott in the bargain. "I'll be there," he said to Matthew, keeping his face and voice void of expression.

"Good. Bryony'll be there, of course, overseeing everything and saying the words. She'll be right busy but you can see her at the feast afterward."

They were going to *eat* after that horrible display? Adam could barely hide his grimace at the very thought.

"We'll be gathering at the square just before sunset," Matthew said. "You'll see everybody walking out from town. Just join in and come along. You'll be welcome."

Adam spent the rest of the afternoon writing a letter to Taylor, telling of his progress and reporting on his plans. His mind strayed often to the prospect of being an observer at a fertility rite, and he considered just how he could possibly go about stopping the proceedings. No doubt the crowd would be worked up into a frenzy and thirsty for the taste of human blood—they wouldn't lightly brook interference from an outsider.

He decided that how it was done didn't matter. His conscience would not permit him to watch without intervening in some way. Let them stone him or worse, he wouldn't allow them to sacrifice the innocent lives of a young boy and girl. Hadn't the world paid enough to these monstrous superstitions?

By the time the sun was setting, his insides were coiled tight with anger and stern resolve. He dressed and went down to the tavern, comfortable with the feeling of both his pistol and his knife tucked securely into his clothes.

The townsfolk were already streaming out toward Talcott Farm. Most of the women carried big baskets covered with cloths, along with big shocks of dried corn. It looked like they were going to an outdoor feast. But he was reminded of the bloody work to be done by the glistening scythes and blades that each man carried along with the tender shocks of corn. He ground his heels into the earth and strode ahead to where the townsfolk were gathering and building a large bonfire.

He spotted Bryony at once. She was gowned all in simple, flowing white muslin, her long hair caught up and wound with spring-green ribbons. Her eyes were sparkling with obvious excitement and the color in her cheeks was high. She looked ravishingly lovely, but Adam shook away his immediate physical response to her. Tonight he'd hold her accountable for all her magical claptrap. The Talcotts had begun this bloody business and he would see to it that Bryony was the last Talcott to ever attempt it.

A crude dais had been built in the exact center of the field, and a thick layer of straw had been laid over the tender, unplanted earth. Some people brought their cornstalks and husks and cast them onto the brightly burning fire, while others stacked theirs together to form a circle of shocks around the fire and the dais. The rich smell of fresh earth and the smoke of the fires mingled in the air.

A girl and a boy, just entering adolescence, were standing by the dais, their young faces solemn with the importance of the occasion. Did they know what they were facing? Adam wondered. Did they understand that they would never know the joys and trials of adult life—of any life—after this night's dreadful events?

Matthew began to bang on an old tin pot, and the silent, waiting crowd gathered in close around the dais. Bryony stepped forward and spread her arms wide.

"Bless us all!" she cried.

"Bless us all," the crowd shouted in response.

Bryony dropped her arms and raised her eyes heavenward. "The signs are good, dear people. We'll have a good corn crop this year."

There was lusty cheering. Matthew raised a hand for silence.

"Lots have been drawn," Bryony continued. "Bethany March and Daniel Conroy have been chosen as our gifts to the spirits of the harvest. Bless them both."

"Bless them!" the crowd repeated. The girl and boy on the dais shuffled at the attention and tried to keep their expressions appropriately sober.

Matthew handed Bryony a leather pouch. From it she drew three kernels of corn. She went to Bethany and Daniel and pressed a kernel into each of their hands. The remaining kernel she took and dropped into a hole that had been dug just in front of the dais. She covered the seed with fresh dirt, patted it down, and stood to recite:

"Mother Nature and Father Creator, we plant these seeds to honor thee. All abundance comes from thee, all sustenance comes from thee, all safety comes from thee. With rain and sun and watchful care, we give to thee thy own fair share!"

As she finished, music rose from the back of the crowd, a throbbing melody of pipes and drums. The tempo was steady, insistent.

Adam watched with keen attention. A man and a woman had stepped up on the dais to stand behind the girl and the boy. They placed wreaths of cornhusks on their heads and took hold of their hands.

Bryony beckoned to them and the four of them followed her toward the bonfire. She raised a soft leather thong and bound it about the wrist of the girl, then knotted it around the boy's wrist. The two older people stood with their hands on the young couple's shoulders, ready to direct them toward the fire. Two more men stepped from the throng and stood before the young couple, scythes in hand.

Adam pushed forward, out of the crowd. He slipped his coat aside and put his hand to his knife-hilt. The music began to swell.

Bryony placed her hands over the thong that bound the boy and girl at their wrists. "Bless the spirits of the harvesters who have gone before us. Bless the spirits of the ones who are to come. You stand on the threshold, young ones. Lead the way to a rich harvest, peace, and prosperity for us all."

The couple was turned to face the fire and the older couple stepped back, away from the brightly burning pyre. The music of the pipes and drums had risen to a fever pitch. The men raised their scythes high.

Adam stepped out from the throng to seize Bryony by the arm just as she lifted her hand to touch the boy. But he was too late. She brought it down on Daniel's shoulder and the boy began to move forward, toward the blades and the fire.

Chapter Six

"Earthe, Water, Fire, and Aire
Met together in a Garden Faire
Putte in a Basket Made of Skinne
If You Answere this Ryddle
You'll Never Beginne."
—*Cassia Talcott*

"No!" shouted Adam, but his cry was lost in the delirious shouts of the crowd.

The young couple began to dance. Shyly, they held hands where they were bound at the wrists, dipping and swaying in time to the throbbing music in the air. The two men clanged their scythes together in a bright salute and the young pair danced beneath the archway of crossed blades. The townsfolk formed a line behind them and joined hands. Around and around the bonfire they all danced, making a long chain of laughing, singing faces. The young couple led them out into the field, where they wove a pattern beneath the emerging stars and then back to the fire, where they circled once more as the music slowed and softened.

The tune was now familiar to Adam. It was an old hymn that he'd heard many times in church as a boy. It was a song of resurrection, sung at Easter, but it had always been sung with solemnity. Here, in the light of the burning cornhusks and the occasional poppings of kernels, the song was raised loudly, but with obvious joy and reverence. Bryony stood on the dais with the parson now, singing and smiling on the people all about her, their hands still clasped from the dance.

When the last notes faded into the sky, the crowd burst into a chorus of greetings and blessings and cheering. The men raced to the corn shocks that were standing tall and gleefully swung their blades to cut them down, scattering husks and stalks all over the earth. The women ran behind and gathered up the leavings in their arms and, laughing and singing, cast them into the fires.

Bryony called for silence. The reverend made a brief, heartfelt benediction, and then Bryony raised her hands once more.

"Come along to the farm, everyone," she called out. "There's cider and smoked ham and a fair night to be celebrated. Good harvest to all!"

Adam watched, dumbfounded, as the crowd dispersed across the field toward the yards of Talcott Farm. The bonfire was left to die down and the leather thong gently unwound from around the wrists of young Daniel and Bethany. Adam felt a confusion of relief, embarrassment, and irritation as he watched the young pair scamper off to catch up with their friends. Bryony waited for Adam by the dais.

"Be careful where you step," she said, pointing to the spot where she had buried the third kernel of corn. "Not only is that blessed ground, it's well fertilized with cow manure."

Adam couldn't help himself. He burst into laughter, shoulders shaking. Bryony cocked her head at him wonderingly. "What is so amusing?" she asked, smiling.

"You. Me. More cow manure. This whole mad place."

"I don't follow."

"This was a fertility rite?"

"Yes. Is it not the way you would do it?"

"I thought rituals to insure fertility and good harvests called for sacrifices."

"Oh. Do they?" Bryony frowned. "This is the way that we've always performed the corn-planting ritual. I'm sure that I followed all the right steps and said all the right words. They're in Mama's book, of course. And the reverend couldn't have said a nicer blessing on the fields. What would you have done?"

"I? I've never done a corn-planting ritual. But I'd always heard that blood had to be split in order to insure a good harvest."

"Blood?" Bryony looked horrified as well as mystified. "How awful! You mean—you would have—" Her mouth fell open. "Like Abraham and Isaac? Little Bethany and Daniel? You would have—Adam, that's terrible!" Anger snapped in her eyes. "That's the most ludicrous, despicable thing I've ever heard of! How could anyone imagine that causing pain and death would bring about a bountiful crop? I'm glad to hear that you've never performed such a rite. I couldn't respect anyone who used magic in such a foul, malicious, cruel—"

"Hold, hold," Adam said, raising a hand. "Let it pass. I have not done it and I would not do it."

"But, Adam," she gasped. "You didn't think that we—that I would—"

"Oh, no, no. Of course not." Adam waved the idea away, using the gesture to pull his coat closer over the hilt of his knife. "Shall we go join the others?"

They crossed the fields beneath the twinkling stars and joined the people at the trestle tables that had been set up in the yard. The townsfolk were already making music and serving up the good-smelling dishes they'd carried in their baskets. Bryony went inside and reemerged, dressed once more in one of her simple gowns and a shawl. She'd left her hair down, but had gathered it back from her face with the light green ribbon she'd worn at the corn ritual.

Adam watched her greeting her guests and wondered at the many sides to Bryony Talcott. She was a believer in magic, one who clung to superstitions, yet she had uncommonly good sense. She was a deceiver of others, but he had yet to catch her in a single dishonest thought or deed, beyond her simple practices of homey "magic." She frequently made a fool of herself by attempting some outlandish practice or spell to find her gift, as she called it. She was as naive as a child about many things. And yet she was as graceful as any woman he'd ever seen, and as wise about some things as the most experienced sage.

She helped out with birthings—both human and livestock—and she knew the coarsest facts of procreation and life. Yet Adam knew that she had never really been kissed, or if she had, it had not been by any man with warm blood in his veins. She showed a charming naiveté about most matters of men and women as partners in love—so charming that Adam was constantly tempted to switch their roles and become her tutor in the magic of the senses.

He was startled at the realization that he was in danger of abandoning his quest and giving in to his desires. Such a thing had never happened to him before. What price would he pay if he were to surrender his tight control and touch her as he so longed to do?

He pondered this question even as he admired the soft curve of Bryony's shoulders and the delightful habit she had of chewing on one fingertip when she was deep in thought. He couldn't be in any danger of falling in love with her, that much he knew. They were worlds apart. Dalliance or the desire to dally was no proof of love. But would it be right to pursue such a dalliance with the woman he aimed to bring low? Would he be able to complete his task, as he knew he must?

He left off pondering this troublesome issue when he saw Matthew beckoning to him. Relieved to have an excuse to put aside his thoughts about Bryony, he went to sit with the old man. Three other men—Marcus Tupper, Jonathan Leary, and Lucas Rutledge—sat with him. They greeted Adam with nods and grins, filled his cup and his plate, and sat up straight, watching and smiling as he ate.

Adam looked up after a few bites and gave them all a questioning smile. They were gazing at him like children expecting a good story. He swallowed. "Is there something I can do for you gentlemen?"

"Well, yes, now that you mention it. . . ." Leary began.

Matthew elbowed Leary in the ribs. "We was just talking about your lessons with our Bryony. Seems strange a man of your powers wanting to learn from our Hag. I imagine you could teach her a thing or two."

That I could, Adam thought, glancing at Bryony as she walked gracefully across the yard to greet the Addisons. He turned back to the men around him. "I have my own ways, it's true. But it never hurts to learn a new trick now and then. Miss Bryony has many gifts I lack."

Adam wondered what was going on among the Four Horsemen, as he had dubbed them. Jumpy at the best of times, Leary certainly seemed in a higher state of excitement than usual. Even Matthew, ordinarily the most sanguine and calm of men, seemed expectant.

"Got some pretty fine ladies up Philadelphia way, eh, Hawthorne?" Marcus refilled Adam's cup with cool cider. "Bet you have your pick of 'em."

"I am acquainted with a few, yes."

"Any special one?" Leary asked.

Adam smiled slowly. "Are you thinking of making a trip to the city, Jonathan? I could make some introductions, if you're looking for some, ah, companionship, shall we say?"

Leary's embarrassed color was evident even by torchlight. "No, no, no," he said hastily. "Demelza'd have my ears."

Adam thought to himself that the formidable Mrs. Leary would have only to look at her husband's ears and he'd hand them over to her himself. But what were the old gents driving at?

"Are you bespoken, that's what he's asking," Matthew said over the rim of his mug.

There it was again. That question. And once again, he wasn't certain how to answer it. "Is there someone you have in mind for me?" he drawled.

The Four Horsemen fell silent. *Ye gods.* He'd guessed it in one.

"I see," he said, chewing and swallowing a bite of ham. "And who is this eligible miss?"

They looked everywhere but at him. He faced Matthew with a quizzical look.

The older man sighed and nodded to the others. "Time to be straight. I think it's the best way." He faced Adam. "It's ordained, son. You're to wed with the Hag."

Adam stared at Matthew, thunderstruck.

"I'm what?" he managed to say at last.

"Matthew saw it in the smokes, not long after Bryony was born," offered Jonathan, a trifle breathlessly. "Bryony's Auntie Beryl saw it, too. A stranger was to come to the hollow and fix up with our Hag."

"Tall, green-eyed. Hair your color," drawled Marcus.

"And a magus, besides," added Lucas.

"You're . . . not joking, are you?" Adam said slowly. Their earnest old faces gave him the answer. "It's ordained, you say?"

"Beryl Talcott was never wrong about a vision in her life," Matthew said. "There was gold edges around the sight, she said, and she saw it more'n once. In the hollow, we take that as ordained." He spread his hands. "And, well, here you are."

"But surely you don't think that I'm . . . that Bryony . . ." He started. "Does she know of this—this prophecy?"

"Oh, no. Beryl swore us not to tell her a word of it. Said it might make the lass skittery and lookin' over her shoulder-like, seein' if there was a stranger coming along."

Adam bit back a curse. This whole venture was getting crazier by the moment. Did they expect him to take all this flapdoodle about smokes and gold-tinted visions seriously? From the cheerful, expectant looks on their faces, it was evident that they believed that Adam would leap up from his seat, drop to one knee before Bryony, and propose marriage on the spot. All because one of their sainted Talcotts had said it was "ordained"!

In his outrage, he forgot all about his thoughts of only a few moments ago. He wasn't having any of this. Cold Springs Hollow would simply have to wait until another tall, green-eyed magician strolled into town. He'd come here to end the Hag's reign, not join in it. And no amount of foolish goading would prod him into setting aside his task here.

Adam peered around him, his gaze coming to rest on Sarabeth Carpenter. With her wide, smiling mouth and laughing blue eyes, she was just the antidote to what was ailing him. And just what he needed to show the Four Horsemen exactly what his intentions were regarding marriage and the Hag.

Matthew and the others watched with interest and then ill-concealed dismay as Adam stood, stretched languidly, and crossed the yard with long, purposeful strides, straight up to Sarabeth of the remarkable bosom and "welcome, stranger" smile. He took her in hand and led her to the area where broad planks had been laid down for dancing. Leaning very close, till his lips almost met her ear, he whispered something that set her into peals of laughter. The musicians struck up a reel and the couple stepped out in time to the lively music, with Adam making it a point to ignore the old men who watched with glum suspicion from behind their mugs of ale.

But he found he couldn't ignore Bryony. Each time the dance whirled them past where she stood chatting with Mistress Addison and some of the other women, he couldn't help but look her way.

His interest was not lost on Sarabeth, who tapped his arm and tugged him away down the line.

"Why don't you just go ahead and get her out of your system?" Sarabeth said with a knowing smile. "Or better yet, why don't you let me do it for you?"

Adam looked down at the other woman with a wry smile. "That's a tempting offer. But there's nothing in there to be got out. The Hag is just a business interest of mine."

"Business?" Sarabeth's eyebrows arched wickedly. "That's a new name for it." She took his arm as they promenaded around the circle. "But I guess you know what you're doing."

"Believe me, I do," Adam said, putting his hand to her waist for a twirl.

But somehow, Bryony's eyes seemed to meet his whenever he turned about, and when the music came to a stop, he found himself so annoyed that he made a curt bow to Sarabeth and strode off toward the woods.

He made his way to a clearing just inside the trees and took a deep, bracing breath of cool night air. It didn't help. What was in those wines they served? he wondered. They tasted like clear, cold apple cider, and yet he felt as loose-limbed and light-headed as if he'd had a bottle of the strongest brandy. More Cold Springs magic, he thought, with a snort of derision.

He strode across the clearing, swinging his arms as he went. His thoughts were heated and restless. Marry the Hag! Get her out of his system!

God, he was sick to death of hearing about the woman, of thinking about her. Yes, she was beautiful. Yes, he could see himself with her in any number of ways. But if it happened at all, it would be in his time and his place and his own—

"Oh, I'm sorry, I—"

He whirled about to see Bryony standing just inside the clearing. Her face was shadowed by her loose-flowing hair, but he knew that honey-rough voice better than his own name by now.

"Don't worry. You're not disturbing me." He couldn't help himself. He drew closer to her, trying to catch a glimpse of those remarkable eyes of hers, as well as the luscious shape that was concealed beneath her light shawl.

"I just came to get some air and to get away from the noise," she said.

"It's beautiful here," he said softly, his eyes never leaving hers.

"Yes. I come here quite often. To be alone."

He caught the slight emphasis she put on the word "alone," but he refused to answer it. He wasn't about to be sent off. He'd stay, damn it all—he'd had enough of other people telling him what he should or shouldn't do. He was sick of questioning his every motive. He was weary of battling his raging desire for her. For once, since the day he had arrived in this confusing little valley, he would do just what he felt like doing.

Bryony had come to an abrupt halt when she reached the clearing and saw Adam. She'd come here to escape from him, from the eyes of all the townsfolk who were watching to see how she was responding to the sight of him dancing with Sarabeth. Yet here he was, looking at her with the most riveting stare, his eyes fairly snapping in the starlight.

Then he came even nearer. There was a wry twist to the corners of his mouth, and his eyes were probing hers, challenging her to withdraw her gaze from his. The mass of his chest and shoulders blotted out the forest behind him, and all she could see was his powerful form silhouetted against blackness and starry skies. She felt a sharp thrill of excitement course through her, making her skin and senses absolutely electric with anticipation. There was a change in him; she could sense it clearly. What would he do next? What should she do? She couldn't keep silent.

"Don't let me keep you if you want to go back," she said, her words coming out breathy and soft as her heart raced in her breast. Why couldn't she seem to move away?

"I think I'll stay."

His voice was hardly more than a whisper, but it sent another jolt of excitement down the length of her body. Could he possibly see how disturbed she was? How could he not, when the feeling was so strong? Again, she felt the urge to resist the power between them with words.

"This is where my mother and father used to come on full-moon nights, to see the moon. And my family used it to adjudge the stars and their prophecies. It's—"

His kiss wasn't a surprise. She'd known it was coming. His lips simply sank down upon hers and captured her senses in one swift, searing instant. She had no thought beyond the soul-shaking power of this simple act and how it was turning her body into a maelstrom of pleasure and excitement and apprehension, all at once.

Bryony had been kissed before. There had been those who'd dared to approach a Talcott witch and touch her. But none had stayed or asked again. Bryony was never sure if that was how it was meant to be or if there was something wrong with her.

But this. This was nothing like those other experiences. And when Adam lifted his mouth from hers, it wasn't to dash away in fear and triumph, as those others had, but to gather her into his arms so tightly that she felt enveloped and lost in his embrace, and to place his lips again to hers, this time with even more devastating effect.

Bryony felt as if her feet had left the ground. She raised her arms and slipped them about his waist, following his lead in their embrace. She lost all sense of time and place as Adam's kiss deepened and his arms held her as if they both might spin off the planet together if they didn't hold fast to one another.

"Sweet. Like peaches," he murmured. She wondered what he meant but she couldn't ask, for he was kissing her again, and now his hands were cupping her face, one thumb caressing the hollow of her cheek.

Heat was rising within her and she knew that this was no ordinary fever. Adam was creating it, rousing it, fanning it as his hands tangled in her hair and brought her mouth hard against his. Her lips, already swollen with his kisses, opened slightly and his tongue slipped inside, giving her a sweet, liquid taste of apples and spices and rousing a soft cry of surprise and delight from deep within her.

Bryony felt her world spinning, tilting, rearranging in the sensations she was discovering in Adam's arms. This was more powerful than any magic she knew, more beguiling. It was almost too much, and yet—

A shout of merriment went up from the party, just yards away. Bryony jumped back, recalling the rest of the world in an instant.

"I'd better go back," she whispered.

"Why?"

Why, indeed. But she knew. It came to her clearly, despite the clouds of sensation he'd summoned up around her. She knew now why she'd been urged to seek her gift before anything else. This—what she and Adam had just shared—was something so overwhelming, so potent and engulfing, that it could easily blot out all other thoughts and desires. Her mind and body and spirit had been filled with him, had longed only for him and his touch. And all that with a kiss! More than that she could only imagine, but she suspected that it would be even more soul-stealing and attention-absorbing than kisses.

"I must get back to my guests. They will need me." She backed off a step or two. Adam followed and seized her arm.

"Can't these people manage without you for once?" His voice was low but challenging.

"Yes," she said, withdrawing again. "But I'm their hostess. It would be rude to stay away."

"What are you afraid of?"

"I'm not afraid of anything. I'm only doing my duty as Talcotts have done for years and years." Her chin came up a notch with the mention of her family name.

"Talcott. That's all you think of, isn't it?" he said, his voice growing cool. "You can always use the Talcott name to hide behind, can't you?"

She stiffened. "I have no need to hide. I have pride in my family. Talcotts founded the hollow. Talcotts have always cared for the people here."

"And a Talcott is all that you are?"

"What do you mean?"

He moved closer. "You're more than a name. You're a human being in your own right. You're a woman. Doesn't that count for aught in your world? Don't you do anything that isn't just what the Talcotts have done, year after year after year?"

She stood her ground, her pride assaulted. "I possess a mind of my own, yes, if that's what you mean. But I am the last of the Talcotts. I have a duty and a desire to carry on our work here to the best of my ability."

"Your work?" Adam smiled, but not with any good humor. "Ah, yes. The Talcott magic."

"Yes."

"Saying silly words at the edges of cornfields and spooning out pap to piglets. That's magic?"

Bryony felt stung to the core. Tears threatened, but she controlled them and her voice. "Perhaps it isn't magic to you. I know you think I'm just a fumbler and maybe I'm not as adept at magic as you are. Maybe I don't have a true gift. Perhaps I never will. But I can tell you this much, Adam Hawthorne: I shall continue to work my 'silly' sort of magic so long as it helps people and preserves my home, and yes, as long as it honors the name of Talcott. At least there is a heart and a soul at work in my magic. Can you say as much?"

He reached out for her again. "Bryony, I—"

He was going to kiss her again. She knew it just as she knew he was mocking her. She put her hand up to her breast.

"Bryony, listen to me. I—Aieeeggsh!"

She spun about and dashed through the trees, hair and skirts flying as she disappeared into the darkness. She could hear him coughing, sneezing, and spluttering behind her for several yards and wondered if he would be all right. Her talisman pouch had been full of mustard, pepper, and ground ammoniac. All were natural and deemed only discouraging, not injurious, according to Talcott lore. She had never had to use such a protection before. Still, he had deserved it!

She came to a stop just under the eaves of the woods. Tears came now, hot and stinging. She brushed them away with both hands, angry at her weakness. How dare he taunt her about her magic, about her family! What sort of man was he? Surely a magus would understand how important it was to give oneself wholly to the magic. Surely he had a family somewhere. Didn't he feel pride in the name of Hawthorne?

Her thoughts were whirling, her emotions rattled. She couldn't think clearly. All she knew was that she'd been utterly taken in by the wonder of his kisses and then, only moments later, been cut to the quick by his disparagement of her magic skills. How could he have gained such power over her? It was a feeling she didn't like.

She straightened her skirts and brushed back her hair, preparing to rejoin her guests in the yard. Adam Hawthorne could take a flying leap at the moon, she told herself. She would carry on seeking her gift.

Adam couldn't fly to the moon. Neither could he find words strong enough to curse himself for being a complete idiot, once he had recovered from her stinging-powder assault. What the devil had come over him? How did Bryony Talcott manage to cause him to say and do the most ridiculous, foolhardy, ill-advised things? And what the hell had she sprayed in his face?

Lord, it was bad enough that he'd kissed her, he thought, mopping at his eyes with his handkerchief. That was his first stupid move. He'd let go of his self-control, given in to his impulses, and kissed her. And he hadn't been satisfied with just one kiss, say, in the interest of knowledge.

No, he'd kissed her again and again and he'd been ready to do just about everything else he could imagine doing with Bryony and her sweet mouth and lithe, luscious body. Ready? Ye gods, his body was still rebuking him for cutting off its delighted, headlong rush to paradise, her protective powders aside. It was madness!

And then he'd gone and hurt her feelings. He knew full well how devoted she was to the people here and how proud she was of the Talcott name. What he hadn't guessed was the depth of her uncertainty about her so-called magic powers. He'd almost let it slip that he didn't believe in magic at all, but she had interpreted his words to be a personal criticism of her talents and her filial duty. She must think him a brute, at the very least.

He ran his hands over his face. This whole affair was becoming more tangled and bewildering with each passing day. All he was supposed to do was come here, find the Hag, unmask her before the town, and go home to collect his money. What was he going to tell his friends—that he couldn't complete his errand because he might hurt the Hag's feelings? Or that he couldn't do it until he'd made love to her?

This last thought startled him with its truth.

Perhaps it would be best to just give up. Making love with Bryony Talcott was the most dangerous thing he could imagine. He'd be better off just getting out of town. He could tell Taylor and the others that the whole town was crazy anyway, so who cared if they were being led down the garden path by a self-styled witch?

Adam shook his head. He wasn't someone who quit at the first sign of adversity. He was a man who believed in solutions, that there were steps to take to change things if one didn't like the way things were going. And although he'd never in all his life dreamed he'd end up in a backwoods hollow, lusting after a Hag and worrying about whether it was permissible to let people go on being duped by a fraud, there had to be an answer to this problem. There had to be a solution. He'd go back to the inn and think it over.

He glanced back toward Talcott Farm. He wondered if he should go to her. *No,* he told himself. He couldn't think straight when she was around. He'd wait until he'd thrashed this out for himself alone. No doubt she didn't want to see him now, anyway. And he certainly wasn't ready for another dose of her peppery assault-potion.

He headed back to the Laughing Dog, his long legs powering him along at a brisk pace. The lamp in his room burned long into the night.

The old gents of Cold Springs Hollow sat up late that night, as well. They had witnessed Bryony's departure to the woods and her distressed return, after which she bade everyone good night and retreated to her house, urging them all to go on with the party without her. Now Jonathan, Marcus, Matthew, and Lucas sat in Matthew's kitchen, their gray heads encircled with thin, curling pipe smoke.

"Well?" demanded Jonathan. "The direct approach sure as the deuce was a washout."

"You've got to admit it, Matthew, it don't look good for our Bryony and that young magus fellow." Lucas scratched his cheek. "You sure you didn't see anything else in that vision of yours?"

"Now, now, let's don't be gettin' hasty," put in Marcus. "These things can take time."

"How would you know?" Lucas asked. "You married your lady the third day she was in the Hollow. And Matt here and his Julia, they was practically plighted to each other in the cradle."

"Still, this is different." Jonathan scooted to the edge of his chair. "Matt, don't you agree this is different?"

Matthew took a long draw on his pipe and let it out, watching it curl, blue and wispy, up toward the ceiling. He nodded. "You may be right about this, Leary. A vision can't show you everything, like it was written down in some book. It's just a picture of what might be."

"Maybe this ain't meant to be," grumped Lucas.

"Maybe. But I don't feel it and I don't see it. I got an idea."

The three others turned their full attention to Matthew. "I'm thinking about the time that my Julia and I was courting and we couldn't find one minute alone together, what with her little sisters tagging along and her father watchin' me like I was plannin' to rob him of his most precious treasure. I was so eager to get her to myself, just for one bit of a kiss, that I was about to bust. You know how it was."

"So?" asked Marcus.

"So, them two have been going about the hollow right and proper, out in the open and in the company of others. They can get away from each other at any time. What they need's a chance. An opportunity."

"But they were alone in the woods tonight and I don't think that went any too well, judging from Bryony's face when she come back."

"That's just what I'm saying. They could get away. But what if they was somewhere together and they couldn't get away?"

"Somewhere alone?" asked Jonathan.

"That'd be right."

"You think that'd make 'em start thinking seriously on marrying up?" asked Marcus.

"That, or killing each other." Lucas gave a sour shake of his head.

"Where?" asked Jonathan.

"Hold on," said Marcus. "Our Bryony's not some doxy. She's a maid and a daughter of the first family 'round here. What's to happen to her after?"

"They get married," said Jonathan. "No shame in that."

"And no one's gonna know, one way or another," Matthew said firmly, glaring around the circle at each man. "Are we agreed on that?"

All heads nodded.

"Where?" Jonathan repeated.

"Needs to be someplace neither of 'em goes very often," Lucas said, musing. "Someplace that can be, secured, I should say."

"Aye."

The four men looked at one another, the lamplight sparkling in their eyes. "The Boat!" they said in unison, and fell to making their plans.

Chapter Seven

"Truth and Roses Both have Thornes."
—*Cassia Talcott*

Adam had just posted a letter to Taylor MacLaren when he saw the wagon coming down from the hills at breakneck speed. At first, he thought it was a runaway; then, as he peered up the road at it, he saw someone in the driver's seat, waving his arm over his head in some sort of signal.

Preacher Kirkland came out from the door of the inn, took one look at the wagon speeding over the rutted road, and ran for the church. Heads popped out of every window and door as the church bell began tolling.

Men came pounding out of the inn, Jonathan Leary puffing in their wake, all of them running to meet the wagon. They surrounded the vehicle before it had even come to a stop and soon were hurrying toward the inn, carrying a woman on a cot.

"What is it?" Adam asked Marcus as the old man came out of the tanner's shop.

"Oh, my. Looks like the Goffs. They live up in the hills, just over the ridge. Looks like their Phronsie is took sick again."

Adam turned and was striding toward the inn when he spied a cloud of dust up the road in the opposite direction. The figure grew and he could see dark hair flying in the wind, skirts fluttering. He knew it was Bryony, riding like the very wind itself.

He ran to greet her and help her off the horse. She was out of breath and only nodded at him as she slid down and ran to the inn, her spelling satchel banging on her hip. Adam handed the mare over to Marcus and leaped after her.

A path had been made for Bryony to come through, and Adam could see her before the hearth, bending over the woman on the cot. Even from as far away as the door, he could hear the woman's labored breathing, as if every gasp were being torn from her throat.

Adam moved closer, standing tall over the crowd to see. Bryony was working rapidly, giving orders in a calm but brisk tone.

"Get me hot water in a basin and several towels," she ordered Demelza Leary. "Andy, your knife."

A man near her handed over his hunting knife and Bryony cut the woman's laces from top to bottom in one smooth, sure motion. She crooned to the woman as she searched through her satchel and pulled out several small linen bags that Adam knew were filled with various herbs.

Demelza returned, towels piled on her arms, and Jonathan followed with a large, steaming kettle. Bryony motioned to Jonathan to put the water on the fire, then reached over to someone's luncheon plate and scooped up a handful of the butter that was left beside the biscuits. She deftly added some of the herbs from one pouch, mixed and warmed it in her hands, then began to spread the ointment on the woman's chest. A strong odor of mint and some other spice that Adam couldn't place rose up around her.

Next, Bryony poured water from the kettle into a small basin and added still more pungent herbs to this, still in their light linen bag. She signaled to the two men nearest her to prop up the woman's head and shoulders, and she placed the bowl under the woman's chin, then draped the towels all about the woman's head and face, sealing her in with the steaming bowl. The woman's chest was still heaving, her hands flailing as if she could pull the air in from around her.

"Breathe freely," Bryony crooned. "Breathe deep in your chest. This potion can make the obstacle loosen and free itself and leave you forever." She took a small stone of pale blue out of another pouch in her satchel and pressed it into the woman's hand. "It's a soothing stone, Phronsie," she said. "Let your fear go into it."

Adam frowned. The woman could not get her breath. How on earth could a rock be of any service to her?

Yet the woman seemed to grow calmer. Her breathing changed from tortured to merely heavy, and her arms began to lower to her sides. The crowd murmured its satisfaction and began to disperse, giving little pats to Bryony and the ashen-faced husband who slumped with relief onto the hearth.

Adam withdrew, taking his thoughts to a table in the corner. He was nursing a glass of brandy when he saw Bryony remove the towels from around the woman's head. She gave her another fresh, steaming bowl of the strong herbs to breathe, gave some instructions to Mr. Goff, and rose to leave.

Adam met her at the door. "Your horse is waiting in Marcus's barn."

She glanced up and flashed a weary smile. "Adam. Thank you for taking her."

He took her arm as she drooped a little going over the threshold.

"It's all right," she said. "I'm just recovering from the race into town."

"What ailed the woman?" he asked. He continued to hold her arm as they turned down the street toward Marcus's house.

"Asthma. Paroxysms of the breath. Or so my mother determined, and she was skilled at finding and naming ailments. I can't be entirely sure of what brings it about, only how to treat it when it does."

Adam frowned. "Asthma. That is a physician's term," he murmured. "How did you treat her?"

"First with a salve of mint, horehound, and the leaves of the blue gum tree. Then with a hot distillation of elecampane, angelica, mint, and comfrey." She glanced up at him, then looked away. "Blue gum trees grow only in Australia. I use the money from the taxes to send for them."

"I see."

"But you don't approve?"

"Of what?"

"Of my using money from the town to work my cures and make up my simples."

"It isn't that. It's—"

They were interrupted by Marcus greeting them outside the gate of his home. They fetched Bryony's horse, thanked him, and began walking the mare back up the road to Bryony's farm.

"You don't approve," Bryony said again, as they left the village main street and took the road.

Adam scowled. "Of using money to work your cures? No. I must say that I can't."

"But how else may I get the medicinal herbs I need?" she asked. "I need Peruvian bark to treat fevers, camphor from the tropics, blue gum bark and other plants that won't thrive in this climate. I can't afford to pay for them myself unless I charge the earth and sky for my cures. So, the town gathers its money together and I send for the medicines we all need. And so we all share the cost."

"Are these magical cures?"

"Magical?" It was Bryony's turn to frown. "Yes, I suppose so. I've heard of doctors who use them and make no claims to magical skill. I cannot truly say they are magical, as I don't know the extent of my talents or if I have a gift of magic, but in the way that I know that my mother used them and by the way that they ofttimes heal in the most hopeless of cases, then I must claim they are magical."

"And that woman, Mistress Goff. Is she a hopeless case?"

Bryony fell silent for a moment. "I should not have used that term—hopeless."

"But she won't get any better?"

Bryony shook her head.

"And she may die of this breathing disease?"

"It is . . . possible."

"I knew of a fellow who died of it. Every fit left him more and more disabled until the life was at last suffocated out of him by it. I've never known there to be a cure."

Bryony remained silent. Adam continued. "So she is indeed a hopeless case." He took a deep breath. "What was that rock you put in her hand?"

"The soothing stone? We call it a moss agate. It's used to soothe fears and to relax the heart and chest. I've seen it work well with people who find themselves overcome with fear or anxiety."

"A rock?"

"A particular sort of rock. One that the Talcotts have used for generations to heal."

"A magic rock?"

Bryony halted in the middle of the road. "What is it you want of me, Adam Hawthorne?"

He shrugged. "I'm trying to learn how you work."

"No. That's not the truth. I may not have a gift but I do have ears that are trained to listen. And you have more on your mind than learning about healing stones or asthma cures. What is it?"

He swung about to face her. "Very well. You went in there and you laid leaves and butter on that woman. You made her inhale a concoction of more leaves. You handed her a stone—a rock from out of the dirt! And yet you know that the woman will die."

Bryony was taken aback by the fierceness of his tone and the hot fury in his eyes. "I said she may possibly die."

"You said it was likely. And you and I both know it is true—she will die. And you walk in there and offer them false hope with soaking hot leaves and shiny rocks!"

"False hope? How can hope be false?"

"What?" He stared at her, incredulous. "Hope is false when the outcome is already known! It is a cruel thing to offer it to people who love and care for a sick one who cannot be cured."

"Cruel? Is that what you think I am? Cruel for offering hope and comfort when I should be telling them to go home and make ready their burial clothes?" Bryony shook her head. "You are the one who is cruel!"

"Telling the truth isn't cruel!" Adam's voice dropped to a hoarse whisper. "Telling the truth means that they know what to do next, how to live their lives, how to go on, even in the face of death! How to accept it."

Bryony backed away from him. "Well, *I* can't accept that. You may say that false hopes are bad, and perhaps they can be, but I know something far worse—no hope at all. And until the day comes when I can look into the future and tell Phronsie Goff and others like her, with gospel surety, that I know the day and hour of their deaths, then I shall continue to offer hope in any and all its forms!"

She swung up on her horse. "You needn't come with me on my errands any longer. I can't be responsible for the peace of your conscience. Good day, Mr. Hawthorne."

She urged the mare into a quick trot and headed for home. Adam turned off the road and made for the banks of the stream, his shoulders rigid as he went.

"One more night, Soot," Bryony said as she dropped down next to the cat on the back stoop. "This is the last time. The last test."

She stared out across the gardens, where the twilight was softening the plants and the orchards to indistinct, violet shapes against the sky. The big gray tom yawned and gave a delicate swipe to his lips with his tongue, cleaning away the last drop of milk that marred his handsome whiskers.

"You don't care, I know," she said, rubbing the cat between his ears. "It's all the same to you just as long as you get your milk each day and some fat field mice to feast on."

But these past days had mattered a great deal to Bryony. After Adam had challenged her about her magic, she had been furious at first; then, calming, she found herself brooding over his words.

Did she offer false hope to the people she cared for? Was she being honest with them when they came to her for aid as their Hag and she could offer only simples and a few comforting words?

Most important of all, would she ever be able to offer them true magic? If she knew she had at least one genuine gift, she would have more than just her name and family upbringing to claim as authority when she went about healing or spelling.

She needed to know. Once and for all.

So, for the past three days, she had been fasting and spelling, poring over the Talcott book and other texts that her family had gathered over the years, meditating and praying. And she had been putting herself to every sort of test she could devise.

She tried reading smokes and got only irritated eyes and reeking clothes for her troubles. She worked with cards and found herself more skilled at a game of solitaire than at any reading of the past, present, or future. Transporting her spirit into the bodies or minds of others, willing plants to bloom, making herself invisible, scrying in a bowl of ink, opening locks with a word, driving snakes out of her garden with a tamarisk stick, sending her thoughts into the mind of another:

all these things she had tried over the past three days, each with the same discouraging results.

Her heart was sinking within her but she refused to think about it, not until this last night was over. She would spend this night at the magic circle in the grove, performing one long, last ritual to reveal her powers. Three was a strong number, the moon was waxing, an east wind was blowing, and by sunrise, the time of all new beginnings, she would know the answer, once and for all. She had decided that this was her last effort. Whatever the outcome of this night, she would face the sunrise tomorrow with the promise of following the truth of that outcome to the end of her days.

She gathered up the things she needed in a willow basket and, with a farewell pat to Soot, turned her steps toward the magic grove. If any place had power, she thought to herself as she drew a large circle in the clearing at the center of the ring of trees, it was this place. The spicy scent of the spruces rose up with every breeze and a multitude of stars twinkled overhead, awaiting the rising moon.

She laid a small fire and began to sing.

Adam kicked at a stone in the path. For the past three days, he had again gone from house to house in the village and out on the farms, asking everyone about Bryony, the Talcotts, their magic, and what the residents believed the Talcotts could do. He had gotten the same answers as before. Someone, somewhere, he reasoned, must have the wit to see that holding on to rocks, burning shoes full of manure, and waving sticks over chickens to make them lay eggs was utter foolishness. At the very least, he had hoped to find someone who was not so satisfied with the Talcotts and their magical claims, someone who had not fared as well by their spelling and cures.

What he found was a gaggle of amused but unconcerned citizens, all of whom, once again, sang the praises of the Talcotts. The worst he could get out of anyone was the comment from Mistress Addison that Bryony was not a superior hand with pigs.

"Pigs!" he exclaimed, kicking the stone another length down the road. "Rocks! Weeds! Cats!"

He had paced his room till the wee hours of the morning last night and had risen before the sun this morning. He was headed to his last destination, his place of last resort—Matthew Cowley's farm. He knew the old man was partial to the Hag, but there was also something special about Matthew, an air of authority about him. The townsfolk treated him with much the same reverence they offered to Bryony, and Adam suspected that not much went on in the hollow that Matthew did not know about. It was time for a few straightforward questions.

He was approaching the road to Talcott Farm when he smelled the smoke coming from the trees. He frowned, wondering who would build a campfire on Bryony's property. Everyone knew everyone else in this place; if someone needed a place to sleep, he had only to ask a neighbor.

Whoever was in the grove making that smoke was a stranger. And that person was but a stone's throw from Bryony's house. The house where she lived alone.

He flung off his jacket and felt for the knife he carried at his belt. Quietly, he moved in among the eaves of the grove.

Bryony fought back the tears as she poked at the remains of the fire. She had vowed she would accept the verdict of this last night and that she would go about her life in peace, certain at last that no magical gifts were to come her way.

But when the roosters began to call sleepily and the birds began to waken in the dogwood branches, her heart was suddenly filled with the pain and sadness of the dream she had lost. There was no gift. She was meant only for herbcraft and animal care.

Anger began to boil up inside her. Years of effort and hope finally dashed, her family's wonderful heritage ended forever—it was too much. She raised the rowan branch she had used as a wand that night and flung it on the fire. In quick succession, she hurled after it the parchment on which she had written her wish to know her gift, the bowls of rice and wine she had used in the ritual, and the wooden bowls full of vervain, anise, hellebore, and sage. With each one she threw, she gave a cry of rising grief and frustration until her shouts rang around the grove, startling the birds up from the trees and preventing her from hearing Adam's approach.

She was about to fling her mother's book on the fire when a strong hand seized her wrist and held it fast. She turned with a gasp to face Adam and recalled how his challenges, his criticisms of her had finally pushed her to the edge. She dropped the book and lashed out at him in fury.

"Go away!" she shouted, swinging at him with her free hand. "You've made your point. I'm not a magus! I'm not the true Hag! I'm just a silly wench playing about with weeds and rocks!"

"Bryony, I—"

"Don't say anything! Get out of here! Get away from me! So even your show magic is greater than mine! So you have a gift and I don't! I don't want you around, do you understand? Get out!"

She was twisting about in his grasp, tears now flowing freely. She wanted to escape his dark green gaze. She couldn't face the mockery that she knew she would find there. Wrenching free, she whirled away from him, dashing toward the trees on the opposite side of the circle.

He caught her and she struggled in his grasp, sobbing and trying to kick him away from her.

"Bryony! Bryony, stop it! You'll only hurt yourself!"

"What do you care?" she shouted. "What could it possibly matter to you what happens to a simple, stupid country wench like me?"

"You're not stupid! And you're not simple," he exclaimed, giving her a shake. "You're just disappointed. Isn't it better to know the truth?"

"Yes! No!" She covered her face with her hands. "I don't know!"

"You do know." He gripped her shoulders. "You do know. I've seen enough, been around you enough to know that you aren't made for lies and deceits. The truth had to come, and sooner is better than later."

"But my family. My friends. The hollow. I've failed them. I've failed myself."

She raised her eyes and saw none of the scorn or smug satisfaction she had expected. To her wonder, she saw some of her own pain mirrored in his green eyes and a tenderness she had never seen there before.

"I know what it's like to feel that you've failed the ones you love most," he said softly. "But you have value beyond your position as any hag or healer."

She looked away, shaking her head.

He drew her closer, bending his head to catch her eye and hold it. "You possess value in your own person, in your own soul. You don't need magic to claim a place in this world. People care for you as Bryony, not just as the Hag."

She felt herself pinned and held by the power of his gaze. She wanted to accept his words of comfort, but she simply couldn't. She had lost her world, her past, her future when the sun rose that morning, and she knew that nothing would ever be the same again. What was she to do? she wondered, tears brimming once more. She dropped to her knees. She didn't know how to be anything other than one of the magical Talcotts.

Adam knelt down with her. She tried to pull away, embarrassed by her tears, but he wouldn't let her go. Instead, he pulled her into his arms, enveloping her with his warmth and strength, and held her.

The floodgates of her sorrow opened and Bryony grieved, there in the grove, leaning against Adam Hawthorne's broad, hard chest. She mourned again the loss of her parents and the rest of her family. She poured out her sorrow at the end of her long quest, at the loss of her dream of fulfilling the legacy her parents had so lovingly raised her to inherit and use. She sobbed for the years lost in struggle. She cried for the loss of that certainty of who she was and who she was meant to be.

And Adam held her, silently, solidly, and let her weep until she had no tears left.

At last, she raised her head. She saw the same tenderness and caring there, but there was something new, something she had caught glimpses of before when he had looked at her, but that she had not allowed herself to think about. She sat back and fumbled in her pocket for a handkerchief, suddenly shy.

She wiped her eyes and blew her nose. "I'm sorry," she told him. "I didn't mean to cry all over your waistcoat like that." She reached up to touch the dark stains on the fine brown wool.

He covered her hand with his own and held it there, just above his heart. She caught her breath. Small tremors were coursing through her. All her defenses were down, she told herself. It was just the aftermath of all the tears, all the testing. She should just pull away.

But she didn't. She couldn't. Instead, she raised the other hand and touched his cheek. She seemed to be falling into the depths of his eyes, as if in a dream, yet she couldn't recall any dream that felt so real, so powerful.

He put his other hand up and cupped the back of her head. Gently, he drew her to him and placed his lips on hers.

It was the lightest of feather kisses, a kiss of air and clouds. There was no demand in it, no insistence, only a beckoning, a calling. Bryony felt an answering call somewhere in the depths of her being. She moved forward on her knees and returned a kiss that gave shape to a lifetime of yearning.

And then she was in his arms, the length of their bodies pressed together as they knelt there amid the spicy fragrance of the evergreens. Bryony knew she had no words to describe the sensations she was feeling. Nothing in her life, not even the kisses they'd shared the night of the corn ritual, had prepared her for the sweet firmness of Adam's mouth, for the breath-stealing power of slipping her arms around his chest and feeling his heart beating so near to her own.

Slowly, easily, she gave in to his urgings and bent backward over his arm. She inhaled long and deep as he pressed soft kisses against her throat, and gave a soft gasp as his lips trailed all the way to the very edge of her bodice.

He tugged at the ribbon that bound her hair back at her neck and let the scrap of satin fall to the ground. His long, deft fingers that had so fascinated her from the first moment she saw them sank deep into the long tangles of her hair and combed it back from her scalp, sending a cascade of pleasurable shivers down her spine. He gathered the hair close in his hand, gently pulling her up to him again. This time, his kiss wasn't of feathers. It was quick and urgent and Bryony's response was equal to it.

She slipped her arms up about his neck and pressed herself against him. She loved the way she felt in his embrace, all fire and air and yet so solidly, firmly real. Her head was light, almost dizzy from his kiss, and her body was heating faster than the sun rising over the hills. She had gone from a shower of grief into a storm of excitement and she was lost to the power of new feelings sweeping over her.

"Adam," she murmured when he again broke his kiss, this time to brush his lips lightly over her earlobes. "Adam, I—"

His lips silenced hers. Her shawl had long since fallen away and through the soft, worn muslin of her gown she felt his hand slide up over her ribs and gently cup her breast. Involuntarily, she leaned into his touch, pressing herself to the heat of his hand, feeling the yearning within her rise and grow. And when he lowered his mouth to the cloth that was straining over the hardened nipple, she cried out softly at the heat he gave to her.

He straightened and cupped her face in his hands. His eyes were shadowed but she could see fires banked down in their depths, fires that were like those she felt within herself, only moments away from igniting and engulfing them both.

"Bryony," he whispered against her temple. "I've been waiting so long."

She wanted to ask him what he meant, but she felt she knew. Besides, he was kissing her again and this time his lips were urging hers to part for him and her lips seemed to have a will of their own. They parted. And as his kiss deepened and his hand slid down to again caress her breast, she was carried beyond all thought. A newer, yet far older, knowing came to her, and, dutiful and diligent pupil that she was, she gave herself up to its teachings.

Adam was in a fiery schoolroom of his own. His body, so long denied by his will, his pride, and his iron reason, broke from its bonds the instant he laid hands on Bryony. He wanted to pour himself into her, wrap himself around her, rub and caress and lick and taste and smell and kiss every last bit of her. He had lost his mind and found something else entirely.

Soft lips, his body chanted at him, swollen in pleasure against his. The tenderest skin, sweet-smelling, and flowery-spicy to the taste. Luscious breasts, perfectly firm and pliant and responsive. Comforting, maddeningly enticing thighs against his, causing his body to tighten and harden and rise up in a mindless, glorious rush of need. His tongue meeting the sweet, cool interior of her mouth—*ye gods,* he thought, even her teeth felt wonderful! Her tantalizing scent, the texture of her hair, the music of her sighs—a whole litany of wonders was being sung throughout his being.

He needed her. Not just needed her—the way a man needs a woman, any woman, sometimes. He needed Bryony Talcott. And here she was, sighing in his embrace, the fragrant heat of her swamping his senses and winding its way around his brain.

He drew her even closer in his embrace and slipped a hand down to lift the hem of her skirts. He was almost shaking with the anticipation of touching the silken-perfect skin he'd glimpsed that fateful morning when he had seen her rising out of her bath.

His eye caught a glimpse of something or someone standing beneath the lacy branches of a flowering dogwood. He started, recalling how he had thought a stranger had been on Bryony's land. He sat up straighter, clasping Bryony about the shoulders.

"What is it?" she asked softly, going still in his arms.

Adam blinked at the spot where he had seen the man—he was sure now that it had been a man—standing just inside the eaves of the trees. There was no one there. But there had been. He knew it as certainly as he knew he was holding Bryony in his arms.

"Adam?"

"I—I thought I saw someone."

Her head snapped around to see where he looked. She scrambled off his lap and stood up, straightening her skirts.

"Bryony, it was no one," he said, knowing he was lying. "You don't have to—"

"Yes," she said breathlessly. "Yes, I do."

He jumped to his feet. "What's wrong? Did I hurt you? I only wanted to comfort you and then, well, it seemed right somehow—"

She reached out and put a hand to his lips. "Shh. Not here." She smiled and her cheeks colored, making her look even more entrancing, if that were possible. "And you most certainly did not hurt me."

She shook out her skirts and went to retrieve her book from the dust by the fire, which by now had died to ashes. Adam followed her.

"Bryony, it was just my imagination. A trick of the eye. You needn't worry that anyone saw us and would say ill of you."

She shook her head. "I don't know that. I don't know anything right now."

Adam frowned. Had he been wrong? Had he misread her sighs, her willing touch and warm response?

"I'm sorry that you were disappointed today. I understand that what you learned is hard to accept."

She looked up at him as she wrapped her shawl about her shoulders. "Yes," she said softly. "It is very hard. But you don't understand."

She tucked the book under her arm and began walking toward the trees. Adam followed after her.

"Bryony, I'm—"

She rounded on him. "Thank you for your . . . comfort. I'll be fine now."

She hurried off into the trees. Adam snagged up her hair ribbon and ran after her. He was confused but he was also wary. If there was someone lurking in the trees still, he wasn't about to let her travel even the short distance from the grove to her house alone.

She stopped in the shadow of the trees, where the light of morning had yet to penetrate. "Please. I don't want you—"

He cut her off. "I don't give a damn what you want. I'm just seeing you safely home."

"I'm not going home. I'm going to the Addisons' farm."

"Then I'll walk you there."

She seemed about to make a fiery retort, then evidently thought better of it. She pulled her shawl tightly about her once more and started off.

Chapter Eight

> "To Bring Rain: When the Moone wears a Halo About Her, Go to a River's Bankes. Beat a Broome upon the Water, Then do Shake it at the Skye. Your Wish, if Wished welle, will be Granted."
>
> —*Cassia Talcott*

"Is that all?"

Bryony looked at Sarah Addison. "I'm sorry?"

"I said, is that all I have to do? Leave a lantern burning in the henhouse at night?"

"Oh. Oh, yes. Well, that, and say the words, of course. Especially in the morning, when the roosters crow."

Mistress Addison spread her hands. "Which words? You haven't told me aught to say." She crossed her arms and squinted at Bryony. "Are you ailing yourself, Mistress Hag?" Her tone was firm, but kindly. "We can't have you gettin' sick on us, not at this busy time, you know."

"I'm fine," Bryony said with a brief smile. "Just a bit preoccupied, that's all."

"Ahh. Well, that's understandable."

Bryony gathered her tools into the satchel and stood up in the cozy, clean little henhouse. The hens, the objects of Mistress Addison's concern, shifted about, giving out sleepy, comfortable clucks. "What's understandable?" she asked absently.

"Oh, let's just say it's the springtime. A young maid like yourself. A handsome young buck hoverin' about and all." Sarah nodded with sage amusement.

"Young buck?"

"The new magus, girl. Don't you think everyone's been noticing you two goin' about together all over the hollow? Oh, not that anybody's thinkin' anything improper, mind you. After all, you're a Talcott and your mama and papa raised you to know the right and wrong of things."

"What things?" She had Bryony's full attention now.

"Oh, you know. Earthly things. Between a man and a woman." The older woman raised her hands. "But as I said, no one hereabouts is thinking anything wrong of you. We're just hoping for the best."

Bryony was utterly at a loss for words. It hadn't occurred to her that anyone would make anything more out of her time spent with Adam than simply what it was: time spent observing her work. Did they imagine that there was . . . that there could be . . . ?

Her cheeks felt like flames. That morning in the woods. Adam had thought he'd seen someone watching them. And they had most certainly not been exchanging spells for the encouragement of infertile chickens.

"Well," she stammered. "Well, you know, there's nothing—"

"Don't you fret yourself." Sarah laid a hand on her arm. "You just go on about your work. Everybody understands if your mind isn't altogether on hens and headaches."

"But—" Bryony gave up. She had no idea what to say to all this. She gathered up her satchel and shawl and hurried out of the Addison's farmyard.

"She still forgot to tell me the words I'm s'posed to say!" Sarah exclaimed as she watched Bryony striding toward home. "Love's a kind of madness, all right." Shaking her head and smiling, she went back in to light the lantern and recite the Ten Commandments over the chickens. It would have to do, she thought, until the Hag was safely wed and back to her old self.

Bryony's spirit was in an uproar.

The past few days had been most bewildering for her. The world turned, just as it always had, the sun rose and set, and the people of Cold Springs Hollow came to the Talcott Hag for help, just as they always had. For them, nothing had changed.

But Bryony went about her old chores and duties with a growing sense of embarrassment and frustration. True, no one asked her to spin straw into gold—an old Talcott family joke—and they all looked at her with the same trust and respect. Yet with each ritual she performed, each cure she presented, she felt more and more dishonest. She was just an ordinary woman who went about with herbs and blessings. And that was all she would ever be. She'd never see visions in Crystal Pond, find water with hazel wands, heal someone with incantations, songs, or her touch.

She'd been too proud, she told herself as she walked home from the Addisons' farm. She'd asked for too much. She'd known from her cradle the Talcott motto: all good gifts are from the Creator.

But the magic had never failed anyone else of Talcott blood. They'd all shown their talents before their twelfth birthdays. Why was she the exception?

She sighed as she unlocked the door of her house and put away her satchel and book in their honored place on the mantel shelf. Ordinarily, she would have taken this time to purify her magic stones and tools after using them all day. But she was losing the heart to perform any of the rituals and tasks she'd done so routinely over the past years. They'd all been in preparation for the coming of her gift as much as a part of her everyday work. Now there seemed no point.

And she had a new worry. Had Sarah Addison

just been prattling on or did the whole of the hollow imagine that she and Adam were—she could hardly think the word—courting? She almost laughed aloud, it was so far from the truth of their relationship.

But was it? another voice inside her asked. Had it ever been the case that she and Adam were just fellow magicians, observing and exchanging trade secrets? Had there been a day, a moment, when she hadn't been so sharply aware of his presence, his face, his eyes, his body, that she had to concentrate with thrice the energy she normally required? Had he ever been far from her thoughts, sleeping and waking, since that night their eyes had met at the inn?

And after their encounter in the grove, disheartened though she was, hadn't she been dreaming each night of Adam? In truth, she'd been waking from those dreams with her body pitched to such a state of excitement and longing that she'd had to recite her old flower-spell primer several times over before she could get back to sleep.

What was between them? she wondered. And how had that changed, now that he and she knew the whole truth about her magic? He hadn't come around once since he'd kissed and caressed her under the blossoming dogwoods. Had that been his way of taking his leave?

She couldn't blame him if he left. There was no longer any reason for him to stay, now that he knew she had nothing to teach him. He had a life elsewhere, and a fine career as a performing magus. A backwoods hollow was no place for him to linger. She knew this.

Then why did her heart want to howl in protest?

She fled the house. She couldn't stand to sit about and worry over things she'd lost. She had to decide what to do now.

She rattled the milk pails and Soot appeared out of nowhere, like a puff of smoky fur. He wore his most wheedlesome expression.

"Don't worry, puss," she told him. "At least Macushla never lets us down."

So that was that.

Adam shut the lid to his trunk and fastened the latches. He looked about his little room at the Laughing Dog, checking for any last items he might have forgotten. There were none.

He couldn't put it off. He'd looked at his situation from every angle he could reasonably consider and the resulting conclusion was, in every case, that it was time for him to leave. He hadn't exactly done what he'd come here to do, but the effect was the same. Bryony Talcott, the Hag of Cold Springs Hollow, had discovered for herself that she was a fraud.

He scowled as he went to the window to look out over the farmlands that stretched away to the foothills. He should feel triumphant, or at least satisfied with the way things had turned out. But even using the word "fraud" to describe Bryony didn't sit well with him. She'd been misled herself, by her probably well-meaning but nonsensical relatives. She certainly wasn't in the same class as most of the cold-blooded schemers he'd encountered in the past. She'd wanted magic to come to her, with her whole heart, and she wanted to use her so-called powers to help others. He couldn't fault her for caring so much. He admired her for it.

But his errand was complete, as of dawn this morning. There was nothing for him here.

Except Bryony.

The thought came to him unbidden. He tried to shrug it off, telling himself that he was just letting some part of his body other than his brain lead him about.

But as much as he tried to trivialize his feelings for her, there was still a stubborn, steadfast element within him that clung to the words: *except Bryony*.

What was it about her? She was beautiful, yes, but he'd seen—and held—women just as lovely before. She was bright. That was pleasant and not overly common among many of the women in his family's social circles. She was gentle. Her slightly husky voice was a pleasure to hear. She was tenderhearted, superstitious, faithful, generous, guileless, fanciful, and hardworking. She was a mix of innocence and simple wisdom, a complicated blend of whimsy and common sense.

"Ye gods." He spun away from the window. He was raving! He couldn't be, it wasn't possible—

He had to get away.

He strode out of the inn and straight to the dry-goods store, which was also the office for the coach line. He had his ticket in hand when he returned, but he wasn't smiling. The next coach, the storekeeper had told him, wouldn't be coming in for another three days.

How was he going to keep away from Bryony for three whole days?

Matthew, Jonathan, Lucas, and Marcus were experiencing no such quandaries. The four of them had started out just after dawn and were now standing before what was known in the valley as the Boat.

It was perched on a crag, just around a bend in the mountains, in the south end of the hollow. Many years before, Phileas Adcock had lived up there. In his fiftieth year, Phileas had taken a notion that Crystal Pond was meant to rise up and rise up big. Taking his ax and his saw and his hammer, he'd felled trees, shaped beams, hammered and nailed for five long years. When he was finished, his modest cabin had been transformed into a ship of impressive size and proportions. Phileas had outfitted it for his wife and sons—though he was a bachelor—and sealed it with pitch so that it was snug and watertight. Then he'd gone through the town, door to door, warning everyone to be on the lookout for a heavy downpour, soon to come.

Someone reminded Phileas that he needed a wife and sons for the journey, and he soon recollected that in order to fulfill the Biblical nature of his prophecy, he also needed two of every animal on earth. He gathered up his best suit for courting, all of the traps and cages and boxes he could lay hands on, and headed out of the hollow, intent on completing his errand. No one ever saw him again, but popular wisdom had it that he'd found a wife in the Northwest Territory and the two of them and their twin sons were busily collecting animals thither and yon.

That had been almost thirty years ago. Phileas, if he was still alive, would have been nearing the end of his life. But no one had torn down Adcock's Ark, and no one had moved into it, respecting that a man must do what a man feels called to do, and that one just didn't fool around with prophetically based architecture.

"'T'ain't seaworthy," said Lucas as the four men gathered at the door.

"Well, of course it isn't," retorted Leary. "Phileas put an end to that when he dug that root cellar down there under the elephants' bunks."

Matthew pushed open the door and the four went inside. Jonathan and Marcus carried lamps and led the way through the lower decks where the animals were to be carried. Single-file, they climbed a narrow stairway to the cabin level, ducking cobwebs as they went, and came out into a dark, spacious room, outfitted with furnishings that were either anchored in place or secured in some fashion against the rolling of the waves.

"I never was too sure about a fireplace on board a ship," said Lucas, who had been to Boston once and had seen some mighty seagoing vessels docked there.

"Probably won't draw all that well out on the water," said Matthew with a nod. "But while Phileas is waitin' for the creek to rise, it's good to have on board." He slung off the burlap sack he was carrying over his shoulder. "I think it's time we got started. That is, if you three agree that this is the place we need."

"If Bryony and her young fella don't get something settled here tonight, then they're not the two I thought they were," said Lucas.

"Hmmph," said Marcus. "If they don't get something settled here tonight, then we're not the four we thought we were!"

"Amen to that," said Matthew.

The four of them set to work. When they were done, they stood back and surveyed their handiwork.

"Looks just like it did when we came in," said Jonathan.

"That it does," said Lucas.

The men looked at the scene before them with satisfaction. Then, one by one, they gathered up their sacks and other tools and went out.

"Fine night for it," said Marcus, glancing up at the gathering clouds.

"Let's just hope it doesn't get out of hand," Lucas drawled.

"What do you mean?" asked Jonathan.

"I mean, let's hope old Phileas Adcock was just a nice old crackpot, like we all believed."

The other men looked at him in a moment of alarm. Then the four of them burst out laughing. They were still smiling when they got back to town.

Chapter Nine

"Thunder frights Beanes into Growing. Beware of Sowing in a Storme, for You Maye Obtaine that which You Fear to Reap."
—*Cassia Talcott*

Bryony frowned up at the sky. The clouds puzzled her. The sunset yesterday had been crimson-edged, the sunrise clear. But now, at midafternoon, rain clouds were gathering over the hollow and the air was growing heavy with moisture.

"Oh, well," she murmured to Soot. "It rather suits my mood."

She'd wandered about the house and grounds all morning, doing her chores in a daze.

It wasn't as if she hadn't seen this coming, she'd told herself. She'd never shown any aptitude for magic, even in the days when she'd been under her mother's and aunts' careful tutelage. She shouldn't be so shocked to learn the truth at last.

Accepting it was the hard part, she thought now, settling herself in the window seat of the front parlor. Her life would be very different from now on. She needed to make plans, she told herself once more.

But she couldn't just yet. Right now she wanted only to mourn and grieve and count the number of hopes that had been canceled at sunrise the other morning. She wanted to bury her head in the sand and hide from it all.

Yet there were other feelings that were twining around the pain of her loss, tugging at the back of her mind. There were vivid recollections of someone's firm, warm lips, someone's stroking hands, someone's body heating hers. . . .

She shook her head, trying to toss off the sudden rising excitement she felt, even in the face of her loss. She didn't want to have to struggle with her feelings about Adam just now. She'd been vulnerable, he'd been there at the right moment, and that was all there was to it.

But what had he said? *You possess value in your own person, in your own soul. You don't need magic to claim a place in this wolrd. People care for you as Bryony, not just as the hag.*

Had he meant it? What about the other thing he'd said, about it being better to know the truth now rather than later? Had he known all along that she wasn't a magician, a true Hag?

Something out the window caught her eye. A

rider was coming up the road to her house at a fast trot, the wind whipping his coat about and threatening to steal his hat. She jumped off the window seat and ran to the door.

"Mistress Bryony!" Marcus Tupper called out. He rode up and she caught the bridle of his horse, holding it steady. "We need your help up at this end of the hollow. Young Phillip Carrowe is missing. His ma says he went out to trap rabbits yestereve and didn't come back. She'd feel all right about it but the lad's never been gone this long and there's a right hummer of a storm coming, looks like."

"I'll be ready in a moment," Bryony said.

She ran inside and fetched her thickest cloak and scarf. She quickly poured an extra saucer of cream for Soot, then bound her hair with a ribbon, twisted it on top of her head, and secured it with several pins.

Marcus was waiting for her outside. He reached his hand down to help her up behind him, and they were off, stopping only long enough for Bryony to grab a lantern from the garden shed.

Adam was beating through the underbrush with a staff, following Matthew deeper into the woods. They'd begun to climb, and the ground was rocky in among the bracken and shrubs.

He'd been walking along the road to Crystal Pond when Matthew had hailed him. The older man had hurried up, somewhat out of breath, and told him about the young boy who hadn't come home from the woods the night before. Adam had welcomed the chance to do something—anything—to get his mind off Bryony and magic and his imminent departure.

"The lad could be anywhere," Matthew called back to him. "These woods can fool even an old tracker like me, especially on a day when a fellow can't see the sun for the clouds."

"Why did he go out alone? You say he was only nine years old?"

"Nine's a fair age for a farmer boy," Matthew said, scrambling over a fallen tree trunk. "And his dad said he could have the money from the rabbits he raised and sold, long as he did it on his own. Powerful incentive for a youngster to get out of his depth."

"I suppose so." Adam felt a drop of rain strike his forehead, then another. "Looks like it's starting," he called to Matthew, who had moved ahead.

"That it is. We're going to have to cover this ground fast, if we want to find him before the storm's in full blow."

Adam caught up to the old man at a fork in the path. Matthew put a hand to his chest. "We'd best split up," he said, puffing. "I'd take the upper but my wind's not as good as yours, young fella. Follow this path to the right. It'll loop around at the top and bring you back down again. Check every bush and little hollow, though, as best you can. If the boy's fallen, he might be lying somewheres we can't see him." He gestured left. "I'll head down this way and tackle the berry brambles. Rabbits like hiding in them and it's possible he went there. We'll meet back at the pond?"

"Right," said Adam.

A few moments later, Matthew's white head and blue coat were out of sight, and the path Adam was following began to rise sharply. The rain was pattering down harder and he had to shade his eyes to search for signs of the lost boy. From time to time, the path would wind out onto a ledge. There, in the open, the wind came at Adam with growing force, and the drops of rain that had pattered through the trees were stinging sharp. He looked up but couldn't see where the trail might lead. The trees were too dense. He plodded on, poking bushes and brambles with his staff.

And then the thunder began to roll.

Bryony toiled up the path, lifting her hood from time to time to peer into the woods around her. She shook a dripping hand off and then cupped her hands together around her mouth. "Phillip!" she shouted. "Phillip Carrowe!"

She was growing hoarse now and her cloak was already sodden. The wind was starting to howl among the higher passes and all of the animals had long since fallen silent and disappeared.

She and Marcus had ridden as far north as they could; then Marcus had gone off to shelter his horse from the growing rain. He was to meet her at the bend in the footpath just due south of Hawk's Rise, but he'd never come. She wasn't worried about him. She knew that the older man was a seasoned woodsman and that it could take a while to find a place where his horse would be safe in the storm.

And it was a storm. She'd felt it gathering all day and now she sensed that it was going to be a bad one. The air felt as if it were full of lightning, crackling and tingling around her head. She knew it would break soon and she needed to find shelter herself before it did. If she hurried, she might make it down the mountain, perhaps as far as the old trapper's cabin just above Matthew's farm. It was almost collapsed, it was so old, but it would offer some kind of protection until the worst was over.

Perhaps that was where Phillip had gone. She was cheered at the thought of finding him at last, safe and sound. Nothing within her told her that he was in trouble.

The thought brought her up short. How could she know that? She couldn't. It was just habit for her. She hadn't any gifts of sight or knowing, she knew that. She just had good old-fashioned hope.

"And that's good enough, I suppose," she whispered to herself.

Thunder sounded, shaking the ground beneath her feet. She quickened her pace. Lightning was imminent and she was out on a crag, with only a few lone trees about her. She had to get to shelter quickly, before the first flash.

The path turned and headed back toward the woods. Though it was still dangerous to be outside, she knew she'd be slightly better protected under the cover of the trees than she would be out here on the crag, in the open.

There were only a few more yards to go. The lightning hit before she expected it, cracking a stone just a few feet away from her. She jumped, startled, and twisted her ankle in a hole. She went down with a cry, sliding off the edge of the path to the rocks below.

Adam was cursing under his breath as he climbed. Where the hell was this loop that Matthew was talking about? The path seemed to wind its way up and up with no intention of ever coming back down until it had reached the clouds.

The clouds. That was a joke. The clouds were so heavy with rain that they were hanging low enough to snag on the trees overhead. Rain had been pelting him for the better part of an hour by now and his hat was tilting a steady stream of water down in front of his nose. The thunder seemed to be rolling closer with every step he took, as if he were about to trespass on the gods' own game of ninepins. He could smell smoke from lightning strikes in the trees beyond his sight. He looked for the boy when he could, but by now he was more interested in getting onto the loop path.

He was just about to give up and retrace his steps when he heard the cry. His heart squeezed tight in his chest. It was Bryony. There had been only one cry, but he knew it as surely as he knew his own name. What the devil was she doing up here in this storm?

He raced up the path, heedless of the storm around him. He burst out onto the rocky crag, looking frantically about him. "Bryony!" he shouted. "Bryony!"

"I'm here!"

He heard her calling, nearby, yet nowhere in sight. He darted forward as a fresh peal of thunder echoed around the rocks.

"Adam! Here!"

He saw the spot where the earth had recently crumbled away and ran for it. He saw her at once, huddled on a small ledge below, her rain-wet face upturned to his.

"Don't move!" he called. "I'll get you up!"

He knelt down and assessed the ground around the edge of the path. It was soft and growing softer in the pounding rain. The ledge below wasn't big enough for both of them and he didn't know if it would hold their combined weights if he went down after her.

He tore off his coat, then his shirt. The rain pummeled his bare skin as he knotted the tail of the shirt to the tail of his coat. He tugged at the knot with all his strength, prayed it would hold, and then flung the end of it over the side to Bryony.

It wouldn't reach. Her fingers, stretched to their fullest length, came up short of the goal. He flopped down on his stomach and hung over the side, both hands gripping the make-shift rope.

"Got it?" he called down.

"Got it!"

"Can you climb up?"

"I'll try."

He watched as she tucked her skirts up into her waistband and hoisted herself up on one foot. She lifted the other foot and cried out as she set it down.

"You're hurt. Just hold on. I'll pull you up."

"No!" she called. "I'm too heavy for you!"

"Just—"

But his words were lost in the next clap of thunder, and Bryony had taken two more steps up the face of the crag before it finished echoing around the hills. He braced himself on his elbows and held fast to the coat as she climbed. Soon, she was close enough for him to reach down to her. He extended one arm, clasped his hand around her forearm, and hauled her up to the edge of the cliff with one mighty heave.

Lightning struck one of the scrubby oaks nearby. Adam jumped up and pulled Bryony to her feet. "We've got to get off this cliff," he shouted over the rising wind.

"Up there," Bryony said, pointing up the path. "I think I see the roof of a house!"

Adam looked where she pointed. There was something there that didn't look like part of the forest, all right. "Can you walk?"

"I think so." Bryony hobbled forward. "Yes. Let's go."

Adam slipped his arm around her, supporting her, and together they stumbled toward the trees. They made it just before another cloudburst broke over the pass, bringing rain so heavy they couldn't see through its heavy curtain. They turned of one accord and headed up the path. They hadn't gone far when Adam gave a shout.

"There," he cried. "I see it!"

He pulled Bryony along as fast as she could go. When she stumbled over an exposed root, he swept her up and carried her the rest of the way to the house just over the rise in the path.

"What the—" Adam gaped at the structure before them. It was the wildest, strangest sight he'd ever beheld, and he wondered briefly if he hadn't been touched by lightning after all.

"It must be the Boat," Bryony said wonderingly.

"A boat? Up here?"

She glanced up at the sky. "Never mind that now. Let's just get inside."

Adam went where she pointed and found the door in the high wooden wall. He set Bryony down while he rattled the latch, then with a muttered oath, simply stepped back and kicked the door open.

Chapter Ten

"Herbes to Cure Love are as Usefulle as Overcoats are to Fishes."

—*Cassia Talcott*

He peered inside the dark building. "It's dark as a pocket inside," he said. "I'm going to prop the door open so at least some light will come in."

He placed a rock in front of the door, then helped Bryony across the threshold. "Let me go first," he told her.

He moved forward with caution, arms out like a blind man feeling his way along. Slowly, his eyes adjusted to the dim light and he could see stairs on the far wall.

"This just seems like a barn or a stable down here," he said to Bryony, his voice echoing off the walls. "But there are some stairs. I'll go up and see what's there. You wait here. If I shout, get out of here as fast as you can. No telling what we'll find in an old abandoned place like this."

"I want to go with you."

"No. You're hurt. You can't go climbing the stairs with an injured foot. Stay here until I can scout it out."

"All right. Adam—"

"What?"

"Be very careful."

He grinned in the dark. "Never fear."

The stairs led up for many feet and each step rose higher into darkness. Adam brushed at cobwebs but kept one hand on the wall, holding his breath to see if the next creaking step would hold.

He reached the top and felt the door, hanging half-open. He pushed it open and called out, "Anyone here?"

His voice echoed back at him. He stepped through the doorway and saw light coming in dim shafts from two narrow windows at the far end. He could make out a hearth and some cabinets on the near wall. His boot heels thumped hollowly on the wooden floor as he went to open them.

To his relief, he found a dust-covered lantern with a stub of candle inside it. He felt about on the mantel and found a flint. When he'd lighted it, he shone the lantern around the room. He gave a low whistle.

"Adam? Are you all right?" Bryony's voice floated up from below.

"I'm coming. Wait there."

He went down and helped Bryony to the stairs. Then, seeing that she was limping worse than before, he thrust the lantern into her hands and swept her once again into his arms.

Bryony gaped at the room at the top of the stairs. She'd heard stories of Adcock's Ark and she'd accepted that it existed, but she'd never seen it before, let alone been inside.

Adam carried her across the floor to the hearth area and set her down on the bench that flanked the dining table. Now that they were inside and she was more calm, she was distracted from her new surroundings by the sight of Adam, raindrops glistening in his hair and on his skin, standing bare-chested before her. She found herself unable to look away from the sight of his broad, well-muscled shoulders and the hard, flat chest that tapered down to his narrow waist. He was absolutely magnificent, she thought. What would it be like to touch that smooth, firm skin . . . ?

"I'm going to try to get a fire started," he said, interrupting her reverie. "There are a few logs here and if I look around, maybe I can find something for kindling. You need to keep that foot up and stay still."

She opened her mouth but nothing came out. After all the years she had spent caring for others, she wasn't sure how to act when someone else, especially someone so temptingly pleasant to look at, cared for her. At last, she found her voice. "Aren't you cold?" she asked.

He glanced down at his bare torso. "A bit. But I don't think there's much I can do about it. I'm afraid I left my coat and shirt out on that ledge where I found you. What the devil were you doing out there, anyway?"

"Looking for a lost boy," Bryony said, rubbing her cold hands together. "What were you doing?"

"The same. Matthew met me coming out of the inn, said he needed help searching the south end of the hollow and the passes up above his place. We separated and the storm broke before I could get back to him. Hope he's all right." He found an old basket in a corner and broke it over his knee, then tossed the pieces in the fireplace. "What were you doing out all alone, with a storm coming on?"

"I wasn't alone," she said. "I was with Marcus Tupper. But he had to get his horse sheltered, so I went on ahead. We were going to meet at a certain spot, but he didn't come and so I started back on my own." She gave his back a tart glance. "I know my way around these hills, you know."

"That may be," Adam said, striking the flint again. "But you didn't know that you were going to fall off that cliff, did you?"

"No," she said, more gently. "I owe you a great debt."

The kindling caught fire and Adam twisted around to look up at her. "It was nothing," he said with a shrug. "I'm glad I was there." He turned back to the hearth. "Where are we, now? You said something about a boat."

Bryony gave a soft laugh. "I knew it was up here, and yet I didn't, if you take my meaning. People had talked of it all my life and said such strange things about this place that I just took it as another old legend. I thought perhaps it had crumbled in ruins ages ago." She glanced around. "Yet here it is. And it seems in fair shape, too."

Adam laid a log on the fire with a grunt, then stood. "I can see that it's all laid out like someone was planning to go on an ocean voyage, though I've never seen any ship's cabin like this one. Who built this place?"

Bryony related the tale of Phileas Adcock and his call to build a latter-day ark. "He was very polite about it, they say," she told Adam. "He always apologized to everyone, and explained that with the measurements he'd gotten from the Bible, he just wouldn't have room for anyone else. He offered lots of advice on converting houses into boats."

"But—this thing won't float."

"No, I don't suppose it will. But Phileas is still out gathering his animals, so I suppose it won't matter much until he gets back."

Adam rubbed a hand over his cheek. "Not too long ago, this whole story, this place, might have struck me as preposterous. Now, it merely seems a cut above humdrum for Cold Springs Hollow." He cocked an eyebrow at Bryony. "Something wrong?"

Bryony could feel the heat rising in her cheeks. She'd been staring at him again, at the rippling planes of his chest as he moved. Could he tell what wayward turns her thoughts were taking?

She shook her head vigorously. "No. Only, I am a trifle cold in these wet clothes."

"Take them off."

"I beg your pardon?"

"Take them off. You know enough about sickness to know that sitting around in cold, wet clothes in a cold room is an engraved invitation to fevers and coughs." He went to a cupboard. "Maybe there's something you can put on in here."

He found a large flannel bed sheet in one of the lower cupboards. He shook it out and hung it before the fire to warm. "It should be warm by the time you can get out of those wet things."

"But, I—" Bryony was at a loss. She knew he was right. She did need to get out of her wet things. And already her ankle was beginning to swell and throb. But undressing in front of Adam? "What about you?" she asked. "You've lost your shirt and coat. You mustn't court sickness, either."

Adam nodded. "I'll see what I can find."

He discovered a rough, homespun robe in another cupboard. To Bryony's relief, he slipped it on, then turned his back and pulled off his boots and breeches. When he turned back around, he was tying the woven belt about his waist, and his bare skin was concealed from view.

"I'm going down below and see if I can find any more wood," he said. "If this storm keeps up, we're going to need a lot more fuel than this to keep warm." He'd found another candle in the cupboard. He lit it, stuck it in a cup from the mantel, and went off, the lantern bobbing in the dim recesses of the room.

Bryony waited until she heard his footsteps on the stairs, then hastily threw off her cloak and scarf and unlaced her bodice. She shrugged out of her bodice and then managed to wriggle out of her skirt without having to put her weight on her injured foot. Even her petticoat and her shift were wet through, so off they came. She stripped off her stockings and sturdy walking shoes, then hobbled over to the fire.

The flannel sheet was heavenly warm and surprisingly soft and clean-smelling for having sat in a cupboard for decades. Old Phileas must have made his cabinets water- and airtight for those forty days and forty nights he'd foreseen, she thought. She wrapped the sheet around her and pulled one of the ends up over her shoulder to tuck under her arm. She reached up and pulled the pins and ribbon from her hair, letting it fall down her back in damp waves. She used the ribbon to tie the sheet snugly around her waist.

She was sitting on the bench nearest the fire, gingerly examining her swollen ankle when Adam returned, his arms loaded with stout logs.

"I found these in a closet or something down below," he said, dropping them on the hearth with a thump. "And he's got—"

He stopped short, looking at her. Bryony met his eyes. There it was again, that look of embers warming just below the green depths of his gaze. She wanted to look away. She couldn't.

"You look beautiful," he said, his voice slightly husky. "Like some lovely Greek goddess come down from on high."

She blushed and smiled. "Do you think Athena wore flannel sheets?"

"She might have." He grinned, too. "It could get mighty cold up on old Mt. Olympus, I'll bet."

She laughed, then winced. He saw her pain and squatted down before her, examining her injury.

"I wish I had my satchel with me," she said. She gritted her teeth as he wriggled her foot ever so slightly. "It's not broken. That's good. But it needs a good poultice laid on it and wrapping."

"Let's see what old Phileas has to offer," Adam said, rising. He went to the cabinets again. "Say, there's food here! We won't starve, at least."

"Food? No one's lived here for more than twenty-five years. It can't be edible."

"You may be right. But I can't imagine jerky wrapped in paper and stored in an airtight box could be all that bad. And there's some hard biscuits. And tea. There's even a full bottle of sherry, corked up tight."

"Bring me the tea," Bryony said. "It's not as good as a compress of marigold, but it should be of some use."

Adam found an old pot that hadn't rusted through and thrust it outside the window to catch rainwater. It took some time, but soon there was enough to brew the tea leaves for a poultice. Bryony tore up a section of her petticoat with the aid of Adam's knife, wrapped the leaves in place, and tied the cloth strips securely about her ankle.

Adam brought out the dried venison, the biscuits, and a sealed jar of strawberry jam. He found a chest that held plates and cups, each nestled into their own slots, to prevent breaking on the long voyage, he figured. He dusted off the table with the hearth broom, then spread out their feast. He found a hook that could go over the windowsill and hung the pot out to catch more rainwater for brewing tea.

The venison was surprisingly tasty and only as tough as ordinary jerky. The hard biscuits were dry, but covered in the jam, or dipped in sherry, they were serviceable. The fire was beginning to reach out and warm the hearth area, and Adam kept Bryony's cup of sherry well filled.

Outside, the storm still raged. He'd thought that it would have spent itself by now, but every time he thought it might be waning, it seemed to redouble its efforts, sending out spectacular flashes of lightning and making the cabin tremble with peals of thunder.

She gazed at Adam across the table. In the golden light of the candle, his hair tousled and loose, he looked more relaxed and at ease than she'd ever seen him. The effect was very intriguing. She wondered what he'd do if she reached out and brushed back that one lock of hair from his forehead.

"So," Adam said suddenly. "Do you think young Phillip has taken shelter somewhere, too?"

"I hope so," she replied, grateful for the distraction. "He might even be safe at home by now. There's an old trapper's cabin down the way, so perhaps he went there. I was headed for it myself when I slipped off the path."

"You didn't know this was here?"

She shook her head. "Oh, I knew that it must be up here somewhere, my parents had told the story so often. But I'd never come across it before. You can't see it down in the hollow for all the trees that have grown up around it."

"What were your parents like?"

She smiled and gazed into the fire. "How can anyone describe her own parents? They were giants. They were the center of all comfort and safety. They were mean old things who wouldn't let me do whatever I wanted. They were strong and weak, good and bad, foolish and wise. Just as we all are."

Adam looked down at his hands. "You loved them very much. I can tell by the way you talk about them. With warmth. Reverence, even. They couldn't have been too mean or weak or foolish."

"No, I suppose not." She smiled up at him. "They were firm in their training of me and I suppose, because I was their only child, they had pinned all their hopes on me. But they were fine and good. Even as their daughter, I know that. My mother was like a flame, always active and in a passion over this or that. My father was more like Crystal Pond, still and deep. Together, they had a power of love and magic that was like no other, I believe."

"Sounds like a most idyllic life."

"You're probably right. That's why I was so lost after their deaths, I think. I never imagined that anyone so vital, so strong, could be taken away so young. I've tried my best to be like them, to make them proud."

Adam looked thoughtful. "I don't know if we can ever please our parents."

"No?"

"It seems to me that strife and discord are part of the way we all learn to become our own men and women. We have to shake off the old in order to learn to stand alone."

"Your parents aren't pleased with you?"

He shrugged. "I think not. But we've learned to get along, to be tolerant. It's only reasonable."

Bryony thought of his words to her that morning in the grove. He'd said that he knew what it was like to fail the ones we love. Had Adam failed his parents?

"So, you never found this place before today, eh?" Adam was looking about the cabin again.

"No. I must have been close many times, but never came across it."

"Never?" He smiled wickedly. "It seems quite a romantic old spot. No trysts with some young swain from Cold Springs?"

She stared down at her plate. "You're mocking me."

He reached across the table and tilted her chin up. "No. I'm not." His voice grew softer. "I know if I were one of the lads around here I'd be doing my best to get you alone."

She pursed her lips and pulled away from his touch. "I don't believe you would. You recall that up until the other day, I was the Hag of the Hollow. Someone not of their world. They were more scared of me and my powers than they were inclined to court me." She sighed. "Of course, now it doesn't matter."

"Are you trying to tell me that not one of those fellows has even tried to kiss you?" He leaned his chin on his hand, his elbow on the table, regarding her with warm interest.

"Oh, yes, that happened. You see, there's a tradition in the hollow that says that if you kiss the Hag on the stroke of midnight on New Year's Eve, you'll have your wish. If you miss the stroke by one moment, either before or after, you'll be blasted with bad luck within the week."

"And someone tried it?"

"Lucius Dreyer. Poor fellow, he was as nervous as a fat goose at Christmastime. I was showing him to the front door when the clock struck. He tripped over Soot, landed the kiss too late, and groaned like a man who's just been told he's got three days to live. He ran out of my house like he feared I'd come after him and turn him into a garden toad."

"And did bad luck find him?"

"I'm afraid so. He was so worried that he hid out in his father's loft for a week. But when his friends came to tell him that the week was up, he danced a jig, stepped on a rake, tumbled out of the loft, and broke his wrist." Bryony giggled. "Poor fellow. I was the one who had to come and set the wrist and bind it for him. I thought he was going to wither away from the humiliation of it all."

"And that's it?"

She felt suddenly shy. "Not until you—we . . . at the corn ritual . . . and in the grove . . . Should there be more?"

"No. No, I suppose not." His voice went soft and husky again.

"And you?"

He was startled. "What?"

"Have you kissed many women?"

Bryony watched him beneath her lashes, too shy to face him, too curious not to watch his reaction. He opened his mouth, then shut it, as if at a loss to answer her simple question. But why shouldn't she ask it? she reasoned. He'd had no qualms about asking her.

Then her heart felt suddenly cold. What if there were indeed many women? What if he—

"Not too many," he answered slowly. "But I'm not a boy, Bryony."

"I know that." She hesitated, then: "Did you . . . touch them? The way you touched me in the grove?"

Adam's face was impossible to read. "Yes, I touched them."

She looked away, toward the windows where the rain was sluicing down over the narrow panes. She heard him move closer to her. Every sense within her came to life with the awareness of him, only a breath away.

He reached out and swept a lock of hair from her shoulder. "Did you like being touched that way?"

No, her reason told her. *Say no.* She couldn't risk having him touch her again. Not that way.

Not when she knew that he would only leave and go back to his home, to his own magic, to those other women who knew all the secrets of touch and kiss and pleasure.

Her traitorous heart took hold, though, and she nodded her head.

He put his hand on her arm and turned her to face him. She wanted to groan like Lucius Dreyer—this could only bring her bad luck. She was already warming and tingling, and all he'd done was touch her arm and look into her eyes.

"Bryony."

"Don't say it," she said, pulling back. "Please don't."

"Say what?"

"Say what you were going to say."

"I didn't know you could read thoughts," he said with a smile. "No more magic, don't you remember?"

His words were gentle, but they stung all the same. "No, I can't read your thoughts," she retorted. "Can you read mine?"

"I've never claimed such power, no." His face was wary.

"Nor have I. But I can guess. And I don't want to hear it."

He straightened, frowning. "I was going to say how much I enjoyed touching you. I was going to say how beautiful you look in the firelight."

"And I said I don't want to hear it! It's not only improper, it's foolish. We won't touch again," she said, with more firmness than she felt.

"You didn't like it when I kissed you?"

"What I like or don't like isn't important."

"It is to me."

"No, it isn't." She inched back on the bench, trying to put more distance between them. "What's important is that now you know that I am not the person you thought I was. I'm not the Hag of the Hollow. You can go on your way, back to your home, or somewhere else, someplace where a true magus can help you with your magic. And I must stay here and—"

"And what?" He inched closer.

"And work as I have been, with my herbs and my simples. Though I have no claim to magic, at least I know that those work."

"And is that what you want?" He leaned toward her. She inched back. She found herself perched on the edge of the bench. "Is that what you want me to do?"

"Yes!" she exclaimed. "I want you to go away and leave me alone!"

He drew back. "All right," he said, his eyes never leaving hers. "But first—"

He leaned over and kissed her with such sweet, swift thoroughness that she had no time to think, only to react. And her reaction gave the lie to every word she'd been saying. Her hands came up, caught his face, and held him while she returned his kiss in kind.

"You want me to go away?" he whispered when their lips parted at last.

"Yes!" she moaned. "Please. You have to. If you don't, I won't be able to stand it when you leave!"

The truth was out and it had surprised even her. She waited for his response, horrified at what she had just blurted out to him. Her confession left her so naked before him, so vulnerable.

Adam let out his breath with a sudden gust. He rose from the bench and strode away into the darkness. She heard him taking the stairs down, his boot heels drumming.

She stared at the fire in anguish, tears blurring the flames that danced there. She'd done it. She'd told the truth. He'd done just what she'd asked, left her alone.

And it was the most miserable, unsatisfying victory she could imagine.

Adam wished he could turn back the clock. He wished he were sitting in the Dolphin Club once more with his friends. And when they proposed that he take a simple jaunt down to a little place called Cold Springs Hollow, he would spit right in their eyes.

He roamed around the lower deck of Adcock's Ark, investigating the vast hold but not really seeing anything. Finally, he gave up all pretenses and went to sit near the open door.

It wasn't just his male needs that were tormenting him now, though his body was trying to convince him to go back upstairs, just for a kiss or two thousand from Bryony's honey lips. It wasn't just his wish to comply with her demand that he leave her alone. He was a gentleman, but this wasn't about etiquette.

It was about the truth of what she had said to him. That she cared for him, enough to know that she would be hurt if he left her.

If he left her.

That was what was nagging at him. He knew that his task here was at an end. He was already packed. She wasn't going to carry on with her magical nonsense, nor charge anyone for an incantation. She had faced up to the idea that she had no magic and had accepted it, though he knew it had been painful for her.

He would leave. Soon.

He'd made a promise to his mother that he'd come back to Philadelphia and begin working at his father's shipping firm. Summer was always a busy time and fall was even more so. He was a man who kept his promises. He'd have to leave.

But he couldn't yet. No, that wasn't the whole truth. He didn't want to leave; that was the truth. He didn't want to leave Bryony.

He groaned. It was madness, but there it was. He wanted Bryony Talcott. He wanted to be the one who taught her all about kissing and touching and the ecstasies that a man and a woman could share. He wanted her around, her amber eyes glowing, her smile shining out just for him. He wanted to protect her, especially now that she seemed so forlorn without her beloved fantasy of magic. He wanted to drink in her soothing, light spirit at the end of the day, to bask in the warmth of her regard.

It was impossible, he told himself with a snort of derision. Even if she would have him, he couldn't stay here in the hollow. He wasn't a farmer or a merchant. He couldn't traipse around Talcott Farm tending honeysuckle and Saint-John's-wort and helping Bryony bring calves and piglets into the world. He had friends and family in Philadelphia. Obligations.

His family. He grimaced at the thought of going back to that cold house, his distant mother, his angry father. . . .

How different it was in the hollow. Bryony's house, the Laughing Dog, Matthew's farm—they all seemed alive and warm and full of the promise of life. If only he could bring some of that cheer into the Hawthorne house.

He straightened. "Why not?" he murmured.

He shook his head. "No. It's mad. Impossible."

He grinned. He closed his eyes, took a deep breath, and then leapt to his feet.

"Bryony Talcott," he cried out, bursting through the doorway above. "Marry me!"

Chapter Eleven

"Words are Parte of the Magic of the Aire, which is Alle Around us. Use Caution in Pronouncing Your Desires Aloud, for you Might Welle Gain what You Request."

—*Cassia Talcott*

Bryony blinked, her eyes still seeing starry images through her tears. "What?"

"Marry me."

Adam came to stand before her, his hands on his hips. For one hysterical moment, all she could think was that he looked like some Old Testament zealot, standing there and commanding her to follow him into the desert for the next forty years.

"Why do you keep saying that?" she asked, bewildered.

"Because," he said in slow, patient tones, "I want you to be my wife."

She stared at him, utterly lost for words. Was he joking? Was he mad?

He dropped to his knees before her. "Bryony," he said, taking her hand in both of his. "Mistress Talcott, will you do me the great honor of becoming my wife?"

"Why?"

He shook his head. "Oh, I don't know. Maybe because you are so guileless as to ask me that question." He reached up with one hand and smoothed her hair back from her shoulder. "Maybe it's because I love the way you smile. And the way you talk to plants. Perhaps it's because I almost lost you today, when you fell over that cliff. Don't ever do that again!"

"You saved my life. I'm very grateful. That's no reason to get married."

"All right, then, maybe it's because I've never before had anyone turn my whole life so completely upside down. Maybe it's because I can't keep my hands off you. Every time I'm around you, from the moment I first saw you at the inn, I've been fighting with myself every day, wrestling my feelings back. I want you so much I can't sleep nights. I want you so much I can't even smell your hair without wanting to toss you down on some bed—hell, on the floor!—and cherish every inch of your beautiful self."

Bryony felt the color in her cheeks rising to stain her whole face. "I must admit that I have wanted to touch you, too," she said softly.

"I'm glad of it. I want you to want me. I want us to spend a lifetime exploring one another."

"But, Adam, that's not enough—"

"Not enough to base a marriage on? Well, what is? I know couples who married just to insure that their family fortunes would increase. I know men and women who married for the sake of propriety—everyone expected them to marry each other, so they did! Their marriages lasted but I don't believe they had half the regard, the passion for one another that we have. Marry me, Bryony."

Passion. Regard. Marriage. Bryony's mind was in a tumult. It was all like a dream—Adam in the firelight, holding her hand, declaring his passion for her, demanding that she be his wife!

There was a crack of lightning outside. The flare lit Adam's face and she saw no mockery, no deception in it. He wanted her. Magic or not, Hag or not, he wanted her for his own.

She knew she should consider it carefully. Rushing into marriage could be folly.

But her heart was so full already. Adam, her magic man, loved her, even when he knew she had no magic of her own to share. After the pain of her discovery two days ago, it was sweet balm to her heart. And she knew, had known from her first sight of him, that she wanted him, as much as he claimed he wanted her. Her body, her mind, her spirit, all longed for this one man.

"Yes."

He sat back as if she had shoved him. "What?" It was evidently his turn to be the slow-witted one.

"I said yes, I'll marry you, Adam."

He was on his feet in an instant, clasping her to him and showering her with kisses. "Bryony," he cried softly. "Oh, my sweet Bryony." He tugged at the sheet and pulled it free from under her arm, then rained kisses on her shoulders and throat. She laughed and squirmed as his kisses tickled her neck. The feeling of his body against hers was radiant, as if he had sent a small sun shooting into her midsection, there to melt and spread its rays throughout her body. He sank to the bench with her in his lap.

Bryony wound her arms about his neck and drank in the pleasure of his kisses, of his caressing hands. *Yes, oh yes,* her mind and spirit sang. This was absolutely right. She was absolutely right in his arms.

His hand slid up her side and cupped her breast. She leaned into the heat of his touch and sighed her pleasure against his temple. It was so sweet, so good. . . .

He was working on the ribbon at her waist when she realized what she was doing. She put a hand up to his chest to halt him.

"Adam! Adam, we're forgetting something!"

"What?" He lowered his head to brush his lips over the soft flesh that showed just above the sheet around her. His clever magician's fingers had already untied the ribbon and he was slipping his hand under the fold of cloth, causing intense, pleasurable white fire to shoot through Bryony's middle. She gasped and reached for her sanity. It was just about within her grasp when she felt his warm, smooth palm slide up over her abdomen and cover her breast.

She writhed in his lap. He had to stop. They had to stop. It wasn't the right time yet.

Ah, but it felt so utterly right. He rubbed the flat of his palm over her nipple and she felt it come to firm, hot attention. Her excitement was mounting by great leaps. His hand slid away and she thought she would have some relief, but then he was caressing her belly, kneading the soft flesh there, then sinking lower to slip between her thighs.

She was still and trembling. The sheet had fallen open around her, exposing her breasts to the cool air, to the warmth of the fire, to the heated regard of his green eyes. His hand at her thigh did not move but rather held there, tantalizing her with its shocking and delightful intimacy.

And then he moved. His long, slender fingers nudged her ever so gently until she parted for him. He was stroking her inner thighs with such complete tenderness, with such thoroughness, that she tilted back against his arm, her eyes closing as she gave herself up to the power of his touch. Her body was almost humming, it seemed, with the intensity of the pleasure he was giving her with his caresses.

His soothing, stroking fingers swept upward, then back, upward a little further, then back, then—

"Ow! Damn it all, what was that?"

Bryony struggled to get upright again. Adam just barely caught her before she tipped off of his lap altogether. "What is it?" she cried, alarmed.

"I don't know." He set her down off his lap and examined his leg. "Blast it, I've been burnt!"

She dropped down and lifted his hand away from the spot. He had indeed been burnt. Not deeply, she noted, relieved, but whatever spark had jumped from the fire had been hot enough to burn through his robe and give him a reddening spot the size of a penny. She dipped the edge of her fallen sheet into the cold remains of her tea and pressed it against his wound.

"Mmmm, that's better," he said.

She looked up at him and saw that his eyes were sparkling with interest. She looked down at herself and gave a gasp. She was stark naked, on her knees before him, one bare breast pressed against his uninjured knee as she ministered to him.

He reached down and gathered her back up into his arms. "Now, where were we?" His hands began to slide down her back.

She squealed and put her hand to his chest, holding him away from her. "Adam! We're not married yet."

"So? What has that—" He froze, holding her where she was. "Do you mean that we, that we can't—" He groaned and dropped his head on her shoulder. "Of course. We can't."

He set her away from him and got up.

"Where are you going?"

He walked to the window, pulled in the pot of rainwater, and dumped it over his head. Then, grabbing a blanket off of the bed, he headed for the stairs once more.

"Adam!" Bryony called out.

"I'm going downstairs. To sleep in the woodshed."

Bryony smiled and blew a kiss at his departing back. She felt her shift and found it was dry from the fire. She donned it quickly, laid another log on the fire, and went to make up her solitary bed.

Not for long would it be this way, she thought. She'd see to it that Adam Hawthorne finished what he'd begun before the week was out. If he didn't, she couldn't be responsible for what lengths her desire for him would carry her.

"Well, what do you think?" Marcus asked Matthew.

The two men were sitting in Matthew's kitchen, savoring his good ale and toasting their old toes while the storm raged outside. Matthew leaned over the hearth and poked the fire, adjusting the logs at just the right angle for maximum heat.

"I think we'd best let Preacher Kirkland know that there's a wedding coming up right soon."

"She'll be all right up there, won't she?" Marcus frowned. "She's a maid and he's jumpier than old Widow Dinsmoore's rooster the day she brought home six new hens."

"Bryony's protected. With good sense, modesty, and her parents' toughest spell of chastity. She'll be a maid on her wedding night." Matthew chuckled. "Our young magus'll be in desperate straits, though; you're right about that. Poor fella, all alone with her up there and not a chance in Hades he's gonna get any relief for his woes tonight."

"Yep. We're gonna have to hold him back or he'll be trying to honeymoon on the church steps, once Bryony's protection spell is broken on the vows!"

The two men laughed. They were the oldest of the four friends, and Marcus and Matthew had shared many secrets over the years. Marcus looked at his companion now and spoke bluntly.

"Are you ever plannin' to tell Bryony?" he asked.

"About our getting them together?"

"You know that ain't what I mean."

Matthew studied Marcus's seamed and weathered old face. "I don't know. I may, someday. But for now, let's see if we can get our Hag married to her magus. Then my story won't matter much."

Chapter Twelve

"The Moon's Blessing is most strong on those Nights when Her Face Shines full and round above. Waxing, she causeth Growth and Hastens Love. Waning, she robbs us of our Powers or causeth the Spirit to release its grasp on Follye. When she hides her Face utterly, make no Spelles, for she will Thwart You withal."

—*Cassia Talcott*

Adam was having a problem with his boots. He'd had them mended, oiled, and polished, and he'd donned them over excellent warm socks of finest lamb's wool, but for some reason he felt as if they were gaping open at the toes and water from an icy stream was pouring over them with gleeful abandon. He thought certainly that Preacher Kirkland would notice his fidgeting at any moment and interrupt the ceremony to ask him what was wrong. But the man carried on, serenely admonishing the bride and groom of the seriousness of the marital estate, and that their consciences should be clear when they undertook such a union, and so on and so forth until, quite suddenly, he turned to Adam and asked him a question.

"Beg pardon?" Adam said, bewildered.

There was mild tittering at the back of the church. Adam turned to Bryony for help but the wonder and warmth in her extraordinary eyes only added to his foggy state. What was happening to him?

"I said, wilt thou, Adam Josiah Hawthorne, take this woman to be thy wedded wife?"

Ye gods. Now he'd really gone and done it. He was being asked the most dangerous question of his entire life and he hadn't the faintest idea how he was going to answer it. Had all this really begun with a simple bet between friends, back in a comfortable club, safe in the civilized, rational world of Philadelphia? How had it gotten so out of hand?

He glanced at Bryony again. She was smiling at him, a tender smile that spoke of confidence and pride and joy. God, she was exquisite! There was a new light in her eyes, a rose-peach glow in her cheeks, and a certain, undefinable allure in her posture. He was close enough to smell sweet lavender in her hair and the spicy scent of the blush roses she held in her hands. From the top of her dark, cloudy hair to the tips of her ivory satin slippers, she was a picture of simple elegance and quiet enticement.

He recalled now what had brought him to this pass—wanting Bryony—and he knew what response he had to make. He had laid a plan to bring her to this very spot under these very circumstances. He wanted Bryony Talcott for his own. Once she was his, and he was sure of her, he could begin to help her break free of the foolish old beliefs her family had foisted upon her. He would take her to Philadelphia, show her the real world, and together they would forget all about witchcraft and herbs and spells and full moons and all the other claptrap she'd had drummed into her head. He would make her his.

The crowd sighed with relief as he replied, "I will."

Bryony looked at him and smiled. The minister then asked if she would, too, and she replied, "I will."

And when Preacher Kirkland pronounced them man and wife, the strangest feeling of all came over Adam. He thought he heard whispering from the rafters.

A trick of the ears, he thought. And that thought was instantly washed away in a wave of the most raging, possessive desire he'd ever experienced. The minister started to say "You may now kiss the bride," but Adam was way ahead of him. Finally, the minister and Matthew managed to pry the couple apart and they were led away to the wedding party.

The party would have gone on for days, if the

guests had their way. The Talcott house shook to its rafters with the sounds of fiddles and pipes and the rhythm of dancing feet. Matthew stood at the bowl and ladled out cup after cup of the sweet wine punch, dispensing wisdom and bad jokes and bits of song, glorying in his role as surrogate father of the bride.

Adam found himself caught up in the celebrations, answering toasts and accepting the good-natured teasing of the hollow-folk. Never had he tasted wine so sweet, he thought in the midst of the revels. And the music—it was marvelous! He had to dance. He had to find Bryony—his Bryony—and dance with her.

The crowd made way for him to go to his bride, and there she stood on the other side of the room, smiling and waiting, as if it were the appointed hour for him to come to her and ask her to dance. He stood for a moment in wonder, just gazing at the tall, dark-haired woman who was now his wife, drinking in the way her golden dress belled out from her long, slender waist, and the smooth, satiny expanse of her breast and throat as they rose above the ivory satin bows of her bodice. She was gold and ivory and precious mahogany, he thought, dazed. She was cream and roses and summer peaches. More than that—she was his!

She raised a carved ivory fan and shadowed her face, her amber eyes sparkling over the lacy edge. Someone gave a loud, pointed cough behind Adam and he started forward, answering her coy invitation.

The musicians began a slow air, an old tune

from the highlands of Scotland, where Bryony's family had lived long ago. Adam took her hand and led her into the stately, swaying steps.

Bryony thought she'd reached the pinnacle of happiness. When Adam approached her, wonder and delight in his eyes, and took her into his possession, it was as if she were being embraced down to her very soul. As they turned and dipped and circled with the other dancers around them, she felt as if she were floating, adrift in her own joy. In his tan coat and close-fitting buff breeches, a simple gold ribbon binding his dark auburn hair into a neat queue, he looked to her like a warm fire in autumn. And she longed to embrace that heat and feel what it could do.

The music came to a halt and Matthew's voice rang out over the crowd. "All right, folks, it's time to say our blessings and good nights. Bryony and Adam'll be weary of us sooner than late, so we'd best get started."

Adam found himself being herded into a crowd of the menfolk, while Bryony was swept away from him by the women. Matthew stood beaming at him, holding a big woven basket.

"Here's blessings for the wedding night and after, lad. First, there's the wine, to sweeten the way and warm you both—"

"Not that you won't be makin' yer own heat!" someone called out from the back of the throng.

Matthew waited for the laughter to die down a little, then continued. He lifted a small packet of paper. "Here's salt to add some seasoning to your lot. And this is hazelwood to ward off evil from your door." He raised a stout wand of polished wood. "There's rosemary, so's you'll always remember the vows you made this day, and a sheaf of wheat so that you'll know faithfulness and good harvests."

"And plentiful seed for gettin' good strong babes!" exclaimed Tom Beebe.

"Now, now, Tom, Hawthorne here doesn't need a baker to tell him what wheat's for, so let's not be resorting to country matters." Matthew thrust the basket into Adam's hands. "Take it all and make this a home again, lad. God bless you both."

Adam didn't know what else to do but accept the old man's gifts. It was all superstitious poppycock, but it would be rude to refuse it in front of all these people. He was too happy to worry about it, anyway. He'd wait until they were gone and dump it all in the garden, maybe. All except the wine, perhaps. They did distill extraordinary stuff here in the hollow.

He looked across the room to where Bryony stood on the stairs, just above a throng of laughing, chattering women and girls. She was taking the flowers from her bouquet and tossing them one by one to the women below, wishing each of them good luck with their husbands and beaux. The women, in turn, were showering her with bright blue cornflowers, rice, and rose petals.

Bryony looked up to catch Adam's glance and smiled. She gathered the last three flowers of her bouquet into her hands and called out to the crowd: "Good night and God bless you all. My husband and I thank you for all the love and kindness you've shared with us this day. May the moon shine upon you and guide all of you safely to your doors."

The men and women began to mingle and pair off, leaving the house with many cheerful wishes for the future of the bride and groom. At last, only Matthew was left.

"Bryony, dear lass, your pa and ma would've been proud enough to burst on this day. Take a kiss from them both." He leaned over and kissed Bryony's forehead.

"Thank you, Matthew," she whispered, her throat tightening with tears.

"No crying, now, girl. This is a happy day for us all. Our Bryony's found her true mate, and Talcott Farm has a fine new master. It's a new day, Bryony. Calls for rejoicin', not weepin'."

"You're right," she said, a radiant smile lighting her tears like diamonds. "It's a new day for certain."

"Adam Hawthorne."

"Yes, sir." Adam came to attention at the stern note in Matthew's voice.

"See that you mind this lass like she was a cache of jewels, you hear? You've got hold of the treasure of the hollow and we won't take it lightly if we learn that she's not been cherished as a proper wife and lady."

"You may depend on it, sir."

"I'm counting on that. I'd best be taking my own advice and getting out of your hair, now. The moon's growing fat outside and I want to stop by my Julia's place before I turn in. Bless you both. 'Night."

"Goodnight, Matthew."

Bryony saw him to the door and then returned to find Adam still by the stairs, surrounded by rice, blue cornflower buds, and scattered rose petals.

"They're for love and abundance," she said, gathering up some of the bright cornflowers. "It's a tradition."

"Who's Julia?"

"Matthew's wife." Bryony came to stand before him on the lowest step. "She died six years ago. He visits her resting place every evening and tells her all about his day and what he plans to do tomorrow."

Adam frowned. "He talks to his dead wife?"

Bryony smiled down at him. "Yes. They were deeply in love. He loves her still, so he shares everything with her."

"And does she—does she . . . share . . . with him?"

"You mean does she talk back to him? Oh, I doubt it. Julia was a wonderful person. I'm sure her soul is at peace. She'd have no reason to speak to the living. Though I feel certain she hears Matthew. She loved him too much to ignore him now."

Adam shook his head. All this she said as naturally and as matter-of-factly as he might describe a visit to his tailor's.

Bryony smiled and placed a hand on his shoulder. "It is getting late, Adam. And the moon is waxing."

Even if he didn't understand her literally, Adam knew exactly what Bryony was saying. The idea of her inviting him to bed—their bed—was instantly exciting to him. He gave up all thoughts of Matthew and superstitions and incantations and followed his impulses. He stepped up to Bryony, swept her into his arms, and hurried up the curving staircase to the bedroom at the end of the hall.

He set her down on the bright woven carpet and gathered her in for a long, silken kiss.

Bryony wound her arms about his waist, her head tilting back to drink fully of the heady wine of his lips on hers. This was what she'd been waiting for, ever since the day she'd first seen Adam Hawthorne and his willow-green eyes. She'd wanted to twine herself about him and feel him everywhere against her, heated, and masculine, and so, so human. All hers, she told herself somewhere deep inside. All hers, and this was one possession she had no intention of sharing, even with her beloved friends and neighbors in the hollow.

The dream was coming true, Adam thought. The dream he'd had of peach-satin Bryony, warm and eager in the circle of his arms, was now made real. He could love her as he wished, tell her anything he wanted, hold her until the deep, bone-reaching warmth of her sweet body soaked into him and stayed put, as if she were a part of him, put there when he and she were first created.

And he found he couldn't move.

"I can't," he whispered.

She drew back, eyes wide with questions, yet still deliciously smoky with the aftereffects of his kisses. "What do you mean?"

"It isn't right."

She gave a soft, murmuring laugh. "How can it not be right? You're my husband. I'm your wife. Or have you forgotten already what we said in church today?"

Adam swallowed hard. His body was at war with his conscience. He'd tricked her into marrying him, somehow. It wasn't right to take her under such pretenses. He hadn't told her everything.

Yet he was on fire to have her, to hold her, to touch and taste her everywhere, to press her down into the cloud-soft eiderdowns and claim every luscious inch of her as his own. And here she was, soft, willing, and so damned warm. . . .

His hands came up to clasp her face, holding it steady as he studied the look in her eyes. There was love there, and wonder, and even a slight flicker of apprehension. But most of all, there was trust and confidence in her amber gaze. Trust that he was in love with her, that she was right in giving herself to him. She believed in him.

The effect was breathtaking. She was more luminous than he had ever seen her before. With each breath she drew, she grew softer, warmer, and more sinuous within his hold. She stepped closer to him, her long, slender hands sliding up over his ribs, caressing and exploring, stirring fires from deep within him. He sank his mouth down upon hers and felt the flames begin to rise.

The sweet force of his mouth against hers stirred Bryony and she opened to him with a sigh of pure pleasure. There was so much she was learning, and so quickly! It was enchantment: his lips on hers, his hands slipping down to caress her waist, his scent—a hint of lime somewhere in it—emanating toward her as their bodies warmed together. She was yearning for him in every delicate nerve and muscle. She felt her body wakening, somehow, growing in power and pure sensation. She wanted more of Adam Hawthorne and his bewitching heat.

"Come, husband," she whispered. "Let's make our marriage bed."

He followed her as she led him to the broad four-poster that waited in the firelight. She took a cup of wine from the bedside table and held it up for him. "This is my great-grandfather's bed, and this is the wine that he laid down when he married my great-grandmother. I share both with you now and always."

Adam thought of Philadelphia, briefly, and of his plans, but as she handed him the cup, she slipped a hand beneath the shoulder of her gown and let it fall along one smooth, pale-peach arm. A quick gesture slid the other shoulder away, and the garment swirled to her feet. She stepped out of it and laid it at the foot of the bed.

Adam felt his heart surge with excitement at the sight of Bryony before him, clad only in the satiny curtain of her dark hair. He swallowed hard, barely noticing the exquisite taste of the fine old wine as it coursed down his throat. Something far more intoxicating was coursing through his veins, and he abandoned all conscious thought in the havoc of its sweeping effects.

Bryony reached out and took the cup from him, turning it to place her lips where his had been. She drank briefly, her gaze never leaving his face. Adam watched, mesmerized, as she set the cup aside and moved to turn down the soft quilts on the bed. He noticed that her hands shook just a bit.

He turned her about to face him. "Are you afraid, Bryony?" he asked softly.

"A little," she said, shivering delicately beneath his touch. "You are my . . . my Adam. My first man."

He drew her to him and enfolded her in his arms. "Don't be afraid, Bryony. I'll make it wonderful for you. I'll make it perfect. I swear it."

She buried her face against his chest and drew a great sigh. "I know you will. I can feel it. But it's so—so engulfing. So powerful. It's more powerful than magic."

Adam caressed her back, his hands slipping down to her hips and then back up to trace the delicate wings of her shoulder blades. "Give yourself to it," he whispered. "We don't need magic here."

She lifted her mouth for him to kiss, pressing herself against him from thigh to chest. He gathered her up tightly, one arm slipping low to clasp her bottom, the other banding her shoulders. She could feel the magnificent heat and strength of his body everywhere, and her tingling, bare skin sensed the power between them increase. She wound her arms about his neck and he lifted her up, taking her fully into his arms and into his crushing, melting kiss.

In the next moment, she was being laid softly on the bed. She kept her eyes closed and savored the sensations of his hands trailing over her body, touching her everywhere. He seemed to be learning every curve and angle of her form, and with each lesson completed, he left a heated kiss, a brand almost, upon the spot he'd memorized. When he touched his lips to her breasts, she moaned and stretched with the agonizing pleasure.

"You like that, do you?" he whispered. She could hear the smile in his voice.

"It's like fire and ice," she murmured. "I'm burning and melting. I want you to stop because I can't stand it, but if you stop I'll go mad from wanting more."

Adam's own body was in such a similar state of anguished desire that he had no words to make his reply. With one quick move, he pulled his shirt off over his head and flung it aside. A moment later, his breeches and stockings followed his boots to the floor. Finally, free of his clothing, he slid down beside Bryony and gathered her into his arms.

Bryony's eyes flew wide open as Adam's powerful, muscled form came into contact with almost every inch of her body. He was all fire and sinew, rough and smooth, hungry and gentle. She closed her eyes again and felt a delicious liquid heat spreading through her as he clasped her firmly, pressing her even closer. He stroked, kneaded, polished, burnished her with his long, hard body and skillful hands.

She gasped as his hand slipped between her thighs and rested there, just below the moist heat of her. He waited a long moment; then, ever so gently, his elegant magician's fingers began a tantalizing dance upward through the dark curls that covered her. She trembled, expecting pain, then sighed, deep and low, as he wove patterns of pleasure, twirling, stroking, coaxing her desire for him.

And she did desire him. Now she knew what it was, what it meant. She wanted Adam Hawthorne to give her his potent, masculine, sensation-evoking body, and nothing else would do. She wanted to know the full joining that awaited them, that was hovering just beyond this moment, when his hands and his mouth promised all.

As if he knew precisely what she was wanting, Adam raised himself up and came astride her. She opened her eyes, adoring the sight of him poised above her, his green eyes smoky with the fires he was holding at bay. She placed her hands on his lean, sinewy ribs, and in that magical moment, he slipped between her legs.

She lay back with a murmur, eyes closed to savor the sensation of his slow, gentle entry. It was not what she imagined, no sudden, violent tear at the veil of her maidenhood. Instead, it was a steady, warming, expanding fullness that roused her even as it soothed the aching emptiness inside her. She was soon crooning in rhythm with his easy motion, lifting her hips to meet his smooth, deft thrusts.

"Bryony," he gasped softly. "Oh, love, you feel like silk."

"I feel like a river of silk," she whispered in reply.

He slid his hands beneath her hips and lifted her, meltingly, into his next downthrust. The power of his pent-up desire almost made his hands shake as the sweet liquid heat of her engulfed him, swamping every thought and reason except one elemental one: this woman was like no other he'd ever loved. There was a longing to this lovemaking, a yearning, and yet the promise of that longing's fulfillment was evident in every sinuous movement of their coupled forms.

A spiral of brilliant heat was taking shape within Bryony; she could almost see it in her mind's eye. It grew and tightened with every delicious stroke and with each whispered love-word that she and Adam shared. Stars were raining everywhere inside her. Rivers of gold were running molten beneath her skin. There was no place to go to escape the pressure that was building and so she abandoned herself to this golden current, riding it up and up, not knowing where it would lead.

Adam's hold on her intensified and she turned to liquid gold, melting into his body as he carried her deeper into the swirling eddies of this maddened river that engulfed them both. She was reaching for something, longing for it, would die if it didn't come to her soon . . . and then, with a final, magnificent thrust of his powerful hips, Adam brought it to her and she became the river itself, hurtling magically into the beyond, becoming a waterfall that plunged ahead and fell free, wild, and golden to the place beneath.

Adam felt rather than heard her husky, shuddering cry and surrendered to the frantic currents within himself. He convulsed suddenly, swept off in a shower of sparks that rained throughout his body, slowing time and holding him there, utterly joined to Bryony for long, pulsating moments. Then he collapsed with her in full, sated, stunned pleasure, their marriage bonds complete in a way that neither of them could fully comprehend or deny.

He tilted to the side, gathered her to him, and together they sank into blissful, dreamless sleep.

Bryony woke in the night, coming to consciousness with a soft gasp. She looked at Adam, slumbering beside her, and knew that no word or movement from him had wakened her. She looked about the room. The candles they had lit had long since guttered into darkness and the only light now was from the setting moon and the multitude of stars outside the window.

She sat up and stared, then rubbed her eyes to remove all traces of sleep. She was tingling all over, suddenly, not from cold, but from sharp, sudden awareness. All her senses were alert.

Outside the window, stars rained. Not just one or two wayward suns that happened to be passing by, but a host of stars, showering their radiance over the earth.

They drenched the skies with silver-gilt sparks, shooting this way and that, falling and climbing, trailing long tails of shattered light. Bryony tilted her head. She could almost hear the music from them, like glass chiming, or the most delicate of spangle-sounding harps.

"What is it?" she whispered. "What is it?"

"Hmm?" Adam stirred softly under the coverlet. His hand reached to stroke her hair, caressing her back and hip.

"The stars," Bryony began. She found she had no words. The tingling sensation was beginning to subside, the music fading in her ears.

Adam raised up and focused on the window just in time to see the last of the wild stars dance out of sight. "Pretty," he murmured. "Comet."

His hand was sliding up her hip, causing Bryony to experience a new and different sort of tingling. She turned to him in the pale light and saw his eyes beckoning her to him. She shifted about and lifted her arms to welcome him.

And all stars and signs were forgotten as they formed their own sun together and let it shower them with heat and light till they were burnished and liquid and melting in its rays. Later, they were cooled and sent drifting to rest by a playful, dancing west wind.

Chapter Thirteen

"A Secret in the Home is Like Rocks Beneath the Tide."

—*Cassia Talcott*

Bryony woke to the trilling of bird song outside the bedroom window. She smiled, stretched, and then jumped as her arm came in contact with a warm, smooth shoulder that was definitely not her own and not Soot's.

She turned onto her side and studied her new husband with wonder and satisfaction. In the past, she'd tried to imagine what it would be like to sleep with a man, to make love. She'd failed utterly, she now knew.

She'd thought it might be painful. There'd been a small amount of pain, but it had been brief and was completely eclipsed by all the pleasure that followed. She'd thought it would be awkward.

There had been moments when arms and legs and her long, loose hair had been a challenge to their maneuvering skills. But Adam had only laughed and made it part of their loving. She'd thought perhaps it would be a disappointment, that all the secrecy and mystery surrounding sex had been a smoke screen to cover up what was no more mysterious than eating breakfast or going for a walk.

She flopped backward onto her pillow. She'd been completely wrong on that count. The exquisite sensation of two bodies joined in love, utterly consumed with shared passion, was so astounding she was still feeling the aftershocks in her mind and body. And making love in the aftermath of a star shower—if that wasn't mystery and wonder, she didn't know what was.

"Good morning."

She looked at Adam. He looked as blissful and contented as she. "We must look like cats in the cream jug," she said.

"We'll have to ask your Soot about that," he said, smiling. "He tried to join us last night, but when he got one look at me, he snorted in disgust and trotted out."

"The ill-mannered old thing."

"Well, I can't say that I blame him. If I'd had his spot in your bed all my life, I'd be more than ill-mannered if I found some fellow suddenly taking my place."

Bryony snuggled against his side. "You won't have to worry about that, ever."

"I should hope not." He stroked the hair back

from her forehead and placed a kiss on the top of her head. "I intend to keep my word to Matthew and guard my treasure jealously."

"I'm glad." She sighed. "I like being treasured."

"Mmm. That's not all you like." His hand made a lazy circuit of her torso.

"True," she said, folding up in giggles as his hand tickled her ribs.

"Well, wife," he said, rolling to his side and propping his head on his hand. "What shall we do today?"

"Oh, my, I hadn't planned that far in advance. What do new husbands and wives usually do on their first day together?"

He rolled his eyes toward the ceiling. "You are joking, aren't you?"

She bit her lip. "No. I'm sorry, but I really don't know."

He bent down and gave her a swift, searing kiss. "Perhaps that will give you a hint."

"Ohhh," she said, chuckling. "That." Her eyes grew wide. "All day?"

"And all night," he said solemnly.

"Oh, my goodness." She looked stricken. "But who's going to milk Macushla?"

"Aiggh." Adam dropped his head to the pillow. "The cow. She's thinking about a cow!"

"I'm sorry, Adam, but she must be bursting!"

He sat up and stared at her in mock sternness. "You can't be the woman I was with last night," he said. "What happened to my insatiable, inflammatory, imaginative, im—im—peccable, I don't know!—lover?"

Bryony bounced out of bed and pulled on her shift and a robe. "She'll be back as soon as the cow's put out of her misery!"

Adam's eyebrows shot up. "You're going to shoot her? That's a bit drastic even in these circumstances, don't you think?"

Bryony stuck her tongue out at him. "Never mind, city boy. Just you be here when I get back!"

Adam let her go and slid back down into the big, cushiony featherbed. He felt better than he had in weeks—hell, years, he thought. Making love with Bryony at last was all he'd imagined, multiplied and expanded a hundred times over. He'd never before felt such complete peace coupled with such raging, erotic pleasure.

She was his. He'd never been a possessive man, certainly never a possessive lover. The few affairs he'd had had begun and ended without much thought or fanfare. He'd never felt moved to pursue a woman if she indicated, even slightly, that her interests were directed elsewhere.

But with Bryony, he felt like he'd tear the head off of any man, woman, child, or beast who threatened to take her from his arms. Their wedding, the consummation of their vows had somehow changed him. He chuckled. He was lustily, greedily in love with his wife. He'd no doubt take quite a drubbing for it when he and Bryony went home to Philadelphia, but there it was: he couldn't help it. Didn't want to help it.

He frowned. Philadelphia. It was a world away. But it had to be faced. He had to go back and he wasn't going back without his own beautiful, sensuous wife.

Bryony came in, bearing a tray of fruit, bread, cheese, and cider. He took one look at her smiling, honey-rose mouth and told himself that Philadelphia could wait.

But he didn't let it wait for long. It was barely a week after their wedding when they boarded the coach for the journey north.

Adam had proposed that they go to Philadelphia on the afternoon after their wedding. "I made a promise to my mother that I would come home and go to work in my father's shipping business. He's had some financial losses recently and he's not getting any younger. We'll need to leave soon."

Bryony had been hesitant. She'd never been out of the hollow. Few Talcotts had. There was nothing they needed from the outside world, as they sometimes called it. She didn't know how she could say good-bye to the people here, or the land itself. The idea of leaving the house she'd been born in, the house where generations of Talcotts had been born and raised, was something she had never contemplated.

Adam was serious, though; she could tell. He needed to get back to his family, his duties. She wondered if he could go and come back, but the idea of being parted from Adam was too awful, especially if he had to make a lengthy stay.

They'd been together such a short time, but already she felt as if he were a part of her, physically and emotionally. The love they'd made, that they both felt compelled to make several times a day, had been more than a mere physical coupling. There was always a sense of profound wonder between them, as if a soul-deep longing was touched and eased for a time. Afterward, they lay together and talked, easy talk and laughing talk and dreamy talk of days ahead. Or, at least, she had talked of days ahead and Adam had been an attentive listener. All day and all night they were together and it filled her hungry spirit in a way she could not have dreamed. No, the possibility of separating, even for a short time, was out of the question.

So, when he asked a third time, she knew she couldn't, wouldn't refuse. And he'd been so glad when she'd said yes. She hadn't anticipated that he'd want to leave so quickly, but, she thought, if he was worried about his father, who could blame him? She understood what family meant.

It had been a scramble to get all her affairs in order in the hollow. Lucius Dreyer and Matthew would share the responsibilities of caring for the farm. Sarah Addison would take Macushla, Soot, and some of the chickens to her farm to stay. Biddy Dinsmoore agreed to care for the special herbs and medicinal plants in Bryony's gardens.

When it came time to pack her personal items, Bryony felt torn. She knew she had little or no use for her satchel, with its rocks, potions, and other magical tools. Yet she couldn't leave them behind. If anything, they represented her family to her and she couldn't let that go. In the end, she packed a small cache of herbs, the Talcott book, and a few other select items that had held a great deal of value and meaning for her. The rest she put away in a chest and left in the house.

Saying good-bye had been the hardest part. By the time she had gone through the town, leaving a packet here, a plant there, Bryony's handkerchief was soaked with tears. Bidding Matthew farewell was the hardest of all.

He had paid two or three visits to Talcott Farm since the wedding, performing chores that permitted the couple to lie in late in the mornings and retire early at night. On those occasions, whenever he'd seen Bryony, he'd looked at her expectantly, as if he were waiting to hear her say something in particular. Bryony had noted these looks, then promptly forgotten them in the delightful distractions of honeymooning with Adam.

She and Adam found him fishing in the pond on the morning of their departure. He hadn't been surprised to learn that they were leaving, but he seemed sad when they approached him on the bank.

"We won't be gone forever," Bryony told him. "When Adam's father is better set in his business, we'll be back, won't we, Adam?"

Adam nodded. "We'll see what happens."

She put her arms around Matthew. He was all the family she had left now, and he was but a distant relation. Yet in the years since her parents had died, he had been like a father to her, looking after her, caring for her, teaching her how to stand alone. Tears filled her eyes and throat.

"Oh, Matthew, I can't tell you . . ." She faltered,

then found her voice again. "I can't thank you enough. . . . Oh, I'm going to miss you so much!"

"It's all right, lamb," he said, his voice gruff with his own emotions. "You'll be havin' a fine time up there in the big city and you'll come back full of new things to teach your old Matthew."

"I will be back," she said firmly. "Don't you go running off like Phileas Adcock, do you hear?"

He laughed. "I've never been called to do that and I don't expect to be. I'm dug in here, girl, same as your people. So just you go off with your fella there and be the happiest lass in all of Pennsylvania." He'd released Bryony and clapped his hands on Adam's shoulders. "You mind what I told you on your wedding night, son. It's a treasure you've got, a prize beyond price. See that she's cherished, hear?"

"I hear." Bryony smiled to see the solemnity with which Adam spoke his promise. To see these two men—the men she loved most in this world—standing together so brought warmth to her heart, even as she sniffed back tears at their parting.

"We'd best get to the coach stop early," Adam said. "My things are already waiting there, but we need to get yours loaded up."

Matthew waved to them until they were out of view. Bryony took Adam's hand as they walked back to her farm. "I wish I knew some spell of protection I could work on him," she said with a sigh.

Adam squeezed her hand. "Matthew? He doesn't need protection. He's got all the protection he needs in his good health, good friends, and his love of life. He'll be fine."

There were more tears at the coach stop as Bryony and Adam climbed on board and waved good-bye to the small crowd that had gathered to see them off. Then they were away, rattling over the rutted road that led up over the pass and into the rest of the world.

"There they go," Jonathan Leary said to Lucas Rutledge.

"I hope Matthew foretold it all right," said Lucas. "I don't like the idea of the last Talcott leaving the hollow."

"We still got Matthew."

Lucas shook his head. "He's not the one and you know it. It's our Bryony we need. It's the Hag that holds the spell over the hollow."

Now Jonathan looked worried. "True. You don't think she'll stay away, do you?"

Lucas glanced back at the coach that was winding its way up the road. "Not of her own will, no. But we got us a long wait before she does come back, and that means we all got to buckle down and weather the storms that are bound to come."

The trip took three days and by the time it was over, Bryony was in such a state of nervous apprehension that she thought she might be ill. What if his parents didn't like her? she wondered. What if she didn't fit into Philadelphia society? What if she made such a fool of herself that she embarrassed Adam?

"You're going to like Philadelphia," he'd told her a number of times already. "It's the national capital and an important trade center, a center of learning and science, and there's so much to see and do."

Adding to her worries was the way Adam seemed to be changing as they drew nearer to the city. With each passing hour, he seemed to grow cooler, somehow, and more reserved. He always held himself proudly, but now he was looking as much stiff as he did proud. Only at night, when they were alone in their lodgings, did he relax and become himself again.

He was just nervous about bringing a new bride home to meet his family, Bryony told herself. He'd come around again when they'd had time to make themselves at home in the city.

There was one last concern that was contributing to Bryony's uneasiness. Ever since their wedding night, she'd been having the oddest feelings. It was only natural, she told herself, that she should feel a bit odd—after all, she'd never been married before, never had a man beside her day and night, never known the extravagant and dazzling pleasures of the marriage bed. But these feelings kept returning, catching her by surprise.

They were like hiccups, she thought with a brief smile. Little hiccups of sensations inside her. Or popcorn popping.

She would feel them at the oddest times, too. She had become aware of them first when she had made their first breakfast as husband and wife. She'd been milking the cow, to be precise, when a little *pop!* had gone off inside her, sending a tiny electric thrill through her arms and hands. It wasn't unpleasant and she shrugged it off, concentrating on finishing her task and making the best breakfast she could devise for Adam.

Along with cheese and bread and cider, they'd feasted on berries and cream skimmed from the top of that fresh-drawn milk. "Devonshire cream!" Adam had exclaimed with delight. "I haven't had this since the last time I was in England. How did you know?"

Bryony smiled. "It's just cream."

"The sweetest, thickest cream in the world. Thank you, my love. It's a wonderful present for our first meal together."

Bryony had tasted it then herself and saw that Adam was right. It was as sweet as if she had added fine white sugar and as thick as the softest custard. She shrugged and made a mental note to check what Macushla had been grazing on of late.

There had been more poppings and tinglings after that, but nothing happened out of the ordinary. And all other thoughts were driven out when Adam had begun to talk of going to Philadelphia.

Now her eyes were wide as they entered that city. Adam pointed out various places of interest to her, and while she had known it would be grand, she'd had no idea that it would be so spread out or so teeming with people. There were people everywhere: on the streets, in carts and on horseback, in shops. And all of them seemed to be in a great hurry to get wherever they were going and to finish what they were doing.

And while there were wonders to be seen outside the coach, she couldn't help but notice the changes that were taking place within it. Each time she glanced at Adam, he seemed to grow even cooler and more still. His handsome mouth had drawn out to a thin line and the light in his eyes was chilly.

The coach took them up a quieter street, and Bryony could see great houses lined up along the avenue, all large, stately, and imposing. They passed through a stone gateway, trotted up a short, curving drive, and stopped at one of the most impressive houses of all.

"This is where you live?" she breathed.

"Yes," said Adam, alighting briskly from the coach. "This is it."

Bryony took his arm as they walked up the steps to the house. She glanced up at him for reassurance and was startled at what she saw in his face. It was taut and stern with a kind of haughtiness she had never seen there before. With each step that took them closer to the house, she felt, as well as saw, his whole body and manner change in this way. A shiver of apprehension shook through her. She wanted to speak, but suddenly the door was opened and she was being ushered inside. She was at last in Adam's home.

Chapter Fourteen

To cure Homesickness, stitch Salte or Earth from thy Home into the Seams of thy Clothing. Also, carry a Pinche of Dirt from thy home Garden and mixe Itt well into a Brew of Coffee or Tea. You will feel at Home in a Trice.

—*Cassia Talcott*

The house smelled of camphor.

That was Bryony's first impression of it. Her well-trained nose identified the overlying scent of that preserving ingredient and it told her worlds about the house and the whole of the Hawthorne family.

"Adam!" A tall, slender woman all in black came hurrying into the entryway. "You're here! You're safe!"

"Yes, Mother," Adam said, going to her and

embracing her quickly. "I'm here."

"But we expected you weeks ago! I thought something terrible had happened to you. What were you doing all this time?" Mrs. Hawthorne's wide green eyes rested briefly on Bryony, then returned to study her son's face with anxiety.

"I was detained. I had an errand to do."

"An errand?" his mother echoed. Now her eyes were turned full upon Bryony.

"Yes. I suppose you could say it was a significant one. Mother, may I present my wife, Bryony Talcott Hawthorne? Bryony, this is my mother, Matilda Cox Hawthorne."

Adam took Bryony by the elbow and pulled her closer to stand before his astonished parent. Bryony summoned her composure, made a brief curtsy, and offered her hand.

"Mrs. Hawthorne. I'm so pleased to meet you. I hope that it isn't too much for you to have a new person in your household, now in your time of grief. If you need my assistance for anything, you have only to ask."

"My time of grief—Adam, what is she talking about?" Matilda stared at Bryony even as she spoke to her son.

"Bryony, this is my mother's normal manner of dress," Adam said stiffly. "She . . . favors black."

Bryony's lips made a round *O,* but she quickly caught herself and, blushing furiously, made her apologies. "Please forgive me, Mrs. Hawthorne. I should have guessed, that is, I didn't know. . . . I'm sorry, let us begin again." She turned on her most winning smile and offered her hand again.

"Mrs. Hawthorne. I'm so pleased to make your acquaintance."

Adam's mother took her hand briefly and nodded, still looking at Bryony with mingled alarm and astonishment. "Adam, why didn't you tell us you were planning to be wed?" she asked, turning again to her son. "We could at least have been a little more prepared."

"I hardly expected it myself. But I met Bryony on a trip to the south, found I cared for her, and the deed was soon done by the reverend in her town."

Matilda bit her lip and frowned. "But your father . . ." she murmured.

Adam stiffened still more, if that was possible. "Father knows I am a man. I make my own decisions. And if I choose to have a wife, then so it will be." He softened a bit. "I'm here, as you asked me to be. I'm ready to learn the business. Let's go on from there."

Servants were summoned and Bryony followed Adam upstairs to his rooms on the second floor. She caught glimpses of the strong, Hawthorne family face gazing out at her from formal portraits along the walls, and she sensed at once that the china bowls and simple, gilt-edged mirrors that graced the tables in the halls were old and fine. But for all its beauty, the house was silent and dim, and she could find no corner where peace and comfort reigned, no heart to match the elegant hearths.

When they reached Adam's room, Bryony looked about her in delight, and then in dismay. The room looked like the palace of a sun king. Everywhere she looked, there were draperies and hangings of warm yellows, golds, and whites. The rugs on the floor were done in deep, rich golds and tans, the sconces and candelabra were burnished brass, and the fireplace was framed in some light, creamy stone. The effect was spectacular, but Bryony felt a shiver course across her shoulders, for the room that should be as warm and welcoming as a sun-drenched patch of meadow was instead winter cold and silent, like a frozen portrait of a bygone era.

Adam turned and saw her standing just inside the door.

"This is where we'll stay," he told her. "There's a bedroom through those doors, and a wardrobe." He began unpacking his valise and carrying things to the tall bureau on one wall. "Your things will be brought up shortly. Make yourself comfortable till then."

Bryony studied him for a moment. He was acting like she was a stranger. Was he ashamed to have her in his elegant home? Had she said or done something to embarrass him? Then she knew.

"Oh, Adam, I'm so sorry that I said that awful thing to your mother. She must think I'm a witless idiot. It's just that back home, when someone dies, we all wear black and—"

"You couldn't have known," he cut in sharply. "Back in the hollow, you would have been correct in your assumption."

"Oh. Well, I'm sorry all the same. I'm afraid I

didn't make a very good first impression as her new daughter-in-law."

Adam straightened from where he was bending over the open valise. "You were fine. My mother has not been well." He came to stand before her. "There is just one thing that I want you to remember, now that you are living here."

"What is that?" Bryony felt as if something awful were about to happen.

"I would prefer that you make no mention of magic or spells or incantations or magic rocks or any of the things you used to do back in the hollow. My family are city people, and well educated, and they wouldn't understand."

"But, Adam, why? Surely they expect that a magus like you would—"

"I'm not a magus." He scowled thunderously. "Not here. Not anymore. Just do as I ask, please, and don't bring it up. If you do, it will do more harm than you know."

Bryony felt cut to the quick, though she couldn't say why. It wasn't as if she were the Hag of the Hollow anymore. She had set aside all her magic when she had married Adam, when she had realized that she had not inherited the special gift she so desired.

Yet Adam was looking at her with such serious intent that she knew this was somehow most important to him. If he needed this, then she could certainly comply. She wanted his happiness more than anything.

She gave him a nod. "All right. If that's what you wish, Adam."

"Will you give me your solemn promise?"

"My solemn word."

Adam's demeanor softened. "Thank you, love. I'm sorry if I sounded harsh just then. I only mean to save you any further discomfort." He reached up and touched her cheek. "I'm trying to protect you. My parents aren't accustomed to your ways, and they can be very . . . opinionated. I want them to get to know you before they hear about the Talcott traditions or any of the things you used to do as the Hag."

"I suppose you're right," she said hesitantly. "Look what an idiot I made of myself when I met your mother. I'll wait to tell them more about myself."

"That's my girl." Adam gave her a brief smile and kissed her cheek. "But don't worry. I intend to make sure that you don't suffer any more such awkward moments. You'll be a lady equal to any in society here in no time. Now, I'll leave you to change while I pay off the coach driver and make sure that the servants know we're here."

He gave her shoulder a squeeze and left the room. Bryony stood in the middle of the thick, luxurious rug and felt bereft of all her familiar, anchoring things. She didn't even have the comfortable, lazy presence of Soot. She heaved a sigh and unfastened her cloak. She washed in the basin and combed her hair, using the toiletries she had carried in her small valise.

When she came out of the wardrobe, the room was unchanged. It was as silent and lovely as a doll's house. Bryony looked around her and then clapped her hands. There was no need to go on feeling this awful, empty chill. There were any number of things that she could do to improve this room. She might not be able to work magic, but she knew how to make a home.

Crossing the room with light steps, she drew aside the heavy gold and white embroidered drapes to reveal shuttered windows. She lifted the latch and pushed the shutters back into their pockets alongside the windows. She shoved the window up wide and breathed in the fresh, sun-warmed air that carried a hint of moisture from the nearby Delaware. She repeated the process at the other windows, filling the golden room with sunbeams that gave it sudden, cheering life and warmth.

Reaching into the folds of her skirt, she pulled out a small packet tied with her favorite green ribbon. She found a lovely Chinese porcelain bowl on the mantel and emptied the contents of the packet into it. The sharp, fresh scent of clean herbs and dried lavender blossoms rose up and blended with the clean, warm air from the windows.

"Flowers," she murmured to herself. The room—indeed, all the rooms she'd seen so far—needed that dash of color and life that only flowers and living plants could provide. A home needed more than just fragile bric-a-brac and fine fabrics to make it beautiful.

She leaned out of the window and peered into the front gardens. No sign of any flowering plants there. Doubtless the garden was at the back of the house, as it was at her home.

Home. She felt a pang of loneliness. She patted her skirts and was grateful that she had stitched some small pockets into the seams, each one filled with a bit of earth and a few seeds from her farm in Cold Springs. The pouches couldn't serve any magical purposes for her, but she liked the idea of knowing that something from her home, from the bountiful earth of Talcott Farm was close to her now.

"Ma'am?"

Bryony looked up to see a young girl dressed in solemn gray standing in the doorway. A snowy white mobcap did its level best to control the girl's mass of curly blond hair.

"Yes?" Bryony asked. "Won't you come in?"

"Oh, no, Mistress Hawthorne. I come to fetch you down to dinner, if you please."

"Oh, my stars," Bryony exclaimed. "I forgot all about it." She ran a hand over her own hair and smoothed down her skirts. "Do I look all right? My trunk hasn't been brought up yet."

"Oh, that'd not be for me to say, ma'am. But we had best hurry, begging your pardon. Mr. Josiah, he's not one for waiting dinner."

"I see. Well, lead the way—I'm sorry, what is your name?"

"Dulcie, Mistress Hawthorne."

"Well, lead on, then, Dulcie. I don't want to keep my father-in-law waiting."

The doors to the dining room were thick, polished mahogany but they couldn't completely muffle the voices inside the room. Bryony winced as she heard the anger in the tones. Still, she nodded to the young maid to proceed.

Dulcie twisted the handle and opened the door, then stood back to permit Bryony to step through. Her eyes went immediately to Adam, who was standing ramrod straight before an older man with equally stiff bearing.

"I don't need your help or anyone else's, you insolent young pup!" The man was all but shouting in Adam's face.

"Perhaps not, but I made a promise to Mother and I intend to keep it." Adam's voice was tight but level.

"And if I say you—"

Adam caught sight of Bryony and cut his father off in midsentence. He reached out to draw Bryony to his side. "Father, may I present my wife, Bryony Talcott Hawthorne? Bryony, this is my father, Mr. Josiah Hawthorne. The third."

"Your wife?" his father thundered. "What the devil are you talking about? You haven't got any wife."

Adam chuckled, but there was no mirth in the sound. "Sorry to disappoint you, Father, but I do have a wife and here she is. I've brought Bryony from her home to the south of here to live with us in Philadelphia. Where I *will* be working for you." This last he said with measured emphasis.

"A wife, you say?" Josiah scowled at Bryony. His bright eyes seemed to take in every stray thread or wayward fold of her outfit. She wanted to fidget under his gaze but managed to hold on to her composure as Adam squeezed her hand.

"When did this happen? I assume I'm to be made a grandfather in a month or two?"

"Josiah!" Matilda exclaimed softly.

Bryony felt her cheeks burning at Josiah Hawthorne's suggestion. Adam took hold of her arm as if to keep her from answering. As if she had any reply to make to such an accusation!

"You might indeed. What would it matter?" Adam said coolly. "The fact remains that Bryony is my wife and she is to be accepted as such."

Josiah snorted. "Taking a wife doesn't make you a man yet, son. Getting a baby on some country milkmaid doesn't make you one, either. It's work that makes a man. Or war. Wait till you prove yourself before you go giving yourself airs."

Bryony stiffened with shock, but Adam's hand held her firmly.

"I served in the war. I've worked. Now I've come home to work for you. And I've brought my wife. If you don't like it, you had better just get used to it, for, as I said, I aim to keep my word to Mother and to Bryony."

Josiah's eyebrows drew down into a furious scowl. "You upstart cur! You come in late for dinner, you drag this—this—creature in with you, and now you stand there and defy me! I ought to—"

"Sit down and eat your meal."

"What?" Josiah thundered.

"I said," Matilda said in a soft, quavering voice, "I think that we all should sit down and eat our meal. Before it gets cold."

Josiah seemed about to gather himself up into

a towering rage, then just as suddenly sat down and turned cold eyes on his son. "Sit down. You heard your mother."

Adam led Bryony to the table and they sat down to plates of chilled soup. Even as she ate and the next courses were brought, Bryony thought the meal would never end. Adam and his parents sat in utter silence, not even exchanging glances over the vast, polished tabletop. She wanted to do something to break through the terrible quiet that hung in the air around them, but she couldn't think of a thing to do or say that wouldn't make the situation worse. So she kept her thoughts to herself, choked down what little food she could swallow around the cold lump in her throat, and rose when Adam signaled he was finished and ready to leave.

What had she gotten herself into? she wondered as she followed Adam upstairs to their rooms. She shivered at the impressions that seemed to come to her from the very walls of the house. Anger. Hurt. Regret. How was she ever to get used to this?

Adam brought her to the door of their room, but he did not go in. "I have business to attend to," he told her. "I'll be back in time to dress for supper. Go in and rest."

He gave her a quick kiss and was gone before she could say a word. Shrugging, Bryony went in and resumed her efforts to make their new quarters into a home.

Adam hesitated outside the heavy door in the north wing of the house, loath to go in and yet needing to know, to see if anything had changed. He'd been away longer than he'd planned. At the very least, it was his duty.

He pulled himself up and gave a soft rap on the door as he pushed it open and stepped inside. The room was warm, but dim, as always, and carried the slight, musty scent of disuse.

"Are you awake?" he called softly to the form in the bed. "It's Adam. I'm back again."

The man in the bed stirred slightly, his tousled blond head turning on the pillow to regard Adam. A flicker of interest seemed to cross his smooth, pale features; then it was gone. He turned his face back toward the wall and he did not move again or speak.

"I know," Adam said, coming to sit on a footstool near the bedside. "It's been too long. But I'm home now, Ross. Home for good. And you'll never believe this, brother of mine. I've brought home a wife."

There was no response from the frail man tucked under the covers. Adam heaved a silent sigh and went on talking.

When he emerged from the room an hour later, he felt spent from his efforts to carry on a conversation by himself. But it was always this way. His older brother was lost to them, beyond recall, it seemed. There was no physical reason that anyone could find why he should not be able to speak, sit, stand, walk, and more. But Ross Hawthorne, Adam's older brother, had not spoken more than two words together since the day he was brought home from the war, gray and undernourished and injured. They'd done all they could to repair his body, but it seemed that there was no reaching his spirit.

Adam's temper rose as he recalled how his parents had attempted to reach Ross and cure him. Having exhausted the skills of all the physicians in the area, they began to bring in all manner of so-called healers and spiritualists and potion brewers. By the time Adam himself had returned home from the war, they had all but exhausted their funds and his father was preparing to borrow against his business in order to meet the exorbitant demands of the latest of these frauds. Adam had looked about him and seen his mother a pale wreck, his proud, intelligent father ready to risk all on a superstitious hope. The house was in disarray, the servants dismissed or vanished as their master and mistress became more and more preoccupied with their own grief and longing. Their friends had been neglected to the point of disaffection or driven off by Josiah's furies whenever an attempted cure would fail. They were both suffering from ill health brought on by sampling Ross's cures, sleepless nights, and prolonged anxiety.

Adam had seen all this and felt a wave of pity and guilt and grief overcome him. He'd torn about town, asking every legitimate physician he could find about Ross's condition. All of them said the same thing: that Ross's mind and body had suffered too much. He was deep in melancholy, beyond the reach of any living being. They'd seen it happen before. They were quite certain of their findings. It was also possible, they hinted, that some of the special cures he'd been given since had done him more harm than good.

Adam came home to find another "spirit physician" ensconced in Ross's room, attempting to cure him with colored waters, complete with a rigged sounding of harp music from a compatriot set up in the rooms above. Adam challenged the man then and there, showed his father and mother the riggings and the accomplice, and promptly hurled the man from the house. To his shock, his mother and father were not grateful. They were, instead, infuriated and hurt. Matilda eventually overcame her anger and listened to Adam's explanations of how these charlatans were taking advantage of their grief and pain. She agreed to stick with tried-and-true physicians after that, although they offered no more hope than before.

Josiah nursed his anger for some time. Adam understood, though he couldn't set aside his own resentment. Ross was the firstborn, the oldest son, the fair-haired child, literally. Ross was the one who had studied and quickly learned Josiah's business, while Adam had pursued his fancy for magic and illusion. It was Ross who could make peace between his hot-tempered father and his stubborn brother. It was Ross who went to war as soon as the muster was called, while Adam remained in Europe to finish out his performance obligations. There had never been a time when Adam hadn't known that his father was comparing the two of them, and it was Adam who was always found wanting.

Adam knew that as a man he shouldn't feel such things. He knew that Ross wasn't in any way at fault for any of it, nor could Josiah change his nature. But he still felt the sting of the injustice and the longing for approval. And in this house, where Ross lay as a living shadow, Adam felt afresh the anger and outrage that his brother should have been subjected to the miserable fiddlings of fakes and frauds.

That was why he had quietly pursued every charlatan and mountebank in five states. That was why he'd turned his back on his own magic, unable to be a part of illusions of any kind. He'd turned instead to revealing these frauds and taken refuge in the study of reason and logic.

And when his parents, weary of facing inquiries from the curious and the few friends that they hadn't alienated in their grief, had decided to let it be known that Ross had died of his injuries and been buried with Matilda's family in Massachusetts, he had gone along with them for the sake of finding some peace with them at last. Only two people outside the household knew the truth about Ross: the physician that Josiah had paid to confirm the rumors of Ross's passing, and Adam's friend, Taylor MacLaren.

But even with all that had been decided, all that had been done, Adam never left Ross's room without feeling both fury and guilt. Despite his studied logic, his powerful will, his keen reasoning, peace was just as far from his grasp as it had been on the day he'd first come home from the war. And it drove him like no other force in this world.

Adam put in a brief appearance at his father's offices, greeting the men who worked there and letting them know that he'd be joining them the following day. His father had scowled and slammed the door to his private office, but Adam ignored him and went about setting up his own desk in a small room at the back of the building.

When he returned to Bryony, he was tired, but in a better temper. He came to her embrace with a sigh of resignation and relief.

"I missed you," she said, giving him a quick kiss. "You've become a habit of mine."

He gave her a brief smile. "I'm glad."

"I'd better get dressed for supper," she said, moving away. "I don't want to be late again."

Adam winced as he recalled his father's rudeness at the noon meal. It probably was best not to anger Josiah any further.

He crossed to the bed and sat down to pull off his boots. He watched with interest as Bryony undid the lacings on her simple gown and slipped the sleeves off of her shoulders. God, she was gorgeous, he thought for the thousandth time since he first saw her. Seeing her slim form emerging from her dress reminded him of his first glimpse of her back in the hollow. He felt suddenly hot, though the breeze from the window was tinged with a chill, and he sat shirtless, in bare feet.

"Come here," he called softly as she stepped out of her dress and stood in her waist and petticoat.

She turned to him in surprise, her hands lifting to undo her hair.

"Come to me," he said, his voice husky and warm.

She let her hair fall free and crossed to him, the pale light of evening setting a fine, pearl-like cast to her peachy skin. He shifted on the bed, feeling the heat centering in him, then swirling upward in a swift pulse to his head and hands. He wanted her with such sudden intensity that he was reaching for her long before she came within his grasp.

He pulled her between his legs and nimbly undid the lacings at the top of her waist. Thank God she wasn't wearing a corset, he thought. Magician or not, he couldn't have waited for the length of time it would take to free her from such a contraption. This way, he could pull the thin fabric aside and bury his flushed face against the cool, smooth skin of her breasts, delighting in the way she immediately arched to him with a soft murmur of pleasure.

But he couldn't wait for such dalliance, however delightful. Soon, he was reaching beneath her petticoat, stroking and coaxing her arousal and tightening with excitement when she warmed to him with gratifying speed.

He wasted no time. He had to have her, had to be joined to her at once, or he didn't know if he could live.

Swiftly, he undid his breeches and slid back, pulling Bryony against him. When she came fully to rest, he quickly rolled her beneath him, lifting her petticoat as he positioned himself above her.

"Bryony, you are so sweet, so sweet," he murmured, kissing the hardened tips of her breasts.

Bryony felt sudden heat welling from within her, racing through her veins to make every square inch of her skin tingle with warmth and pleasure at Adam's touch. Everything felt so good! She wanted to somehow make him melt into her pores, to drink him in, to inhale him, to take him wholly within her being. She wanted the fullness of his loving and she wanted it now.

"Come to me," she whispered. "Oh, please, Adam. Come to me now."

He swiftly obliged her, joining their bodies with a single thrust that caused both of them to cry out with the sheer ecstasy of the act. Adam felt as if he were made of fire, and yet it didn't burn, only filled him with intense, pleasurable heat. He pushed himself up on his hands and gloried in the simple sensation of being completely enveloped in Bryony's satiny body. He didn't know if he could ever get enough of her.

Bryony arched beneath her lover, savoring the distilled moment of their joining. Adam filled her so wonderfully, and when at last he moved, it was as if circles of hot, liquid sunshine were spreading out from the center of her. How good it felt just to move in rhythm with him! How sweet it was to hear the love-words he was pouring into her ear: endearments, promises, demands.

And how quickly the fire began to kindle upward

between them, making them clasp one another in fierce need, rocking them, and finally causing them to burst into a blaze of sensations. They shuddered and cried out, found the sweet pinnacle of their lovemaking, and collapsed after many long moments in ecstasy. They lay tangled on the satin coverlet, utterly spent and silent.

Adam drew a deep breath. At least he had Bryony. At least he had this wonder that they shared. He could survive.

A knock at the door interrupted their afterglow. Muttering in annoyance, he crawled off the bed and tottered to the door, fastening his breeches as he went.

"Yes?" he demanded as he flung the door wide.

Dulcie shrank back a little in fright at the sight of upright, fastidious Adam Hawthorne shirtless and barefoot, flushed and tousled from making love.

He blew out an exasperated breath. "Yes, Dulcie," he said with strained patience. "What is it?"

"Mistress Hawthorne sent me to tell you and Mrs. Hawthorne not to be late to supper. That's—that's all."

"Supper?" Adam turned and took a quick glance at the clock. "Ye gods, you're right. All right, Dulcie. Tell the mistress that we're on our way." He closed the door.

"I don't know what came over me," he said as he hurried to the wardrobe and yanked out a clean shirt. "I don't want to give Father another chance to rant tonight. I've had enough trouble today."

Bryony stared at him in wonder. Sitting on the bed, her clothes tangled around her, she still felt the wonderful languour that followed their loving. Indeed, she felt as if she didn't ever want to leave this bed, especially not if Adam were in it with her.

But he wasn't. He was bustling about the room with the determination and energy of a man who had just come from a brisk and bracing walk in the cool of the evening. Was there something wrong with her, or was it just one of those things that was different between men and women?

Sighing, she slipped off the bed and padded to the wardrobe. By the time she had chosen a gown and was headed for the pitcher and bowl to wash up, she, too, was feeling refreshed and energetic, though apprehensive about meeting his parents again.

Perhaps it had been a bad morning for them, she told herself. Most likely they'd be more relaxed and welcoming this evening, as they lingered over supper.

Cheered by these thoughts, she dressed quickly and was in time to see Adam finish up his toilet and go to the door. She smiled at the sight of him in his elegant brown suit, his hair burnished and tied neatly with a black velvet ribbon.

"We'll just make it," he said, opening the door and standing aside for her. "Remember now, not a word about magic or other Cold Springs folderol."

Bryony felt as if he'd splashed cold water on her. The passionate, giving man she'd just made love to had disappeared and in his place stood this stern stranger. What was happening?

Adam took her hand as they went down the stairs and gave it a kiss. She smiled. So she hadn't lost him entirely. She'd survive.

Supper, however, proved to be another ordeal of silence. Josiah grunted his greetings at the two of them as they entered the dining room, then spent the rest of the meal scowling down into each course that was served. Matilda sat with a formal, frozen smile on her face, exchanged a few comments about the weather, then seemed to drift off into a reverie.

Bryony's feelings were a mixture of relief and embarrassment, for the most part. She was relieved that she was not asked to make sensible, rational conversation with the Hawthornes, and that they were not watching her as she tried to recall all that she'd been taught about proper dining etiquette in the far-off days when mother had been intent upon schooling her for every contingency. The selection of glassware alone was enough to keep her occupied, let alone figuring out what some of the food was that she was being served.

Yet she was embarrassed by the silence, feeling sure that she was the cause of their reticence and that she should be doing something to enliven the proceedings. What that could be, given the limits that Adam had given her on the way down the stairs, she couldn't begin to fathom. At home, the topics of fertilizers and crops and animals and gardens and babies and, of course, healing and magic, were considered perfectly acceptable for discussion over dinner or over the back fence. What on earth was left for folks to talk about? Maybe she wasn't the whole cause of their silence, after all. Maybe civilization had robbed them of dinner conversation.

When the meal was over—at least as far as Bryony could tell—Josiah shoved back his chair and threw down his napkin. "I'm going back to the office. We're going to the magistrate tomorrow over this Schuyler Bailly affair and I have to finish the papers."

"Oh," Matilda said. "But wouldn't you rather stay here and welcome our guest? Perhaps Bryony would like to play chess."

Josiah gave her a sour smile. "First of all, Tilda, she isn't a guest; she's Adam's wife. She lives here now; let her get used to it. Second, I doubt that they play chess in that backwoods little hamlet she hails from. Last, I have work to do if I'm to keep our expanding little family in shoe leather." He gave a piercing glance at Bryony's waistline as he passed her, heading for the door.

"Good night, Father," Adam said after Josiah had gone out. "So pleasant to chat with you, as always."

"Adam." Matilda's tone was gently reproving.

"Mother, I'm taking Bryony shopping for some new clothes tomorrow. Where shall we go? I want her to look like a proper Philadelphian woman."

"Oh." Matilda looked over at Bryony with vague surprise, as if seeing her for the first time. "My dressmaker is Mrs. McCauley, just by Elfreth's Alley. The milliner on Market Street is good, and so is Madame Gile. And I suppose you could go to Mr. Axton, the shoemaker, if she wants shoes." She blinked at Bryony. "Are you sure you want to get new clothes just now, dear? In your condition, perhaps you had better wait until after—"

"Damn it, Mother, she is not pregnant!"

"Adam! There's no call to be indelicate." Matilda looked at him in shock.

"I'm sorry, Mother, but sometimes it's the only way to get your full attention. Bryony is not with child, no matter what Father says. She has only some clothes she wore in the country and now she needs some decent clothing to wear in the city. That's why we're going shopping."

He rose and stood behind Bryony's chair. "I believe we'll retire for the night and get an early start in the morning."

He reached down to pull out her chair at the same instant Bryony pushed herself back, so anxious was she to escape the room. Adam muffled a yelp as the chair made contact with his shins and his toes.

"Oh," Bryony gasped, twisting to look up at him. "I'm so sorry!"

"It's perfectly all right," he said, teeth clenched in pain. "Sit still and I'll help you up."

"Oh."

She managed to rise with a semblance of her natural grace and together they exited the dining room, saying good night to Matilda as they went. Once on the stairs, Bryony apologized again.

"Never mind," Adam said, cutting her short. "Just remember that in the city, a lady waits for the man to lead the way. That's all you have to know."

"I see." She followed him up the stairs, trying to commit to memory all the new rules she'd learned that day. Had she really only been in this house a single day? So much had happened.

He pushed open the doors to their room and stood aside. She pulled up abruptly and stood still in the hallway.

"Aren't you going in?" he asked.

"Of course I am. As soon as you lead the way."

He glared at her, as if trying to see if she was mocking him. "All right. Here's how it works. When it comes to getting up from the table, let the gentleman lead the way. When it comes to doors, the lady leads the way."

"Why?"

"Why?" he echoed. "Why, indeed. I don't know. That's just the way it is. That's the way it's always been. The lady goes through the door first." He motioned her inside.

"But what if there was a burglar or a wild animal on the other side of the door? Would I have to go in first, then?"

"Ye gods." Adam gave her a gentle push inside and shut the doors behind them. "I'll let you know if there's likely to be a wild animal on the other side of a door in this house."

"Thank you, Adam."

"You're welcome."

She moved serenely to the wardrobe and began to undress for bed. Adam went to shut the windows and shutters, which were still standing wide open, competing with the warm fire that Dulcie had lit in the hearth.

When he had finished washing and undressing down to his long-tailed shirt, Adam returned to the bedroom to find Bryony already in bed, her lovely dark hair fanning across the white linen pillowcases. He recalled his exasperation with her and all her odd ways, but his irritation didn't last long once he'd slid into bed beside her and felt the soft warmth of her along his side.

No, he told himself. He wasn't up to this. They hadn't been in this house so much as one day! He couldn't go on making love to her as if he were a dying man and she his last hope of life, then get up in the morning and try to shape her into the wife he needed her to be. It was too confusing. He would keep to himself and keep his mind on business. Lord knew that tomorrow, his first day at work for his father, would not be an easy or a pleasant one. He could use the rest.

He turned away from her and closed his eyes, forcing himself to count slowly in his head so that he could fall asleep from the monotony of it. He reached one thousand and forty-seven and finally drifted off.

He dreamed he was holding Bryony close in his arms, kissing her delicious mouth, tasting sweet peaches and cream. Her soft breasts moved against his chest, and her long, silky thighs entwined him. He was fully aroused, he was entering her with a long sigh of relief and joy, he was rocking to sleep in the pleasure of her sweet, giving body. He was rocking to sleep, he was rocking, he was rocking. . . .

He was awake and making love to his beautiful wife, moving like a wave in her slender arms, breathing the love-warmed scent of her hair. And when he reached his peak, he heard her soft cry joining with his and he sighed once more and drifted back into deep, restful sleep.

Chapter Fifteen

"There's More to A Marriage than Four Bare Legges in a Bed."

—*Cassia Talcott*

Adam was gone by the time Bryony woke the next morning. She writhed and stretched beneath the soft linens, recalling the long, slow love they'd made last night, drifting in and out of sleep until the pleasure had demanded their full attention. How nice it was to know that what they shared in bed wasn't at all diminished, despite the troublesome feelings in the house.

She sat up and looked about the room. The drapes and shutters and windows were all closed, and the fire was dying in the fireplace. It was slightly damp and chilly in the room. She shivered and felt about for the nightgown that Adam had slipped off of her in the night. It was nearly seven o'clock, she noted. She couldn't recall a time when she had slept so late.

There was clean, cold water in the basin by the wardrobe. Bryony took the copper kettle that was hanging over the fire and splashed hot water in to warm it. She set the kettle on the hearth and turned back to the basin. Her eyes widened and she stood stock-still, her mouth forming a perfect *O*.

She stood staring at the water, feeling once again the sensation of soft, drifting clouds around her and a golden tingling inside her. In the water, clear as a painting or a scene out of a window, she saw figures and faces, houses and trees. It was this house, the Hawthorne house, she saw in the water that was still rippling from the water she'd added. Two boys came bursting out of the door, one blond, the other auburn-haired. They raced down the steps and out to the street.

The scene blurred, then cleared. Bryony saw the blond boy, now a man, dressed in a uniform. He was standing by a tree, and moonlit shadows played across his face. She saw those comely features, so familiar and yet not, twisted in a grimace of horror and grief. He put out his hand and he seemed about to speak. Bryony leaned forward unconsciously, in order that she might hear him. A lock of her hair touched the water and the scene rippled away, leaving only the image of plain water and the smooth creamy white of the basin.

She raised her hands to her cheeks. What on earth had she just beheld?

"It can't be," she whispered. It couldn't be. She'd tried scrying time after time, scrying in the loveliest spot in the world, Crystal Pond, where her ancestors had viewed images of far-off times and places for generations. She had seen nothing more remarkable than the reflection of passing clouds and birds reflected in its pristine waters.

But this, this was like nothing she'd ever experienced before. It was—

She backed up and sat down on a chair.

It was magic.

Her heart was racing. She wanted to jump up and run about the room, burst out and tell someone, anyone, shout it out the windows! She darted up, then froze.

She was in Philadelphia. In the Hawthorne house. And she had made a solemn promise to Adam that she wouldn't even mention her failed magic or her family's history to anyone here.

She sat back down in the chair, then bounced up again to peer into the basin. There was nothing to see, only water.

She hugged herself as a shiver coursed down her spine. Perhaps it had been her imagination. Perhaps it was a trick of the light or the reflection of a painting on the wall.

She glanced about the room. Nothing. No paintings, and only a bit of light from the small, high window. No lamp or candlelight played on the water. She knew there wouldn't be. Every instinct within her told her that she had indeed just seen something extraordinary in the waters of a porcelain washbasin. She had been given a gift. Whether she would ever see another vision again, she couldn't guess. But for now . . .

She drew a deep breath and plunged her hands into the now tepid water. She washed quickly, dried off, and laced her bodice. Then she went, as if in a daze, to the sitting room and plopped down on the settee.

If it was indeed magic, then what had she seen? She guessed that the auburn-haired boy running out of the house had been Adam as a child. But who was the blond? Was he the same person as the soldier who stared from among the trees with such grief and sorrow? Was he somewhere here in Philadelphia?

She wanted to giggle. Here she was, experiencing her first successful creation of magic, and she realized that in all the years she'd been training and trying, she had never really thought about what she'd do once she'd found her gift. It had been enough just to have it. But she knew she had to find out about the scene in the basin. Her mother had always said that the good Lord didn't send out messages just for the nonce. Bryony had spent her life training and preparing to be the Hag of the Hollow and she knew that magical gifts weren't meant to be refused or ignored. She had to learn what the image meant.

She bounced out of her chair and headed for the wardrobe. She was dressed in a twinkling, her hair gathered back in a soft chignon at her neck. Her feet skimmed the stairs as she descended, suddenly feeling as if she had a purpose in the strange, cold house in this vast new city.

Matilda Hawthorne stared at her new daughter-in-law in shock. "What did you just say?"

"I asked who Adam's companions were when he was a boy," Bryony said, finishing the last of her breakfast. "Were there other boys who were his special friends? I know what it's like to be the only child and I treasured every chance I got to meet with other children in the hollow."

She glanced up at Matilda and saw that her usually pale face had gone ashen. "Is something wrong?" she asked the older woman. "Are you not well?"

"No. That is, no. What—" Matilda cleared her throat and took a sip of tea. "What makes you ask such a thing?"

"Oh, I only wondered. I want to know more about my new husband and his life. I think it is especially important for a wife to know her husband's friends, don't you think?" Bryony hid her discomfiture at lying by stacking her breakfast plates and reaching for her own teacup.

"Ah. Perhaps. But surely childhood companions are best left to childhood. Adam is a grown man."

"Yes. I'm sure you're right." Bryony looked down at her hands, disappointed.

"I've been a wife a bit longer than you have, child. And I've been the hostess to many of Josiah's business partners and acquaintances. That's what a husband of Adam's station needs most in a wife—a helpmeet in his world."

"Do you think so?" Bryony studied Matilda's face with puzzlement. "But what of love or friendship between a husband and wife?"

"Honor, respect, and duty come first." Matilda pushed her chair back and rang the bell for the server. "Love may come after. There's hard work and hard times to be borne in this world and we wouldn't make it far on kisses and soft words alone."

Bryony nodded, feeling both chastened and bewildered. As the serving girl took away the plates, she pondered her mother-in-law's words. She'd seen her own parents kissing and exchanging soft words many a time when she was growing up. She recalled how her father's eyes would light up whenever her mother drew near and how her mother's cheeks would color like poppies at some of the things her father would whisper in her ear.

But her parents had not been of Adam's station, true enough. They had been simple folk, farmers, for all their education and magical talents. Matilda Hawthorne was a proper Philadelphia woman. Surely she knew what a man like her son expected in a wife.

"Good morning, Bryony," Matilda said, rising. "I'll be in my study this morning. Adam left word that he would be here to pick you up for this shopping expedition at eleven-thirty, so you'll want to run up and change to be ready in time."

"Yes, I will. Thank you." Bryony rose and followed Matilda out to the hall.

"The coach will be waiting at the front entry," Matilda said. "Collins, the houseman, will let you out."

Matilda floated away, her dark maroon skirts hardly rustling over the thick hall runner. Bryony watched her disappear into the west passage and then trudged upstairs to her room, pondering her mother-in-law's advice and trying to come up with another way to learn about the blond boy in her vision.

"I suppose I shall just have to ask Adam," she told herself. She'd just have to make sure that her true purposes were concealed.

However, she didn't have a chance to ask Adam the time of day when he returned. He was in a cold temper when he swept her into the waiting coach and she was carried with him on a brisk, cold breeze of efficiency.

Driving through Philadelphia on a busy workday was a wonder for Bryony. The churches alone caused her to stare with wonder at their tall spires, and the business district with its bustle was a sight to behold. Matthew would love to see this, she thought. She stored it all up to tell him when she got back home.

Adam gave her little time to sightsee. Whisking her out of the carriage, he took her arm and hurried her into the dressmaker's shop.

"I have only four hours off from work," he said as they stepped inside the bright little shop with its elegant hangings. "We'll have to get you outfitted in that time or wait until I can get time off again."

"Four hours!" Bryony exclaimed. "If I can't pick out a new dress in four hours, I ought to be retired to the rocking chair."

"We'll see," Adam said.

She did see. Adam ordered out model after model to show Bryony a bewildering variety of gowns—morning gowns, tea gowns, riding dresses, walking outfits, ball gowns, nightgowns, dressing gowns, as well as capes and shawls. Then came the lingerie—silk stockings, satin corset covers, silk garters and shifts, taffeta petticoats, panniers! The art of corseting alone, Madame Gile confided, was the single most important part of dressing that a lady could learn. Bryony marveled that such instruments of torture could be so fantastically beautiful, yet she puzzled over why a corset should take up so much of a person's time and attention.

Adam ordered fabrics and dresses with a decisive nod or shake of his head, seldom consulting Bryony on what she wanted or needed. Indeed, Bryony wasn't sure what she wanted or needed, and permitted herself to be led by both Adam and the proprietress.

From Madame Gile's they went to the bootmaker, where slippers and boots of satin, kidskin, and calf were measured and ordered. Next to the milliner's shop, for lace mobcaps, picture hats, tall hats with plumes, and even a nightcap of gauzy India muslin.

It was at the wigmaker's that Bryony protested at last.

"I don't need a wig, Adam," she said as they stood surveying the tall, elaborately dressed and curled wigs that stood in the shop window.

"Of course you do. Everyone wears them at parties and for formal wear."

"You don't."

"How do you know?"

"I've never seen any in your wardrobe or in our rooms. You don't even powder."

He glanced down at her and something like a smile appeared to play at the corners of his mouth. "You've been paying attention."

"Yes, I have. I want to be a proper Philadelphian, Adam, for your sake. But you're proper enough for me, and if you don't wear wigs or powder, then I shan't either. Besides, the powders they use are death to the scalp—they smother and itch. And all manner of creatures may reside in those wigs and a lady might never know it until one of them crawled out and bit her at the dinner table."

"Don't be absurd," Adam said. Privately, however, he recalled one occasion when a small creature had indeed emerged from a lady's wig at a formal dinner party, and his feeling of revulsion when the otherwise lovely woman turned to him and smiled coyly, unaware that a beetle was inching its way across the satin bows of her coiffure.

"Very well," he said. "We'll leave out the wig this time." He took out his pocket watch. "It's time for me to return to work. I'll walk from here and you can go home in the carriage. Just tell the driver I'll need him at six o'clock."

Adam kissed her briefly on the cheek, then suddenly put his hands on her shoulders. "You were perfect this afternoon. Do you like the things I bought for you?"

"Oh, Adam, how could I not? They're splendid!"

He kissed her swiftly, on the lips this time. "I'm glad. You'll be the belle of the city, you'll see. We'll talk more tonight, after supper."

He squeezed her hands and strode away, signaling to the carriage driver to help Bryony into the carriage with her packages. Bryony stood staring after Adam for a moment, the warm touch of his kiss on her lips and his words of praise echoing in her mind. She had Adam's approval, a hundred beautiful new things, an elegant new home, and a carriage waiting to drive her anywhere she liked.

So why did she feel so empty?

Bryony spent the next few days testing her newfound talent. She'd been afraid that the vision she'd seen in the basin had been a fluke, a one-of-a-kind, one-time chance occurrence. To her delight and awe, she found that when she used the methods she had been trained to use in scrying—meditating, silence, soft singing or chanting—she could indeed see visions in the basin. And not only the basin. She began to see, unbidden, reflections of other places and times in mud puddles and spilled cider, clear soup broths and watering troughs. She had to begin shutting the visions out, rather than calling them up, or she feared she'd get too addled to function as either a human or a Hag.

A Hag. She hugged the idea to herself. The line was not dead. At long last, she had come into her inheritance. She felt like skyrockets were going off inside of her when she thought of it. She had true magic at her command.

She didn't dare tell anyone else, though she was bursting to. She'd made a solemn vow to Adam, on her family's name, that she would never speak a word about magic to anyone now that she was in Philadelphia, and she would keep that vow. At last, though, she couldn't stand not sharing her news with someone, so she wrote a long letter to Matthew detailing her newfound gift.

The knowledge of her gift gave her new confidence and heart. In the long days while Adam was away at work and there was no one around to see or hear her, Bryony began to test her skill, to perfect it. Moreover, she decided to try out other forms of magic and cures to see if she had, by any wild chance, another gift.

When they had arrived in Philadelphia, Bryony had hidden a small cache of herbs, powders, and other magical objects she'd carried from the hollow in the bottom of the wardrobe, behind her old clothes. Now she brought them out and set to work.

She started with the simple spells and elements of magic that made her feel more at home in the strange rooms she shared with Adam. She tucked bits of sage behind the mirrors and washed the woodwork with clean water, mint, and lavender. She said prayers and incantations over the doorways and windows and placed tiny hidden pinches of nettle, ivy, hellebore, and thyme as guards against sadness, evil, or sickness entering their chambers.

Their big bed called to mind their wedding night. She had longed to perform a bride's ritual that night but had no faith in her magic to say the words or lay the special herbs in place. She knew now that making love with Adam surpassed any magic she'd ever imagined or known, but just for the sake of tradition—and caution—she performed the ritual now.

"Here is rosemary for the end of childhood," she said softly. She tucked a small cambric bag beneath the mattress in the corner she deemed to be the closest to due north. "Thyme is for happiness," she said, moving to the east-facing corner. "White roses for pure love," she said over the south corner. "And lavender for cleansing peace," she said as she went to the western corner. "Lavender to cleanse us and to soothe my fears on my wedding night," was what the bride usually said in this ritual, but it didn't seem to fit. She paused, looking at the soft linen pouch in her hand. An alternative quickly came to mind. "Lavender to soothe away my fears in this new place," she said, and tucked the pouch away.

She stood back from the bed for a moment, hands on her hips. A smile played about her lips as she recalled the way in which she and Adam had spent most of the previous night. Her body tautened and heated just at the mere memory of the way he had taken her up and set her astride him, urging her on to the most glittering heights of abandon and pleasure.

She reached into her old satchel and pulled out a fifth bag of herbs. "We may never have need of this," she said with a chuckle, "but it can't hurt." She thrust the bag straight into the middle of the mattress. "For heat and passion that never fails, foxglove shall warm us." She laughed again. "And what fun it will be to put that bit of herb-magic to the test!"

There were incantations to recite, rituals to be refreshed. She went searching for rocks and feathers in the gardens and found several useful trees and shrubs as well. She consulted the family book and even tried a few spells she hadn't tried in years.

She never imagined that she could be glad in any way about the time she'd spent working alone in the hollow after her parents died, but it served her well in this case. It was no trouble to set to work refreshing her magic in the solitude of her room.

She was torn, though. She'd given Adam her word that she would never again mention magic to anyone. He'd made it clear by cutting her off several times that he didn't even want her to speak of it to him. She wasn't breaking her word, exactly, but she sensed that he wouldn't be pleased if he knew that she was practicing her skills again.

After thinking it over for a few days, she decided to hold her counsel until she had further explored and refined her skills. Then when she had undisputed proof that her talent was real and lasting, she would broach the subject to Adam.

As for Adam, he was feeling baffled. He was acting like a schoolboy just discovering the delights of the opposite sex. He was insatiable. Every night, he went willingly to bed with Bryony—he had no intentions of living like a monk—but this was ridiculous! She was like some powerful drug in his bloodstream, stirring him to new heights of pleasure, prompting him to laugh and tickle and stroke and romp, for God's sake, with his *wife!* If this kept on, he thought, they'd soon be hanging from the ceiling, trying to see if they could come up with yet another way to reach that golden, glittering pinnacle that spun them out heavenward and drew them back together in a bond of intimacy that was unlike anything Adam had ever felt.

Each morning, it was more and more of a struggle to get out of bed and get dressed and rush off to the sober offices of Bacon and Hawthorne Shipping. He was missing breakfast every day because he was always too late to stop before he had to meet his impatient father at the front door. And every morning, his father wore the same sour expression that said he knew exactly what Adam had been doing all night that had so tired him the morning after.

But Adam simply couldn't help himself. It was too delicious to sink into the eiderdowns with Bryony and give himself up to a world of sensations, where no columns of figures marched before his eyes, and no watchful, paternal eyes followed his every movement. It was getting so he would drift off in a daydream of anticipation each day as the clock hands twitched nearer to six o'clock.

But each day he would also remind himself of his mission to bring Bryony out of the dark ages of her upbringing and into the light of the age of reason. He would hurry home with resolve struggling to override desire, sternly plotting out the next lesson that he, Pygmalion, would teach his Galatea. But by the time he'd come home, visited Ross, changed and dressed for supper, and dined, it was almost time for bed. And there Bryony would be, supple and naked and inviting in that warm golden bed, her lush amber eyes sparkling in the firelight. He would pull a book off the stack that was piling up at the bedside and prepare himself to read to her and question her about the superior reasonability of his beloved philosophers.

"All right. This is from Lucretius."

"Mmm. Born ninety-four years before Christ. He was a student of Epicurus."

"Correct. Must you do that?"

"Do what?"

"That. With your foot."

"This?" She gently massaged the arch of his foot and the inside of his ankle with her toes.

"Yes. It's very distracting."

"I'm sorry." She scooted up a bit, her breasts pressing softly against his upper arm. "Go on."

"All right. Lucretius. From *De Rerum Natura*—"

"That means *On the Nature of Things.*"

"That's correct." He frowned at her. "How did you know that?"

"You have to know Latin and some Greek in order to study the old herbals. Mother and Father taught me some, and Matthew did, too." She languidly tucked a lock of glossy hair behind her ear.

"Matthew Cowley?" He felt a sudden, tempestuous desire to nibble on her ear and shook himself mentally.

"Yes. Matthew's more than tolerably educated. He and my father studied together as children."

Adam was hardly paying attention. He would permit himself one kiss, he thought, for he didn't want Bryony to feel his lessons weren't motivated out of love.

He bent and kissed her, savoring the sweet, cool taste of her mouth. With effort, he returned to his book.

"All right. Lucretius wrote: 'What else can give us more sure knowledge than our senses? How else can we distinguish between the true and the false?' By this he means that we must use our eyes and our ears, our senses of taste, touch, and smell to understand the world. That's why they were given to us. Any knowledge that we get any other way is not true knowledge, but a falsehood. Do you understand?"

"Yes, I think so. He means that we were meant to taste, touch, feel, hear, smell, and see the world. That way, we will come to know how the world really is."

He kissed her again, for being such a clever student. She pulled back when the kiss was done, eyes still closed, a soft smile curving at the corners of her mouth. The coverlet had slid back a bit, and those soft, creamy breasts were revealed in all their sweet perfection, the blush-rose aureoles almost visible above the edge of the bedclothes. . . .

Another kiss wouldn't hurt, he decided. It certainly warmed him so that he could sit up and read in comfort.

"All right," he said at last, clearing his throat and sitting back up. "Lucretius. *De Rerum Natura.* 'What else can give us more sure knowledge . . . than . . . ' "

"You read that."

"I did?"

"Mm-hmm. It was about how we need to hear, and see, and smell. And taste. And touch."

"Taste. Touch," he echoed.

She was looking up at him with those wondrous eyes, her silky body resting alongside his, and, damn it, she was lying there *breathing,* so that those high, perfect breasts rose higher and then sank out of sight, tantalizing him with the promise of a glimpse of those lovely budding nipples, and it was all so unfair and so temptingly good and—

And he'd be lost before the second page, rolling over to devour her with lush, hungry kisses. Before he knew it, they would be lost in the myriad intricacies and inventions of lovemaking, utterly engrossed in the true pursuit of knowledge—via the senses. Lucretius might have been proud, but it drove Adam wild when he left the bed in the morning and realized that once again, he'd given in completely to his carnal instincts and was thereby no further along in his efforts to change Bryony into a full-fledged member of civilized society.

Yet she seemed to be improving, despite his lapses, and soon he decided it was time to show her a bit of what the good life in Philadelphia could be like. His friends and acquaintances had been becoming more and more inquisitive about his bride, and the remarks about bridegrooms and their occupations were beginning to grate. He decided it was time to accept one of their invitations and take Bryony to her first Philadelphia party.

After a week or two of concentrating on her magic, Bryony was beginning to grow restless. Adam and his mother had made it clear that she was not expected to participate in running the household. Indeed, for all she saw of Matilda during the day, Bryony thought perhaps the house ran itself.

Boredom was dangerously close and everything in her rebelled against it. If she didn't do something soon, she'd be reduced to pacing the floors. What did people do when there were no people or animals to care for, no gardens or fields that demanded their attention? She could read, she supposed, but she was used to doing that in the evenings, after her chores and obligations were done for the day—it wasn't something she wanted to do all day long.

She wanted to pursue her quest for the boy in her vision. She planned to ask Adam, but she wasn't sure yet how she could do that without having to explain about her vision. She decided that she'd best wait to discuss that with him when she felt ready to talk to him about the arrival of her magic.

She'd only seen a small part of the big house thus far. If this was to be her home, she reasoned, she ought to know all about it. Besides, she was already getting weary and impatient with just sitting or pacing in the rooms she shared with Adam.

She trailed down the stairs, studying each of the faces portrayed there. The family resemblance was strong, even in the portraits that looked quite old. The Hawthorne blue eyes and strong chin appeared again and again, as did Matilda's dark auburn hair and green eyes. Adam's ancestors looked out on her with cool, uncaring tolerance. Would she ever feel at ease in this house? It wasn't that she felt unwelcome, exactly, but more as if she were an aberration, some mistake or intrusion that, in time, would go away of its own accord.

She shook off these dreary thoughts and walked briskly down the rest of the stairs. There were doors on either side of the foyer. The right-hand one was standing slightly ajar. She knocked lightly, and when there was no answer, she slipped inside the room. It was a lovely parlor, all done in sky blues and sea greens, but like so much of the rest of the house, it was closed and cold and dark. She crossed the foyer to the other door and found a vast and impressive library, with a leather-topped desk and two comfortable settees flanking the fireplace. Again, it was dark and cold, and the fireplace was so pristine it looked as if there hadn't been a fire in it for years.

She went to the opposite stairs and climbed to the floor above. That part of the house was much the same. Room after room of exquisite decoration and ample comfort, and almost all of them appeared to have been shut up for quite some time. Some of the furniture was even draped in cloths, as if the occupants had left the house on an extended journey. She went back downstairs and entered the south wing, which extended out from the same side of the house as their rooms upstairs.

Occasionally, she passed a servant in the halls, but they only nodded and brushed past her, barely meeting her eyes. She found no sign of Matilda or Josiah, though she discovered what she assumed was their bedchamber. She was beginning to feel as if she'd laid a spell of invisibility on herself.

The north wing was much the same as the south wing where she and Adam stayed. But as she came to the far end of the hallway, her senses began to tell her that something here was quite different from the rest of the house. The hallway smelled so strongly of camphor, or at least so it seemed to Bryony's sensitive nose, that she felt as if she were in a preserving room or something worse.

There was no longer that sense that she was all alone. But the emotions she felt were not cheerful or companionable or even neutral. Instead, she found herself clasping her suddenly cold hands together as a wave of bleak, unutterable despair washed over her.

"What is it?" she cried aloud, softly. "Who's here?"

Chapter Sixteen

"Grief Imprisoned may Kille the Heart."
—*Cassia Talcott*

She approached the last door on the hall. It was an ordinary door, painted the fresh, clean white of all the other woodwork in the hall. She cocked an ear and thought she caught the sound of music from within. Then there was silence, followed by the sound of footsteps down the hall, beyond the opening to the north wing passage.

Unaccountably, she felt guilty for being in this part of the house. She jumped and ran down the hall to another room, slipped inside, and stood listening behind the door. Dulcie's voice came from the hall, calling back to someone in the kitchen. Bryony peeked out and watched until the little maid had turned and gone back to the kitchen, then let herself out and slipped back to her own room, grateful not to have been caught spying. But her curiosity had been aroused and she wondered what had happened or was happening in that wing to give her such a sense of bitter pain and hopelessness.

Adam came home late, his forehead creased with tension. Bryony poured him a glass of sherry and sat down quietly beside him. He sipped the drink in silence.

"We'd better hurry to supper," he said at last. "Father is in a temper that would cow a saint, and he's ready to seize on any excuse to tear into me."

"Why?"

"I made a business decision he didn't like. Took me to task. Told me he'd make sure that no one dealt with me without him being present."

Bryony shook her head. "He's got the most tightly locked-up spirit I've ever seen in a man."

"Don't let him hear you say that. He'll have you tightly locked up in a trice." He launched to his feet and went to refill his glass. "I've had an invitation. Would you like to go to a party?"

"A party? When?"

"In two weeks. At Taylor and Tammy MacLaren's house. They've not been married too long, either, and have just moved into a new home. It's a housewarming of sorts."

"I'd love it!" Bryony jumped up from the settee. "I've been wanting to meet your friends for so long!"

"Well, most of Tay's friends are friends or acquaintances of mine, so you'll meet them there as well as anywhere."

Bryony looked at him quizzically. "Don't you want to go?"

He took a drink, then nodded. "Yes. I'm looking forward to seeing Tay, at least."

She put her hand on his arm. "If you're worried that I might embarrass you—" she began.

Adam waved her words away. "No. No, I'm not." He gave her a brief smile. "I couldn't be prouder of you. You'll be just fine."

"Then why is it that I feel as if you don't want to go to this party?"

He shrugged. "No reason. It's just my mood tonight. I don't feel precisely festive."

She kissed him on the cheek. "Then let's go down and be there before your father arrives, shall we?"

Adam grunted. "He'll find fault with that, somehow." He set down his glass and went over to the bed. "Have you seen my watch?" he asked, looking around the bedside table. "I believe I had it in my waistcoat pocket when you so shamelessly wrestled me onto the bed last night and had your way with me."

Bryony giggled as she stood at the mirror, putting up her hair. "Yes, you poor soul, and how you groaned and moaned at my ill treatment of you! You didn't—" She broke off with a start as she turned and saw Adam pulling back the bedcovers to search the mattress.

"Here," she said, hurrying over to him. "Let me do that. I'm almost ready. You go change and I'll search for your watch." She took the covers from his hand and shooed him away from the bed.

He looked at her in confusion for a moment, then shrugged and went to the wardrobe. Bryony sighed with relief. In another moment, he might have decided to turn the mattress over, or check inside it. She didn't like to think what he'd do if he found the pouches of herbs she'd tucked into it.

She shook out the pillows and found the watch. Adam gave her a quick kiss of thanks, finished his dressing, and led the way downstairs.

Adam had guessed correctly. When Josiah saw them both seated in their places at the dinner table he gave them a sardonic smile. "Can't wait to get at the victuals, eh? One more transaction like the one you made today and we may be eating scraps from John Stockwell's table before the year is out."

Adam refused to rise to his father's baiting. "Good evening, Father," was all he said.

Bryony was pleased with the way he rose and went to greet his mother when she entered the room. Matilda scarcely seemed to notice, but Adam took her arm and seated her at the table all the same. There was some feeling there, she decided, though it was less than robust in its expression.

She looked from Matilda to Josiah. It had not been too hard to imagine her own parents as young lovers. But the Hawthornes—it was beyond her ken. Surely they had experienced some of what she and Adam shared, at some time in their lives. They'd had Adam, after all.

She started as she felt Josiah's icy gaze upon her.

"What is it, girl?" he demanded. "Don't like our soup?"

"It's fine," she said, hurrying to lift her spoon and taste it. "Thank you."

"Then mind you eat it and stop gawking." He turned to his wife, cutting off any reply that Bryony might have made. "Saw that idiot Schuyler Bailly today," he told her. "Still has some notion that—"

"You will apologize to my wife."

Josiah looked up at his son with a scowl. "I'll what?"

Adam laid down his spoon. "You will apologize to Bryony."

"What the devil for?"

Bryony touched Adam's arm. "No, Adam, it's all right."

"No, it isn't." Adam kept his eyes on his father. "You were rude to my wife."

Josiah waved away his words. "She doesn't know any different. Besides, she was staring at me, and where's the manners in that?"

Adam pushed back his chair. "You will apologize to her."

Bryony didn't know where to look. She glanced at Matilda and saw her staring down at her soup bowl, silent.

Josiah's eyes burned into Adam's. Adam rose from his chair and put his arm under Bryony's.

"Very well, very well. I'm sorry," Josiah barked. He raised his eyebrows at Adam as if to say "There. Are you happy?"

Adam sat down again. He nodded to his father. He retrieved his spoon and resumed his dinner.

My heart, what a pair of pepper pots, Bryony thought. Were they at all aware that they shared the same temper? Adam's was just as hot as Josiah's, she sensed, but she knew now that part of his coolness was calculated to resist and to annoy his father's heat. She wanted to laugh.

She glanced at Matilda again. The tiniest smile seemed to play around her lips just before she took her next sip of soup. Bryony smothered her own smile of amazement and delight.

Life, she thought to herself. It was a weak flame, but underneath all that starched linen, the Hawthorne family still had the elemental spark of life.

Bryony had something new to ponder over dinner. With her own thoughts to content her, she didn't mind the silence of the others.

Adam spent every day except Sunday at his work. He seemed to be throwing himself into it with full force, trying to squeeze as much satisfaction from it as he could find, though Bryony guessed that he wasn't finding an abundance.

She tried to keep herself occupied while he was away. She explored the back gardens and found them beautifully kept but devoid of flowers or any sort of herb. She decided that Adam wouldn't object to a few flowers, so she planted some of her seeds from home in an out-of-the-way corner. It didn't get as much sun as she would have liked, but the soil was good. She found a pleasing ritual for growing plants in her mother's book and laid down a protective spell around the little plot to keep out the bugs.

To her delight, the plants pushed through the soil within two days' time. By the end of the week, healthy young shoots of marigold and violet were standing proudly at attention in the shady corner.

Her new power was heady, but not all of her attempts were successful. She tried a spell for invisibility and found it only rendered her slightly dizzy. An effort to make a mirror speak to her resulted in a profound weariness of the sight of her own face.

But she kept practicing. And the longing to tell someone, to share her magic, was growing stronger with each passing day.

Finally, it came to her. She was fairly certain that the herbs in the mattress had been working their magic. She couldn't so much as lie down on their bed for a quiet nap without needing to hop up soon after and splash cool water on her face. And when she and Adam were there together it was as if they were discovering each other anew each night.

If her magic worked on Adam unawares, she reasoned, why couldn't it work on the other members of the Hawthorne family? She turned to her mother's book and began to study. She was searching for a spell that could somehow encompass all the family at once when she heard the calling.

The sound was inside her, she thought as she rose from her chair and set aside her book. Tears sprang to her eyes. It was the loneliest, most forlorn sound she'd ever heard. She let the calling lead her.

She knew where she was going before she had descended the stairs. The room at the end of that long silent hall was where she must go. She didn't hesitate. She trusted her magic and her intuition.

Before she even realized she was doing it, Bryony had grasped the door handle and pushed open the heavy door. It opened easily, and warm air rushed out to touch her cheeks and hands. She seemed to come out of her trance as the heat seeped into her chilled skin. Why was there a fire in this closed-off part of the house? she wondered. But her surprise at finding a heated room was nothing compared to what she beheld as she stepped across the threshold.

An onslaught of sensations, some pleasant, some frightening, came at her. Her ears recorded the deep, pressing silence of the room, but at the same time, far off, in some deep recess of her consciousness, she heard again the delicate, laughing notes of music she'd heard out in the hall the other day. The air in the room was closed and stale and once again, Bryony found the scent of camphor to be the overpowering topnote—camphor, she thought dimly, the odor of things set aside, preserved, old, dead. One quick shiver chased another down the length of her spine as these thoughts came to her. The warm air before her and the cooler air of the hall behind her magnified the sensation that she was leaving one world and stepping into another. Last, her eyes took in the beauty of the room, with its heavy brocade hangings and deep jewel tones, and then came to rest on the pale, emaciated figure lying utterly still beneath the elegant bedcovers.

She caught her breath. "Oh, I'm sorry! I didn't realize that anyone was here." But although she knew she should turn and go at once, she couldn't force herself to move back. Instead, she found herself moving ahead, into the magnificent, forbidding room. The door swung shut behind her.

The blond head on the bedpillows turned slightly, and Bryony saw two blue eyes, circled with pale shadows, meet her own. There was no mistaking the resemblance to Josiah's eyes, though these eyes held none of his fiery anger. This was another Hawthorne son!

"My name is Bryony," she said, almost without knowing it. "Bryony Talcott Hawthorne. I'm Adam's wife."

Something flickered in the man's eyes, then quickly faded. He didn't speak.

"Oh!" she said. "Perhaps I've made a mistake. I'm always doing that here, it seems; there's so many rules about how to behave. Perhaps you can't hear. Can you hear?" she asked, raising her voice.

The man only looked at her with the same steady, bland gaze. Bryony babbled on, her nervousness growing.

"What am I saying? If you can't hear, you can't very well tell me that you can't hear, can you? I must find a piece of paper and write you a message. Now, where would I find a pen and piece of paper?" She bustled further into the room, heading for the bureau near the heavily draped windows. "My guess would be in here."

"Top drawer."

"Top drawer? Thank you, I'll—" She stopped short and whirled about, red-faced. "You do hear! And speak. Oh, forgive me, sir, I—"

The man only looked away, as if suddenly weary. Bryony felt another rush of that deep despair she'd felt in the hall and all the way up in her room. This was its source. But what could possibly have happened to make a young man like this give in to such complete melancholy?

She felt torn. She wanted to stay and comfort him; everything in her being and training told her that she should. But she wasn't sure she was welcome here or if there was some rule about her being here. What would Adam say to her? What would his parents say?

She looked again at the slender, pale face and felt the shifting, bubbling feeling inside her again. The magic was with her again, the golden magic she had felt on her wedding night and when she'd seen her first vision in water. She hesitated, debating for but a moment, then surrendered to it and felt the cool, golden light inside her intensify.

She summoned up her courage, fought off another wave of the engulfing despair, and walked straight over to the bedside. She found a footstool and sat down on it, looking the man right in the eye.

"May I ask you a question?"

The young man closed his eyes, then opened them again. She took it as a yes.

"How long do you plan to lie here?"

Bryony watched carefully, holding her breath. The words had just come to her out of the blue. She knew the question was rude and impertinent, but she saw what she was hoping to see in those still, blue eyes. A faint flicker of outrage and pain, of healthy Hawthorne anger. Still, the young man didn't speak.

"Good," she said softly. "You haven't given up on life altogether. Though sometimes I imagine that you've wanted to. You don't have to answer me if you don't wish," she told him gently. "As Adam can tell you, I can talk enough for two when I wish. I've been wanting someone to talk to, so perhaps you won't mind listening to me. I'm new here and I don't know anyone, so I get a bit lonely, I confess."

As she was speaking, Bryony was taking an inventory of all she could see of this man. He was pale and thin, and his skin had the translucent look of someone who had been secreted away from the sun and the air for quite a long time. His blond hair was a fine color, but the texture was dull and lifeless. His lips had little color, his fingernails the same. He bore no visible scars. His voice, when he had spoken, was soft and a bit rusty, as if long unused. He could move his head and his eyes and mouth, but she didn't know about the rest of his body. His scent was definitely wrong for a young man of his age, all musty and dry and edged, again, with camphor.

A multitude of questions crowded into her mind and heart. But she could see that the young man was already tiring just from the effort of looking at her. She smiled at him.

"Perhaps I can come back at another time," she said, reaching out and touching his hand on the coverlet. It felt cool and lifeless to her fingers. "If you don't mind. I could use a friend."

The blue eyes blinked at her again, and she accepted the signal as an invitation to return. The pale lashes drifted down and she saw that he was on the verge of sleep.

"I don't know your name," she said, leaning toward him.

"Ross."

And then he slept, she knew, so she stood up and slipped quietly from the shadowy room. Once out in the hall, she felt tears come to her eyes, unbidden but not unwelcome.

She wiped her eyes and headed back down the hall. The halls and rooms were as empty and silent as before.

Ross Hawthorne, she thought as she returned to her rooms. Adam's brother. He had Matilda's delicate looks and Josiah's blue eyes, while Adam had Josiah's bolder features and Matilda's deep green eyes. The resemblance was undeniable. But why had Adam never said that he had a brother?

Why was Ross secreted away here in this isolated part of the house?

There must be another rule about it. Perhaps this was the way Philadelphians cared for their ill, in quiet rooms, shut away from the world.

Whatever it was, Bryony thought, it wasn't for her to question—at least that was what she was sure she'd be told if she mentioned it to anyone. And she also felt sure that she'd be forbidden to discuss it or to visit Ross again.

Well, she thought, she had no intention of doing that. She had little enough to do of worth around this place. She was going to keep her own secrets now. She'd been called and she was going to visit Ross Hawthorne as often as she could. And if she was going to visit him, she knew she was bound by her Talcott blood to do all she could to help him. She would be the Hag again, even if for a few brief moments a day. The Hag of Hawthorne House!

The thought cheered her and she entered her rooms smiling and humming. When Adam came home that evening, he found her curled up on the settee before the fire, looking like Soot after a visit to the creamery. The effect was charming, they were late for dinner once again, and Bryony made a mental note to check the settee for stray herbs that might have escaped from their bed.

Chapter Seventeen

"To Foretell the Future, Rise at Dawne and Heed the Bird's Calles: Cries from the North denote Tragedie; from the South, Goode Crops; from the East, Goode Love; From the West, Goode Luck."

—*Cassia Talcott*

Bryony waited before she visited Ross again. She spent the days in careful observation, noting the routines of the household. She saw that Matilda regularly spent the early afternoon hours in retirement in her sitting room. The bedrooms had been cleaned and the servants tended to be in the back of the house during those hours, often doing tasks in the kitchen and pantries and the washroom. It would be the ideal time to visit Ross, she determined. At last, she gathered up her courage, went quietly to the north wing, and slipped, undetected, into his room.

Everything was as it had been when she left it last time. Ross lay in the bed, pale and listless as before.

"Hello," she said. "I hope that you don't mind that I've come to visit again."

There was no reply, not even a fluttering of his lashes. Bryony went on bravely. "I brought something for you to see. It comes from my home—Cold Springs Hollow." She took the stool at his bedside again and pressed something into his hand.

His fingers curled over the object, ever so lightly. Bryony smiled in encouragement. "Isn't it a nice stone? If you hold it up to the light, you can see right straight through it. I used to pretend I could see fairies and pixies—piskies, I called them—through it when I was a little girl. My mother gave it to me."

Ross didn't respond, but he didn't drop the stone, either. Bryony had chosen it carefully from among the collection she still kept hidden at the bottom of her wardrobe. She'd said a quiet prayer over the crystal that morning, along with an old incantation that called upon the clarity of the stone to help dispel dark sorrows.

"I imagine that you were as surprised to see me as I was to see you when I was here last time," she said. "I've only been here a month or so, and Adam and I have been married only a little longer than that. I've never been to a city before, so Philadelphia is a wonder to me! Back home, everybody knows everybody else, but here, I don't see how a body could learn half the names of everyone in this city if they tried a lifetime."

Bryony talked on, telling a little of life among her beloved hollow-dwellers. She watched for signs of interest or protest and saw none, but bit by bit, she saw Ross's long, fine fingers close over the smooth, clear stone and hold it fast. The sight of those fingers, so like Adam's, touched her heart, and the golden, bubbling feeling of her magic rose up inside her once again.

When she came the following day, she brought a bag of soft-scented herbs she'd tucked into her clothing. She hid the bag in a fold of the drapes that were tied back at the head of his bed and smiled as the delicate, woody fragrance wafted over Ross's head, causing his nostrils to quiver slightly in response.

From then on, each time she visited him, she brought with her some object or token that gently demanded that he bring his dormant senses to life. She carried in books and read him bits of stories, though he tended to fall asleep, lulled by her voice. A sweet taste of a jam tart, the rough texture of a conch shell, the many colors of a piece of fine cut glass, the sharp, invigorating scent of a pine twig—she used anything she could think of to quietly lure him back to life.

And as his senses returned to activity and he took note of these new objects in his environment, she was taking careful note of how he moved, and what he could or could not do with his body, and whether some sign of the returning fires of life were present in his cool blue eyes.

She made certain that none of her efforts would

create suspicion in the house. She put away the objects she brought, tucked herbs into dim corners, and carried off any remains of food or plants she brought with her. Each day, she returned to her rooms well before Adam came home, with new things to think about and new plans to make. She made notes and tucked them away in her mother's book, documenting her progress.

She longed to share with Adam the excitement of this unfolding process, but she held back. She just wasn't sure of his response, especially since he was working so hard to teach her the art of city living.

She would have to be content with what she had, and wait for the right time to tell Adam what she knew and what she was doing. If she excelled at her "lady lessons," as she called them, and worked hard at fitting in with his way of life, then perhaps he'd be more accepting of her old ways.

So Bryony threw herself into the process of getting herself civilized. She dressed with care each morning, took pains to read the newspaper after Adam had read it—though she found it sadly lacking in wholesome gossip—and followed his instructions on etiquette everywhere they went.

When he reminded her the following night that they were invited to a party, she was delighted at the prospect of spending an evening with him. "Oh, but, Adam, are you sure that I'm ready?" she asked again. "I don't want to do anything that might embarrass us."

He rolled over to take her into his arms. "I

haven't a single qualm about you, love. Everyone is going to be enchanted with you."

She smiled over his shoulder at his choice of words. Then, just before they were swept off into other endeavors, she had an idea.

It was dangerous. It was daring. It might backfire on her.

But as Adam kindled the lovely heat between them, and together they fanned the flame to a soaring height, she decided she had to try it.

"Mrs. Hawthorne, it is a joy to meet you."

Bryony found that she liked Taylor MacLaren at once. His warm brown eyes and genuine smile made her feel immediately welcome.

"You must let me introduce you around, Mrs. Hawthorne. Everyone was surprised when Adam announced he'd brought a wife home from his travels, but it's easy to see why he felt he couldn't leave without you. He looks quite the satisfied married man, I must say." Taylor beamed at his friend and Adam shot him a warning glance.

"Did Adam tell you that I just bought this house? My wife and I have been living in my bachelor's apartments while it was being fixed up. This is our housewarming party." Taylor offered Bryony his arm. "Would you care to see some of its features?"

"I'd like that very much. Adam, will you come with us?"

"Ah, Hawthorne, Beau Weston's been asking after you all evening. Seems he has something urgent going. I'll be sure that your lady is well looked after." Taylor pulled Bryony's arm through his own.

Adam looked like he wanted to seize Bryony's arm and pull her back against him, but he saw Beau Weston bearing down on him. Taylor took the opportunity to steer Bryony into the drawing room and soon they were lost among the press of silk- and satin-clad guests.

"Hawthorne. Been looking for you everywhere. You're never at the Dolphin these days. Married life must be damned agreeable, eh?" Beau was resplendent in a purple brocade coat with drifts of lace at the cuffs and neck.

"More than you'll ever know, Weston," Adam drawled. "Tay said you had some urgent business that was burning in your elegant bosom?"

"I should say." Beau brushed a speck of wig powder from his undeniably elegant shirtfront, then continued. "I have a good one for you this time. This fellow is the genuine article. A true miracle man. And he's heard of you and is ready to cast down the gauntlet."

Adam scowled. "Spell it out for me, Beau."

"It's just as I say. There's a fellow down in Chester. Saw him myself. He can bend a solid silver spoon in half using just the power of his superior mind. Absolutely the most amazing thing. But I knew you'd want a piece of him, so I told him all about you. He wants to meet you. Says you'll go away convinced."

"I doubt that. But I don't think I'm interested in any spoon-benders or table-raisers just now. I've gone in with the old man now, you know, and that keeps me pretty tied down."

"Along with a pretty new bride, I'll bet! But you can't say no to this one. He's got money of mine, rather a large piece, I might say, not to mention all the others who've failed to prove that he isn't just what he claims to be."

"More fool you for throwing your money away on mountebanks. I've warned you enough times."

"But aren't you the least bit curious? Where's the old rouser to the cause I used to know? Dear Lord, that little country wife of yours hasn't bewitched it out of you, has she?"

"What do you mean by that?" Adam asked sharply.

"Well, no offense, Hawthorne, but you've been keeping to yourself ever since you came back here with that little fascinator. And now you don't seem to have any hunger for the chase—what else can a fellow conclude but that yet another of the mighty has fallen to the charm of having a pretty wife at his beck and call?"

"Never mind my marriage, Weston," Adam said, relieved. "Let me think about this, all right? And not a word to anyone else yet. I don't want this noised about until I've made up my mind."

Beau clapped him on the back. "That's more like it. Oh, this will be fine, I predict. It's good to have you back."

Bryony was enjoying her tour of the house. Taylor MacLaren, for all his teasing of Adam, was proving to be a thoughtful and interesting companion. His new home was filled with innovations, and his easygoing disposition was reflected in the warmth and comfort she saw in every room. She liked the way he spoke of his wife, Tammy, as if she were his friend as well as his partner in life.

"How long have you known my husband?" she asked as she paused to admire a huge Oriental bowl filled with tulip shoots.

"We were boys together at school. We all used to ride together and it was Adam who taught me to hunt."

"We all?"

"Well, Adam, myself, and other fellows in town our age." Taylor hurried on. "He was always the one to dare the devil. Many's the time I thought we'd have to carry him home in pieces, but he always landed on his feet, like a cat." Taylor offered her his arm and they strolled down the long hall, viewing the portraits and paintings that hung there, lamps canted with precision to show each work of art off to its best advantage.

"Adam was always a quiet fellow, in his way. He was forever looking, watching, making note about how this was made and that was accomplished. Then, by Jove, he'd go home and the next day, he'd reproduce the same feat, in detail, or he'd show us a sketch he'd made of an animal or a machine, right down to the least feather or nail. He once spent a week on the docks, just watching the sailors working the lines, tying off and making knots. Later, I found his room filled with bits of rope, each one tied in a perfect replica of a different seaman's knot." Taylor's eyes twinkled. "But then, I suspect you know much of this already."

Bryony shook her head. "No, I didn't. Though I'm not surprised. Adam is so gifted at his magic and a magician must exercise both courage and careful practice."

"Yes, shame he gave all that up," Taylor said. "He was one of the finest performers I'd ever seen. And he loved it so. But, still, things change, and now he has you to occupy his time and attention. And I can't begrudge him a moment of it. How do you like my skylight?"

"Skylight?"

"Yes. Look up."

Bryony looked up to see a large, square hole cut in the ceiling. She gave a delighted little cry when she saw that she could just make out the stars through the glass overhead.

"A skylight! What a beautiful name. And what a wonderful invention." She gave him a quick, worried glance. "It's quite safe to have a window in your roof, isn't it?"

"Quite. Fellow who designed it took no end of trouble with mathematics and what all to be sure he got the structure supported around it."

She smiled at him and tapped his arm with her fan. "And this fellow would be you, wouldn't it, Mr. MacLaren?"

He bowed. "I confess it was. And I'm just immodest enough to show it to every living soul who crosses the threshold. My wife had to scold me for dragging tradesmen through the parlor to see it just the other day."

"I'll warrant she's terribly proud of you, even so. What a clever thing to construct."

"Will you and Adam have a house of your own soon?"

Bryony's smile faded. "I think not. At least, Adam has never spoken of it."

"Well, he's new at this being married business. And new to business as well. No doubt when he's found his feet and his father's finances are back in order, Adam will be looking for a fine new place to be alone with his bride."

Bryony decided to take a chance that Taylor was as good a man as he seemed. "Mr. MacLaren, has Adam's family always been so troubled?"

Taylor gave her a brief, startled glance that quickly changed to his friendly smile. "No, I'd say not. Growing pains, I guess you'd call it. Things were all right when Adam was a boy, but with a man like Josiah, the mildest of sons would still be bound to butt heads with his father."

"But Matilda, Adam's mother. She's so very sad."

"Ah. Yes, that is a trouble. She's such a beauty still. All of us boys were half in love with her in the old days." He ran a hand over the smooth mahogany finish of the table. "I can't say what happened to make her retire so completely. And I'm not sure that any of the Hawthornes, with that stubborn pride of theirs, would be likely to tell their problems to an outsider."

"An outsider?"

Taylor looked embarrassed. "I was referring to myself. I'm sure that Adam will share all with you, if he hasn't already. He just needs time. He doesn't give his trust easily." He smiled. "Don't worry. A little patience is all that he needs. You've won his heart, that's clear enough, but it may take him a while to learn to confide in you."

"Does he confide in you?"

"Not completely, no. He certainly didn't tell me he'd fallen in love and married you. I didn't even know that he'd brought you home to Philadelphia until I encountered him at his father's offices."

Bryony studied Taylor's face. He was an honest man; this much she could sense. But he wasn't sharing the whole truth with her. What was he hiding and why? She was growing weary of secrets.

Still, something told her not to press the issue with Taylor. If he was keeping secrets, it was out of a desire to protect Adam, she sensed, and not out of any delight in deception.

"Come," she said, linking her arm in his once more. "Let's see what the others are up to. Someone said something about a game of cards?"

Adam was glowering at his hand when they arrived at the card table. Beau Weston, his lady friend Alison Curson, and Wade Sewall were playing with him, though they looked more lighthearted than he.

Bryony went to stand beside him and laid her hand on his shoulder. He glanced up at her. "You're back."

She caught the undertone of anger in his voice and decided to ignore it. "Yes. What are you playing?"

"Fair chance," Beau told her. "Shall you join us, Mrs. Hawthorne?"

"If someone can teach me the rules," she said with a smile.

"You've never played?" Beau's smile was wicked. "Then come to me, ma'am, and I'll show you how it goes."

Adam reached out and clasped a hand around Bryony's wrist. "She'll partner me, Weston."

Beau raised his hands with a laugh. "As you say, gov'nor. As you say."

Adam pulled out a chair for Bryony and called for another drink. She guessed that he'd already had quite a few but she knew he had a good head. She sat down and listened as he tutored her in the fundamentals of the game.

The first few hands were amusing. No one seemed to mind Bryony's awkwardness as she struggled with the rituals of dealing and discarding, betting and raising the stakes. She even won a hand.

It was after they stopped for a bite to eat that the trouble began. A servant passed around a tray of pastries. All of them helped themselves, except Adam, who found himself another brandy, instead. They were chatting and laughing as the sweet, crumbly desserts disappeared. No one noticed that a bit of Bryony's roll took an unexpected dive, straight down into the bodice of her dress.

She didn't dare retrieve it. She simply brushed at the lace around the low-cut neckline in hopes of dislodging it, then gave it up as lost.

They resumed their card game. Bryony gave a cry of delight as she bested all of them in short order and took the hand. They played on, and Bryony found she couldn't lose.

Her heart began to pound as she realized what was happening. The magic. Something had triggered it and suddenly she was claiming purse after purse from Adam's friends.

She glanced at Adam. He was staring at her with an expression she could not read. But it didn't look like either fond pride or amusement.

She tried to lose. She truly did. Finally, she began to make such silly bets and discard the most obviously valuable cards that the others in the group began to protest.

"Now see here, Hawthorne, what's the idea of bringing this alluring little cardsharp among us?" Beau asked. He was laughing, but Bryony heard real suspicion in his voice as well. "This isn't another new line of work for the Astonishing Balthazaar, is it?"

Adam set his glass down hard. "What's that mean?"

"He means," said Wade, "that your wife is either deuced lucky or she's got a bit of your magic touch with the cards, old man." He grinned. "No offense, of course. We're all friends here, eh?"

"You're saying that I'd use magic to cheat you out of your money?" Adam's words were ominously quiet.

"No," Beau said, lifting his drink. "But you might use a beautiful lady to distract us all!"

The glass went flying from his hand before he

could get it to his lips. Bryony sprang up. "Adam, no!"

Adam stood beside her, his fists clenched at his sides. He looked down at the little pile of cash and chits in front of Bryony's place. With one sweep, he sent it all flying.

Then he turned and stalked away toward the door. Bryony cast an apologetic glance at the others and hurried after him.

Taylor intercepted them in the foyer. "Adam," he said amiably. "What's this I hear about a fracas over filthy old money in my house?"

Adam faced him, his eyes dark. "I'm sorry, Tay. Make my apologies to Tammy, please. Bryony and I must be going."

Taylor glanced at Bryony. She nodded. "Yes, Mr. MacLaren. I think we'd best be off."

A servant brought their coats. Adam donned his in silence, made a stiff bow to his friend, and went out. Bryony shook her head. "I'm sorry" was all she could say.

Taylor walked back to check on the card players and found them fully recovered and quietly engaged in a new game. He strolled out of the room and back into the gallery, pondering Adam's sudden departure.

He stopped before the Chinese bowl and frowned. The crimson, ruffled tulip blooms were full and lush, at the freshest point of their peak.

Less than two hours ago, when he'd strolled through the gallery with Bryony Hawthorne, they'd been mere shoots, not even budded, lacking more than a week to their opening. He recalled how she had touched them and, smiling, laid her cheek to one sleek, cool stem. Could it be . . . ?

He chuckled to himself. He could imagine what Adam would say if he came to him with the claim that his new bride had magically forced open his tulips. "Oh, by the way, old friend, does your wife do roses as well?" Taylor murmured.

But there had been an incident with spilled wine earlier in the evening. Perhaps it had been simple embarrassment at having overturned her drink at a party where she was a newcomer. Perhaps spilling things always upset her so. But her face had gone so still when she had knocked over her wineglass, and she had stared at the puddle that had formed on the tabletop for so long he'd thought she was going to faint.

She hadn't. But when he'd touched her arm and spoken her name, she had raised her eyes to his and he'd known, absolutely, that she wasn't seeing him.

What did it mean? Was lovely Bryony prone to fits?

"What gorgeous tulips!"

Tammy came up beside him and slipped her arm under his. "Are these the ones that came from Holland last fall?"

He nodded. "Parrot tulips, they're called. Have you ever grown tulips before?"

"My father cultivated many of them at our country house."

"Do they open in a matter of hours?"

She thought for a moment. "They do bloom quickly. And like most spring flowers, they don't bloom long. A matter of days, yes. But in a matter of hours?" She shook her head.

"That's what I thought." He shrugged and slipped his arm about her waist. "I must have a green thumb."

"No doubt it's your skylight," Tammy said teasingly.

"No sauce, wench," he said with mocking sternness. "That skylight is a brilliant addition to this gallery and will be the wonder of generations to come."

"I'm sure of it. I can hear our grandchildren now: 'Grandpapa was quite mad, wasn't he, Grandma? To put a big old hole in our roof?' "

"Minx!"

She dodged his playful swat to her backside and darted down the hall, laughing. Taylor dashed after her, and the mystery of the tulips was soon forgotten. At least for that night.

Bryony didn't know how they were going to get up the steps. Adam had insisted that the coachman let them out a half-mile from home so that they could enjoy this "truly wonderful night!" as he had proclaimed. The liquor had reached his head at last and he'd gone from glowering to giddy in less than half an hour.

This "truly wonderful night" was threatening a cloudburst any moment, Bryony thought grimly as she guided her swaying husband down the lane toward their house. And, as his feet weren't working too well in unison, she didn't see much hope of getting up the front steps of the house without some major mishap.

"Sweet Bryony," he murmured, leaning on her shoulder. "You were quite the belle tonight. Nobody, not even Beau Weston, could hold a candle to you."

"Thank you," she said dryly. "Mind the shrubbery!"

They snipped off one of Mrs. Davenport's prized hydrangeas but it couldn't be helped. At least they hadn't crashed right through the whole bush, Bryony thought. The house was in sight, now if they could just get up the drive and up those—

"Bryony. Bryony, Bryony."

"Yes, Adam?"

"Bryony, I don't deserve you."

"Don't be silly. Here's the entry, in we go. . . ."

"No. Truly. I'm not the sort of husband you deserve. You deserve a—a prince. A king! Not some old foul-tempered clerk in a fusty old ship—ship—shipping firm."

Bryony ignored him. "Here are the steps; can you make it up?"

"'Course." He stood before the lowest step, swaying and squinting. "Which ones?"

"Take the ones on the right," Bryony said. She was so tired by now that she was beginning to feel a little giddy herself. "If they don't work, we'll cut new ones in the morning."

"Damn right we will!" He pounded her on the shoulder. "That's my girl. If it doesn't fit, by God, we'll force it!" He placed a hand over his heart. "It's the Hawthorne creed."

"Come along, Mr. Hawthorne," she said, tugging at his sleeve. "You're a credit to your ancestors, rest assured."

They mounted the steps and, taking them one laborious step at a time, made it all the way up to the third and final step. Adam peered at the front door. "Who lives here? Bryony, it's late, m'love. We can't go to another party tonight." He patted her nose. "You little vixen, you. You've been at the wines, haven't you? That's all very well for you; you can sleep in tomorrow, whereas I have—"

Bryony was trying the door as he spoke. "This is your house, Adam," she told him. "We need the key."

"My house?" He gave her a cool glance. "Of course it's my house. Where's the key?"

"Your pocket," Bryony said with a sigh.

He regarded her with suspicion, then checked his waistcoat. "'Tisn't either."

Bryony reached into his coat pocket. There was nothing there. She made a methodical search of every pocket and seam where he could possibly hide a key. The results were most disappointing.

"Oh, it's all right," Adam said expansively. "We'll just wake up Mother and Father. They'll let us right in."

Bryony grabbed his arm before he could knock. "Oh, no, we won't," she whispered. "It's two in the morning, you're blind dr—er, somewhat under the influence, and they already think I'm dragging your good name in the dirt! We are not waking them up."

"Bryony." He beamed down at her. "You are the sweetest, the best, the tastiest little morsel of—"

"Save it," she hissed. "Just stand back for a moment and let me think."

She had to get this door open. If they went in any other way, they'd only have to waken the servants, who would be sure to talk about it in the morning. If they stood out here in the avenue any longer, the neighbors were bound to hear or see them. She was going to have to do something dangerous, but necessary.

She felt around inside the pocket that was sewn into the lining of her cloak. Her fingers closed around something slender and smooth, like a sliver of ivory. She drew it out and, under cover of the lace of her sleeves, she pressed it into the lock. "Open lock, I beg of thee, just as the swallow must fly free," she murmured.

"Wha'zat?" Adam asked.

"Oh, nothing," she said. "Look, the door was open after all." She held the door open and motioned for Adam to step inside.

"What a clever wife I have," Adam said, weaving his way over the threshold. "Opens locks with just a word to the birds."

"Don't be foolish," Bryony said, though her heart leaped at the thought that he might have understood what she had just done. "The door was stuck, that was all. Now, be quiet, if you will, sir. We still have to get upstairs to our room."

She palmed the swallow's bone and slipped it into her pocket as she ran to prevent him from crashing into a table holding an antique brass bowl. Crawling, climbing, stumbling, they made it to their rooms without meeting anyone. Bryony closed the doors behind them and leaned against them with a sigh.

She looked at the bed and saw that Adam had fallen across it and was already fast asleep, snoring lightly. She shrugged.

"At least my door spell worked," she said to herself as she went to pull off his boots.

It wasn't until she undressed herself that she saw the secret of her sudden success at cards. "Cinnamon," she groaned, taking the little morsel of pastry out of her bodice. "'A touch of cinnamon draws money to itself,'" she murmured, quoting the Talcott book.

She'd have to be more careful, she thought. Her magic was alive and working, but she didn't have full control over it. If she was to practice in secret, she'd have to be more vigilant, even in the most innocent of situations.

Chapter Eighteen

"A Goodly Parte of All Magick lies with the One who casts the Spelle. Prithee, Learne Common Sense. The Value will prove Itselfe prodigiously. And soone."

—*Cassia Talcott*

"MacLaren! What brings you down here to the dirty business world?" Adam rose from his desk and went to greet his friend with a smile.

"I came to see how your head was doing today. That was more wine than I've ever seen you take. Leastways, not since we were young and foolish bachelors."

Adam rubbed a hand over his forehead. "I did stare a good many glasses to their bottoms, didn't I? But I don't seem too far from myself this morning."

"Glad to hear it. Did Bryony mix up some kind of a potion for you?"

Adam almost dropped the chair he was pulling up for Taylor. "What do you mean?"

"I mean that's what Tam does for me when I've imbibed beyond the prudent man's glass after supper. Noxious stuff, but puts me right as rain. Nice to have around, these wives, eh?"

Adam relaxed and motioned for Taylor to sit. He wasn't about to confess that he didn't remember much of what happened since just before he and Bryony left the party. But he could only assume that he hadn't told Taylor anything about Bryony's past.

He returned to his desk chair, sat, and spread his hands wide. "Now. What can I do for you? I don't believe that you came here just to inquire after my health or discuss matrimonial bliss. Need help getting rid of some of your father's old, worn-out money?"

Taylor grinned. "I'm already one of your prime investors. And the name of MacLaren is not associated with the tossing of money about like chaff. But, in fact, I did come here to talk about marriage."

"Oh?" Adam leaned back in his chair and grinned wolfishly. "Anything I can help with? Your little Miss Sandborne turned out to be more than easy on the eyes."

"Mrs. MacLaren, I'll thank you to remember. And I might be tempted to call you out for your disrespectful tone regarding my wife, if it weren't for the fact that you are so obviously besotted with your own."

Adam felt wary. Taylor was a good friend, but his calm brown eyes saw much more than most people suspected. "It's true," he replied, making his tone light. "I find I've made a rather nice match for myself."

Taylor snorted. "A rather nice match! You were all but ready to chain her to you by the time you left last night. I thought you were going to draw on Weston just for kissing her hand."

"I let you go off with her alone, didn't I?"

"True. But then, you know me well enough to know that I'd never make an advance to your Bryony, lovely though she is."

"So. Do you have a point to make here, MacLaren?"

Taylor brushed a fleck of dust from his coat-sleeve. "My conversation with Mrs. Hawthorne the younger was very pleasant. And intriguing." He turned his eyes on Adam. "Am I correct in guessing that she doesn't know what you were doing in Cold Springs Hollow?"

Adam considered his answer carefully. He knew it was no good to lie to Taylor. Taylor was too clever and too honest himself to miss it. And, as he had said, he and Adam knew each other too well. "Yes and no. She knows that I came there in search of her family, to learn about them. Which was true. But does she know that I came there to reveal her as a fraud? No."

"But she married you. She loves you, even after you held her up as a fake before her whole town?"

Adam looked away.

"Ahh." Taylor steepled his hands before his

chest. "This *is* a story, isn't it?"

Adam looked around to see if they could be heard, but the door to the office was closed tight and he could hear the hum and clatter of activity from the workroom beyond. He took a deep breath and let it out.

"The circumstances in the hollow were not, well, not typical. Not what I had expected. I went there with every intention of following my usual practices. But when I met Bryony, I found I couldn't do things as I ordinarily do."

"I can imagine it set you back a bit when you learned the Hag of the Hollow was a young beauty."

Adam nodded. "You could say that. And one of the very first things she said to me was that she possessed no magical powers. She believed in all of it, of course, and she was hoping that somehow she would find her one special gift, as she called it, that would prove she was the legitimate heir to this legacy of witchcraft, handed down from her parents."

He leaned forward and rested his elbows on the desk. "Her whole family was taken from her in an outbreak of the fever. She was her parents' only child and she lost all her remaining relatives along with her father and mother. She admired and loved them with all her heart. She would try any mad trick to see if she had gained one of their so-called gifts."

"And what did you do?"

"I spent time with her, learned that she was skilled in simple herbcraft and that she was trusted by the people there. She managed to heal by their faith in her and the value of some of the truly medicinal plants she used. I still intended to go on with my job there, until one day, I found her near her house, heartbroken and exhausted from trying to summon up magic. She surrendered all her claims to magic on that day and vowed that she would never again seek to practice it."

Adam rose and began to pace. "I'd begun to care for her. I wanted to take her away from there, where she'd be reminded of all she imagined she'd lost. I wanted to show her that people got on with their lives every day without resorting to crystal balls and smoke tricks."

"So you married her to save her from herself?"

Adam shot a glare at his friend. "No. I said that I cared for her! But I was afraid that she'd be sad there and I had to get back here to begin working for my father. I'd promised my mother I would after she told me the firm was in trouble last fall. So Bryony and I were married in the hollow and we came away."

"And you've never told her the truth about your work?"

Adam shook his head. "There was no longer any point. I wasn't going to reveal anything about her, she was coming with me, I was going into business. It's in the past. It's behind us."

"How will you keep it a secret? Someone is bound to mention it if she goes about in our set."

"I've already talked to Weston and the others. They've said they'll keep mum. No one else knows around here. I've always kept my projects a secret here in the city. No one else knows, that is, except you." Adam came to a halt behind Taylor's chair. He waited, not willing to face his honest friend with his request. "Will you tell her?" he asked softly.

Taylor was silent for a long moment. Then: "No. I won't. Not if you believe it might hurt Bryony." He twisted around to look up at Adam. "And she would be hurt, wouldn't she?"

Adam grimaced. "Yes." It was the first time he'd truly admitted it to himself, though at heart he had known.

"Are you going to take on that fellow that Weston was talking about last night?"

"The spoon-bender? I don't know. I doubt it." Adam crossed the room once more. "I have too much work here. And I don't like to leave Bryony just yet. She's still in awe of this big city, as she calls it."

"Ah, so we're softening, are we?"

"What do you mean?" Adam growled.

"I just mean that you don't seem to have that old hunger in you that you used to have. That anger that drove you to bring the truth to light, no matter the cost."

"I don't know what you mean. I just know that I have obligations here. I'm a man of my word. I promised my mother I'd stay here and help Father with his business, whether he liked it or not. And I made marriage vows to Bryony."

Taylor held up his hands, smiling. "Just speculating. No offense intended." He grew serious again. "I'll do my part, I promise. But secrets are dangerous, Adam. The longer they're kept, the more powerful they can grow."

Adam scowled and strode to the narrow window that looked out to the busy street. "I'll tell her. Someday. When she's more used to our life here. When she's had time to put all of that old magic nonsense out of her head. We'll laugh over it, most likely."

Taylor didn't reply. Adam turned and spread his hands. "That's all there is. You can rest at ease."

Taylor shook his head. "There's another thing that worries me."

Adam was growing irritated. "Ye gods, man. Are you turning old womanish now that you're a married man?"

"Maybe." Taylor stood his ground. "You know that I'm the only one who knows the truth about Ross, outside of your family. The rest of the world believes he died and was buried with your mother's people in Massachusetts. Have you told Bryony?"

Adam stalked away again. "What is there to tell?"

"Does she know that you have a brother?"

Adam was silent.

"You haven't told her anything, not even that your parents had another son, or that he went to war, or that—"

"No!" Adam barked.

"Good Lord, Adam! He lives there in your house with you! Don't your parents even speak of him?"

Adam shook his head. "If they do, they do it in the privacy of their rooms. There's never been a word of him. Just the knowledge that he's up there, lying in that room, weighs heavily enough on us all."

Taylor came behind him and laid a hand on his shoulder. "That must be damnably hard. But all of Philadelphia knew Ross Hawthorne and that he went to war and they believe that he died of his war wounds. You can't tell all of them to be silent."

"I know. I'll tell her. But in my own way, in my own time." He turned to Taylor and clapped him on the shoulder reassuringly. "Bryony and I haven't known each other as long as you and Tammy. We weren't childhood sweethearts. We're just getting to know one another. There'll be time enough for hard truths. I can face it, but I'd rather not rush it."

Taylor smiled. "All right. If you're sure it's the best way."

"I am."

"Well, I've done enough meddling in your affairs for one day," Taylor said with a grin. "But I wouldn't do it if I didn't think she was perfect for you, Hawthorne."

"So good to have your blessing, *Reverend* MacLaren," Adam said, bowing low, hand on his chest.

Taylor gave him a gentle bang on the head with his cane and headed for the door. "Oh, there was one other thing I wanted to ask you. You said that Bryony was gifted in herbcraft and that was all?"

"Lord, but you're full of questions today, aren't you? Of course. Herbcraft and simples. That's all. How could there be more?"

"Just curious. And you say that she renounced all her practices when she married you and came here?"

"That's what I said." Adam looked at him quizzically. "Why?"

"Oh, no reason. You don't know anything about tulips, do you?"

Adam closed his eyes. "Go home to your lady, MacLaren. Have some good strong tea and settle your brains. You're beginning to worry me."

Taylor laughed as he went out. But his forehead was creased with worry all the way home.

Despite her close calls the night of the MacLaren party, Bryony felt compelled to carry on with her magic. She'd been thinking about the idea she'd had the night before the party and she decided that now was the time to put it into motion.

She took the last of her herbs, made up some new cambric pouches, and carried them all to Matilda and Josiah's bedroom. She wanted to giggle as she placed the little packets of magic under the mattress, but she reminded herself that this was an important endeavor. She kept a sober countenance as she quickly pronounced the spells and blessings, but when she returned to her room, she had to bury her head in a chair cushion to muffle her unseemly laughter.

Her next opportunity to work a bit of magic

came as a surprise. She had received a delivery the Monday after the party, from Taylor. She'd been both puzzled and pleased when she opened the box and found it was full of tulip bulbs.

She'd shown them to Adam and he'd shaken his head. "MacLaren's gone a bit mad on flowers and architecture," he told her. "But he's a harmless madman. Humor him."

She took them out to the back garden. By rights, it was too early to plant them for the spring, but she decided she'd take a chance on raising some up in the coming fall. She was carefully turning over the earth, singing a little blessing song over the bulb as she set it in its hole, when she heard a soft step behind her.

It was Matilda, dressed in black as usual, but looking less vacant, less dreamy than Bryony had ever seen her. Bryony sat back on her heels and wiped her hands on her apron.

"I hope you don't mind that I'm planting these here," she said. "Adam said it would be all right."

"Yes, I suppose it's all right." Matilda pointed to the box of bulbs. "Tulips, aren't they?"

"Yes," Bryony said with a smile. "Taylor MacLaren sent them to me. All different colors, I believe, and some I've never seen before."

"I used to have them all along the walk, over there."

Bryony nodded. "That would be a good place for them. They didn't get too much sun?"

"No. The house shadowed them in the afternoons. And I used to put hyacinths in among them."

"Why did you stop?"

"Why did I stop what?" Matilda looked at her mildly.

"Why did you stop planting flowers? What happened to them all?"

"Oh. I dug them up one spring. Just before they bloomed. It didn't seem right somehow, that year." She shrugged. "I just never got around to doing it since."

Bryony extended her spade to her mother-in-law. "Be my guest."

Matilda looked at the spade with a mixture of fear and longing. "Oh, I couldn't."

Bryony only held the spade up higher.

Matilda took the spade in her pale, slender hand and slowly, slowly gripped the handle. She sank down beside Bryony and began to dig.

The two of them worked all morning, side by side. The box was only half-empty when Dulcie called them to dinner.

Matilda handed Bryony's spade back to her. "Thank you, dear," she murmured.

Bryony watched her drift away and then hurried to get cleaned up and consult the Talcott book before Adam and Josiah arrived for the meal. By late that afternoon, she had laid another new spell upon the Hawthorne house and grounds.

Taylor's words had begun to nag at Adam. He heard them as he sat at his desk, trying to make sense of page after page of numbers and cargo lists. They intruded at the most inopportune moments with Bryony. They pestered him on the solitary walks he sometimes took during the dinner hour.

He believed in the truth, didn't he? In facing things honestly and realistically? Hadn't he been working to accomplish just that when he'd met Bryony in the first place?

He'd told Taylor that he'd tell Bryony about his efforts to destroy the work of magicians and healers in his own good time. But the longer he thought about it, the more he wondered if there would ever come a good time. Should he tell her now and be done with it?

His dilemma was made more complicated when he ran into Beau Weston on his way to dinner.

"Have you thought any more about seeing this fellow in Chester?" Beau asked him after they had exchanged greetings.

Adam shook his head. "I've been too tied down with the business." He cleared his throat. "Ah, Weston. About what happened at Taylor's the other evening—"

Beau waved his hand. "No, no. Say no more. Wade and I baited you, though all in fun. And we know how you feel about people who use magic and illusion for gain. Which," he added, grinning, "is why I'd like you to have a go at this Benedict fellow. He's gained quite a bit from this spoon-bending gambit and if he's a fraud, I want to know about it. So would a great many others, I'll wager."

Adam hesitated. "You know that Bryony doesn't know about these excursions of mine."

"So you told me. And I'm prepared to be the soul of discretion."

Adam hesitated. "Give me a bit more time. I have some other business to clear up first."

"To be sure. But not too long, I hope. Chester isn't far from here and it won't be long before folks in the city will be talking about him and clamoring to have him here."

"He must be quite a showman," Adam said wryly.

"No comparison with the Astonishing Balthazaar," Beau said. "But no slow-coach when it comes to embellishments."

They parted and Adam went to dinner at a nearby tavern rather than going home. He had a great deal to consider as he ate his solitary meal. On one hand, he wanted to see this fraud. There was no doubt in his mind that the man could no more prove that he could bend spoons with the power of his mind than Adam could fly. Also, his regular visits to Ross reminded him of his original purpose in taking on these jobs. He had a score to settle with these miserable cheats.

On the other hand, how was he to tell Bryony? With this Benedict the Spoon-bender just over in the next town, she was bound to hear something about him. And she would certainly hear it if Adam went and publicly revealed the man as a fraud in front of Beau Weston's friends. He would have to tell her about his unusual sideline.

But how?

The time just wasn't right. He needed more

time to know that she wasn't still clinging to her old superstitions.

Something else nagged at him. Something he could barely recall, about Bryony and magic and the opening of a door. About that card game.

It eluded him. It must have been a dream. He dreamed of Bryony quite a bit, even when she was sleeping beside him, so it was a likely explanation.

He left the tavern and walked briskly to his office. He had a few more things he needed to do before he could tell Bryony all.

"So, what shall we do today?"

Bryony was perched beside Ross's bed. The drapes were open and the summer sunlight was streaming in over the carpet and dancing on the patterns in the coverlet.

Ross was sitting up in bed, turning over the pages of the Talcott book. He pointed to an entry titled "bryony" and gave her a pointed look.

She tilted the book so she could read. "Yes," she said, "I was named after the bryony root. All the women in my family have plant names. Cassia Talcott began this book. My mother was Amaranth. I had an Aunt Coreopsis, an Aunt Beryl, and an Aunt Trillium. It's a good thing there are a lot of plants on this earth, because I'd hate to have to name my daughter Mugwort or Skullcap."

"Your daughter?"

She smiled and shook her head. "No. Not yet. But I have hopes. A baby in this house would do it a world of good." Bryony leaned toward him. "Would you like to be an uncle?"

Ross looked away. She sensed his retreat into himself. "Are you still so sure you shouldn't be alive?" she asked softly.

He looked at her, startled for a moment. Then he closed his eyes and pulled his spirit inside himself once again. Bryony knew that he wouldn't speak again, or even look at her, no matter what she did, when he went into this state.

She wanted to shake him. She wanted to shout at him to tell her what secret story he was holding inside. If she could just learn what it was that he saw and felt, perhaps she'd know how to help him.

The magic struck her with a force she'd never felt before. At the peak of its tingling, golden whirlwind, she understood what she must do. She would go inside Ross Hawthorne. She would see the world through his eyes.

She trembled as the magic subsided. She'd never done a kything, a transportation of her spirit. She'd tried it, back in the hollow, but she'd always been disappointed. But now that she had her powers, perhaps she would be able to perform the ritual with success.

"I'll be back," she told the silent Ross. "And when I come again, we'll talk, at last."

She was in her room, poring over the Talcott book, when Dulcie knocked at the door and brought in a note for Bryony.

"How wonderful!" Bryony exclaimed, reading it over. It was an invitation from Tammy MacLaren, asking her to tea the following afternoon. "Wait just a moment while I write a reply," she told the maid.

She dashed off an acceptance and gave the maid instructions to deliver it at once. She sat back down to read her book but her mind was on the invitation. How nice it was to have someone extend hospitality to her at last! Back in the hollow, a newcomer barely would have crossed the threshold of his or her new home before the neighbors would have come calling, a fresh-baked pie or a jug of cold cider in hand.

She shrugged. Things were different in the city, Adam had told her again and again. It just took city people a lot longer to do things, she decided, probably due to all the rules they had about what was or wasn't proper. She was glad that they were ready to accept her as proper, at last. Perhaps if Adam saw that she was not going to embarrass herself or anyone else, she could begin to share some of her magic, in the open.

Bryony dressed with care for her visit to the MacLarens. She chose an open gown of light turquoise with a snowy white quilted petticoat showing below the lace-covered stomacher. She felt a bit silly wearing the green silk mask beneath her broad, bergere hat, but Madame Gile had insisted it was the only way to protect the skin from the sun, and she had seen other women wearing them as they passed by on the avenue.

Matilda met her in the foyer as she was leaving. "You look lovely, dear," she said. "I wanted to ask you, if you don't mind, could I . . . ?" She held up a garden spade.

Bryony smiled and nodded. "Please do. Mr. MacLaren sent so many bulbs! We'll have a whole meadow of tulips out there, come fall."

Matilda turned and drifted away. Bryony felt a glow of satisfaction at the success of her new spell. She reminded herself to thank Taylor again for the bulbs—he'd put wonderful tools into her hands.

When she arrived at the MacLarens', a servant took her wraps and then led the way into a sunny sitting room decorated in Chinese yellow. Tammy came to greet her, hands outstretched.

"Mrs. Hawthorne. I'm so glad you could come!"

"I was so pleased to be asked, Mrs. MacLaren."

The two women looked at each other and burst into laughter. "Isn't it the oddest thing, being married?" Tammy asked. "Every time someone calls me Mrs. MacLaren, I keep thinking they're talking to my mother-in-law!"

"I don't feel nearly old enough to be a Mrs. Anyone," Bryony replied. "Please call me Bryony."

"If you'll call me Tammy. Come and sit; there's so much I want to ask you!"

The two of them took their places at a beautifully laid tea table by the window. Bryony admired the lush garden view from their seats.

"Oh, yes, Taylor loves his plants. And my father is a devoted horticulturist, so he keeps us supplied with new and exotic green things." Tammy said, pouring tea into delicate flowered cups. "I have to confess that I barely know a rose from a dandelion, myself."

"You must thank your husband again for the tulip bulbs he sent to us. I can hardly wait to see them bloom."

Tammy handed her a cup of tea, followed by a plate of small cakes. "Tay was delighted to do it. He said that you had a special way with tulips."

"I?"

"Yes," said Tammy, sipping her tea. "He was just grinning like a chessy cat when he sent them off to you."

Bryony made a moue of puzzlement. "I can't think how he could know that. I don't believe I've ever had tulips in my garden at home."

"Now, that's what I'd love to hear about," Tammy said, helping herself to cakes. "This little hollow where you were living. It sounds idyllic, from what Nicodemus Harper told Taylor."

"Nicodemus Harper?" Bryony wondered if she was sounding like a dunce, always asking for explanations.

"Oh, you may not have met him. He's a leader here in the city, works with the President and all. He was in your hollow several years ago, I understand, and he was quite taken with it. He told Taylor that it was the prettiest place he'd seen in all of his travels."

"It is lovely," Bryony said. "My family's lived there for over a hundred years."

"How marvelous! And here I'd thought it was this tiny frontier village. Your family came from England?"

Bryony related a closely edited version of the Talcott history. Tammy was a rapt listener, interrupting only to ask a pertinent question or refill Bryony's cup. Bryony soon turned the tables on her and began to ask about Philadelphia. Tammy related several adventures she'd had in the new nation's capital and Bryony admired her storytelling skills and her forthright manner.

"And were you frightened when the British invaded?" she asked. "The war hardly touched us, though soldiers marched through the hollow on their way to the Brandywine."

"Oh, heavens, I was petrified! We never knew from one day to the next if we were going to be turned out of our houses." She sighed. "We lost so many fine young men to the war. I do hope time bears out that their deaths weren't in vain."

"Amen," Bryony murmured.

"Oh, of course, you know how it is. Adam and his family suffered so much when Ross came back home. When they lost him at last, Taylor thought Adam was going to go out of his mind."

"Lost him?"

"Yes. Poor Matilda and Josiah, they just closed themselves up in that house after they came back from the funeral and never came out, except when Josiah went to work. Ross was such a fine person, so fun-loving and handsome. All of us girls were in love with him at one time or another. We couldn't believe anyone so young and dashing could ever die." Tammy's eyes were misty. "We lost too many boys of our set," she whispered. "Thank God Adam and Taylor were spared for us, yes?"

Bryony's mind was reeling. Tammy thought Ross was dead. Dead! Not an invalid. How could Tammy be so misled?

"I'm sorry," she said. "I guess I don't know all—"

"Oh, I can imagine that Adam's kept his grief to himself. He was always a close one. Taylor thinks you've been good for him, though. He was saying the other night that Adam was beginning to be more like he was before the war and Ross's death." Tammy looked up to see a servant enter. "Yes, Tucker?"

"Begging your pardon, ma'am, but Mrs. MacLaren is arriving."

"Mother?" Tammy rose. "Oh, heavens, she's early." She turned to Bryony. "I'm so sorry. I promised my mother-in-law we'd go shopping together this afternoon."

Bryony rose, still stunned from Tammy's revelations. "It's quite all right. I must be going, anyway." She reached out her hand. "Thank you so much for the lovely tea. I hope that I can return the invitation soon."

"I'd love that," Tammy said, following her to the foyer. "Just send me a note."

"I will."

The coach was brought around. Bryony climbed in and waved good-bye to Tammy. She told the driver to take her out to the city limits before going home, then collapsed back in the seat.

What on earth was going on in the Hawthorne house? Ross wasn't dead! He was sick, he was sorely troubled, but he certainly wasn't dead. And yet Adam and his parents had let everyone in the world believe that he was. They'd even had a funeral for him!

Bryony shivered at the thought of pronouncing a loved one dead long before that loved one's spirit departed the body. No wonder the whole house seemed so weary and sad. They'd all given up hope.

But why, she wondered, had Adam never told her about his brother? Why hadn't he told *her* that Ross was considered dead? Was she not even to be extended that modicum of trust, of faith?

She felt a wave of anger course through her. How dare they play God with Ross's life? How dare they treat her with so little respect as to think she wasn't worthy of learning the truth about the family? How dare they give up hope on Ross?

Well, she wouldn't give up. If they were going to hold rituals of death, she was going to hold one of life.

Chapter Nineteen

"Sorrow does not Kille, yet It may Blight."
—*Cassia Talcott*

When she arrived home from the MacLarens', Bryony went about her business as usual. Adam came home and they dined with Matilda and Josiah. Matilda and Josiah went off to their room as soon as dinner was finished, and Bryony noted with triumph that there was a bit of color in her mother-in-law's pale cheeks this evening, and she had added some touches of lace to her usual dark gown.

She and Adam went to their own rooms. Adam was especially quiet. She left him to his thoughts as she laid her plans for the following day.

Adam gathered her into his arms when they got into bed. Bryony was only a little disappointed when he fell asleep without making love to her.

Her heart was full tonight, but she wasn't ready to share it.

Bryony did not forget her vow to herself. She wasn't going to permit Ross Hawthorne to live out his life, shut up like a shell unto himself. She spent several more days studying, meditating, and praying. Then the day came.

Bryony spent the morning fasting and summoning up the image of Aunt Coreopsis. She placed her plan before her, asking for blessing and guidance from her gentle aunt's enduring spirit. Now, as the house began to settle into its early afternoon routine, she felt ready at last to try to truly help Ross.

She came into his room as usual and was pleased to see that he was propped up in bed, holding one of the many rocks she'd given him over the past weeks. He greeted her with a brief smile.

"I have something to ask you," she said, taking her seat on the footstool by his bed. "You may say no and I shan't be in any way offended."

He cocked an eyebrow at her and she felt a little triumph at the return of natural curiosity. But his face so immediately sank back into its sorrowful complacence that she hurried on with what she had to say.

"Do you believe in magic?" she asked.

Ross gazed at her, then frowned and shook his head. "No."

She grimaced. "Well, that will make this a bit more difficult. Let me ask this—do you believe that I believe in magic?"

He nodded at once. She grinned. "I thought you might have gathered that. I do. I not only believe in it, I have the power to use it. I want to ask a great favor of you. If you will allow me to attempt it, I may learn something that can be of help to you." She leaned forward and laid her hand over his. "You see, I also believe that you want to be well again. If you didn't," she added bluntly, "you would have up and died long before this."

Ross's mouth turned down and Bryony laughed lightly. "Josiah's son, to be sure. But that's neither here nor there. What I wish to do is employ a magic skill I possess. My aunt taught me a great deal about it, I have prayed on this, and I believe that now is the time to do it."

Ross was silent.

"Oh, what is it! Yes, of course you must know that for us to begin. It is a projection and sharing of the spirit, called kything. I have the skill to place my spirit within the body of another and see and feel and even think what they are thinking." She raised her hand. "It is not an evil magic, if that is what you fear. A Talcott may not use magic for any purpose of gaining unfair advantage or doing harm to anyone in any way. Our magic will not even work for ill."

A hint of bitter amusement showed in Ross's face. "Can't harm me more."

Bryony took his hand again. "Then you'll let me try? I vow there will be no pain to you. Aunt Cory said that people never seemed to even know that she was there. What do you say?"

Ross stared at her for a long time. Even behind

the lusterless blue eyes, she could tell that his mind was at work, weighing the matter. At last he shrugged. "I'll do it for you."

Bryony beamed. "Thank you, Ross," she said softly. "I'm honored by your trust."

She went about the room, gathering together the things she would need. She lit a good beeswax candle and circled it with a ring of purifying herbs. Then she took up the box that lay on the table next to Ross's bed and set it on the coverlet before him.

"I need something of yours to do this magic," she said. "And I believe that what I need is in this box."

Ross's face went paler. Bryony tensed. What if this was too much to ask of him? What if he refused?

But Ross reached up with one thin, shaking hand and pulled a chain out from beneath his shirt. He slipped it over his head and handed it to Bryony. She took it and used the key that hung on it to open the box.

Bryony's heart twinged with pain as she beheld the contents, though the objects meant little or nothing to her. On a bed of deep green velvet lay another key, a lock of hair, and a small, smooth piece of wood. Gently, she moved the lock of hair to one side and lifted out the key and the piece of wood.

"Just rest," she told Ross as she pulled up a chair at his bedside. "I don't know how long this will take. Have no fear."

Bryony held the key and the wood, one in each

hand, and laid her hands loosely in her lap. She had worn a white linen gown for purity and a ring of coral on her left hand to keep peace around her. She closed her eyes and let the visions come.

She was floating in moments, a soft sound of breezes and tinkling glass all around her. She was disoriented but unafraid. Somewhere, she felt Aunt Cory near her, smiling. She took comfort in the sign and began to focus on Ross. She felt her shoulders sagging, felt her heart go heavy.

The darkness came suddenly. She heard it as much as she felt it, a deep, sucking void all around her. She was out of the realm of breezes and gentle music and whirling downward into a maelstrom of feelings. There was passion and love, rage and pain, panic and fear, bitterness and regret, guilt, and shame, and sorrow. And above and around and through it all was cold despair.

Bryony felt tears behind her own eyes, hot and stinging, but they would not fall. She felt herself moving again, then settling. She was there. She was within him.

She saw the room around her, the hangings, the coverlets, the walls and ceiling as they looked from among Ross's pillows. Then, in startled amazement, she saw herself, sitting with eyes closed, head bowed, on the chair beside her.

She turned her gaze in another direction. It was too disconcerting to see her body through Ross's eyes. Yet before she could look away entirely she felt something else. She felt the slightest, faintest glimmer of hope.

Blue waves of icy sorrow swept in and carried

the feeling away in an instant. *Rest,* she said to Ross with her mind. *Let our thoughts flow like water.*

Ross obeyed her and closed his eyes. But the rest brought no peace. Images began to form before Bryony's inner sight. A bleak, cold room, cramped and wet. A lovely, laughing young woman. Running, feet drumming over frozen ground. Shouting, screaming, then searing pain. She looked down and saw a red rose of blood blossom below her shoulder. Then cold and darkness again, the cramped wet room.

Too fast, she called out to Ross.

But Ross had been carried away, his story too long untold, and Bryony had no choice but to go with him. The floodgates had opened.

Adam prowled the offices of Bacon and Hawthorne Shipping. His conversation with Taylor still plagued him, making him short and snappish with the clerks. *Had* he gone soft since he'd met Bryony? Did he turn down the job in Chester because he didn't want to face the issue of magic again? Had he lost his hunger for truth, for proof?

He didn't like the implications. He didn't like the idea that he might have lost his edge, lost the impetus that had driven him for so long.

He scowled as he sat down at his desk once again. He was the same man he'd always been, he told himself. He hadn't forgotten the brother who lay in that lonely room even now, out of reach of all help and hope. He hadn't set aside his hatred of the people who had bilked his parents and fed their desperate hopes with fraudulent claims and silly acts.

And while Bryony might have been raised with such folderol, she had left all that magic claptrap behind in Cold Springs Hollow. She had faced the truth bravely and accepted that there was a better, more reasoned and honest way to live.

Honesty. That was what it all came down to, didn't it? he thought, shuffling more papers around on his desk. He had urged her to face the truth and accept the honest facts of life. And he couldn't imagine anyone so faithfully truthful as his wife.

But Taylor had challenged him once more last night, demanding to know if he, Adam, had been truthful with Bryony. Why didn't Bryony know anything about the time he had spent unmasking witches and magicians and false healers? he had asked.

Adam didn't like the answer. He was ashamed. He was ashamed to tell Bryony that he had endeavored to rout out and destroy the lives and reputations of people like herself and generations of her beloved Talcott family. He didn't want to see her face when he told her that he had come to Cold Springs Hollow to bring her low.

"Damnation," he muttered, crumpling a shipping bill in his fist.

He'd prided himself on his ability to look truth squarely in the eye. He'd urged Bryony to do the same, claiming in lofty tones that it was the only way to live.

And he still believed it was. What he needed to do was bring his truth to her once and for all. No more hiding and concealing his past. He had to show her that he was no hypocrite, demanding that she hold to standards that he himself could not maintain.

He shoved his chair back and reached for his hat. "Barkin, I'm going out. I should be back in an hour or so. Tell my father if he asks that I've gone to clear up an important debt."

He couldn't wait for the coach to be brought around. He set off at a brisk pace for home.

Bryony was lost.

Ross's memories had engulfed her and filled her mind with their darkness and their pain. She was with him, she *was* him, sitting in that icy room, her uniform ragged and inadequate to keep the cold from penetrating into her very bones.

But she had rage to warm her. The Hawthorne temper was simmering in her, lively and hot. She looked at the man seated next to her. Her heart contracted with pity at the bruises that marred his young face.

"Say, Conklin," she heard herself saying. "What do you call a hundred members of Parliament all chained together at the bottom of the ocean?"

The man raised his weary eyes to meet hers. Bryony grinned. "A good start," she said.

The man began to laugh. But his laughter quickly turned to hacking, wheezing coughs and when he took his hand away from his mouth, Bryony saw specks of blood on his fingers.

"It'll be time soon," she said, not knowing what she meant. "Hold on, lad. You'll be sipping ale and tossing your sweet Betty before you know it."

The room began to melt and shift around her. It was a gorgeous spring day and she was walking beside the lovely young woman she had seen earlier. Waves of love lapped around her now, and she felt the startling intensity of Ross's desire for this woman. How different it was for men, she thought; then her own consciousness was washed away and the girl dropped her hand and faded into the shadows of the far trees.

"Don't go," she cried aloud, and heard Ross's voice speaking the words. "Oh, God, Elyssa, come back!"

But the swirling darkness had her again. The icy room, the chains she now saw on her ankles. The key. The key from the box. It lay in her hand and she looked down to see a man in a dirty British uniform lying on the floor at her feet, his head crushed and bleeding on one side. She stared in horror, raised her hand to push her blond hair from her face, and saw the brick she had managed to pry from the wall over many long days. There were bits of blood and hair on it.

No time to think. She was running through the dark, dragging Conklin with her. Conklin was wheezing and coughing up blood; he could barely run.

There were more men outside. Eight more of them, she knew that somehow. There was an open field and just beyond, outlined by the pale moon, a thicket of trees. That's where they had to go.

Shouting. Musket fire. Conklin dropped at her feet.

"No!"

She stooped to help him. Conklin shoved her away. "Run!" he croaked.

"I can't leave you!" But she did. She kept running. She couldn't pull him with her.

She was running, racing barefoot over the icy ground. The chafed spots on her ankles began to bleed. A sharp report rang out. A flaming hot wasp's stinger entered her back. She looked down and saw the blood coming below her shoulder. She kept running. She kept running.

She reached the trees and looked back. A soldier stood over Conklin's inert body. She saw the musket go up and then come down with a fury toward Conklin's lolling head. She screamed but even as she cried out, she was turning and running, tearing through the brush, heading deep into the woods.

Miles passed beneath her feet. Days and nights seemed to melt and blend over her head in a sickening whirl of suns and moons. She was sick, growing weaker by the second.

And then she was being handed into a cart and she lost all the images at once and sank into blackness and the stormy colors of despair.

Adam scowled at Dulcie. "What do you mean, she didn't go out?"

"Well, Mr. Hawthorne, sir, I mean that she didn't call for the coach, she didn't take no horse, and her hats and cloaks are all where they're supposed to be."

Adam bit back a curse. He'd already looked in their room himself. He'd searched the garden, the parlors, and even checked to see if Bryony had joined his mother in her sitting room. Matilda had told him she'd seen no sign of her for hours now. Where would she have gone?

He set off up the stairs. Perhaps she was in the library. She often borrowed books to read, though she said she preferred to bring them back to her own sitting room rather than sit in the vast, unheated library with its dark leathers and mahogany bookcases.

But she wasn't there now. He felt a growing apprehension within him. She was somewhere in the house; he sensed it. She had wandered out; she hadn't been abducted. She was . . .

His footsteps turned of their own accord to the north wing. When he reached the hallway that led to Ross's room, he heard a scream. He broke into a run.

Where was she?

Bryony was weeping, aching, heartbroken. And she was lost in the dark. Voices rose and fell around her, light occasionally pierced her sight and then was snuffed out. All was lost. They were all dead—not just Conklin and the guard she had killed, but all the others who had put their trust in her, their captain. She had promised them freedom and she had delivered them into the hands of death.

Wailing sounded in the distance. Winds lashed at her, tumbling her this way and that in the cold darkness. She couldn't move, couldn't speak. She was trapped in this howling place of pain and she knew she deserved to be there. She would stay and await her turn. A corridor of midnight stretched before her and she floated toward it, her heart gone and her hope utterly banished.

If only she would die and put an end to it.

Chapter Twenty

"When Your Heart is Afire, some Sparkes will Flye out of the Mouth."
—*Cassia Talcott*

Adam stood in the doorway of Ross's room, openmouthed with outrage. In that instant, Bryony slumped over in her chair and slid to the floor in a heap.

Adam was at her side in two long steps, scooping her into his arms. He turned to the bed. "Ross, what the hell is happening?"

Ross seemed to be struggling up from deep water. "Magic," he mumbled. "She's . . . in me. . . ."

Adam didn't wait to hear more. He dashed into the hall, shouting for help. Dulcie and Collins came racing up from the kitchen. "See to my brother," Adam said to Collins. "Dulcie, come with me."

He raced down the hall to the front parlor, crashed through the doors, and laid Bryony down on the couch before the fire. "Get Cook to run for Dr. Morrison," he barked at Dulcie. "Fetch some brandy and another blanket. Go!"

He grabbed the afghan from the back of the couch and began tucking it around Bryony. She was pale as ivory and like ice to his touch. She didn't move, she didn't speak, she hardly seemed to breathe. It was as if she had vanished inside herself.

"Bryony," he said, rubbing at her hands. "Bryony, wake up!"

Dulcie came hurrying in, the brandy bottle and a glass on a tray. She quickly poured the drink and Adam seized it and held it to Bryony's pale, bluish lips.

"Drink it," he said, tipping her chin up. "Damnation, Bryony, drink it!"

He managed to get some of it into her. It came trickling out at the corner of her mouth.

"No, you don't," he exclaimed. "You will drink it, miss, if I have to put a pipe down you and blow it in!"

He tipped the glass up once more and this time the amber liquid flowed in and stayed. After a long moment, he saw her swallow.

"Praise be," Dulcie murmured.

"Where's that other blanket?" Dulcie fetched it from the hall. Adam laid it over Bryony and tucked all the ends in snugly around her. "Build up the fire," he told the maid. "Make it roar! God's blood, she's like ice."

Dulcie scurried to do his bidding. Adam began scrubbing at Bryony's cheeks, reciting a long litany of dire curses. "Bryony," he growled. "Don't do this to me. Wake up, love. Wake up!"

But she lay still and limp, as if her will had been utterly eclipsed and life was only moments away from its last ebb. Despite more brandy, the heavy blankets, and the roasting fire, she was not getting any warmer. Her skin, normally so peach-fresh, was even more pallid than when he had found her.

"Bryony," he whispered, his desperation growing with his fear. "What were you doing in there? Why can't you speak to me? Why are you so damned cold?"

He leaped up and made a turn before the fire. Then, with another snarl, he climbed onto the couch with her and surrounded her with his embrace, wrapping his arms and legs about her. His anger and fear kindled hot within him and he clutched her to him, willing his body to give her his heat.

"Come on," he murmured in her ear. "Wake up, wife. It's time to greet your husband." He gave her a little shake. "Bryony. It's morning, love. Time to get up."

His voice shook. It wasn't working. She was scarcely breathing. He turned her to face him, both of them crowded together in the small space. He took her face in his hands and kissed her, her cold lips shocking against his urgent warm ones.

He heard a small breath escape her. Wildly,

he followed his instincts and began to kiss and caress her. "Come, love," he whispered in her ear. "You know what I want. You know what we love to do together. I won't let you go until I've tasted you again. I won't let you go until I've buried myself deep inside you once more and then once more and then again and again and again." His hands traced their way to her hips and he pressed her closer. "Feel me," he urged. "Make me grow for you. And I promise I will cherish you everywhere, kiss you everywhere, make you pant and sigh and cry out with my loving you. I love you, Bryony. Come back to my love." He sank his lips once more onto hers and clung to her with such fierceness that he thought his own bones might crack.

Bryony heard the voice, far off, as if in another life altogether, another world.

"Bryony, it's time to wake up, love."

Who was Bryony? she thought. He didn't know any Bryony.

He didn't know? She didn't know?

She felt herself tumble slowly in the dark. It didn't matter. Nothing mattered. Time was growing shorter and the darkness deeper. Nothing would bother him ever again.

"Bryony!"

She stirred. Who was that? She felt she wanted to go and find out.

"Bryony, damn it, get back here and satisfy your husband!"

She felt a ray of light pierce her inner vision,

hurting her head. What now? Who was disturbing him?

"That's my love." The voice was coming closer. Or was she drawing closer to the voice?

The darkness was thinning. She began to feel again, first an icy blast, then a welcome ripple of heat. What was happening? Where was Ross?

She felt something. Something very solid and real. Arms around her.

"Bryony, come back. Keep coming. Keep coming to me."

She felt a horrid jolt of pain and slid back into her own mind, her own body, in one dizzying, stomach-churning mental motion. She was still pinned, though, and she couldn't seem to move her arms. But there was more—

Adam! Her heart shouted for joy. It was Adam! She knew those lips, knew that voice, knew that warmth, knew those arms, knew that—

"Oh, my goodness!"

"Bryony!"

"Adam, oh, Adam!" She buried her face in his chest and burst into tears.

Then the doctor arrived, Matilda at his heels, and there was a flurry of activity. Dr. Morrison checked Bryony for every injury and malady he could think of but could find no ill results. He took Adam aside as Dulcie fussed around her mistress, offering hot tea and tucking pillows in behind her.

"You say she was unconscious when you found her?"

"Not just unconscious," Adam said, rubbing a

hand across the back of his neck. "She seemed, well, I know this sounds ludicrous, but she seemed almost dead. If I couldn't hear her heart just faintly beating, I would have said she was dead."

"And yet she seems quite fine now." Dr. Morrison nodded to where Bryony sat before the fire, roses in her cheeks once more, sipping tea. "What happened?"

"I wish I knew. My only guess is that she had some sort of a fit or perhaps a . . ."

"A what?"

"Spell," Adam said, his voice expressionless. "A fainting spell."

Bryony felt an explosion was coming. For two days after Adam found her in Ross's room, she waited, wondering when Adam would speak. He was kindly and solicitous of her by day and in the night, when he was deep in sleep, he clutched her to him as if she might disappear at any moment. But he didn't speak to her, except to ask after her health, tell her some bit of news from the office, or discuss the weather.

Bryony felt she would soon go out of her mind, but she kept her peace and pondered all that she had seen and felt when she had occupied Ross with her own spirit. It was a wonder to know that she did indeed have the skill; there was no question of that now. Still, what she had learned of Ross was of far greater importance.

She had known that he had suffered but she hadn't known how deeply scarred he had been. She had felt realms of physical and emotional pain that had no equal in her own experience, not even when her parents had died.

She tried to sort all the pieces together. She knew their sum, but she could not make out the whole shape of his story. He'd been a soldier. He had been beaten, shot, imprisoned. He had loved someone and lost her. He had tried to escape. He had tried to rescue someone. He'd killed a man. He had run away.

She wanted to learn the story but she knew enough to realize that each day, each hour, Ross Hawthorne lived in guilt, and regret, and despair. Her first instincts had been correct: he was waiting to die.

But it wasn't his time. There was more that he had to do. And now that she knew some of his story and his pain, she could set about helping him heal.

There was one more piece of the puzzle she longed to see, however, and she knew she wouldn't find it in Ross's room or within his spirit. It was here, in the room she shared with Adam and in the rooms where Matilda and Josiah lived and ate and slept and worked. It was the piece that explained why a family would hide their own son away and tell no one, not even a new member of the family, that he existed and how he lived.

She had no more time to ponder the matter or to plan, though. The explosion came two days later.

"Bryony."

She looked up and saw Adam standing in the doorway of the parlor where he had carried her the afternoon she had been lost in Ross's tortured spirit. She set aside her book and waited.

"I have to ask you something."

"Go on," she said. "You know that I have no secrets from you."

He scowled. "No, I don't know that. How long have you been seeing my brother?"

She lowered her head. "Yes. You're right. There are many secrets between us." She looked up at him as he came to stand by the fire. "I discovered his room quite by accident about three months ago. I was lonely here and needed a friend, so I began to visit with Ross. I was shocked to learn that you had a brother, let alone one closeted away in this very house. You'd never spoken to me about him. Your mother and father never speak of him. So I let him remain a secret, too." She frowned. "Now I wish I hadn't."

"Yes. You should have come to me at once."

"I know. But I was afraid you would be angry with me and that you would forbid me to visit him. Was I wrong?"

Adam shrugged. "Possibly not. But didn't you also keep your visits a secret because you were going in there and trying your magic claptrap on him?"

Bryony was stung. "It is not claptrap. How can you say that?" She rose from her chair. "There is another secret I haven't told you, Adam. I've kept it from you because until now I scarcely believed it myself, but I am possessed of magical talent. And not just one gift. Many gifts."

"Bryony, that's madness. You said you'd relinquished all of that nonsense that day in the grove by your family's house. You tried and tried and there was no magic to be found. Why didn't you stop?"

"I did. It simply came upon me."

Adam looked away in disgust. "Bryony—"

"No, Adam. It did. It was shortly after our wedding, perhaps even that very day, I'm not sure. But slowly, things began to happen. I found I was seeing visions in mud puddles and water basins. I caused plants to blossom at Taylor's party. Trees began speaking to me. Locks open when I say but a word to them. I'm astonished that you didn't notice it yourself!"

"And why didn't you tell me that these things were happening to you?" Adam's expression was stony.

"Because I had given you my word. I made a vow to you that I wouldn't mention magic here in Philadelphia and that I'd do my utmost to be like the people here. And I have done just that, haven't I?"

"That's beside the point," Adam exclaimed. "Whether you mentioned it or not, you went into my brother's room and you tried to work one of your wild spells on him. Didn't you?"

Bryony cocked her head and narrowed her eyes. "I worked more than one spell on him, Adam. And if you cared anything about your brother, you would have noticed that those spells have worked."

"Rocks and weeds and perfumed oils and candles cannot change my brother's state! They cannot change anything!"

"No, but the love and the power of magic behind them can change things."

"They—" Adam paused and drew a deep breath. "Just what were you doing in there the other day when I found you?"

"Transportation of the spirit. Mine into his. My spirit entered his body and saw and felt as he does."

"Bryony, that's ridiculous."

"Call it what you like, but do you agree that you have never told me one word about your brother, nor have your mother or father or your friends or the servants in this house?"

"Only one or two of the servants know about Ross. And they would never tell."

"And do you agree that Ross seldom speaks more than three words in a space of hours?"

"Given. What is your point?"

"Then how do you account for my knowledge that Ross was captured and imprisoned during the war? That he and a man named Conklin escaped together along with eight other men? That all of them died while escaping, save for Ross?"

Adam only stared at her, eyes cold. She went on.

"How do I know that he was in love with a lovely young woman with flame-red hair and that he lost her? How can it possibly be that I know he pried a brick from the wall of his horrible cell and that he used that rock to smash a British guard over the head and steal the keys to their freedom?"

She walked around to the back of her chair and rested her hands on its back. "How might I have learned that to save his sanity, to keep his hope alive, he had spent hours, days with Conklin, planning the houses they were going to build when they got free? They picked out every nail, every roof shingle, every stick of furniture and laid them in place, waiting to be free again."

"He might have told you. Taylor might have told you."

"No one but Tammy MacLaren has told me anything. And all she told me was what the world thinks it knows about Ross—that he's dead! Yes, Ross might have told me. But he didn't. He cannot. Most of the time, he can recall very little of what happened to him during the war. But when I joined my mind and spirit to his, I saw it all. He shared it with me."

Adam had turned and was staring down into the fire. Bryony waited.

"If you know what my brother has gone through," he said at last, "how can you do what you have been doing to him?"

"Doing to him?"

"How can you go into his room, to his sickbed, and wave your silly stones and potions over his head and promise that his life will be restored to him as it was before the war?"

"I would never do that."

He twisted about to face her. "You have. You just said you've been working your spells on him."

"I have. But I've never promised him that I could give him back his old life. He wouldn't want it even if I could. Just the same as you and I and everyone else, Ross is older now. The mere passage of days would have changed him, had nothing else. I can't restore his youth or his innocence or his friends and companions to him. No magic can work that way."

"What will it take to prove to you that there is no magic?" he shouted. "Life simply happens; there is no way that powders or chanting or little rocks can influence the way the world moves at all!"

"Yes, they can!" she replied. "They do! I know. I've seen it hundreds of times. My family has been influencing the way things go in this world for hundreds of years." She stepped closer. "It may not work the way you think it should or even the way we want it to, but it can work and it does. I know this. I have the Talcott powers."

"Bryony, it's nonsense. Magic will not restore my brother's mind. Magic cannot start a fire. Magic doesn't make the crops grow. What is destined to be will be. That's all."

"I don't believe you. How can you say this? You're a magus yourself."

"No, I'm not," he groaned, turning to face the fire. "I used to be an entertainer, a trickster who amused people with his antics. The magic you saw me perform in the hollow was mere illusion."

"I don't understand."

"I used to be a magician. I performed all over. But I gave it up. I didn't want to be a part of that trickery any longer." He put his hands up on the mantel. "I know all of the tricks, Bryony, do you understand? And that is how I have used my talents up until a few months ago, when I came back here to work for my father."

Bryony came around to stand at the opposite end of the long hearth. "What has any of this to do with my gifts? Or with Ross?"

Adam let out a long breath. "I have another secret. One I intended to share with you, when the events of the last few years were far behind us."

Bryony waited. Adam continued. "For years I was a magician, an entertainer; you know that much. I performed everywhere, all the colonies, in England, in France. But when I came back from the war, I set it all aside. I took on a new task. That of using my knowledge of magic and trickery to unmask the frauds who claimed to be witches and sorcerers and emissaries from the spirit world. I went wherever I was summoned and I put to rout all the cold, bloody fakers who preyed on people's hopes and desperation."

"Go on." Her voice was soft, controlled.

"It became my goal and my profession to prove that magic was nothing more than foolery and that at their worst, those who claimed to practice it were nothing less than blackhearted thieves. I saw poor people bilked out of a lifetime of savings. I saw families destroyed when the healers, their last hope, came and fanned the flames of their longing and then left, taking their money and their hope with them in their heavy pockets." He turned to face her. "I was very good at it, Bryony. I am known for it."

She gazed at him, her mouth slightly open, as if she had suddenly lost her breath. She shook her head. "Adam. Say it isn't true. Say that you didn't—"

"I did," he said. "I was told that there was a whole family of such frauds in a little town called Cold Springs Hollow. I allowed my friends to persuade me to go, one last time, before I had to go to work for my father." He gripped the mantel, his knuckles showing white. "I came to the hollow to reveal to all that the Hag of the Hollow was a miserable cheat and a fraud. That all the Talcotts had been duping the people in that little valley for—"

"Stop it!" Bryony raised her hands to her ears. "Don't tell me this!"

"It's the truth! Aren't you sick of the secrets between us?"

She took a step toward him. "You did this? You planned to make a fool of me? To shame the name of my family? Why?"

He winced at the bewildered hurt in her voice. "I did. At first. But when I got to know you and saw how deeply this magic nonsense had its grip on you, I couldn't stand it. You were so beautiful and bright and kind and yet you wouldn't, couldn't see what it was doing to you. Your mad, futile quest for your so-called gift was destroying you, wearing you down. I wanted to get you away from the hollow and show you that the world gets along just fine without incantations or other silly tricks." He spread his hands. "And I fell in love with you."

"You fell in love with a fraud?" she asked. "A blackhearted thief? A deceiver who preys on the weaknesses of suffering people?" She shook her head in wonderment. "No wonder you were so comforting that day in the grove. You were celebrating my failure!" She paced away, twisting her skirt in her hands. "And you brought me here to save me from myself and the poison of my family? How noble of you, Adam."

"No, Bryony, I swear, I did it because I was in love with you. I didn't want to be without you. And I didn't want you living in the hollow, thinking about all you imagined you had lost." He stepped toward her. "And hasn't it been better? Haven't you seen that it's all right not to rely on superstitions? Hasn't living here in Philadelphia shown you that? That people can survive and even thrive without a witch or a magus to tell them what to do and when to do it?"

"No, I haven't." She turned to him, struggling to keep her anger and pain from turning into tears. She wanted to hold fast before him. "What you've shown me is a family destroyed by doubts and fears and resentments and what-might-have-beens. I see my husband hating his father. I see your brother suffering, lost inside himself because all the lot of you can do is wring your hands and say 'Poor Ross!' I see your mother wandering about this house like a lost soul." She placed her hands on her hips and eyed him squarely. "I may be a foolish country girl, unable to let go of old ways and too naive to know the ways of the world, but I will tell you this, Adam Hawthorne. I don't see that your world is in such good shape for all your reason and rationality. I saw a lot more love and caring and folks helping others and respecting others in a single day back in backwater, backwoods, backward Cold Springs Hollow than I've seen in all this time in your fancy Philadelphia!"

Adam stiffened. "Then why don't you do something? Go ahead! I dare you! Take a magic rock and heal Ross! Give my mother back the joy she once had. Show me some magic words to say to make my father—" He broke off.

"Love you?" she asked softly. "Why not? Magic brought you to me. Magic made you fall in love with a plain country witch when you could have had any of the beautiful, accomplished ladies here, or in Boston or New York or Charleston."

"Don't be ridiculous."

"Am I being ridiculous? Perhaps I am. But the next time you're drawn to a faraway place to meet with a witch, perhaps you'd better think twice about how you ended up there. And the next time you see someone open a locked door with a sliver of bone and a few words, perhaps you'd better give a little thought as to how that happened. And next time you're sleeping alone in that bed, up in that cold, dark room of yours, perhaps you should ask yourself why it is that you can't keep your hands off of me when we're in it together. Then take a peek under the mattress. Magic is everywhere, Adam!"

"Bryony, you can't—"

"Don't you dare tell me what I can and can't! I've seen what life is like when people refuse to see the magic in the world, within themselves. Magic is all around, Adam, even in Philadelphia, but I'm going back to where folks see it and use it and thank the Lord that it exists!"

He heard a rustle of skirts, turned, and saw her vanish out the door.

Chapter Twenty-One

"No Questioner can Hope to Banishe all Woe. Nor should Any try, for a Single Teare may moisten the hardest Earthe and make it readye for the Spring."

—*Cassia Talcott*

Bryony wiped her eyes and raised the leather shade to look out at the rain-drenched countryside through which they were passing. It was the same as before, all dripping trees and muddy, running creeks, and she felt as if she were just a part of the whole, weepy mess.

She was glad to have the coach to herself at last. The last passenger had alighted an hour back and almost as soon as the wheels had begun to turn again, Bryony gave in and poured out the tears that she'd been holding in since she'd climbed aboard the coach in Philadelphia.

Adam had proven false. It had been a horrible revelation. If he had been false with another woman, she might have understood, been able to face it, maybe. But he'd been false in a more hurtful, deeper way. He'd pretended to love her and to believe in her. He'd tricked her, mocking her family and their gifts with his sham. He'd taken her away from her home, her people, not to cherish her as his wife, as he had promised, but to change her into someone else entirely—he was ashamed of her as she was. Moreover, he was not only ashamed of her magic, but he'd sworn himself an enemy of all magic and all persons who had made magic. He took money each time he held one of them up to ridicule and scorn!

She bit her lip. And then there was Ross. Adam had let the world believe that his brother was dead when all the time he had been lying in that lonely room, cut off from people, from life.

She wanted to take Adam Hawthorne and shake him until his eyes rolled. How dare he—he—

How dare he still cause her heart to thrill at the very idea of him?

She loved him. That was what hurt most of all. Her pride had taken her away from Philadelphia and that dark, unhappy house, but her heart was still there, held solely in Adam's keeping. The memory of the love they'd shared, the laughter and merriment and the hours of passionate coupling held her heart in those rooms above that icy hall. If only she were carrying a baby, some part of Adam that she could take with her, she could find some scrap of happiness. But she knew without a doubt that no baby had been conceived in any of those ecstatic moments together. She was alone.

There was nothing to do now but go home to the hollow and start over again. She couldn't pretend that nothing had happened; everyone knew that it had. But she could be at peace there, among people who needed her and cared about her. True, the Talcott line would fail, but she could leave a legacy of healing and comfort and magic that would serve the memory of the name as long as it should last.

She let the tears come again as she thought of how Matthew had been convinced that she and Adam were fated to be together and that their joining would be the basis of a new and stronger line. How hopeful they all had been. How disappointed they all would be when she told them how foolish those hopes had proven.

She shook herself gently and wrung out her handkerchief. She couldn't go on feeling sorry for herself. At least she had a home to come to and people who loved her. It would be a welcome change from the bitterness and sorrow of the Hawthorne house.

How would Ross fare? she couldn't help wondering. Would he tell anyone of their visits together? Would he ever get better? It was another regret that she had carried away from that house. She hoped that somehow, some way, Ross would find the strength to return from the hell he had been living in for so long. She prayed the Hawthornes would come to their senses and treat him like a living being once again.

Would anyone find her secret plot of herbs in the back garden and tend to them? She'd never told anyone that they were there, but perhaps Adam's mother might chance by there.

And what about Matilda and Josiah? She had been positive that the love herbs she'd slipped into their bed had been working. Matilda went pink-cheeked as a girl when Josiah looked at her in the mornings these days. And in the evenings, too.

It didn't matter, she told herself as the coach rattled on toward the hollow. That part of her life was over now and she must put it aside.

Matthew was waiting for her outside the Laughing Dog when her coach pulled in, although she hadn't sent word that she was coming. She didn't get the chance to question him about it when she climbed down to take his large, weathered hand.

"There's no time to waste," Matthew said before she could get a word out. "The fever is back and it's worse than ever before."

"How bad?" she asked, reaching for her satchel.

"Three dead and I don't think Demelza Leary will last past sunset." Matthew's face was grim.

"Take me home to get my remedies and I'll get right to work."

Horace Benedict was in his element. The house was elegant, the company of the best, the food and drink superb. What was more, all of these wealthy, silly, would-be aristocrats had paid money to see him perform. It was perfect.

Except for that one man at the side of the drawing room. The one with the dark auburn hair and the darkly glittering green eyes. He was watching Horace like a fox watches a rabbit hole. His look made Horace wish he'd worn a cooler waistcoat and breeches.

That ass Weston had brought him tonight, that much Horace knew. He'd never seen the fellow before. But if he was a friend of Weston's, Benedict reasoned, he was rich, that was certain. And watchful or not, he might be an avenue into the center of Philadelphia society, a place Horace Benedict desperately hoped to reach soon.

Horace went on with his performance, bending pins, then needles, then nails. He was about to move on to his grand finale when, from out of the corner of his eye, he saw the man with the fox's eyes go over to Beau Weston, lean down, and whisper something in his ear. Then the man left.

Well, that's a relief, Benedict thought. He moved to his set of spoons.

"A moment, sir!"

There was a murmur from the crowd as Weston rose to his feet. "If you please, Master Benedict. I would so love it if you would do me the honor of using one of my spoons."

Benedict started, but quickly recovered his composure. "Oh, Mr. Weston, I couldn't possibly. It would be a crime to ruin one of your fine Sheffield pieces."

"I'll consider it a crime if you refuse me," Beau said with a charming smile. He was already making his way up to the table where Benedict was plying his trade by candlelight. "Please. If you'd be so kind."

Benedict shook his head. "I'm afraid it might not be accomplished with an object that doesn't belong to me. The spirits can be quite temperamental about sending their powers if all is not as they expect it to be."

"Oh, what a shame. Here, I tell you what, old fellow. I'll make a present of it to you." Beau pressed the spoon into Benedict's hand. "Now it is yours and yours alone. Your spirits may work away with a will!" He turned to go back to his chair. "Oh, but you may want more light, sir. Pray let me get you another candle." Beau bent down and pulled the shuttered lamp from under the table.

Benedict choked. It was his hidden heat source. He placed the objects on the tabletop, just over the opening that was blocked from view by the other candlestick. With their thin pewter softened from the heat below, it was no problem to bend his objects without any obvious movements of his hand or fingers. What was Weston trying to do?

He decided he had to save face. The audience was beginning to murmur and discuss among themselves, always a bad sign. He wanted their rapt attention. He took Weston's heavy silver spoon with a tight smile and held it up before the crowd. Weston moved off to one side, very near the spot where the man with the fox look had been standing.

Benedict closed his eyes. He called on the spirit world to grant him the power to change immovable metal with just the power of his faith and mental strength.

Sweat was pouring down his face before he had to give it up. The audience had watched politely for a while, then gradually turned away and began to chat about the weather, the business climate, local politics, and gossip. Weston approached him, smiling.

"Not so good, eh, Horace?" he said, keeping his voice low.

"You—you—" Benedict spluttered.

"Yes, well, don't exert yourself, old man. You've worked hard enough for one night. Here's a penny for your troubles, sir. If you go now, maybe you can find your way out the back before these good people come after you and demand their money back."

Benedict went gray at the thought.

"Oh, and Horace?" Beau's smile broadened. "Don't show your face anywhere around here again. I won't be so gentlemanly next time."

Horace Benedict bolted for the back door and went out into the night, headed for the western frontier. Beau Weston continued to smile. He'd just decided to begin a new and delightful career.

Adam had been out most of the night, first with Beau Weston in Chester, then walking back and forth along the waterfront in Philadelphia. It was a dangerous place to be walking at this late, late hour, but Adam's mood was so dark and his manner so forbidding that any who came close enough to attempt anything questionable were immediately driven off with one fierce stare.

When Bryony had left, he'd been thunderstruck, then outraged. What a ridiculous female tantrum she was throwing, he'd ranted to himself. He was the one who had feared for her life when she had sent herself into the silly trance. He wasn't the one who was clinging to outdated, nonsensical superstitions despite all evidence and teaching to the contrary. He wasn't the one who had been sneaking off to visit his brother and trying out all manner of nostrums and mock cures on a helpless invalid. He was the one who was trying to protect his family and carry on.

But as the days passed and there was no word from Bryony, he began to wonder if there was more than one tale to tell in this matter.

Bryony's words on the last day finally struck home and now, as he paced about the docks, he was turning them over and over in his mind. What had she meant about him being drawn to Cold Springs by magic? He'd heard a secondhand report of witchcraft in the western hills and he'd gone to investigate, because that was what he did. That was all.

But then there were the Four Horsemen, the four old men, led by Matthew Cowley, who had quite matter-of-factly told him that he was fated to marry "their Bryony." And damned if that wasn't just what had happened.

What was it she had said about a locked door and a sliver of bone? He'd been so top-heavy that night coming home from Taylor's party that he hardly remembered how they had gotten home. Yet he had recalled something about a lock and some words to the birds, hadn't he?

Magic is all around, she'd said. But how could that be?

Then there was Ross. Ross, who had hardly spoken in years, had been agitated for several days after Bryony had left. Adam had gone to visit him one evening after work, just as he always did, and found him sitting up in bed, holding a small cambric pouch in his hands. And to Adam's astonishment, he had demanded to know where Bryony had gone. Adam spent that evening in Ross's room, listening with alarm, anger, and then wonder as Ross related how Bryony had been visiting him, attending him, treating him as if he were a living, breathing human instead of just a sad object in a bed.

And Ross swore on his life and the lives of the friends he'd lost in the war that Bryony had indeed, somehow, come inside his mind. He'd been worried that the experience had been too much for her and that was why she hadn't come to see him.

When Adam told him that Bryony had left and why, Ross had thrown the pouch at him, then all of his pillows in quick succession. "Dunce!" he had raged, his rusty voice packing a world of disgust and indignation into a few words. "Ass! You just let her walk out of here? Are you mad?"

Adam couldn't have been more astonished if the carpet had raised up and flown him around the room. He'd retreated soon after, seeing that Ross was weary from his outburst. But he cherished that burst of anger when he'd gotten over the shock. That was the Ross Hawthorne that he knew!

He turned away from the waterfront and started up Chestnut Street. Ross was right. He was an ass.

Stupid pride and stubborn will had caused him to lie to Bryony about everything. He'd been so proud of his efforts to reveal deceits and delusions that he'd missed the delusions that he'd created for himself.

That was why he hadn't stepped up tonight and unmasked that shammer, Horace Benedict. He'd handed the job over to Beau and Beau had been delighted to take on the task. Let him have it, if he likes, Adam thought, making his way toward home at last. He himself no longer had any interest in it.

He thought again of the light in Ross's eyes when he'd talked about Bryony. There had been more light and life-force there than Adam had seen since the day he'd returned from the war to find his brother in his room, sick, gray-faced, and silent. Bryony had managed to rouse him from his stupor, tempt him with food, and bring him among the living—such as they were in the Hawthorne house. Was it magic? Or was it merely the magnificent power of her loving spirit?

Tempestuous nights in her arms also came to his mind. She'd awakened fires in him that he'd never known to exist, and together they'd explored unparalleled heights of sensuality, intimacy, and loveplay. His heart and mind were so full of her that it was as if she had invaded his very soul, but instead of conquest and havoc, she'd set up a home there. He was bound to her and felt himself a most willing captive. Was that magic? Or just the right woman coming along at the right time?

She'd touched his mother's sadness, too, somehow, he thought. The stark gray and black gowns had begun to give way to lavender and mauve, with a touch of lace now and then. She'd been out in the garden again. Was it Bryony's magic? Or just time healing the old wounds of their past?

"Ye gods," he whispered.

He was questioning nearly everything in his life. The very foundations of his beliefs, the shape of the world around him, was changing and expanding and it was more than a little unsettling. Bryony was turning everything upside down. He'd spent his adult life fooling people about magic, or trying to disabuse them of their foolish beliefs in magic, and here he was today, married to someone who claimed she was a witch, passionately in love with her, and still more doubts were creeping in through the cracks in his armor of skepticism and rigid reasoning. He was entertaining the possibility that this someone—someone he loved—could actually work magic.

He strode through the foyer and straight up the stairs to his room. He went to the bed and sat down on the satin coverlet, shaking his head with disbelief at himself. There it was, just as she had said. He could feel himself flushing and stirring, and quick, vivid images of Bryony naked and smiling in his arms flashed across his mind. He leaped off the bed and thrust an arm beneath the mattress.

"Why, the little—" he breathed, pulling out the small linen bag of herbs. He sniffed its contents. He had no idea what was in it, but whatever it was, it seemed to have an effect on him.

Or did it? For all he knew, what aroused him was the recollection of all the marvelous, delirious nights he'd spent on this bed, embracing silken Bryony, adoring her beautiful body and sweet, warm spirit.

It was ludicrous. Preposterous. He knew better!

And yet . . . He recalled the conversation he'd had with Matthew that first day in Cold Springs Hollow. What had they been arguing about? Adam had said that he only made people believe that magic was taking place. Matthew had replied, "What's the difference?"

Belief was the key. He'd made no magic, yet he'd done it with such skill that people believed they were witnesses to magical forces at work. Suppose Bryony did something similar, but more powerful? Suppose she made real magic, but did it with such skill that nobody saw there was magic at work. Maybe that was the nature of real magic—that it was so subtle and so closely aligned with nature and the spirits of the people involved that it became an invisible and seamless part of the whole. Except if they believed—then it became real and clear and natural.

What was the difference, indeed? What was it he wanted in this life, if not Bryony's love, his family's happiness, and his own peace of mind? Which would he prefer—a lifetime without Bryony, watching his family slowly crumble into dust, secure in the knowledge that he was right about this magic business? Or to spend a lifetime with someone who brought joy to everyone around her—especially his troubled family—and whose love filled him with wild passion as well as deep satisfaction and peace?

Call it love, call it character, call it magic—what mattered was that he was beginning to believe that it worked, and that it was Bryony who made it work. He was in love with a witch. She was his beautiful, sensual, spellbinding witch-wife.

And he was going after her. Now.

He strode out the door and burst into the hallway, bellowing for his horse, his coat, his hat. Servants came scurrying from all four corners of the house, alarmed at the sudden disturbance of the usual somnolence of the Hawthorne house.

"Get me my coat and gloves!" Adam shouted, swinging a startled Dulcie up into the air. "And enough food to last me to the frontier. Hurry now, there's a good girl." He set her down with a laugh and gave her a gentle shove in the direction of the pantry.

"Adam, what is it? What's happened? Is something wrong with Ross?" His mother came hurrying in, a clutch of vivid red tulips in her hands.

"No, Mother, Ross is just fine. He's going to be just fine. We're going to see to that." He strode to the secretary and began pulling out paper and pens. "I'm leaving a note for Father. Give it to him when he gets home."

"Where are you going? You gave your word that you wouldn't leave him alone to work that business by himself—"

"I have to go, Mother. I have to go get Bryony. I have to—" He paused and turned to face her. "I have to go get my wife."

Matilda stared at him for a long moment, then slowly set the tulips on the hall table. She moved toward her son with firm, purposeful steps.

"You're absolutely right to go to her, Adam. I've been wondering when you were going to come to your senses about Bryony, but I knew that I couldn't tell you what to do. You wouldn't have listened."

Adam took both her hands in his. "I know. I've been a pigheaded idiot."

"Oh, no, dear. Just a Hawthorne." Matilda's eyes danced and a sweet, mischievous smile played at the corners of her mouth.

Adam stared in wonder at the lovely change in his mother's face. He couldn't recall the last time he'd seen that smile, but he recognized it as the smile of the mother he'd so loved as a child. Here was another miracle to lay at Bryony's feet.

If she'd see him. He squeezed Matilda's hands and moved back to the desk. He scrawled a quick note to his father, folded it, and tucked it into his mother's apron pocket.

"I'm leaving as soon as I can get my gear together. I can't say when I'll be back. But I will be back, I promise."

"Or we could come to you."

He gaped at her. She smiled again. "I know. I've been a ghost in my own home too long. We all have. It's time we cleared out for a while and let this old musty place air out. I imagine Cold Springs Hollow might be a lovely place to visit."

"It is, Mother." He enfolded her in a huge bear hug. "It's . . . magical."

Chapter Twenty-Two

"To Expedite a Legal Matter, Enter into Courte wearing the Colour of Oranges and essence of Skunk Cabbage on thy Personne. To Expedite Matters of Love, Come Naked."
—Cassia Talcott

Adam found her by the scrying pool. She had wrapped herself in her shawl and was huddled against the base of an oak tree, the scattered leaves a soft, rustling bed beneath her. She seemed to be asleep.

He approached as silently as possible, was reaching out to touch her hair when her remarkable eyes fluttered open and stared intently into his. He drew back his hand but didn't retreat. He knelt on the ground before her and returned her gaze.

"So," she said wearily. "You're here after all.

Well, I'm too tired and too busy to listen, Adam. Go back to your beloved Philadelphia and leave me to my misguided, heathenish ways."

"Bryony," Adam said, reaching out to brush away a leaf that had landed in her tousled hair. "I'm sorry. For everything. For my disbelief. For lying to you. For betraying you. For failing to see who and what you truly are."

"Fine. You're forgiven. Now, please go away."

She started to scramble up but he gripped her hand and wouldn't let go. She wanted to run, to scream, to slap at the strong, capable hand that held hers so insistently. But she found she couldn't. She was just too tired, she told herself. She didn't want to have to run away today.

She settled back down among the leaves. "Now I suppose I shall have to listen to your story."

"Bryony, I love you."

She shook her head. "You don't. You couldn't love me and be so wrong about who and what I am. You hate magic and my magic is as much a part of me as my heart or my brain. It's only logical, then, that you hate me."

Adam nodded. "I know that now. And you're right. I didn't love you when I asked you to marry me and leave your home. Not as I ought. Not as you deserve. But I was still an arrogant pup who was hell-bent on proving to the world that I knew what was best for everyone. I was bent on having my revenge."

Bryony couldn't help herself. "What revenge?"

He cocked an eyebrow. "Will you hear me out?" he asked warily.

"I suppose I must," she said. "I doubt if you'll leave otherwise. Go ahead, tell away." She settled herself with her hands folded in her lap like a bored but obedient schoolchild.

Adam ignored her pose. "You know about Ross and you know that he was injured in the war for independence. Did you also know that my brother was a fine man, full of honor and sober dedication? He was the sort who could have made peace between the Capulets and the Montagues with naught but a word and a smile. Did you know that he was—is—my father's favorite, literally the fair-haired boy? For years I struggled in his shadow, loving and admiring my older brother, but feeling slighted by a father who had no eyes for any but this firstborn son. I was jealous, to say the least. When I met the great magician Jacob Meyer and became his pupil, I felt at last that I was worth something, that I had a place in life. And I was content. Ross was to go into partnership with our father and I was happy in my magic."

Adam paused and pulled a twig from the ground and began stripping it of leaves. Bryony went on listening in silence, her face impassive.

"Our family was at peace until the war began. I was in England, doing magic shows in London until it became too uncomfortable for a Yankee to be in British society. Ross, however, had gone into the military as soon as our father would permit him to leave. Ever dutiful, ever diligent, ever a leader, he became a brilliant officer. He was beloved by the men he commanded and he looked after them with care.

"But he and his men were caught at Camden, in South Carolina, and sentenced to be prisoners of war there. I, in the meantime, was in service to the south. I didn't hear of his capture until much later.

"The prison camp was a hellhole. Conditions were so bad that even the rats died of starvation and disease. The English tortured Ross and Conklin because they thought they were carrying secrets for General Gates and General Morgan. They may have been, but the English never learned a word. Despite torture and starvation, Ross summoned up his strength and led a daring escape with many of his men. But as they were fleeing, all of them were captured or shot while Ross looked on, helpless in hiding. He went immediately back on active duty, though he'd been greatly weakened. He was wounded in the battle at Guilford Court House and sent home, deathly ill."

Bryony watched Adam's face. His features were still, but she could detect the hurt and anger within him, the loss. She felt her heart contract in sorrow for all he had suffered, for all that her friend, Ross, had suffered. No wonder it had been so painful for her to look inside Ross's being. He had been consumed with grief and sorrow and guilt for so long.

Adam continued.

"I came home some months later. By that time, the doctors had pronounced all his wounds healed, except that he couldn't walk, could barely sleep, and had bouts of violent raving when he wasn't sunk into a melancholy so deep that no one could reach him. He drove off everyone, including his fiancée, Elyssa."

He paused, lips pressed tight. Bryony saw the tears that were just behind Adam's eyes. Involuntarily, she reached out and touched his hand.

"This is the hardest part to tell," he said, his voice shaking just a trace. "It's—damn, I just have to come out with it. I came home to find my parents closeted in Ross's room. A man was in there, waving a branch over my brother and sprinkling him with some kind of colored water and some dirt that he claimed came from a site in the Holy Lands where John the Baptist walked. He'd rigged up a cord to signal a comrade outside so that whenever he pulled on it, a harp would play, thereby indicating that the angels were working a miracle on my brother. It was the lowest sort of calumny. I challenged him to prove that he had ever made anyone well in any way, but he said that the Lord works in mysterious ways. I said that his own ways were no mystery and that he couldn't cure a Virginia ham. I yanked his accomplice into the room, harp and all, matched the dirt in his box with the dirt on my own boots, and threw him out of the house."

"How did your mother and father take that?"

Adam's face darkened even further. "They were enraged. My mother tried to defend the fellow, saying that he was their last hope. I said that if he was their last hope then it was time to leave Ross to God."

"Adam!"

"I know. It was cruel. But, damn it all, this was my brother! And I soon learned that this fellow was but the latest in a long string of humbugs to whom my parents had given their faith, their trust, and their money. One of them had come near to poisoning him by purging him with lobelia. God only knows what damage he inflicted on my brother! My father had gone so far into debt for their shams that he had sold off part of his business—the business he'd built with his own hands, the business that was to be Ross's legacy. But my mother was so hurt and angry that she slapped me for my pains and fled to her rooms."

"And Josiah?"

"My father asked how I dared come in and challenge their actions when all I'd ever done in my life was play at games and practice my silly tricks. If I had been at home when I should have been, if I had gone to war at my brother's side, perhaps none of this would have happened."

"Oh, Adam."

"I can't say I blame him, looking back at it now. He went on to demand whether I could heal Ross. I told him no, I'd never be like these other rascals and claim that I could do such a thing. It was pure thievery, I said, for them to have taken my parents' money and claimed that their nonsensical methods could cure Ross's ills. They had made a fool of him, I said." Adam drew a deep breath. "Well, my father, as you know, can bear almost anything except to be thought of as a fool. He came close to striking me, too; then all the fight seemed to go out of him. 'Go do whatever you wish,' he said. 'I'll have no more to do with you.' "

"That must have hurt you very much."

"I can see why he said it. Ross was his favorite, his heir. Who was I to tell him that what he was doing to save his beloved son was foolishness?"

"That's very understanding of you."

"That's hindsight. At the time, all I could think of was how this fraud had entered my family's home, gained my parents' respect and trust, and how he'd stolen that trust along with their money. That was my brother he was practicing his nonsense on! I could not forgive myself for not being there to ward off these charlatans, because I, of all people, would have been able to see through their smoke and mirrors.

"I went in and saw Ross, saw the evidence of those fakers who had been there, messing with him, and I saw what a pitiable state he was in. I vowed then and there that I wouldn't let another person be taken in by these monstrous tricksters. I'd make it my task to find them out and rout them. I would show others that facing the truth was far preferable to the sick fantasies woven by these snakes."

"And that was what you intended to do with me?"

Adam looked up into her eyes and Bryony saw the honest pain in them. He nodded, twisting the twig until it snapped. "It was a gamble, as you know, as well as a personal challenge. But I hadn't counted on you being you. I fell in love with you, Bryony. But I was still so blind that the only way I could have you and live with the vow I had made was to make you over into something you were not."

Bryony shook her head. "Love. How can such a wonderful emotion be the cause of so much pain and confusion?"

"When it finds itself in the hands of a rank amateur, like myself, love can't help but become a slave to confusion and error." He looked away from the golden eyes that were studying his face with such serious attention. "I know I've betrayed your trust, Bryony. And yes, much of it was in the name of love, poor grasp of it that I have. I came to this hollow out of anger at the loss of my family and my brother. For love of them, I went after everyone who laid claim to magic—until at last I encountered you. And when I couldn't resist loving you, I tried to win you away from your magic, to make you mine, not understanding that without your magic, without your beliefs, you would not be the woman I loved. I feared that I might lose you and my pride. I hounded you about learning all those so-called civilized things because I was afraid to admit that I'd fallen in love with one of the very people I'd sworn to be my enemies. I would make you over into the image of what I thought I wanted, without regard to what you wanted or needed, and without regard to the truth that I held deep in my heart."

"And what truth was that?"

"That you are a witch, a Hag of the Hollow, a member of the magical circle, a healer. And that was what was drawing me to you—not your beauty alone, not your quick mind and good heart alone, but also the instinctive—ye gods, I said it!—instinctive knowledge that you could perform real magic and were in touch with powers and forces far beyond my ken. And that I needed that in my life just as much as I needed old Cicero and Lucretius."

Bryony stared at him in wonder. Was this the same man who had shouted at her only a few weeks before? The one who had shaken her and told her that she was living in a fantasy world that would be her destruction? "What has changed your mind?" she ventured at last.

"I wish I could say that I reasoned it all out in my superior brain," Adam said with a rueful twist of the lips. "But it took a long time for it to creep in and sink into my heart. Most of all, I believe it was my big brother who drove the point home."

"Ross?"

"Yes. Quite the chatterbox these days, my brother. Pestered me day and night about you: where had you gone, why didn't you come visit him, did I know that the juice of something or other plant would bring about a cure for warts, or some such thing." Adam took both of Bryony's hands in his. "You did it, Bryony. You did heal. You healed Ross Hawthorne when everyone else in the world, including—especially—his no-account younger brother had given up all hope."

"What—what do you mean?"

"I mean just what I said. You touched him, you touched his life, you touched his spirit, you touched his mind—and he is talking and sitting up and threatens to turn handsprings as soon as he can get enough to eat at last."

"Adam! Really?"

"Before God and Matthew's grandfather fish, I swear it." Adam's eyes were shining. "You have the gift, Bryony. Ross told me that he started to feel better when he met you, but that he really felt changed when you went inside him and took on the pain and horror he'd been keeping inside all this time. He felt his burden lift at last. He's on the mend. He may yet walk, love, and there's more."

"More?"

"More. Mother has been going about with dirt beneath her fingernails for weeks now—she's dug a new garden in the back of the house and is busy day and night preparing it for next spring. And my father, well, he hasn't changed all that much, but he has been needling me about the whereabouts of my 'lady-wife,' as he calls you, and the man seems to be hovering about my mother in the most attentive fashion of late so that I can't help but wonder if they haven't discovered some of your herbs from under our bed."

Bryony went scarlet. Adam only laughed. "I knew it! It would take magic to put a smile into my father's eyes once more and you have done it." He reached out and gathered her into his arms. She came without protest, her eyes still wide with wonder. "You, my beautiful witch-wife, are the source of all my joy and if that isn't magic, I don't know what is. Please say that you will stay with me always and work your enchantments on me to the end of our days."

Bryony buried her head in the comfort of his chest, letting the bands that been clasped about her heart loosen and fall away at last. He gathered her close and she rested there, feeling whole at last.

Adam felt her in his arms, felt how thin she had grown, and noted the dark smudges beneath her eyes. She had been working too hard, neglecting herself. He gathered her more tightly, as if fearing that she might slip away from him.

"Bryony, lass." They both jumped as Matthew stepped out from behind the tree, his footfalls as silent as the air around them.

"What is it?" Bryony scrambled to her feet.

"It's Marcus. He's taken a bad turn."

Bryony turned to Adam. "I have to go."

"Of course you do. You're the Hag," he said. "But I'm coming with you. I have a score to settle with you, Matthew, and with Marcus, and the other two of your little gang. I'm here to see that none of you gets away before I've brought you to task for meddling in my life."

Bryony gaped at Adam, but there was no time to say more. Matthew led the way and the three of them hurried away.

Chapter Twenty-Three

"All goode Witches need Possess a Broome and a Mirror. A Broome used in Vigilance may work Wonders upon a dirty Floore. A Mirror will, with Wisdom, help her See the Truth in Others."

—*Cassia Talcott*

Bryony ministered to the old man with herbs and with incantations. Matthew and Adam aided as best they could as the hours dragged on and Marcus's fever and deep, racking cough consumed him.

As evening fell, Bryony knelt beside the bed for a moment, her head on her hands. She turned and looked up at Matthew with a puzzled frown. "Matthew," she said, "you have to help me now. I don't know enough to do what he needs of me."

Matthew looked stricken. "No, girl. I've never been—"

"But you have the power. That's it, isn't it? You're a Talcott, Matthew. You're a magus." She rubbed her reddened eyes. "How could we all have been so blind?" She stood and took Matthew's gnarled hands in hers. "Do it for Mother and Father, Matthew. Do it for Rosamunda and Julia. Do it for Marcus."

Matthew shook tears from his bright old eyes. "But I failed your mama and papa, lass. I tried it then, I was so desperate to save them."

"But you have me, now," Bryony said. She tugged him toward the bed. "And I have the power, too. We can do this together."

Matthew looked at her and then looked at the gray face of his friend in the bed. He nodded.

Adam watched, spellbound, as Matthew and Bryony washed their hands in fresh lavender water and then rubbed their hands briskly with a snowy white square of lamb's wool. They prayed together briefly, then went to the bed and pulled back the coverlet. With Matthew's big hands laid over Bryony's, they began at the top of his head and slowly skimmed their hands over the length of Marcus's body, their palms only an inch or two above him. As if doing a dance with their hands, they skimmed again, then circled back and began to hover over his chest.

Adam felt himself holding his breath. He had no idea what they were doing, but it was beautiful to watch the tall old man with his silver head bent over Bryony's dark one, their hands joined and moving with one accord.

At last, at a murmured word from Matthew, they lowered their hands to Marcus's chest and gently held them there. Adam watched, rapt, as they closed their eyes and simply touched their friend. Time seemed to stretch or stop, he didn't know which, but it was fully dark outside when Matthew and Bryony lifted their heads and their hands and stepped away from the bed.

"What do you think?" Bryony asked.

"Time will tell." He laid his hand on Bryony's shoulder and turned her to face Adam. "Take her home now, lad. She's near spent. I'll keep watch."

Bryony gave the older man a kiss on the cheek and went out. Adam looked at Matthew with mingled awe and curiosity. "Why didn't you tell anyone?" he asked.

Matthew shrugged. "I never had the calling. I just had the blood. It came to me the same as the color of my eyes or the number of my teeth." He nodded toward the door. "But her—she had the calling. Right from the day she popped out of the egg. There'd be no denying her."

Adam opened his mouth to say something more, but Matthew raised a hand. "Go take care of her. We got years to gab on this, you and I."

Adam smiled at the old man and followed his wife out into the night. They walked home to Talcott Farm in silence, the cool wind bringing hints of autumn to their senses.

Soot was waiting at the door, just as always, and he eagerly conducted both of them into the kitchen, where the all-important task of pouring his dish of milk was completed to his satisfaction.

He seemed not at all surprised to see Adam, and after an inquiring sniff or two at Adam's boots, strolled to the hearth for his nap.

Bryony felt suddenly shy, as if this man were not her husband and they had never before spent an evening in each other's company. But the gulf between them was still present, she could feel it, and only their past together could have created that gulf.

She found some food in the larder and served up cold meats, cheese, and dried fruits. Adam accepted his food with a smile. "This reminds me of our first breakfast together," he said, drawing chairs up before the fire.

Bryony was silent, picking at her food. She hadn't been eating much since she came back to the hollow, and she found she still had little appetite. Adam's appearance had surprised her. She'd been so busy caring for the fever victims that she hadn't bothered with any other activities such as scrying or image-conjuring. Aside from her nightly dreams of him, she hadn't expected his coming.

All he had shared with her this afternoon had touched her. She knew now the full extend of the suffering he and his family had gone through, and how he had struggled with his passions and his grief. But where did it leave her?

"You've been working hard. It's influenza, isn't it?"

"Influenza?"

"Yes. That's the name the doctors in Europe have given this sort of fever and wasting cough."

"Oh."

"It's what your parents died of, isn't it?"

She nodded, pushing her food around on her plate. "And all the others who were left of my family. All my aunts were old and had no children. I was—I am the last Talcott."

"What was that you and Matthew did for Marcus tonight?"

"Touching," Bryony said simply. "Good old-fashioned laying on of hands. It is the simplest and the most difficult of all skills."

He set his plate down on the hearth. "After your family died, you must have felt a bit like I did when I learned that Ross wasn't recovering. I wanted to do anything I could to change the world, to change myself, to change others, just to feel as if I had some power in this world."

She shrugged. "Yes. I suppose so. I wanted to do all I could to restore the magic they had fostered in this hollow for so many years. I wanted them to be proud of me."

"I'm sure they would be. I'm sure they are."

She shook her head. "I don't know." She raised her eyes to meet his. "I spent so much time dreaming and working. Then I thought I'd never have the gift, and I gave up. That was wrong of me."

"I didn't help much, did I?"

"You may have," she said. "By prodding me, by getting me to let go, I may have opened the door for my magic at last. But when it came, when I knew I had not just one gift, but many, I was too proud, Adam. I wanted to try everything at once, whether I was ready for it or not. I tried spells on people without considering whether they were ready for the results. I was vain." She clutched the sides of her plate. "Ross could have been hurt by my kything with him. I had never tried it with anyone else, anyone less troubled. I hadn't practiced. I hadn't thought about how Ross might react. All I could think of was how angry I was that you and your parents had given up on him and how I would show you all that there was life there, after all."

"And you did."

"But I risked his well-being, my own, your family's. I know that now. I owe all of you an apology."

"Apology accepted."

She looked at him in surprise. "Just like that?"

"Just like that." Adam took her plate and set it on the hearth with his. He went to squat before her. "Haven't we spent enough time talking and apologizing and explaining?" He took her hands in his. "I told Matthew, promised him I'd cherish you like a treasure. I'm a man of my word. Come, wife. Let's go to bed."

She stared at him; then her lips began to curve upward. "Just like that?"

He swept her up off her chair. "No, love. Just like this."

They were up the stairs and in the big soft bed only moments later. Soot waited a discreet ten minutes or so, then rose, stretched, and went to clean their plates.

Chapter Twenty-Four

"In Wintertime comes the Miracle of the Hawthorn Tree, with its snowye Blossoms growing out of Seasone, so the Story goes. Also at Christmasstime, take the Holly and the Ivy into the Householde and let the Master and Mistress of that House joine even as the thorned Holly and the winding Ivy do entwine. From such Joinings are Babes well made, and the New Year made Joyfull and Glad."

—*Cassia Talcott*

Adam stared in wonder as the woman alighted from the coach. She was dressed in garnet red from head to toe, with a gauzy white wool veil tied over her broad picture hat. She waved a white ermine muff at him and beckoned for a kiss.

"Mother?" he asked wonderingly, moving to greet her.

Her laugh rang out across the fresh powdered snow. "Yes, son. It's your own old mother. Come help her down before she dives into some snowbank and catches her death."

Adam hurried to her side and helped her down to the wooden walk, still gaping in wonder. "What's the matter?" she asked pertly. "Didn't I send word that we were coming?"

"We?" he asked, looking dazedly at her remarkable hat and flushed cheeks.

"That's right, brother. We."

Adam turned to see Ross standing in the door of the coach, readying to step down.

"Ross?" he whispered.

"Happy Christmas, beetlebrains. Give a fellow a hand, won't you?"

Adam leaped to his side and held out his arms.

"Well, I love you, too, baby brother, but not that much. Save your hugs for Bryony and just help me down."

Adam felt his throat tightening as his brother put a hand on his arm and, using his cane, came to light on the frozen ground of Cold Springs Hollow. He was walking. Just as Bryony said he would.

"Ross, when . . . ?"

"After you left. I thought about what you said about giving up reality so that you can see your dreams more clearly. I thought it was about time I came out of my reality and tried on a few of my dreams."

"But I wrote that to Father in a note when I left. How did you—"

"I read it to the whole family."

Josiah Hawthorne stepped down from the coach and stood with his hand on Ross's shoulder. Adam wondered if in fact he was only dreaming.

"Father. Father, I—"

"Later, son, later." Hawthorne's tone was gruff, but his eyes held a new, softer light. "Let's get our bones out of this icy wind." He glanced around. "Where's that little witch-wife of yours? Where's our Bryony?"

Adam grinned. "I left her home mending her broomstick."

"Damn good thing, too. Don't want any daughter of mine out traipsing around in this blizzard. Have I got any grandsons yet?"

Adam, to his astonishment, felt himself reddening. "None yet that I know of, sir." He smiled. "But I'll be sure that you get a full report when I do."

"See that you do. Now, are we going to stand around here until we become living statues or are you going to take us home?"

Adam looked at Ross, who was grinning broadly. "I suppose Father will want to drive?"

Ross snorted. "Not if I get the reins first."

"Oh, stop your dallying," Matilda broke in at last. Her smile was fond. "Take us home, Adam. We've brought Christmas with us."

Adam swept her up in a hug. "That's what you think. Wait till you get a taste of Talcott tradition.

You'll beg for mercy before the twenty-fifth ever arrives."

Bryony was waiting at the door for them when they arrived. Her eyes filled with stars as she saw the four of them seated in the wagon, but they changed to shining tears when Adam stood aside and let Ross step down and take his first halting steps toward her. She flew to him and nearly knocked him over in her joyous embrace.

"Oh, yes, this is a fine thing," Adam said, pretending to pout. "Do I ever get greeted that way? Of course not. This is typical of you, Ross."

Bryony stuck her tongue out at him and went to greet his mother. Matilda hugged her fiercely and the two of them wiped at the tears that were glistening on their faces.

"Mrs. Hawthorne." Josiah's voice was stern in the cold air.

"Yes, dear, what is it?" Matilda asked.

"Not you. Her." He nodded imperially to Bryony. "Come here, girl."

Bryony shot an anxious glance at Adam, but went to Josiah at once. The older man peered at her with judicious consideration.

"Bryony Talcott Hawthorne, you once said that I was a starving soul who could never get his fill."

Bryony looked flustered. "Ross, you weren't to tell him that!" she began.

"Hush and listen to an old man, even if he is a fool. It's only respectful."

"Y-yes, sir."

"You were absolutely right, you precocious little chit. I had everything and yet I was as shriveled up inside as if I were starving. Well, I hope you're satisfied, because the worm has turned. I intend to taste the joy of life, just as you do. And anyone who gets in my way will have to explain himself, understood?"

"Yes, sir." Bryony smiled, eyes sparkling with fresh tears.

"Ye gods, here come the waterworks again," Josiah growled. "Inside with you, girl, or those tears will be icicles. In fact, my legs feel like icicles even now. Adam, what's the meaning of keeping your wife and family standing out in the ice and snow? Didn't I teach you any manners? Get inside, all of you!"

Bryony giggled as Josiah stomped ahead and barged into Talcott House ahead of them all. Ross came up beside her and she took his arm.

" 'The worm has turned,' " he said, shaking his head. "I should live so long!"

"Oh, but he has, Ross. I can see it in his eyes and all around him like a—like a—"

"Halo?" Ross looked horrified as well as amused.

"A crown," Bryony said firmly. "You must admit, he's rather royal."

"That he is, sister-in-law. That he is."

"Oh, Ross, I'm so happy for you." Bryony hugged his arm. "I'm so glad you're here. It's been so long!"

"Too long. Adam kept writing and saying you

were both coming back soon, but you never did. So we came ahead to you. You told me so much about this place I could almost picture it in my head. Now that I'm really here, well, nothing could convey how beautiful it is. No wonder you had to come back, Bryony. And no wonder Adam had to come as well."

Bryony hesitated a moment. Adam had come for her, he'd said. But he hadn't said he'd come to stay. He'd come to take her back with him to Philadelphia. Now that things were settled in the hollow, and she was sure of her magic and the power she had to keep and protect her home, could she leave here, even for Adam?

"It's a beautiful time of year," was all she said as they went up the steps. "Everything seems to be at peace."

"Where are you going?"

Adam sat up in bed, the bedclothes still warm and tangled from an especially passionate bout of lovemaking, after which both he and Bryony had fallen asleep almost instantly. Now he watched her graceful, naked form moving about the bedroom, gathering up her clothing from where he'd cheerfully tossed it aside earlier.

"I have to go out," she whispered, coming to the bedside. "You go back to sleep."

"Only if you'll join me," he said, reaching to pull her down on top of him.

She giggled and writhed seductively against him. "You don't want to sleep, though, do you?" she murmured.

"Well, now that you mention it . . ." He cupped her bottom and pressed her against his hardening arousal.

She placed a silky kiss on his mouth and gave another rapturous wriggle. "You're incorrigible. I like that in a husband." She pushed up and hopped off the bed. "But I must go out."

"Where?" Adam growled. "Damn it, woman, are you going to leave your only husband utterly unsatisfied and aching?"

She turned to him, hands on her hips. "You sound just like your father!"

He stared at her, aghast. "I do not!"

"You do. And you're hardly unsatisfied, if I recall your words to me but an hour or two ago. What were they? Oh, yes. 'Ohh, Bryony, love, that was sooo good. I'll never move again!' " She gave an exaggerated yawn.

"All right, that does it." Adam swung out of bed and lunged for her.

She squealed and danced out of his reach. "No, you don't. I have a solemn task to undertake and I won't be hindered by your boundless lust. You'll have to wait until I get back."

"A solemn task, eh?" Adam stood with arms crossed and regarded her. "And just what does that mean, as if I couldn't guess, little magician of mine?"

Bryony looked at him standing there, naked and glorious in the dying firelight, and almost forgot what it was she had to do. But she rallied her wits quickly as a cold draft slipped under the door and chilled her bare feet.

"It's the solstice," she said. "We celebrate Christmas and the change of seasons on this night as well as the twenty-fifth." She pulled on warm woolen stockings.

"Outdoors?" Adam asked incredulously.

"That's right." She bounced up from the footstool and grabbed his hands. "Come build a bonfire with me outside, and I promise we'll come back here and build one in that very bed."

It was an offer Adam couldn't refuse. Before long, he was standing out in the yard behind the house, the winter moon blinking at them from behind the scudding clouds above. A huge fire glowed before them, and Bryony threw back the hood of her cape in its warmth. A sprig of holly was twined in one of her brown locks, as well as another twig he didn't recognize.

"What's this for?" Adam asked, wrapping one arm about her and toying with the sprig in her hair.

"Holly? Holly is for the winter and to welcome strangers into the home. It is evergreen and means eternal life, even in the dead of winter. It's special for Christmas."

"And what is this other?"

"Hawthorn."

"How flattering. What does it mean?"

"Mmm, I don't know if I should tell you."

"Why not?"

"Because it might not come true. And even if it did, I'm not sure that it would be a good thing."

"I don't understand. It sounds as if you're working a spell that you don't want to work."

Bryony sighed. "I do and I don't." She stared at the fire, then off across the snowy fields to the woods beyond. "The hawthorn twig is for a rich harvest come the spring, and that is good. It is also for happiness and blessings in the union of a man and a woman."

"And isn't that good?"

"Only if they both want it."

He turned her to face him, lifting her chin so he could look deep into her eyes. "I want it, Bryony. I do."

"Children, Adam? That's what hawthorn means. Will you want witch-children, who'll need two parents to help them grow into their gifts?"

"Witch-children or the ordinary kind, as long as they're ours."

She glanced away. "But will they be accepted in the city?"

"My family will love them no matter what. As they love you."

"That's not what I mean."

"Tell me, Bryony. Tell me clearly. You know I'm not as good at reading other people's minds as you are."

She faced him. "I don't think I can go back with you."

"Bryony, I—"

"No, hear me out, Adam, please. I left Philadelphia because I was angry and hurt and I wanted to run home and hide from all my problems. But I couldn't run away. I brought them with me, and they still had to be solved. But now that I'm here, and now that I had to pay such a dear price to safeguard my home, I don't think I can leave it and go to live in another world. The influenza left the hollow weakened. I need to stay and help build it up once more."

Adam frowned. "What if I asked it?"

Bryony bit her lip. "No, Adam. I don't believe I could. At least not for long." She gazed up at him, her torn and very vulnerable heart showing clearly in her amber eyes. "It's hard to say it. You are my husband. I would come with you, of course, if it was the only way we could be together. But I believe I would pay a high price if I went."

"You mean you would lose your gift?"

"I think so. It would be greatly diminished, certainly. Talcott blood and sweat and tears are in this land, along with the bones of our dear ancestors. We are part of the hollow and it's a part of us. I need to be here to feel complete, whole." She hesitated. "And I want to raise our children here."

"Bryony, are you—"

"No. Not yet. But it could be soon." She gave him a wry smile. "The signs say that a rich harvest is coming, at least for the fields."

Adam released her from his embrace and strode to the fire. She watched him anxiously, fearing to say anything more for fear of upsetting the delicate balance of things as they stood now.

"I've just regained my family," Adam said slowly. "My brother is recovering, my mother returning to life. My father is behaving as a human being rather than a tyrannical, money-making machine." He tossed a branch onto the fire. "And none of us is getting younger. Except Matthew, maybe."

Bryony smiled but kept silent. He needed to be with his family. He wanted to go back to Philadelphia. How was she to trade her life for love?

"But this is where I began to live again myself," he said suddenly, turning toward her. "This is where I learned that the world is more than just what my eyes can see or my ears can hear. This is the place where I found out I had dreams, just like everyone else. This is where I found you."

He stood before her, arms at his sides, face half-lit from the light of the fire. "I want to be here, love. In Cold Springs. I want to make this our home. I want to see if Matthew is ever going to catch that damned fish. I want to see if Millie Beebe marries Lucius Dreyer. I want to be here when Phileas Adcock returns with two of every animal on earth. I want to see our children building bonfires and playing with magical rocks and planting herbs in the garden. I want to see you, love. I want you at my side every morning, noon, and night. I understand that who you are is deeply tied to this hollow. And I love who you are. I don't want to change that."

He moved swiftly to her and seized her face in his hands. "You are a witch, Bryony. You've cast your spell and bound me to you and to the land here. And I intend to see that you're never able to throw any counterspell on me—you'll never get rid of me, even if I have to become an out-and-out wizard to best you. I'm going to love you until I die, until our bones are dust, until, until—"

"Forever," Bryony whispered.

"Until forever!" he said fiercely.

"But what about Philadelphia? What about your family?"

"They're here now, aren't they? They can visit, we can visit. Hell, they can come live here if they want. I have a feeling that Ross might do just that, judging from the way he was drinking in this place all day. But my mind is made up, Bryony. I'm dug in. I'm here to stay, with my beautiful, spellbinding, enchantress wife."

She threw her arms about him and they shared a kiss so full of power and love and fulfilled longing that it left them both dizzy and clinging to one another in the flickering light of the flames. Bryony moved away from Adam and picked up a wreath she'd laid near the fire.

"Holly and ivy, together we sing," she chanted softly. "Crown of winter and hope of the spring."

"Bring it along," Adam said, pulling her close and turning toward the house. "We'll hang it over the bed for luck."

"The moon is full," Bryony said, her smile mysterious and full of a new glow. "That's another good sign."

"I don't need any signs to tell me," Adam murmured against her hair. "We're going to plant a seed tonight, on the very first night of winter. And come the fall, we'll reap a fine harvest."

Bryony turned starlit amber eyes up to gaze at him. "You're awfully sure of yourself."

He pulled her toward the sleeping house. "If you want magic, love, just come along with me.

The Astonishing Balthazaar still has a few tricks left to show you."

And so he did. But not before the Hag of Cold Springs Hollow had astonished him in her own unique and magical way.

Author's Note

I hope you enjoyed reading *Enchantment*. I had great fun looking up spells, proverbs, magical practices, and herb-lore for this book. Cassia Talcott's *Compleat Book of Spelles, Herbes, and True Wisdom* is a fictional work wholly of my own invention, as are all the other spells and cures in this book. I am not a witch, a magus, an herbalist, or a physician, nor are my publishers, to the best of my knowledge. It is *not recommended* that you attempt any of the spells or cures in this book without consulting a trained pharmacist or doctor.

I owe a special debt to several authors and herbal specialists for the invaluable resources that I was able to use in "conjuring" up my story. The sources I consulted include: *Good Magic,* by Marina Medici; *A Victorian Grimoire,* by Patricia Telsco; *Therapeutic Touch,* by Dolores Krieger;

Cunningham's Encyclopedia of Magical Herbs, by Scott Cunningham; *The Illustrated Plant Lore,* by Josephine Addison; *The Book of Home Remedies and Herbal Cures,* by Carol Bishop; *The Complete Book of Magic and Witchcraft,* by Kathryn Paulsen; and *Flim-flam!* by James Randi. All of them were enlightening and entertaining.

I love to hear from readers! You can write to me in care of Leisure Books, or at: P.O. Box 1733, Round Rock, TX, 78680-1733.

Prologue

Indian Territory, 1877

The two men glared at the Indian who stood between their freedom and a king's ransom in gold.

The Indian was tall, his skin the color of dark bronze, his eyes as black as the bowels of hell. His voice was like slow thunder as he ordered them to get out of the cave and leave the gold behind.

Charlie McBride was willing. Life was more precious than gold. Any fool knew that.

Any fool except Denver Wilkie.

As soon as they cleared the cave, Denver drew his .44 and fired at the Indian. Denver was a crack shot and the bullet struck the Red Stick in the chest, just left of center. Blood oozed from the wound, spreading like crimson tears over the warrior's buckskin shirt.

The Indian fired back. His first bullet struck Denver in the throat, unleashing a fountain of blood.

The second smashed into Charlie McBride's shoulder. He staggered backward, tripped over a rock, and landed on his rump, hard. More frightened than he'd ever been in his life, Charlie stared up at the Indian, certain he was about to be given a one-way ticket to hell.

For a moment, the two men stared at each other, and Charlie felt as if the warrior was probing deep into his soul, prying into the innermost secrets and desires of his heart.

And then the warrior lowered his rifle. "Take only what you need," he said at last. "If you take one nugget more, my spirit will haunt you for as long as you live."

His mouth as dry as the dust of Arizona, Charlie McBride could only nod.

"My body—" The Indian was swaying on his feet now. "Do not leave it . . . out here. . . ."

Charlie nodded again. "I'll bury you," he said. "You have my word on it."

"Inside the cave," the warrior said, his voice growing faint. "Swear it."

"I promise," Charlie said, but the Indian was past hearing.

Slowly, the life faded from the warrior's eyes, the strength left his legs, and he fell slowly, gracefully, to the ground.

Although he was growing a little light-headed from the blood he'd lost, Charlie McBride kept his promise. He jammed his neckerchief over the wound in his shoulder to stop the bleeding, then wrapped the dead warrior in Denver's faded Hudson's bay blanket. He left the Indian's body on a natural shelf deep in the bowels of the cave, across from the treasure he had died to protect.

Then, his saddlebags filled with a fortune in gold, Charlie McBride rode away from the mountain.

His first stop was at the land office, where he bought 200 acres of land, including the Indian's mountain, even though he knew he'd never set foot in that cave again.

Chapter One

Montana, 1994

She felt it again, a warm breath whispering against the side of her neck, and then a chill, as if a cold winter wind had found its way into the cavern.

For a moment, Kelly didn't move, only stood there. With her lantern held high, she was unable to shake the feeling that she was being watched, that unseen eyes were contemplating her with equal parts of curiosity and malice.

But that was ridiculous. There was nothing to be afraid of, she told herself. Nothing at all. If her grandfather was right, no one but members of the family had been in this cave for more than 100 years.

Taking a deep calming breath, she placed the lantern on the ground and returned to her study of the body that occupied a narrow shelf along the side of the cave wall. The body, wrapped in a faded Hudson's bay blanket, was located exactly where her Grandfather had said it would be.

In her mind's eye, Kelly could see the ancient remains on display in the local historical museum, along with a small white placard that named her as the contributor.

Kelly shook her head. She had never truly believed her Grandfather McBride's ramblings about the riches supposedly hidden in a cave in the mountain behind the ranch. She had thought all his talk about a wealth of Indian gold guarded by the ghost of a savage Lakota warrior to be nothing more than the confused yearnings of an old man's mind—a jumbled mix of old legends and fables handed down from one generation of McBrides to the next.

A long sigh escaped Kelly's lips as she stared down at the blanket-wrapped corpse.

She believed her grandfather now.

Answering some call she didn't understand, Kelly drew a corner of the blanket back, then blinked in surprise. She had expected to find no more than an emaciated corpse, a skeleton clothed in tattered shreds of deer hide; instead, she saw the well-muscled body of a man dressed in a buckskin clout and fringed leggings. His moccasins were unadorned. He was tall, long legged and narrow hipped. His hair was black and straight and fell well past his broad shoulders. His jaw was strong and square, his cheekbones prominent, his forehead wide. His nose was long and blade straight.

Kelly stared thoughtfully at the dark stain on his shirt front, then frowned in bewilderment. Why hadn't the body decayed? She had the strangest feeling that the Indian wasn't dead at all, that, like Sleeping Beauty, he was merely sleeping away the centuries, waiting to be awakened by love's first kiss.

With a shake of her head, she put away such fanciful thoughts, and then, impulsively, she touched his cheek with her forefinger. His skin was supple and . . . warm.

Warm when it should have been hard and cold. When it shouldn't have been skin at all. After all these years, the body should have returned to the dust from which it had been made.

A shiver of unease skated down Kelly's spine, and she glanced around the cave, every instinct warning her to run. Abruptly, she jerked her hand away from his cheek. Then she saw it, a small buckskin bag resting against his chest.

Curious, she opened the small sack and emptied the contents into her hand. For a moment, she could only stare at the large medallion resting in her palm.

Fashioned in the shape of an eagle with its wings spread wide, the amulet was about three inches in diameter. And it appeared to be made of solid gold. Even in the flickering light of the lantern, the fetish seemed to glow with a life all its own. It felt warm as it nestled into the palm of her hand.

Kelly stared at the eagle for a long moment, and then, almost of their own volition, her fingers folded over it, and her gaze was drawn to the numerous bags of gold dust and nuggets stacked one on top of the other against the far wall. There was enough money there to pay off the mortgage on the ranch, enough to settle her grandfather's hospital bills. Enough to keep her in comfort for the rest of her life.

Her hands were trembling as she pulled the blanket over the face of the dead man. She couldn't put his remains on display. She knew somehow that he wouldn't want that. Tomorrow, she'd bring a shovel and bury the Indian in the farthest corner of the cave, where he could rest undisturbed.

Kelly sighed. The body had rested there, undisturbed, for over 100 years. She wasn't going to bury it so *it* could rest in peace; she was going to bury it for her own peace of mind.

As she stepped away from the narrow shelf, she felt the warm breath against her neck again.

Put it back.

Kelly whirled around, her gaze searching the cavern's dim interior for the source of the deep male voice. But there was no one there.

Suddenly anxious to be gone from that place of death, she slipped the medallion into the pocket of her jeans. After folding her grandfather's map, she stuck it inside her shirt.

For now, she would leave the treasure as she had found it.

For now, she wanted only to go home.

Her bootheels made soft crunching sounds as she hurried toward the entrance of the cavern. The cave was long and narrow, with a high, rounded ceiling and a sandy floor.

Blowing out the lantern, Kelly left it on the ground inside the mouth of the cave. The opening was only a few feet high and barely wide enough for her to fit through. It had taken her over two hours of intense searching to find the cave at all, and then it had been by sheer luck.

Kelly squinted against the sunlight as she stepped out of the cave. For some reason, she had expected it to be dark outside.

Her grandfather's old gelding, Dusty, whickered softly as she stepped out of the cavern. She patted the buckskin's neck, suddenly glad for the presence of another living creature, and then she swung effortlessly into the saddle and reined the horse toward the Triple M.

Riding away from the cave, Kelly slipped her hand into the pocket of her Levi's, her fingertips moving over the golden eagle.

From behind her, she heard a low rumble, like thunder echoing off the mountains, and then she felt it again, that chill that was colder than the north wind.

Seized with a sudden uncontrollable fear, she drummed her heels into the gelding's sides and raced for home.

Chapter Two

she ate dinner later that night, Kelly studied
e golden eagle, intrigued by the intricate carv-
g. It was the most beautiful thing she'd ever
en, tempting her touch again and again. She
arveled at the rich feel of the gold beneath her
gertips, at the delicate lines that formed the
d's deep-set eyes and sharp beak. The wings
re exquisite, the talons honed to fine sharp
ints.

Rising from the battered kitchen table, she
ickly washed up her few dishes, took a long
surely soak in a bubble bath, then settled into
d with pillows propped behind her back so she
uld read.

But she couldn't concentrate on the book. She
pt thinking of the body in the cave. How long
d it been there? A hundred years at least, she
ought, because the Triple M had been in her

family about that long. Why hadn't the bod decayed? She stared at the eagle standing agains the table lamp beside her bed. Why had the bod of the Indian felt warm to her touch?

Kelly shook her head. Surely that had been product of her overactive imagination. But sh had not imagined that long, lean body. He mus have been quite an impressive man in his day tall and broad shouldered. She knew someho that his eyes had been as black as sin, that hi teeth had been straight and white, and that whe he smiled. . . .

She laughed softly, uneasily. What was th matter with her, fantasizing about a man who' probably been dead for over 100 years! Fir thing tomorrow she would bury the body. made her uncomfortable just knowing it wa there.

She was about to switch off her bedside ligl when she saw a dark shadow at the window. A the air seemed to leave her body, and her hea suddenly seemed too big for her chest as sl watched the shadow pause, then move on.

For a moment, she was frozen with fear. The she bounded out of bed, ran into the living roor and grabbed the shotgun from the rack over tl fireplace, grateful that her grandfather had taug her how to shoot.

Heart pounding, she stood behind the fro door, listening, waiting. For the first time, sl realized just how alone she was. Her close neighbor was five miles to the south. She couldn pick up the phone and dial 911 for help.

Far in the distance, she heard the lonely wail of a coyote, and then there was only silence, a silence as deep and dark as the grave.

She stood there for a quarter of an hour, her whole body tense. And then, gradually, the sounds of the night returned. She heard the frogs croaking in the pond behind the house, the song of a cricket, the soft sighing of the wind, and she knew somehow that whatever had been lurking in the shadows had gone.

It took her a long time to fall asleep that night, but when sleep finally came, she dreamed of a tall, dark-skinned warrior with hair as black as midnight and eyes as deep and dark as fathomless pools of liquid ebony. . . .

In the morning, her fears of the night before seemed foolish. Kelly had never been one to be spooked by shadows in the night. She'd lived alone in Los Angeles ever since her father had died five years ago. Lived alone and liked it, but when Grandpa McBride's health started failing, she had tried to convince him to come to LA and live with her. But her grandfather had refused to leave the Triple M. Like Kelly, he had cherished his independence. She knew he would have died alone if the hospital in Cedar Flats hadn't called to inform her he was there. She'd taken a two-week leave of absence from her job with Wolfe, Cullman, and Chartier and flown to Montana to be with him.

Kelly felt a familair tug at her heart as she thought of her grandfather. In days past, when she was a little girl, her family had spent their summers at the ranch, and Grandpa had charmed her with tales of the Old West, repeating the colorful tales his great-grandfather, Charlie McBride, had once told him, tales of Indian fights and buffalo hunts and mountain men.

Her grandfather had been on his deathbed when he'd told her about the gold his great-grandfather, Charlie, had buried in a cave in the mountain behind the Triple M.

"Gold?" Kelly had said with a grin. "If there was any gold up there, don't you think someone would have found it by now?"

"It's there, girl. My great-grandpappy told me so."

"Why didn't he spend it?"

"He was afraid of it, afraid of the ghost who haunts the mountain."

"Ghost!" Kelly had exclaimed.

"I've seen him, Kelly girl," her grandfather had said, his gnarled hand squeezing hers with surprising strength.

"Really?" Kelly had asked, leaning forward. "When? Where?"

"When I was younger and braver. I followed my great-grandpappy's map and found the cave. The gold's in there, girl, a fortune, just like he said."

"And you never touched it?"

"Oh, I took a little dust now and then, when I needed it. But something told me not to try to take more than I needed. Now it's yours, Kelly. Use it wisely."

Those were the last words her Grandpa Frank had said in this world. He was asleep when she went to visit him the next morning. He'd opened his eyes, smiled at her, and then, with a sigh, he was gone.

And now the ranch, and the gold, belonged to her.

After a quick breakfast, Kelly went out to the barn and saddled Dusty. She had a grave to dig, and it was a long ride to the cave.

Kelly approached the cavern with a growing sense of unease. Chiding herself for her foolishness, she slipped on a pair of heavy work gloves, removed the shovel she'd tied behind the saddle, and ducked into the cave.

Pausing near the entrance to light the lantern she'd left the day before, she felt her heart begin to pound as shadows came to life on the walls. The cavern was roomy inside, high enough for her to stand erect once she was inside.

Nothing to be afraid of, she told herself. The dead can't hurt you.

Her booted feet made hardly a sound on the soft, sandy earth as she went deeper into the cave. She wouldn't have to dig a very deep hole, she decided, just deep enough to cover the body.

Her heart was pounding like a runaway train as she drew near the ledge, and then her breath caught in her throat.

The ledge was empty.

The body was gone.

Not believing her eyes, Kelly ran her hands over the surface of the earthen shelf, searching for some sign that a body had actually been there, that she wasn't losing her mind. Nothing.

And then she saw it, the faded Hudson's bay blanket, crumpled in a heap beneath the ledge.

For a moment, Kelly felt relief. She hadn't imagined it after all. The body had been there, and now it was gone.

Bewildered, she stared at the blanket. Gone, she thought. Gone where?

Lantern in hand, she searched the floor of the cave for some sign that an animal had dragged the remains away, but there was no sign of animal tracks, no footprints other than her own.

She laughed at that. Of course there were no footprints. Ghosts didn't leave footprints.

With a cry, she turned on her heel and ran toward the entrance of the cave, scrambling out of the narrow opening as if Satan himself were snapping at her heels.

She dreamed of the Indian again that night. She was walking in the moonlight when suddenly he was there beside her, his black eyes glowing like dark fires. He gazed at her for a long moment, the awareness growing between them, and then, quite unexpectedly, he brushed his knuckles against her cheek. The touch exploded through her like lightning, and while she was trying to recover, she heard a voice echo in the corridor of her mind. A voice that was husky with warning. His voice. *Put it back.* And then he was gone.

She woke to find the sheets tangled around her legs, her brow damp with perspiration.

Unconsciously, she reached for the golden eagle she'd placed beneath her pillow, and as her hand closed around its smoothness, she heard the warning again. Only this time it wasn't a dream, and she didn't hear the words echoing in her mind.

She heard the words, spoken clearly, from the shadowed corner of her room.

"Put it back."

On the verge of terror, Kelly scrambled across the bed and switched on the light, her eyes wide as they searched the room.

There was no one there.

Chapter Three

Harry Renford stared at the young woman seated before him with obvious disbelief.

"Pay off the loan?" he said, repeating her words as if he hadn't heard her quite right. "You want to pay off the loan?"

Harry sat back in his chair, his hands folded on the desktop as he studied her face. Kelly McBride was a pretty girl, with long, curly brown hair and large blue eyes. He'd known her grandparents, Frank and Annee, for years. Annee had died almost ten years ago, but Frank had stayed on at the ranch, alone. He'd gotten pretty feeble in his old age, but he'd refused to leave the Triple M, and the ranch, located some 30 miles southeast of town, had fallen into a state of disrepair.

Old man McBride had died three weeks ago,

leaving behind a mountain of hospital bills and a sizable mortgage. It had been in Harry's mind to buy the Triple M when it went on the market and discover for himself if the rumors of a hidden gold mine were true. It had seemed a safe investment. If there was no gold, and he doubted there was, Harry planned to turn the Triple M into a guest ranch. But then Frank's granddaughter had shown up to claim the old place. He'd made her what he considered to be a generous offer for the ranch—an offer she had politely, but firmly, refused, thereby upsetting his carefully thought-out scheme.

Harry shifted in his chair. He wasn't a man who liked to see his plans upset, especially by a young city girl who probably didn't know the difference between a dandy brush and a hoof-pick.

"Well, that's fine, Miss McBride," he drawled. "Just fine. But where, if you don't mind my asking, did you get the money?"

"I don't believe the source of my funds is a requisite for paying off the loan, Mr. Renford."

"No, no, of course not. Well, it will take me a day or two to get the necessary papers drawn up. Why don't you come back on, say, Friday afternoon?"

"Fine. Until then, Mr. Renford."

Outside, Kelly drew a deep breath and let it out in a long sigh of relief. She was glad to be out of Harry Renford's sight. She didn't like the man, though she didn't know why. It wasn't his looks, she mused. He was quite a handsome man, with a shock of wavy blond hair that was just turning gray at the temples, a charming smile, when he cared to use it, and light gray eyes. It was his eyes, she decided now—they were cold and unblinking, like the eyes of a snake.

Well, as soon as she paid off the mortgage on the ranch, she wouldn't have to deal with him again. Tomorrow she would drive into Coleville and see about selling some of the smaller nuggets. She didn't dare do it here. Cedar Flats was a small town where everybody knew everybody else's business. She didn't want to have to answer any questions about where the gold had come from.

Frowning, she started down to the sidewalk to where she'd left her car. In a few days, she'd have to decide what to do about the ranch. When she'd first arrived, it had been in her mind to sell it, but once she'd seen the place again and remembered the good times she'd had there, she'd known she couldn't sell the old ranch. It had, after all, been in her family for over a century. Still, it was horribly run-down. The house and the barn were in need of painting inside and out; the corral fences needed new rails. There was no stock to speak of, except for Dusty and a couple of aging chickens.

Nevertheless, she was here, and she was here to stay, even though it meant relocating, quitting her secretarial job with Wolfe, Cullman, and Chartier, and finding other employment.

Kelly laughed softly. She didn't need to work anymore. Having access to those nuggets was like having a trust fund. She was set for life.

She was unlocking the door of her car when a man appeared beside her.

"Miss McBride?"

Kelly hesitated a moment before answering. "Yes?"

"I'd like to talk to you."

He was Indian, she thought, noting his dark skin and high cheekbones, though there was nothing particularly sinister about that. There were lots of Indians in Cedar Flats. Most of them lived out on the reservation.

"Talk?" Kelly said. "About what?"

"The Triple M."

Kelly glanced around, reassured by the presence of other people nearby. "What about it?"

"I'd like to buy it."

Kelly glanced at his faded green shirt, the sleeves of which were rolled up to his elbows, exposing bronze forearms thick with muscle. Frayed blue jeans hugged his legs; his feet were encased in a pair of run-down black boots. She doubted if he could afford to buy a cup of coffee.

"I'm sorry," she said politely. "The ranch isn't for sale."

She opened the door and slid behind the wheel, but before she could close the door, the man took a step forward, placing himself between her and the car door.

"Could we go somewhere and discuss it?" he asked.

Kelly shook her head, thinking that his voice was as deep and rich as dark chocolate fudge.

"Please."

The word seemed torn from his throat and she had the sudden unshakable feeling that this was a man who hadn't done much apologizing in his life.

She looked at him then, really looked at him for the first time, and felt a shiver of apprehension skitter down her spine. He looked remarkably as she had imagined the dead man she'd found in the cave would have looked when he was alive.

Kelly's heart began to pound as she noted the similarities. Like the body in the cave, this man was tall and dark. His thick black hair fell past his shoulders. His legs were long; his shoulders were unbelievably broad beneath the almost threadbare shirt. He seemed made of solid muscle. His eyes were as black as obsidian, just as she'd imagined those of the dead man would have been. His nose was straight as a knife edge, and his mouth . . . oh, my, she had never seen such a sensual mouth on a man in her whole life.

He stared down at her, one black brow arching slightly, as if he knew exactly what she was thinking.

"Are you sure we can't discuss it?" he asked in a voice as seductive as candlelight and champagne. "Maybe grab a cup of coffee in the motel coffee shop?"

"I'm sure," she said, wondering if he was truly suggesting what she was thinking. "Now, if you'll excuse me—"

Kelly stared pointedly at his muscular forearm,

which was resting along the top edge of the car door.

His dark eyes flashed with anger as he stepped away from the car.

In an instant, Kelly shut the door and locked it. Shoving the key into the ignition, she gave it a twist, put the gear shift in drive, and pulled away from the curb.

But she couldn't resist a look in her rearview mirror. For some reason, she had expected him to have vanished from sight, but he stood in the middle of the narrow two-lane street, staring after her.

Kelly let out a long, ragged breath as she turned the corner at the end of the block. Whoever the man was, he intrigued and frightened her as no one ever had.

Lee Roan Horse felt his brows draw together in a frown as he watched the light blue Camaro careen around the corner and disappear from sight.

His first meeting with Miss Kelly McBride hadn't gone quite as planned, he thought wryly. For a moment there, she had looked at him the way most white women did, with a mixture of interest and curiosity, and then, for no reason that he could fathom, she had stared at him as if she were seeing a ghost.

So, he mused, what now?

Hands shoved in the back pockets of his jeans, he crossed the street to where his battered Ford truck was parked and climbed inside, only to sit staring out the windshield, his finger tapping on the steering wheel. She had something he wanted and he had two choices—ask for it, or take it.

He'd tried asking. . . .